HEADPRESS24

POWERED BY LOVE

HEADPRESS 24 **POWERED BY LOVE**

Published in November 2002
by Headpress

Headpress/Critical Vision
PO Box 26
Manchester
M26 1PQ
Great Britain

Fax: +44 (0)161 796 1935
Email: info.headpress@telinco.co.uk
Web: www.headpress.com

Editor **David Kerekes**

**British Library Cataloguing
in Publication Data**
A catalogue record for this book is available
from the British Library.

ISBN 1-900486-22-9

ISSN 1353-9760

Buy online:
www.headpress.com

Contents

Editorial

Many thanks to all those people who wrote in to congratulate us on the *Last House on Dead End Street* feature in HEADPRESS 23. The deluxe DVD of the film will have hit the streets (and internet stores) by the time this editorial makes it into print. Our extensive retrospective met with an almost unanimous thumbs-up — with the exception of one person, who slapped a Cease And Desist order on us. As a consequence, while legal teams argued the toss across the Atlantic, HEADPRESS 23 fell into a two-week limbo Stateside. We didn't accede to the demand, and — for the time being at least — HEADPRESS 23 remains freely available. It might always remain available, but why chance it? If you haven't already got a copy, best get one now! Hell, even if you have got a copy, get a second one! And the reason for the Cease And Desist order? Well, it's a long story but what happened is

THE FILM IS CALLED BUTTMAN'S
European Vacation III. It begins at
the Barcelona Erotic Fair, 1995. The
camera is in motion, up and down the
winding streets in the old part of
town. Every so often the camera jerks
just a little bit, and the picture jumps
a fraction — particularly when heading through a cobbled square, up some
stairs, through a heavy door, and into
the busy throng of the fair.

Who's Buttman?

by Laurence O'Toole

Inside, there are people everywhere. Porno
people, which means there's a lot of flesh on
display, plenty of short skirts and long legs
caught in the viewfinder. The camera min-
gles. At one point it bumps into the butt of
Nina Hartley, American porno actress and
free speech campaigner. She turns and smiles
at the guy who's holding the camera, and
they exchange pleasantries. Seems like they're
old acquaintances. The camera moves on,
becomes briefly intimate with a few more butts
and watches some erotic dancing on a podium at the hub of the fair. Later, backstage,
talking to one of the dancers, telling her how
she really ought to appear in one of his videos, the guy with the camera remembers to
introduce himself, "I'm Buttman," he says
matter of factly, "I'm here for a reason. I like
butts'.

... In Las Vegas, Buttman's camera is following Suzy Matthews down the street. She's playing a sexy woman in a white and black polka dot dress, on vacation with her husband. It turns out the both of them are big Buttman fans. Wouldn't you know it! Matthews lifts up her skirt and shows Buttman her backside. "Oh my God, oh my God, you have a great... Oh my God." Soon after the couple agree to letting him film them having sex in their hotel room.

... On Victoria Embankment, beside Westminter Bridge and looking across to the Houses of Parliament, Buttman is alone again with his camera and getting nowhere. He approaches a woman standing nearby. They talk a while, compare parliamentary systems, and then he asks her if she'll let him see her butt, just a little bit, but she walks off, disgusted. Buttman rebuffed.

... And finally, at home in Malibu, and Buttman's taking time out from the pressures of being a peeper. In his pool, lolling on a inflatable lilo, sucking on a beer, his eyelids start to droop, he falls asleep. Pool, sleep — it could only be Buttman's Wet Dream. He dreams of a tropical paradise, and a barely clad Krysti Lynn cavorting under a sunlit waterfall. Till the sound of loud knocking interrupts his sleep, bringing him back to the harsh waking realities of being Buttman. It's Krysti Lynn — had to be really — come knocking at his door, wondering if he'd like to make another video with her.

And so on, and so on. By which time readers are probably thinking to themselves exactly who is this guy with the camera and the dirty mind. Who is this so-called Buttman?

John 'Buttman' Stagliano is the most successful man in American film pornography of the nineties, with undoubtedly the most regularly mispronounced name — the g is a silent g, and the first syllable's sort of pronounced 'star'. On the internet, at the newsgroup *Rec.Arts.Movies.Erotica*, a site that prides itself on having a nose for the good stuff, and for sniffing out the fakes from a mile off, a reviewer called Imperator gets it across in a nutshell: "When in doubt, rent Stagliano... Stagliano continues to rule contemporary porn."

I'M SAT IN JOHN STAGLIANO'S FRONT room. His front room is big and long, featuring a large dance floor, a big fireplace, and lots of blue furniture. I recognise the long blue sofa I'm sat upon from some of his videos. If furniture could talk, this one could tell of many hardcore sessions. Stag's blue sofa has seen some action in its time: three ways, four ways, anals, double penetrations... And now me, on a sunny Californian morning, my walkman primed, my list of questions at the ready.

How famous are you, Mr Stagliano? "As famous as anybody in porno."

How successful are you? "Very. More successful than virtually anyone else. And I'm sort of bragging now, I know, but I'm also telling you the truth."

According to a lot of his fans, John Stagliano is "the luckiest guy in the world". In fact some go as far as to suggest that Stag's got it so good, that his kind of luck's simply out of this world, some kind of cosmic good fortune, something a bit celestial. "John, honestly, I watch your movies," writes a fan, "I see the things you do, the things that happen to you, and I reckon sometimes you must think you've died and gone to heaven."

The way to heaven for Stagliano was through making porno movies. This Italian-American, born and raised in Chicago, owns and runs Evil Angel, a video producer and manufacturer which presently commands a good sized share of the American porno market, as well as selling product in territories all across the globe. From Australia to Amsterdam, Japan to Brazil, the Evil Empire is a name to reckon with in porno. Except, of course, for the British Isles. For, in the UK, and over in Ireland, it is against the law to sell the kind of movies John Stagliano makes, that is, in other words, hardcore pornography.

A few weeks prior to meeting with Stagliano I had sat-in on committal proceedings at Old Street magistrates in London. A bunch of wideboys were up for importing and intending to sell indecent and obscene material. Previously, I'd read some of the customs reports, a couple of which concerned seized movies produced by Evil Angel, movies by Stagliano and co. The obscene contents likely to offend, deprave and corrupt, and generally cause mass hysteria up and down the land, depicted erect male members, spread labia, scenes of fellatio, cunnilingus and penetrative sex. This is what we are being protected from: filmed sex for sale.

I mention this to Stagliano. How do you feel about the fact that your movies are against the law in Britain?

"Well, of course, it surprises me. To be honest with you, I don't really understand why. I like England and English culture. I

John "Buttman" Stagliano

All images used in this article are © Evil Angel Video and E A Productions

find it to be a very sophisticated country, the people likewise. It is interesting to think that this modern nation, adjoining other modern nations which are advanced and free-thinking, choses to be repressive in terms of pornography."

Though these market restrictions lose Stag a chunk of potential income, it is the principle of the thing which seems to irk him. One gets the impression that he is perhaps slightly affronted — how can a nation he respects, be so disrespectful to him in return? Where any lost revenue is concerned however, he doesn't seem to be losing any sleep. After all, Stagliano already has over a million dollars stashed away in the bank. There's the groovy house in Malibu as well, with all the trappings and furnishings: the pool, the sun deck, the great view, the art, the voluminous stash of vin-

tage porn, all of these are aspects of what in *Face Dance* , Stag's biggest movie, he calls "my reward for being a pervert".

But not every pervert, not every porner, can expect to do so well, or could even dream of making such a packet. Stagliano made a packet out of porno by doing something new. In 1989 the former stripper started making hardcore porno movies about a shy, horny guy with a camera whom he called Buttman. These are movies which he writes, produces, directs, edits, films, manufactures, owns and features in as Buttman — not that he's any kind of control freak, you realise.

To date there are close to thirty Buttman movies, set in places as far flung as New Zealand, Prague, San Diego and London. As with the location, the content of a Buttman tale can shift around a bit. However, the basic set-up remains sweet and simple: it involves Buttman — the man who loves butts — going out into the world at large, with his Hi-8 video camera, to seek out and approach attractive women. These women, who just happen to be passing by, will be persuaded, after a bit of cajoling, to show Buttman their behinds. And then, later on, they let him film them having sex. Maybe they'll be having sex with Stag's friend, Rocco Siffredi, the Italian heart-throb, currently porno's reigning studmeister; maybe they'll have sex with someone else, another porn performer, or with their own boyfriend, lover, or husband. Whatever, Buttman will be there, filming the heat and the passion, the penetration and the orgasm, getting the best sex shots he can. Porn *vérité* it is described by some, this porno style invented by Stagliano where the camera is part of the scenario. *AVN* calls it gonzo porno.

Essentially, Buttman is a walking, talking male fantasy apparently played out in real life. Camcorder man with a female butt fetish as big as the grand canyon, and a few neat chat-up lines to get the ball rolling. So much said about porn, be it in defence, or hostile, forgets how porn is a thing of fantasy, a whole series of fantasies.

Like the one about the male stripper in *Buttman's Inferno*, where the female audience goes mad and they start devouring him live on stage. Or, the one about the personal appearance session at an adult video store where the fans not only got to have their picture taken with the big porno star — the excellent Angela Vickers — but actually end up nobbing with her.

The latter scene is pure Buttman: the snooping around the video store in first person point-of-view (POV), the tease of sex being in the air but not simply served up to the viewer on a platter, the ingenious blurring of what's reality and what's the fictional set-up. The blurring is essential. Stag creates new porno fantasies that are also semi-plausible and then he films them like they are for real. These are fantasies a viewer can believe in.

How it works is the scene will get going and be sort of realistic. There's a guy, or maybe a couple of guys, and they're a bit hopeless, bumbling around, making jokes, until a dream girl walks by, and they approach her in the nicest possible way, "Miss, I seem to be lost"; and rather than being rebuffed, she is flattered, and she talks to them. And, at this stage, we are still in a realm not *too* far removed from reality. Until she agrees to Buttman filming her butt-cheeks up close — "Oh my God, what an ass" — by which time the switch from camcorder man realism to fantasy pornotopia has already happened, but was effected so adroitly, that most often than not you're carried along with the flow and you're probably in there in the heart of the fantasy, and you've stopped asking yourself is this for real, did any of this actually happen, and are moving towards Stag's next level, the sex level.

The first time I saw a Buttman movie, I have to confess, I don't think I really got into the sex aspect, or the fantasy aspect either. I was too bothered trying to figure out what was going on, how much was for real, and how much was a con. And this Buttman character, I kept wondering, was it a dreamed-up character, or was Stagliano simply playing himself? (as well as playing with himself on occasions).

"Buttman is me through and through," says Stagliano. "Except for the part when he goes up and talks to the girls on the street, which, I guess is pretty much what people associate with Buttman. I just wouldn't do that in real life. I probably shouldn't say that," he confesses, "probably the biggest compliment I get, and it happens all the time, is that fans come up to me and say, are those girls real? Did you really go up and talk to that girl, or was it set up? Well, of course, it's all set up."

Stagliano gets letters from fans who want to be Buttman, but who don't appear to be having much success. "'Oh John I'm having so much trouble," they write 'I go out on the street with my camera, just like you do, and I'm not getting anywhere, can you help me?'" What have I done!" Stagliano jokes "I've created a monster."

So now I know for absolutely certain, it's all made-up. However, even knowing for certain, getting it straight from the Stag's mouth, that it's truly just an elaborate fiction, there is still a bit of me that doesn't want to hear this, the part that replays in my head that scene in the strip club, and wants to believe that at the very start of the scene, when the featured male stripper was late and the screaming gathering of women were about to go mad, when Stagliano handed over his camera to his friend — coming out of retirement briefly, going up on stage and doing a strip — and the women loved him to death for it, and then the real stripper arrives and gets on with the show and the real wild action commences… You want to believe this, or at least some of it, sort of happened, that it wasn't all set-up.

There are many reasons we want to believe what we see on screen, a prime one with the Buttman series is down to Stagliano's clever manipulation of the first person, quasi documentarian style of film making. What you see in a Buttman movie is only what he sees through the lens of his camera. The film is shot entirely from the first person point of view of Buttman. There are no master shots in a Buttman movie, no pretence at objectivity; the viewer is pretty much always aware of the existence of the camera, because the cameraman is Buttman, who is also asking all the questions, leading things on, and making things happen.

John Stagliano takes this on the hoof, documentary, video diaries-style, jerky hand held camera film making process for a ride. What was supposed to be the essence of unadulterated representational truth telling becomes in his hands a great big game of post-modern porno tease. To those who think they already know what porn's about, who think it's always dumb, tedious, repetitious, all gonads, and a big empty space between the ears, they ought to check out a movie by John Stagliano and see if they still find it so basic, so easy to read, so totally unsophisticated after all.

But let's not get carried away here, let's not run the risk of losing the plot. The main

thing about a Stag movie is he shoots good porno. He's a hit because his movies are hot, they make people horny. Buttman is a creation that cannily spans the divide between the rawness and immediacy of amateur porn and the technical quality, sophistication and beauty of Hollywood style professional fantasy porno.

In the American porn zine, *Batteries Not Included*, porno reviewer Tammy Cole describes the onset of tedium that sometimes comes through watching too many same old porno movies:

> … you ask yourself, isn't sex fun anymore?… That's the feeling I had when I popped Buttman's Ultimate Workout into the VCR and refilled my coffee cup… [I] glance at the screen and pour scalding hot coffee over my hand. Worse yet, I keep pouring… Blowing on my scalded wrist, I move feebly back to the chair and sit on the edge transfixed as I watch the mind of John Stagliano take me where I've never been before. "What an ass! What an ass! What an ass!" someone mumbles. I realise it's me… You have never, ever, in your wildest fantasies come close to the sexual commotion depicted herein… If Russ Meyer is the tit man of the century, John Stagliano is the ass man of the millennium.

If you talk to regular video pornography users, couples or solos, gay or straight, they'll tell you a lot of things about what they like, and what they really loathe. Although two people never say exactly the same thing, there are a pair of requirements for porno that come up with impressive regularity: porn fanciers like their screen sex to be hot and heartfelt and they want it to be technically of good quality. Amateur porno is popular because the sex is for real, uninflected, beyond some of mainstream porn's rigid conventions, a breath of fresh air after way too much of porno-by-numbers. As they say in pornoland, Amateur gives you "more bangs for your bucks". And then, about a million miles down the road, there's the high end product, porno deluxe, shot on film, glam porn with high production values, stories, locations, slow-mo, computer effects, and beautiful, beautiful megababe porno superstars wearing pounds of make-up, big hair, siliconised breasts, having beautifully photographed sex with hosts of other beautiful types . It's a quality piece of fantasy product: "more glam for your bucks."

EACH END OF THE BUSINESS HAS ITS FANS, and its critics, but neither can do both at the same time. High end porn comes across sometimes like pretty performers more into looking pretty than getting, as Candida Royale describes it, "really down and dirty". Amateur will feature raving sex fiends but the beauty aspect can be a little meagre at times, too homely for comfort, whilst the camera work does get a little wayward.

This is where the Stag movie comes in. When Buttman's on song, you get the best of both worlds, am and pro. Stag recreates the freshness and intimacy, the unbridled heat of amateur sex, 'real sex', but he also gets the

best sex shots, the best angles, as well as creating some of the most innovative porno fantasy scenarios.

The fictional set-up of a Buttman movie sees him on the streets, at a club, in the park, crawling through bushes with his camera, looking for some action. Once he has located his desideratum the scene evolves without any absolute certainty as to how it might work out. This slight element of doubt contributes to a sense of drama running through the whole scenario — will he be found out, will he be sent packing, or will she show him her butt — which helps the pretence at reality to be maintained.

In due course a hardcore scene ensues which seeks to mesh that pretence at reality with a soliciting of real sex performances. This subtle play on fictions and realities is partly aided and enhanced by the way the film is shot in Stagliano's faux amateur style. "A

Nikki and Anna from John Stagliano's Buttman magazine Vol 1 No 3

Buttman movie looks amateurish, for the most part, because I'm in it with the camera, talking to people… as if I'm an amateur, as though it's not a set-up scene."

Stag recognises a debt to the eighties boom in Amateur: "A lot of the first Amateur stuff, and some of the stuff still coming out today, really was someone's home video from Oklahoma, of someone having sex. Ninety-nine per cent is shot really badly, but sometimes it's really hot and interesting to look at. The people are not performing" .

This was a big influence on Stag's porno work . "Amateur sex is real sex, and getting real sex is what I'm all about, whilst doing it really professionally. My final product is sophisticated, I hope. Well filmed, well edited, where the pop shots aren't missed, and the girls are not am girls from down the road, they're fantasy girls, dream girls. But the sex is real."

A paid-up Method porner, as a young man Stagliano took acting classes with a teacher whose credo was "no acting please". He believes in the Method as a way of getting reality acting from performers. "It's all to do with getting in touch with what we're really feeling, let the emotions flow freely — the psychotherapy approach to creativity, getting people to stop acting and start fucking." Furthermore, "what the Buttman concept allows me, better than any other format, is to find this reality, is to find some real moments of sex".

When I asked if he always found them, he laughed and said no. Later he confessed that there is a limit to what you can hope to get out of people who perform sexually. That, if the sex lacks something, then you have to supply the heat through some quality filming, a lot of smart editing too.

From a critically detached perspective — i.e., if you're actually watching and not getting aroused — there's some truth to the allegation that in porn too many sex scenes are alike: "Blow-Dog, Mish-Pop", a young turk porno director described it to me, "Formula porno: first blow-job, then shots of fucking doggy-style, some missionary, and finish with the ejaculation shot, the Pop shot: Blow-Dog, Mish, Pop!" Sex scenes can start to look pretty interchangeable, and one becomes a little bit fatigued. With Stag, when he's really doing his things, his work truly stands out. In *XXX, A Feminist Argument for Pornography*, Wendy McElroy admits that each time she watches the opening scene from *Face Dance 1*, she is left open-mouthed.

So, how do you go shoot good sex, what's the secret?

"Well, being into porno kind of helps. I don't think there are really that many people in this industry that jerk off to porno, who look at shots from the point of view of asking themselves does this really turn me on?

"For example, I will try and get both a good view of the actual penetration *and* the girl's face, her expression, or the guy's face, his expression, have all of this in the same shot. It takes finding the good angles Most people, instead, they'll shoot one minute of penetration, and then cut to face of performer pretending to be aroused, pretending the pen shot and expression took place at the same time, whereas in fact they'll have been filmed one after the other. Then they'll piece all of these shots together and think they have a sex scene. That's porno. Well no it isn't, because they haven't got a mood, they didn't get the ambience of the sex scene, it's just porno by numbers. It doesn't turn me on."

BEING TURNED ON, IS THE REASON STAG got into porno in the first place. He loves it, a fool for erotica. "One of the keys to my success, and people can tell, is that I really enjoy what I am doing." Former partner and lover, Brandy Alexandre agrees "Thing that really singles John out from the others, is that he really, really likes porno. He's an enthusiast, a naughty boy peeper, a real lover of women. At least fifty per cent of people in industry find porn loving comes a distant second to the love of making money. For John, clearly it's the other way round."

LATER THAT DAY STAG WAS DOING SOME editing in the Butt den and ensconced in his recliner chair, surrounded by TV screens and editing facilities, an edit console in his lap. The movie is called *Nudes-a-Poppin'*. Forty women descend upon a nudist colony in the mid west once a summer for a stripping contest. Stag and a pal go every year to film the proceedings. Now I am watching Stag knock the raw footage for *Nudes-a-Poppin'* into shape. There's a segment containing three naked girls dancing on the stage, doing poses, performing some minor acrobatics. Stag fast forwards, back and forth, back and forth, across the same bits of footage, editing things down, linking things up. At a certain point he stops, freezes the frame. Apparently transfixed, he lifts up out of his chair and gets up close to the screen and just stares. "I don't know about you," he says to me quietly, "but, these three girls are really turning me on." And you realise the Buttman's the real thing, he's not faking nor bullshitting, living up to his own image, he's just into it.

It perhaps begs the most obvious question. So, after many hours spent talking to the genial Buttman himself, finally I asked it. What are the correct lineaments of a videogenic female posterior? Or, in another language, what is it that makes a butt great? — "It has to be full, round, and stick out a bit. It can wobble, but not too much." Furthermore a woman can have cellulite. He's no cellulite fascist. "But then again I don't want to see too much of the stuff."

He agreed however, that in a sense such criteria are pretty much after the fact, that ultimately the attraction of a butt resides within the realm of the ineffable. "It comes down to being moved".

IN A WET AND BLOWY SAN DIEGO, Buttman's on the trail of Krysti Lynn, the 'tease from hell'. He stumbles across another equally obsessive butt-fancier hiding out. Krysti Lynn catches the both of them watching her. She calls them freaks. "Why are we freaks," cries the butt-nut, "just because we worship the butt?"...

There was a time in porno when the butt, the backside, rear, ass, bottoms were not the focus of attention they are these days. You just need to look at movies from the golden age of porn, from the seventies through to the mid eighties, movies such as *Opening of Misty Beethoven* or *Devil in Miss Jones*, to notice how you barely get one single shot of either Constance Money or Georgina Spelvin's rear. "You'd get anal sex, plenty of that, but the shots were always of pounding, and never of butts pure and simple."

Stag not only found porno seriously wanting for this omission, he saw it as being a crime against human nature. "Butts tell a man a woman's healthy. He is drawn to her biologically, genetically, her good butt tells the man that she will be strong and breed well." Stag is a big fan of the thoughts of Camille Paglia, but more about that later. Worshipping the butt gives Stag the kind of porno insight you can't buy, nor fake. "You see, a guy can decide to shoot a butt, and he can choose the wrong angle, and the reason he does this is because he's not into butts the way I'm into them, he hasn't spent hours and hours staring at butts like me." It is this undissimulating passion, wrapped up with the pursuit of excellence, that has put Stagliano where he is now, right at the front of the pack.

Contrary to popular belief, the streets of pornotopia are not paved with gold. Not every pervert in porno gets rewarded with a smart house out in Malibu. Once upon a time, it's true, there were people making a quick killing in the skin game, without needing to be a porn genius. But that was the early pioneering years of porno, and those frontiersman times are long gone. These days, porn in the USA, apart from the intermittent rash of legal hassle and moral condemnation, is a well established industry, a mature market with far tighter profit margins that are getting tighter all the time.

Competition in porno is tough; this is a market forever on the verge of total glut, with seven or eight thousand titles released onto the market in 1997. To make your product stand out from all the rest, from the truck-

John Stagliano — swamped by bottoms

bondage; Greg Dark, Alex de Renzy, Joey Silvera, and the directorial outings of Rocco Siffredi. All are constituent parts of the Evil Empire, and making Evil Angel a porn industry leader with Stagliano its CEO, fussing over figures, release dates, ad space, percentages and assorted executive headaches; hardly the thing one associates with the eternally adolescent grown-up who lives to love butts.

Does this make Stag chairman of the bored? "Sometimes. There are moments when I feel like running away. But there's another part of me that enjoys running a company. After all I started out in adulthood dreaming of completing a doctorate in economics."

The Buttman phenomenon is more than just an American dream come true. Not only does Stag travel the globe to make his Buttman movies, but the Buttman phenomenon is a global success story, with sales as far and wide as Italy, France, Australia, New Zealand and South America. In Brazil Buttman's a kind of phenomenon, Stag releases a movie a month, there's even a comic called Buttman.

All from a guy who the first time he saw a hard core porn movie thought it was completely gross and ugly, all scarily red and full of close-ups of weird-looking bodily functions. The same guy who when he first came to Los Angeles to attend UCLA, didn't even realise that Hollywood was in LA as well.

John Stagliano has certainly come a long way. It all started at a modern dance class. Studying economics was fine, but John liked to be physically active. He took dance class, mainly because all the girls in the class wore body-hugging leotards, and because there

loads of porno-by-numbers videos and the sheer dross, requires that you have something special to offer.

Buttman movies go into the shops in larger amounts and at higher wholesale prices than just about anyone else's, and they sell not for just a few weeks, as is the norm with most product in porno, but month after month. Movies he made five years ago continue to sell today. This is very rare in this massively fast turnover industry. What's more, Stagliano's company, Evil Angel, produces, manufactures, and promotes not just his own movies, but a whole prestigious roster of other porn film makers including the movies of John Leslie, ex-actor turned moody porno auteur; Bruce Seven, the boss of American

weren't that many girls doing economics or playing basketball at the time. The dancing agreed with Stagliano. He began also to attend acting classes and to do some nude modelling. The economics degree was ditched for a life of fun and fucking.

Stag was a good-looking guy, with twinkle toes and a love of expressing himself sexually. During the late seventies he became a male stripper, working in LA, Las Vegas and all over North America. In '79 he appeared in the first ever Chippendale show in Los Angeles. Back then male strippers were not the muscle-bound beefers doing the rounds today. It was a time of Saturday Night Fever, of lithe guys, fleet-footed and cute, winning dance competitions and coming out west to make a living.

Stripping saw Stag develop his understanding of the theatrics of putting on a show that was truly arousing. His performances might sometimes involve dressing up as a woman, or as a zealous, self-abnegating priest who was struggling to contain his lusty, carnal thoughts. Stag's biggest, best trick was playing a cop, whom just when the women in the audience were starting to get horny would come charging in pretending he was going to bust the show, only to then whip his dick out. "If it is realistic, the place goes mad. It's this swing between guilt and lust."

The swings are a big deal for Stagliano. Like a lot of porners, Stagliano resents the fact that there are some who will try and censor him, those who seek to tell him what to do. However, at the same time he is convinced that it's the sexual repression, the erection of erotic taboos within American society, that makes his jobs as a porner a lot easier.

Stag's love of porno stretches all the way back to Chicago, being brought up a good Catholic boy during the late fifties and early sixties. An church altar boy, he would while away the time at mass dreaming of girls in tight sweaters, and he's been a regular smut hound ever since. All that tedium and Catholic guilt made Stag into a pornographer. He feels sure that had he been brought up in an environment of free love and sexual candour

there'd have been no Buttman today. "Sexual repression provides a lot of fuel for sexual arousal, the swing from being repressed to letting it all go, to being really turned on."

At one point in his adolescence, the guilt he felt was so bad that he stopped masturbating altogether. After reading a lot of books about moral honesty and personal integrity, he was determined to be a good person in life and do the right thing always. Wanking made him feel bad and so he stopped — for two years!

Another period of relative sexual abstinence commenced when in the early to mid eighties, as Stag turned thirty and started to think about doing something with his life, he gradually moved out of the waning stripper business and into porno. It sounds wildly implausible, but he swears it's the truth.

"A lot of guys get into porno because they think they're going to be around all these beautiful porno women. And that's fine, you know, porno women are the best in the world. However I actually gave up a lot of sex and sexual adventure entering the porno business, because I moved out of stripping, where at the time, you could easily have two or three flings a week without having to hardly think about it. Moving into porno, as bizarre as it sounds, was a case of moving into a business where there was less sex, less getting out and about, and more need to focus."

Stagliano is porno's finest example of how the stereotypical image of the typical ugly porno geezer getting lots of beautiful women because he's got power is not so true, not anymore. This is a guy who made a living from his looks and his sexuality, long before he made porn movies.

"I only say that about giving up sex when moving into porno to make me seem more pure in my motives," he jokes, "But, thing is I wanted to make good porno... I was very interested in making a good piece of work, and not in the least bit interested in screwing the women I was hiring. It was business to me, and if I wanted to date an actress, I'd wait till the film was finished before I'd ask her out."

Just as some guys go into porno for the wrong reasons, a lot of talented people don't go near the industry because they don't want the stigma. Stag considers himself perfect for porno because he's not afraid of these stigmas. " I made a decision early on in life not to worry about what other people thought of me. That's no way to run your life."

He told his mother what he was doing, her father, in turn, was a bootlegger during prohibition. She says she doesn't care a whole lot for what he does, but she did say "well, at least you're making a lot of money" .

I wondered about the right words to use to describe his product. People are forever quibbling over words and names. The day before at Vivid Video they had told me how the word pornography was the worst.

How do you feel about the words porn and porno, are you a pornographer? — "Yes, of course I'm a pornographer. Porno's the word, it's what I make. Adult entertainment doesn't so aptly describe for me what porn explains or advertises, which is, material that is made specifically to sexually arouse somebody. That's my definition, and I'm happy with it."

The porno stigma can still be difficult in daily life, on a plane journey, in a taxi, at a party. Stag likes dance and told me he would like to teach dance, would like to work with kids, but thinks that that is pretty much cut off from him: "people don't like the idea of a porno-maker being in with kids."

However he remains sanguine: "In the nineties I think people are more accepting of porno. It caused a lot more offence in the late seventies and early eighties than it does today. Or maybe I've become more self-assured, more confident because I've become more successful." (There's something quintessentially American, or is it Southern Californian lodged in this comment, this observation of how he feels he is treated. The main thing here may well be success, the pecuniary wealth. In the eighties, pre-Buttman, not only was he a pornographer, but a poor pornographer — now that is truly obscene!).

Stag's start in the business came in the shape of small circulation magazines, containing porno stories he wrote with accompanying hard core photo stories. Next came low-low budget independent video productions. His first ever movie, part financed by his share of the winnings from a contest run by *Playboy* for the best stripping couple dance routine, Stag was only supposed to produce and write, but the would-be cameraman proved not to be so good at filming the sex, he missed the first cumshot in fact, so Stag stepped in.

Success didn't come quickly, for most of the eighties Stag independently made a porn video once every so often, and struggled along, making some moderate hits, and some costly flops. These were not days of early success. To make matters worse for a while shooting hard core in LA became a very dangerous business. People were going to jail for shooting hard core. For all of 1986 Stag and pretty much everybody else stopped making hard core in LA because the police had taken to busting porn people on charges of pimping.

Once he had to abandon a shoot just before it got started because one of the actresses had refused to show up having being tipped off they were about to be busted, and Stag looked out the window and saw men in dark suits sitting in a car opposite the building. It took one brave or foolhardy porner to fight the law all the way to the state supreme court to demonstrate that he was making movies and had nothing to do with prostitution.

During his lean years Stag learned how to get by, to grind out a career by cutting production budgets down to the barest minimum. He would do all his own camerawork, becoming good with sound, editing his and other people's movies, utilising the new video technology till it had almost become second nature, when he knew where all the buttons on the camera were without thinking, "it's like it's become part of me, like a motor activity". These were his prentice years. Sometimes he'd shoot a movie with a video pack strapped to one shoulder and the sound recording instruments strapped to the other shoulder — it was a lot of weight to bear.

When you see Stag negotiate Soho mar-

ket on a Saturday afternoon so adroitly…
it's because he put his hours in, till by late
1988 Stag was ready to go it alone.

The final push came when one of the big
porno companies turned down one of his
movies. They wouldn't distribute it. They kept
telling him his product wasn't right, they
didn't feel they could sell it to the cable net-
works. Needless to say, Stag did not agree.
What's more, he suspected he'd been stiffed
by them, that they hadn't paid him all he was
owed. It's a common gripe in porno. Cheques
bounce, verbal deals are reneged upon, everybody suspects they've been shafted at least
once in their career — no pun intended. The
actress Brandy Alexandre puts it like this,
"the truth is that to every snake in porno
there are twenty pussycats, problem is, it's
too often the case that it's the snakes that
hold the purse strings."

I asked Stag how much dishonesty there
is in the industry. He acknowledges there's
some, mentioning a few big names who he
knows owe him money, ripped him off at some
point. "I have to say this, however, that of all
the places I've been to, I think I've met more
unscrupulous people in England than anywhere else in the porno business — probably
because it's so underground. In England so
many people in porno are lying and cheating.
Three people in London have called up girls
saying they're John Stagliano, in town to
make a movie, this has never happened anywhere else."

Finally Stagliano got too pissed off with
the sharp practises to hang around any
longer. He went off and set about starting up
his own company, convinced that his material was hot and would make him a wealthy
man. When Stagliano tells you about his career — which he will at great length, given
the chance — of the years leading up to Evil
Angel and the Buttman movies, what comes
across is a sense of the steady convergence of
various key factors: his butt-lust, the absence
of butts on the market, his familiarity with
the new, lighter technologies, his disaffection
with the state of things. Everything was in
place, waiting for the right moment, the big

idea, his hardcore killer application.

Utilising the debt facilities of thirteen
credit cards Stag raised $60,000 and set about
making a batch of movies to launch his company. One was tentatively to be a film about
a guy with a camera who gets into trouble
and who also has a thing for butts. "At the
time, it had just become acceptable with the
appearance on the market of smaller vidcams
to have unsteady camera work. There were a
couple of TV commercials running round
then which employed the technique."

Previously, other than perhaps in the
movies of Jean-Luc Godard, being made
aware of the camera was not the done thing,
not even in porno (at least, not on purpose).
Stagliano was dating Brandy Alexandre at
the time. One night they had gone to see the
first Batman movie. On their way home he
says she suggested he call this new movie of
his The Adventures of Buttman. He didn't
like the title at first. "I thought it was kind of
gross."

Alexandre has been out of the porno industry for a few years now. She declined to
talk with me in person, she said she'd put on
some weight since quitting, and felt insecure
about not looking like the porno superstar
anymore. We spoke on the phone. Brandy
suggests that she came up with more than
just the name, but the whole concept. "I told
him to shoot the movie entirely in first person POV, and not back and forth between
Buttman POV and your regular mastershot
camera work like he was planning on doing."

She also claims she came up with the notion that this roving guy with the camera
should be a lover of butts, "like John's a lover
of butts, a guy who's a bit shy, a bit hapless
and luckless, just like John is, who tends to
peep around a bit…I suggested all of that… I
bet he didn't tell you that," she said. Later
she concedes that this is unlikely since he
doesn't agree with her version of history.
(When Stagliano first suggested I speak with
Brandy, he said she'd have a few things to
say about him, some stories to tell, "Believe
me, she won't just say nice things about me".)
The version according to Stag is that he was

toying with making the first person POV part of the movie for some time. The idea pretty much originated with Antonioni's *Blowup*, the art house classic of swinging sixties London. *Blowup* had made a big impression on the teenage Stagliano, "the nude scene in it drove me nuts!"

There's a scene in *The Adventures of Buttman* that's a steal from *Blowup*. It's the famous scene set in a park in south London when the fashion photographer David Hemmings photographs something but doesn't know exactly what. Later, back at his studio, he blows up the image to reveal a hand sticking out of some bushes, holding a gun. The Buttman version sees our hero making his screen debut playing about with his video camera at a party. His snooping lands him in a bit of trouble and he is thrown out — a typical Buttman incident. He goes into a local park and is experimenting taking pictures of the moon, when he's distracted by the sound of rustling in some nearby bushes. He pans to the right, films something, but is not sure what until he returns to his studio, where a closer look reveals a woman's butt sticking out of the bushes.

Later Stagliano's character returns to the scene of the crime, where he meets the butt's owner, the porno actress Tracey Adams, and they go back to his cottage and have sex together. Later still, there's another woman. Having noticed his anatomical predilections she declares, "you're Buttman". And the rest, as they say, is porno legend.

THE SCENE IN *ADVENTURES OF BUTTMAN* between Stagliano and Tracey Adams is a rare instance of Stagliano having sex in one of his movies. It happens, but not very often. The reason being, he admits, is that he's not very good on camera: "I can't stay hard. I'm too self conscious, and not virile enough. If I could fuck like I do in real life, that would be fine, but as soon as camera is on, even if there's no one else in the room it cramps my style."

The irony is there for all to see — of the

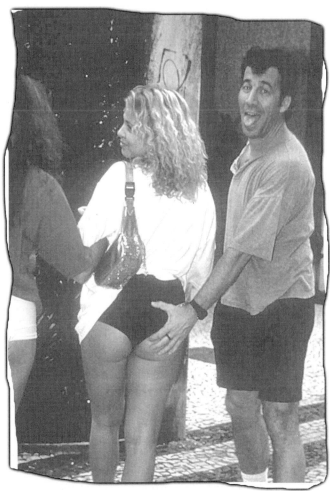

Cheeky!

porner who shoots people having sex all the time, but not himself. Stag is quick to see it himself. There are however, other reasons for his absence: "I'm the cameraperson, that is my main function. I'd rather have better looking, better endowed, younger guys fucking, and I'll do the camera work, and concentrate on getting the best shots."

But what happens if one of these younger,

virile types has one of them non-virile moments, when he can't get it up? — "If a guy has a problem getting hard or staying hard then what you have is a very big problem. You can talk it through, take a break, have a beer. Reassure him. And sometimes this will do the trick. Other times you just have to give it up, and write if off as a loss."

ADVENTURES OF BUTTMAN

THE ADVENTURES OF BUTTMAN WAS released in late '89 alongside some other movies Stagliano had made and stockpiled to launch Evil Angel. Unlike these, which did reasonably good business, *Adventures* just kept on selling. Likewise with the second Buttman movie: *Bend over Babes*. "The shops just kept on selling out and ordering in more."

Things were going so swimmingly that Buttman could start to think globally, be packing his suitcase and heading overseas. During the nineties, Stagliano has ventured far and wide, taking Buttman across Europe, to South America and Australasia, though so far he remains resistant to the idea of venturing east of Prague, confessing to being rather scared of the Russian Mafia.

It's a much made criticism of American porno: all the movies look like they're made in the same place. Back in the days when it was mostly a NY based product, you would get a lot of cramped interiors, sweaty wallpaper curling at the edges and bad grey light. Then porno relocated to California and the same half dozen Californian bedrooms started showing up in every new movie, the same ugly bedspreads, same cheesy knickknacks.

In contrast the best of Euro porno, currently doing rather well over there — with the likes of Ben Dover, Joe d'Amato, Private, and the Video Marc d'Orcel range — tends to shoot outdoors a lot, using to the full exotic locations like castles, bridges, hunting lodges and historic city centres for backdrops. It brings another feature to the pleasures of porno: porno as travelogue.

Stagliano always remembered the complaint of a room mate at college, who found a lot of porno was so miserable because it was always stuck between four walls. His yen for being a peripatetic porner, however, started all the way back during his teenage years, when the junior Stag would peddle across Chicago on his bicycle, seeking out the seedier parts of town, the kinds of places where there was a possibility of scoring a dirty mag from under the counter. "As a consequence, for me, it was always exciting to go to new places, which is one of the major reasons why Buttman is forever on the road."

Such roving did, however, have to wait for the Hi-8 camera to come out on the market, with its video cassettes that can pass as audio cassettes at customs. Stag admits he remains anxious whenever leaving and returning to America, but he worries most of all when coming to England, fearing that someone at arrivals will recognise him, that he'll be summarily turned away as an undesirable porner, "'Oh we know what you're going to do, get out of here!" In fact I worry about telling you this, because I don't want to give people reading any ideas."

So far, Stag's porn journeying has remained free of law trouble, and from 1991 a series of foreign hits started rolling off the Buttman production line, into the shops and out again — *European Vacations, Rio Carnivals, Buttman's British Adventures* and the like, joining up with a extending line of homegrown hits, movies like *Ultimate Workout, Butt Freak,* and *Buttman v Buttwoman.*

According to Brandy A. the first batch of Buttmans were genius work, "John revolutionised porn." It's funny to think back on how at first the Buttman movies were supposed to be Stag's filler titles, to be fit in between his real movies, like *Mystic Pieces, Shadow Dancers, Rock n Roll Heaven,* movies with casts, scripts, stories. Yet it was to be his knockabout, butt-fuelled experiments in new ways of filming porno that made the big sales.

There's a mesh of interconnected reasons why the Buttman movies took off in such a big way. The shorter version is it all comes down to Stagliano's decision to place himself inside his movies. Stagliano crossed the line, taking his portable videocam and becoming an actor in his own porno fantasies. Like a lot of big ideas, it was also a pretty simple idea. But in porno terms this was a giant step. It simply hadn't been done before.

For someone who doesn't follow porno so closely, a Buttman movie might not seem so fantastically revolutionary. This is partly because, almost ten years on, we are now far more familiar with the experience of being made aware of the presence and existence of the camera. The whole genre of the jerky, hand-held, active first person POV is virtually commonplace. (*Man Bites Dog, Roger and Me, Video Diaries.*) This is particularly so within porno, where someone's good idea seldom goes uncopied. These days in American X-rated video, nearly everyone with a Hi-8 camera, a modicum of front, a line or two of decent patter, and no shame at all, is doing what Stagliano first did with Buttman. There's Seymore Butts, Philmore Butts, Ed Powers, Randy West, Jon Dough, and Britain's Steve Perry with the 'Ben Dover' series.

They say imitation is the highest form of flattery. So, is Stag flattered, or just pissed off? — "It doesn't bother me, not at all. To be honest, it makes going to video arcades much more enjoyable. Nowadays I find a lot more stuff I can jerk off to. And anyway it's an idea and you can't copyright that. It's a technique that anyone might want to use."

The Buttman technique takes the viewer inside the movie, heightening the experience of looking. "In *Buttman* people are aware of the camera, they feel the movement. The quick zooms and quick focussing — it makes the camera seem alive, makes the action more alive, makes it more real. All of this is contrary to set-up shots, when the camerawork is static." Stagliano continues, getting deeper into the technique. "Buttman walks into the room, sees a girl, the camera checks her tits, then her face, down to her tits and up again and so on, that's how it is filmed which is kind of like how our eyes work in real life, visually this is a lot more interesting. Con-ventionally, you'd show a girl in a room, a guy walks in, you see him walk in, you see him look, and what he looks at, you still have close-ups on parts of the body, but it's not the same, it doesn't move the same way, not like eye movement."

With the success of the first two Buttmans, Stagliano took the decision to stop scripting his movies. Creatively Stagliano enjoyed making these kinds of movies. But they weren't so successful. He came to the conclusion that porno isn't really to do with such things. "Porno, it isn't about intellect, moral complexities, and moral problems, it's about arousal, and if you're going to use a story, it must be a very sexual story that leads up to a great sex scene."

He continues. "For years people were saying you got to have a plot. They'd criticise a movie for having no plot. I mean, who gives a fuck if it doesn't have a plot. That's the most ridiculous criticism I've ever heard! What you need to ask yourself, is, does it have any sexual tension in it? Does it have any good build up and tease?" Stag is equally quick to dismiss porno that is in too much of a hurry to get to the fucking. "I could almost jerk off better to the beginning of sex scenes in porno, the lead-up, the teasing, the kissing, the taking off of clothes."

"My job in porno is knowing how to build up that erotic energy, the suspense, the tease, the tension, using dramatic set-ups, a bit of characterisation, psychological detail: "Is she going to take her clothes off or not, are they going to fuck or not? That's what's really exciting in real life, is if you're in a room with someone and you're going to try and seduce that person, you're going to try and make them have sex with you, but you can't be sure you'll be successful and that's what I try and get across in my movies.... Plot and stuff, I don't care, that stuff is bullshit."

It's a bit like Clinton during the '92 election, I suggest. Whenever he'd feel himself about to waffle, embarking on some high-blown oration, he'd quickly remind himself what really counts in elections, "It's the economy, stupid', he'd say to himself. Likewise with porno: "It's the sex, stupid."

"Exactly, that's all the people who rent ultimately care about."

Which doesn't mean that porn's stupid or boneheaded?

"Absolutely not. That's a very unsophisticated point of view."

As far as Stag's concerned the people who say stuff like that betray themselves. "I like to compare people who make good porno movies and appreciate good porno movies to the way people fuck. For some a good fuck is simply pounding away, for a lot of people good sex is sensuality, ambience, consideration, appreciation.

"The biggest problem with porno for years was doing these silly little stories with scripts with people who can't act! Plus, most of the time, you're shooting it on video which is faster than film with sixty pictures per second, whilst film has only twenty-four .Video's real life. There is this sense with film of removal from reality, richer colours, more stylised, and less brutal on bad acting I guess."

Without a script, Stag has the basic Buttman concept to which he'll add the barest outline of a situation, a scenario, looking to find the heat through impro and mood.

He'll ask a performer if they have any skills that can be used in a fictionalised setting. Some of the guys might be dance instructors, or fitness trainers, which Stag could try and work into the forthcoming scenario so that they might perform more naturally, be more convincing within their 'role'. Some girls will have done some office work prior to getting into porno, waitressing, dancers. Maybe they can play a musical instrument. "One girl had once worked as a realtor so we made that as part of the situation. It keeps it more real."

Again it's Stag the method-porner, with the option of pursuing his reality thing as a director from actually inside the movie, as the filming is occurring. By saying something as Buttman to one of the performers, saying something unexpected perhaps, which may push their performance in another direction, he can direct a scene without having to stop it, talk about it, and start again.

All this talk of method and directing sounds a bit high-art, rather highfalutin. Certainly it is true, as Wendy McElroy has observed, how porners have a habit of telling you their philosophy concerning porn. It stems perhaps from a need to boast, to have their work and themselves taken more seriously, not to be dismissed out of hand. Stagliano, though, feels there are more practical issues at stake — rooting out the bad acting, the conventionalised/institutionalised sexual responses he sees too often in porno. When casting for a new movie, the first thing he looks for, he admits, is a desirable performer, a good butt. "Anything else I can work around." Once this particular primeval need has been satisfied however, he tries to cast people who haven't worked with many other directors before. Ideally it will be their first time.

"Once a girl has done a lot of movies she performs and groans and looks immediately turned on. A girl who performs on set with a whole load of people hanging around, milling around, like in a carnival situation, which is what too many porno sets are, she protects herself with controlling her performance, making it into a process and not a natural response. The last thing I want to see is a girl doing something because she thinks that that's going to please us."

Another thing Stagliano doesn't want to see is silicone. Breast enhancements has to be one of the biggest bones of contention in porno at the moment. The fans loathe plastic in their videos, at least judging by the numbers of complaints you hear about. There are whole web sites on line dedicated to the restoration of real bodies in porn. All these people complaining and yet, at the same time, all these performers going under the knife. It's a funny thing. I asked Stagliano what he thought about it all — after all, he did make *Buttman's Big Tit Adventure* against all advice and made a fortune from it.

"I like big women. If I had to conceive of my ideal woman, it would be someone like Anne-Nichole Smith with real tits. Blonde voluptuous women, that's my thing, my fetish. However, I can't tell you how much I dislike silicone. For some girls, it makes their breasts look better, for some it makes them look worse. For all girls, it makes their breasts a lot less fun to play with. I would rather have my girlfriend with saggy, natural tits, than great big 'done' tits. I see these girls with gorgeous natural small breasts saying they're going to have a boob job and I say don't do it. What are they going to think about them in ten years."

Brandy Alexandre feels the same, "all the women in porno these days are getting their tits done, it's really boring."

All this plastic on screen and in magazine spreads and on the dance circuit, was this a case of porno sending out the wrong kinds of signals? — "I don't think so," says Stagliano.

"Why blame porno for this. People are always too quick to blame porno. It's not much better in the regular world of movie making. Look at Melanie Griffith and Pamela Anderson, they say Demi Moore and Madonna had theirs done, and what they chose to do as women has a lot more impact than anything a star in porno chooses to do."

Once the business of shape, career and cosmetic surgical history has been successfully covered, it is at the casting stage that the business of contracts is gone into. Stagliano, like most directors, will talk about the scene he has in mind with the models, and at the same time goes over model release forms and contracts, ascertaining what hours they will work, what they get paid, who owns what, and what they will be expected to do in the sex scene. "So that everybody knows what's going to happen and nobody feels manipulated..."

How much does a woman expect to earn from appearing in a Buttman movie?

"Usually $400 a scene for a new girl. Sometimes a girl will name a price, I'll say it's too low, I'll pay you more, sometimes they name a high price and I let them have it, as much as $1,000. To do an anal scene she'll ask for $400, I'll offer her $600 because an anal scene is demanding and I want them to feel happy. Up to a point, however. I don't want to be suckered, I don't like it if a girl works for me for $1,000 and then goes and works for someone else for half that... that's not fair to me."

How much are 'the talent' making in porn these days?

"In the mid eighties people like Traci Lords and Ginger Lynn were big and working every day of the week, making a lot from porn

Buttman magazine pin-up

Jessica

BUTTMAN

alone, a thousand bucks a day. Maybe if a new girl comes into the business and she's really hot she might make $10,000 a month for a few months, and then the scale slides, because people get used to you."

"Most girls work a lot in porn and only make a few thousand bucks a month. But that's as performers. The last five years or so has seen this incredible boom in features dancing, with porno performers out on the road. Celeste, Woody Long's wife [the guy who drove me out to Stag's house], she was a one-time Vivid contract player. She did a scene for me, starting out in her career, then she got her nose done, tits done, went on the road, now she earns maybe $4,000 a week, and will probably be making double that

the driving, out there making good money for themselves. It's so insulting to speak of them always as poor little girls, they work hard — and they're doing it for themselves.)

Stagliano has an upright reputation in the industry, as someone who's good to work for.

"Working with John was fun," remembers Brandy Alexandre. "He was respectful, gracious, he didn't push you, he coaxed, and was very boyish and charming. He charms the girls, makes suggestions. He doesn't bark orders. He doesn't treat women like chattel." (Brandy Alexandre) The good working experience seems to come across in the final product, you only have to see the smile on Patricia Kennedy's face at the start of *Buttman versus Buttman*, or Zara Whites and Alexan-

Buttman on the job

amount from tips, and will be able to spend around thirty to thirty-five weeks on the road in the year. And in between times, they make movies."

(The general idea is that women in porn are being coerced, subjected to violence and pressure to perform, when in reality a half to three-quarters of their working month they're off dragging an enormous lighting rig around America, usually with their partners doing

dria Quinn in *Ultimate Workout*. The writer Tammy Cole considers the latter: "These girls cannot be acting! They gotta be paying him. They are enjoying it too much! Not just enjoying, they are revelling and rejoicing! It's evident with every body movement, every facial expression."

And what about safe sex in porno?

"The self-imposed norm within the industry is a HIV test every six months, DNA test every two months.... I also require an anti-body test every thirty days for performers, which is a lot cheaper. These things are more important than rubbers, which are very non sexual, and some girls are allergic to them."

For a man who makes a point of setting trends and making the running in terms of good ethics, Stag is disappointingly inflexible on safe sex. "I have shot with rubbers four or five times, with people I really wanted to use. But if people say they want to use rubbers, then usually I won't hire them."

The director Gino Colbert, who directs both straight movies as well as the gay movies for which he is famous, for which he was made an *AVN* hall-of-famer, tells me the straight industry are basically stupid, or ignorant, or both, where safe sex matters. "They just don't understand. They still seem to think that it is some kind of gay-only complaint."

Colbert always offers performers the choice of using condoms. With *All About Teri Wiegel*, he said four out of the five couplings declined the offer. They said condoms affected their performance, making them feel less sexy. Colbert reckons the big thing that straight needs to do is sexualise people in condoms, and to stop saying rubbers aren't erotic. Typically, Stag argues that for gay movies safe sex is a must, and with a transsexual movie he's was about to produce at E A the decision had been to go with rubbers. "Transsexuals tend to be very sexually active," he tells me.

And porn performers, I suppose, aren't sexually active in their work. A scene in *Face Dance* comes to mind. Near the start of the movie Rocco Siffredi is kidnapped at airport arrivals by a seductive intermediary sent by Buttman. He is blindfolded and driven to Buttman's abode, where he features in a Stag party game, called the face dance — organised to celebrate Rocco's coming to America. The game involves four blindfolded men with four women butt-dancing in their faces. The women rotate, changing partners till they've done all four guys. In due course the blindfolds come off and the situation evolves into a choreographed orgy, whilst Stagliano watches and films. It's basically another male

fantasy taken to the limit. The kind of bachelor party game every American college fraternity, every Animal House probably dreams of happening. Here, not only is the wildest fantasy enacted, but it involves the most attractive women, and is there, preserved on videotape, to be watched again and again.

The face dance goes on at length, likewise the sex chain which follows, which also involves an awful lot of swapping and switching of partners. The length has to be some kind of record, even for an orgy scene. Every individual on screen, it would seem, gets to be intimate with everyone else. Now, the point is, if this doesn't count as sexually active, than what does! If anyone on this shoot had been infected or carrying anything, all eight of them would have been at the very least exposed, before the shoot was done.

People in straight hardcore are quick to stress that though there may have been incidents, some scares and the like, so far no straight actor in porno has been infected making porno. The only reported AIDS death in straight porn was John Holmes, who, they say, got infected through being an IV drug user. Assuming all this is true, you still can't help but feel that it's some kind of miracle, whatever kinds of precautions are taken. A few years ago, the actress Busty Belle put it in a nutshell: "I don't care if you had an AIDS test two weeks ago, who were you with last night?"

FACE DANCE

FACE DANCE I AND II IS STAG'S MAGNUM opus. Made in 1992, the scripted, shot on film, high-end, porno extravaganza weighs-in at a massive four hours forty minutes long. A non-Buttman movie (though actually featuring Buttman as one of the narrative strands) *Face Dance* is a highly wrought and multi-layered piece of work, comic, dark, arresting intense. Definitely a little wayward and flabby, at times a little self indulgent in spots, at other times *Face Dance* amounts to a razor sharp, compelling and mesmeric experience. It certainly feels like Stag's finest moment in porno.

It's the story of the horrors of movie production. Rocco plays an Italian porn actor who comes to America to make a regular, non porno movie, and finds himself tangled-up in a lot of neurotic mess. The director's a malevolent, manipulative son-of-a-bitch. He is obsessed with pushing the actors to breaking point, bullying and belabouring the talent to find 'the inner-truth' of their character, during interminable rehearsals that always seem to turn into screwing sessions. He's fucking with Rocco's mind.

Meanwhile, the producer (played by Tiffany Million, one-time female wrestler) isn't proving so helpful with her flimflams and her power games: either she's insisting Rocco hides his porno background from the movie's financiers, or she's subtlety mocking his stud credentials.

Rocco's not happy. Rocco doesn't want to stay, he wants to go back to Italy, get back to making good, old honest porn flicks. But he can't get away, and they keep pushing him and pushing him, till he's all fit to blast.

Rocco's agonies, account for one of the three narrative strands of Face Dance. In complete contrast, another strand features a series of laid-back, knockabout Buttman segments, filmed in and around Buttman's abode — Rocco's sanctuary where he goes to ease his pain and get some light relief. The third and least satisfying part of Face Dance concerns some farce filler concerning the shenanigans of the secretarial people at the film production company. Some of these scenes are quite hard to watch — exactly what you get when you try to do porno screwball with no script and a lot of weak acting.

It's the darker fantasy scenes in Face Dance which catch the eye, and which make the lesser parts tolerable. Full of manic energy, with the emotions cranked up extra high, and featuring Joey Silvera's excellent performance as the bastard movie director, they feature a staggering series of choreographed sex scenes. Ultimately, with Stagliano, it's not going to be the stories that make or break it, not like they do maybe with movies by people such as John Leslie, Paul Thomas, and Candida Royale.

The sex in Face Dance is probably the best Stagliano's ever shot. At times the whole purpose seems to be to find interesting and intense new ways of filming sex. If the big face dancing scene, already mentioned, is just a little sloppy, just a little too drawn out, then the opening and closing four-way scenes (which function as a kind of framing device for this most extended of porn movies), are peaks, whilst the chequered dance floor routine is probably the most technically bravura piece of sex photography you're ever going to see in porno.

Two couples are fucking on a shiny, waxed, black and white dance floor, but fucking like it was a dance routine, a slow-burning, steadily evolving dance routine. Stagliano switches between various group-shots and close-ups brilliantly. The group shots are cross-sectional compositions mixing sharp angles with an uncluttered depth of vision, accommodating in any single frame one couple in the foreground right, one couple middle ground left, and, between the two, at the back of the shot, Joey Silvera watching, and playing with himself as he watches. Add to this the dark lighting, the black and white squares on the chequered dance floor, the smoky dance mirrors and the arrangement within the frame of the silver dance poles, and then add on to this the way Stagliano cuts and switches between such group shots and close-ups, fanning the heat, where his camera prowls and circles between and around the bodies in motion, and you get a sense of the kind of visual impact which starts to build as this long and appropriately unhurried scene approaches its climax. All kinds of kaleidoscopic fornicating patterns form and then split to reform in new ways, on and on and on.

This builds to a quite startling pitch, unlike any other piece of sustained porn work . It is little wonder he won awards, little wonder too, that part of him wants to be more than just Buttman, and that he dreams of doing mainstream erotic dance movies. Stagliano took a long while getting Face Dance just so, for him at least, the editing alone must have taken for ever. But it was worth it. Though there are serious flaws in terms of bad writing and bad acting and some slug-like pacing, there are moments of time in *Face Dance* when you feel as though you have left porno and entered mainstream Hollywood's hidden place, it's secret, dark erotic chamber. Though 100 per cent a hardcore porn movie, *Face Dance* is also something else, like a hardcore porno movie about to cross over and become a mainstream erotic movie, with all the hardcore intact.

Face Dance is both a very signatured piece of porn auteurism, psychobiographically telling much of it's creator's life and aspirations, whilst also functioning as a kind of opulent, over-the-top porno progeny of the collective musings of Prince, Bob Fosse and Jean-Luc Godard (circa *Passion*). It's like the three of them teamed up and tried to imagine what a porno movie they'd make together would actually look like, and then asked John Stagliano to make it. With *Face Dance* John Stagliano made what is felt by many to be the best straight porno movie of the nineties, as well as up there and ranking alongside breeder porn's all time greats, *Devil in Miss Jones I* and *II, Opening of Misty Beethoven, Seven into Snowy, Baby Face, Pamela Mann*. As they say, if you're going to rent one porno movie, (and you've got four hours forty minutes to spare)...

SCOPOPHILIAC !

There's a scene midway through *Face Dance*, when the fun and games of Buttman mixes briefly with some of the weird stuff out of Rocco's movie. It's late one night and Rocco arrives back at Buttman's abode. He finds Buttman hovering outside in the dark, peeping in through the window with his camera, eyeing up some potential funny business going on indoors involving a couple of girls. Buttman's unaware of Rocco's presence, and for a while Rocco says nothing, he just stays back in the shadows, watching Buttman peeping in. Time sort of hangs for several seconds, action suspended, before normal service is resumed with the two of them hooking-up together in matey union of peepers. Though short lived, it is a curious moment: quiet, tense, vaguely unsettling.

It's not the only time Stag's dropped a double peep view in a movie. And he's not the only person to be doing such things in porno. In fact, in porno, the viewer's never too far away from a reference to the tangled business of watching; another reminder of how what we are all doing, one way or another, is peeping.

Previously critics with a psychoanalytical bent have had themselves a field day with porno and the complexities of voyeurism; that dark, Freudian drive to look. However, where Buttman is concerned — when apart from the scene in *Face Dance*, the references to voyeurism are handled with a lighter touch — another route is preferred. After all, this isn't Alfred Hitchcock, and it isn't schlocky Brian de Palma either, this is Buttman, and the term isn't scopophiliac — 'peeping tom' will do just fine.

Buttman is your commonplace, neighbourhood peeper. The kind of horny guy who's forever idling away the time, peeping over garden fences, scrabbling through bushes, up grassy banks and the like, furtively approaching the windows of private residences where he's got a feeling something 'nasty' is going on. Buttman scurries, he scopes, he snoops, it's what he does. Watching a Buttman movie brings the excruciating pleasures and pains of peeping right up close to the viewer's eyes. Is John Stagliano then, really just another peeping tom?

"I've always liked to sneak around, to take pictures, to go down to the beach in LA, to bikini contests, snapping pics of girls' butts on the sly, when they're not aware of it."

He tells me he's still got a whole boxful of these pics he took from years back. "This was always my obsession and (with Buttman) I could put it into a dramatic context... Voyeurism is very important to the success of Buttman, working as part of the erotic build up, the first person POV, of sneaking around, of not just getting into the sex straight away."

Foregrounding voyeurism in this way, is

this a rather dangerous game? Don't you run the risk of making the viewer uncomfortably all too aware of their bad habits? Or, worse, might it make them comfortable with such activities? Does rehabilitating voyeurism threaten to kill the goose that laid the golden egg?

"I'm not sure I do that in my movies. I'm not sure if I want to make it seem okay to look, because it's a lot more fun sneaking a look. I think that just walking down the street, girl-watching, is an incredible lot of fun, and that's what a lot of my movies are about, and if they help people feel okay about that, then fine."

Stag is also interested in the view that being a peeper for porno, and basically having had access to porno, has possibly kept him from being an actual peeper in real life. I ask him at one point, Do you think porn was good for you?

"Definitely. Without it what would I do with all my ideas, where would I take them. Porno's a good expression for that kind of stuff, without it, I might have to do it in less socially acceptable ways in the real world, like being a peeping tom or something like that."

Though Stagliano denies any attempt to accommodate the gawper, to find ogling and peeping a kinder press, the Buttman movies definitely play a bit like this. Butt's the rubber neck who never gets sent packing, who never really gets into trouble. With this Stag tunes in to one of porno's biggest fantasies which, not uncoincidentally, also happens to be a lot of young males' ultimate fantasy — where the average guy can sneak a peek at a vision of beauty, maybe even strike up a conversation, and not be rebuffed. Buttman does this. He does it all the time. He pulls it off.

Which makes him such a success story, possessed of a large band of loyal fans. Buttman's out there, doing it for the guys.

And making a financial killing from it, too. Over time Stagliano has become not very upwardly mobile, but steeply. And he's not at all shy about it either. In an interview with *Filmmaker* magazine in 1993, when asked what the future held for him, Stagliano said, "I don't want to keep making this kind of

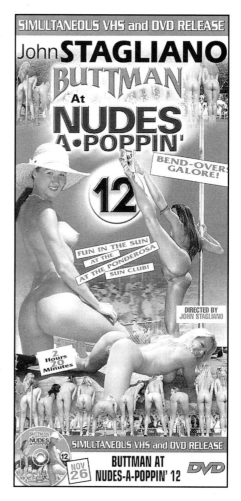

money, it seems kind of weird." Such an embarrassment of riches has to add to the appeal of his movies. Buttman's fantasies not only lead to gorgeous women and great sex, but a heap of cash. No longer do we seem to be watching just another hardcore video featuring a guy with a camera who gets lucky — whose camera snooping didn't get him beaten-up or arrested, but a big time porno fantasy about a camera-snooper making pretty good, and whose camera snooping actually made him into a very wealthy individual.

BUTTMAN'S INFERNO

BUTTMAN'S INFERNO... THE OPENING *sequence of the movie. Another perfect, sunny day in southern California, except for the fact that there's a forest fire raging, and the Santa Ana wind is blowing the danger ever nearer to people's homes. The scene is chaos. Helicopters flying overhead, firetrucks on the streets — like LA during the riots. Everyone's getting in their cars, getting out of there fast. Meanwhile , with his buttcave seemingly about to be barbecued, Buttman's thinking out loud to himself, "if only we had a girl here now, we could shoot a great scene."*

It's interesting how the Buttman fantasy has evolved in terms of an increased economic well-being . There was a time when Buttman hardly had two beans to rub together. In *Buttman v Buttwoman*, Buttman got fired by Bruce Seven, and then he lost his

STREET DATE: **APR 5**

John
STAGLIANO

BUTTMAN'S
Big
ADVENTURES #5

ALL NATURAL
VOLUPTUOUS
VIXENS!

BIG TITS!

BIG ASSES!   **BIG FUN!**

house and became one of LA's homeless people, seen wandering the streets of Santa Monica, rooting through garbage looking for food.

Of course by this stage in his life, Stagliano was actually already a very wealthy man, and the reality of the particular movie was completely the other way round. He was in charge, he hired Bruce Seven. But southern California is a fiercely free market kind of place, where capitalism lays waste to losers, and it is this scary knowledge that's humming away in the deep background of the Buttman fantasy. With *Buttman's Revenge*, Buttman finally made it big. With the runaway success of *Buttman's Big Tit Adventure* against all the odds, his ship finally came in . Welcomed back with open arms by Bruce Seven, Butt finally got himself a luxury home. But even then it was little more than a year later when he nearly lost it again, during the raging Malibu forest fires.

If you've seen a few of Buttman's movies, it probably means you've not only seen his home a good few times. Recent movies regularly feature Stag's place. There's Buttman at home with Krysti Lynn, 'the tease from hell', trying to get some editing done in the den whilst Krysti is fooling around out on the sun deck, distracting him from his work by playing with herself, or having sex with her dance instructor. Then there's Buttman chilling out by the pool, dropping off to sleep, commencing his 'wet dream'. When American *Penthouse* did their big glossy profile of Stagliano a few years back, he was photographed wearing a dinner jacket, bow tie and Hawaiian trunks, draped over the side of the pool and sipping champagne.

Buttman in heaven, or Buttman — really big show-off?

Obviously it makes sense to film at home; it's a lot cheaper, and it means you don't get stuck on the freeway for hours on end. However there's more than just penny-pinching going on here. For a start Stag's proud of his house, the success it symbolises — he's showing it off, and, maybe ever so slightly, ever so nicely, rubbing the viewer's nose in it. Yet it's more than this too. The dreamhome is part of the arousal. Buttman's abode works as a kind of alluring extension of the fantasy scenario of Buttman's excellent life. Porno desires, porno dreams are more than just a series of uncomplicated libidinal hankerings, they are aspirational fantasies, intricately tied in with other kinds of urgent needs, wishes and wants. Buttman movies are consumer, capitalist wank fantasies, just like a whole lot of other American consumer capitalist wank fantasies peddled by the regular non-porno media — movies, TV, magazines and pop videos. Just like the hegemonic mainstream whose mores his hardcore sensibility partly transgresses, Stagliano's movies offer the seductive and arousing hallucination of blissful, careless living, of luxury homes, fine furnishings, beautiful people, great fucks, sun-kissed travelogues, of the achievement of uncomplicated and carefree states of being.

In the mid eighties, when the authors of *Porn Gold* interviewed Rupert James, editor at Rodox (the hardcore magazine publishers in Denmark), he volunteered the following on the subject of capitalist fantasies in pornography. "The style of mags has more or less stayed the same, but the quality has improved tremendously. Our productions are beginning to look more and more like *Dallas* or *Dynasty*." James continues, "If you take our magazine stories ten years ago, they were usually shot under fairly humble circumstances, normal flats… Whereas now everybody arrives in Cadillacs and Rolls Royces at a big house in the country… So there's a double edged fantasy in it now. There's not only the sexual fantasy, there's also this escape into the world of the wealthy."

We live in times of tremendous diversity, for sure, and American culture is as diverse and verticalised as any. But, were you to dabble in a hefty bit of reducing and boiling down, then quite probably the twin peaks of a young American male's fantasy — het or gay — would pretty well run to about something like this: get laid a lot, and make a heap of money. Young straight men love Butt movies. A large percentage of Stag's renting, buying market

are such young men — be they single or in relationships — and still virile enough, still rampant with hormonal urges to entertain the kind of fantasies, if not realities, of multi-partnered, pornocopian promiscuity that the Buttman scenario embodies.

Is Buttman all about never having to grow-up? — "If you consider growing up to be settling down and having kids and moving to the suburbs, then yes Buttman's partly about not growing up."

A remark from earlier comes to mind, about Stag and Buttman being totally the same. Likewise the things Brandy Alexandre told me concerning the two years they were going out together, how he's a nice guy, charming and all that, but unable to commit in any way. That their relationship became too open for it to last. Whenever he'd cheat on her, he'd do it in secret, and she'd have to drag the truth out of him, each and every time. "I'm not sure if it's men can't say no," she says, "or men simply have to be deceitful. Maybe it's both."

Over time Brandy remembers how she found herself giving ground, the rules being repeatedly re-negotiated, and ultimatums allowed to slip: of letting him cheat, giving him that licence, but only if it was going on in another city, when he was Buttmaning abroad, and so on, or, if it had to be local, only with strippers, or hostesses, but not with people she knew. When she finally drew the line at him screwing with women in the industry, who maybe she had to work with the next day, he then fairly predictably did exactly that, having an affair with Patricia Kennedy from *Buttman versus Buttwoman*, an infidelity which brought their relationship to a close.

"John's a very decent person, and fun to be with, but he's really crap at relationships."

After the death of Krysti Lynn at the end of 1995, Stagliano admits he started giving the 'c' word some serious thought. He part reckons he's maybe ready to commit, completely. He'd like to have children, he says, and if Lynn were still alive, then maybe they'd have had children together. He says this, but then he almost immediately starts to back off, putting a price on it. "There's forty per cent of me that would love to settle down, be totally monogamous, start a family, but there's the other sixty per cent tugging away, that requires the occasional out-of-town splurge."

He's a bit of a 'titty bar' addict. Now and again the ex-stripper likes to frequent strip bars. He enjoys going out of town, by himself, to places like Seattle, Tampa and Las Vegas, "where the girls dance real nasty". Following the death of Krysti Lynn, he felt able, he says, to make a pig of himself whenever he fancied, and had only just recently himself a hatful of fun in Amsterdam.

"I can't help it, there's a part of me that still wants to play".

Not just sex play either, for porno's Peter Pan (somewhere the comparison had to be made) also loves his sports. Once he realised the basketball was coming on TV he couldn't get rid of me quick enough. And then there's the baseball. Every year Stagliano heads off to baseball summer camp for the over-forties, where they play baseball all week long, get a little coaching from some pros, and strain the odd hamstring. Summer camps like this cost a fortune, but then America's executive class needs some time to be kids again, to let off steam. Last year Stag's team won the end of camp tournament. He's very proud of this fact. Stranded in the middle of the long, wooden dancing space in Stag's front room, amidst the practice dance rail and the big mirrors is a free-standing drinks bar. Upon which stands his summer camp tournament trophy, and a baseball signed by last summer's pro. Though the trophy's much smaller than any of the countless big porn statuettes he's won, they're all collecting dust in the hallway back at the office, whilst this one's here, taking pride of place.

I found this endearing, but also rather funny. It's a bit rude though, isn't it, going to someone's house, and finding things to feel superior about. After all it's just his way. Like the day before, on our first meeting, in his office at the Evil Angel buildings, when I'd literally found Stagliano down on his hands

and knees, surrounded by a storm of paper, trying to work out which piles were to be left on his desk, and which piles were homework. His bag looked a bit like a school satchel. His staff — mainly old stripping chums from way back — kept asking questions, making demands. He seemed a bit puzzled by it all, scratching his head. He said these days all he really wanted was to play hockey.

Maybe it was all a big act, but he really was like a boy playing the part of the man. When Stagliano took me on a tour round the building — enthusiastically pointing out the

new mega-sized video duplication machines he'd just installed, the coffee machine and the snack dispenser, his awards, the baseball hoop by the loading bay at the back, where they try and play whenever there's time — the experience was akin to being shown around an adolescent's bedroom. Until of course, the next day at his house, when he actually showed me his bedroom, quickly shuffling a heap of messy clothes out of sight, when he thought I wasn't looking. And I thought some more of Tom Hanks and *Big*, the sweet natured, eighties feel good movie, when Hanks plays a boy stuck inside the body of a full grown man. When I said I liked his TV set, this great big monster screen planted right next to his bed, he was chuffed. He told me he loved to lay there at night watching sports, immediately flopping down on the bed for a demonstration of his preferred position.

I wondered if I should have said 'cool!' or something in return.

Of course this isn't the whole of the story. Like the fans who write the letters saying Stag's got it great, thinking his life must amount to a slice of heaven, day after day after day. But they aren't in on the editing process, the long hours spent, not trotting about the streets, but stuck indoors, working alone, the monotonous hassle anterior to the final smooth assembly, cutting and compiling, back and forth and back and forth, knocking the raw footage into fantasy shaped narratives.

Stag isn't just a boy who really doesn't want to grow-up. The thing is he is also a business man, a pretty smart businessman, and his Evil Empire comes with a staff and a whole load of commitments, and obligations to the other porno auteurs like John Leslie and Greg Dark whose movies he manufactures, promotes and distributes and has to watch the figures on closely. The adolescent stuff needs to be contained, he can't just drop everything and go rushing around the place 'goofing around'. Especially after the less than amicable departure of Patrick Collins, business manager and ex-friend. Collins started out minding the shop. But now he is a porno director in his own right, who in 1996 took his Elegant Angel wing of the empire and walked, going on record as saying Stagliano couldn't run a business and would fail without him. Which means the two of them aren't friends anymore. "Patrick's a

bully," says Stag, "and he wasn't doing his job properly, hadn't been for a long time. Since he left, sales have never been better. I should have fired him years ago."

Such bullishness apart, Stag went on record within the industry saying he felt be-

Buttman on the job

trayed by his colleague's precipitate departure. A sense of betrayal compounded perhaps by the feeling that the timing wasn't very bad, coming as it did during a period of calamity and loss for Stag. One evening in December 1995, the actress Krysti Lynn was driving back from a bar to his house, with a friend, when she lost control and the car plunged down the side of a hill. Both Lynn and her friend were killed. The wreckage wasn't found for two days. The road is narrow and very winding and dangerous and she was doing more than 100 mph.

Stagliano wrote a long and poignant piece about her for *AVN*. Typically he didn't pretend all had been fine between them. They'd been living together for a couple of years, but the relationship hadn't always been easy, or a thing of joy. Lynn was actually about to move out at the time, and they were both dating other people. The idea had been that they'd work together on a music video for her — he was working on the script for this the night she died — and a non-porno feature about erotic dancing directed by Stagliano and starring Lynn. And then maybe they'd think about dating again. He spoke of how Lynn had had her share of drink and weight problems, but had finally started to get her life in good shape and was even helping to re-motivate Stagliano with his long planned non-porn debut. She was however a force of nature, he told me, a turbulent, impulsive character and driving too fast and recklessly was the way she was. "She did it to herself," he replied when I said how sad it was. "She really can't blame anybody else. She was twenty-four and she was beautiful."

He had a copy of the issue of *AVN* carrying his appreciation of Lynn on the coffee table. In it he also mentioned how in the early days together she'd pushed him into being more domesticated, more of a regular homemaker, buying food and cutlery and furniture and things. When I came to visit there was no food in the place, not a scrap, just a stack of vitamin bottles and plenty of diet Pepsi stacked-up in an otherwise empty fridge. I noticed a small series of post-its pinned to the fridge door, with Gatsby-like self-improvement maxims written on them, things like, "it's process that counts, not results." It's a cliché but Stag's dream house was a tad spooky, shell-like, had the kind of ambience you get with a place that nobody's being living in for some while, whereas in

fact Stag spends a fair bit of his time working out of here . Though very tidy, the rooms were dusty, and the place had 'bachelor' written all over it. I wondered if Stagliano felt a little bit lonely. Is that the killer truth about the luckiest man in the world. Maybe his grieving has only just started, but maybe this is a case of a grieving that has sort of drifted and become a kind of loneliness.

Around the house there were small heaps of Lynn memorabilia. Especially the bedroom, with videos, promotional material, private photos and stuff. He gave me a Brazilian wallet calendar for 1996 with a picture of Lynn frolicking on a beach in Brazil, some glossy flyers and brochures advertising films she's been in. When I mentioned how I hadn't seen *Buttman's Wet Dream*, he rooted out a copy of it for me from out of the pile of vids by the bed and when I came to play it the tape was already halfway through, stopped right after a long scene involving just him and Krysti joking around the house together. At one point he went to look for some more videos for me, saying that's where Krysti keeps them, present tense, as if she hadn't been dead for many months now. Looking out the big windows at the enormous sun deck, the sculpted swimming pool, the big ocean down below, I thought of that song, 'Dream-Home Heartache'. But then immediately started wondering if I was being a bit too quick in jumping to conclusions, and wondering if perhaps in a way that's what I wanted to find in the dreamhome, some sorrow, wondering if that is what we always sort of enviously hope to uncover.

It's true we all do that, but then the circumstances were peculiar, not what I'd quite expected. Meeting a guy called Buttman for the very first time at his HQ in the heart of fun-loving pornoland, you don't expect to end up talking about bereavement and bereavement counselling, which is what happened. Coming out to meet with him, I thought I'd meet a guy as light as candyfloss who liked women's butts. But he wasn't like that.

The melancholy, I suppose is there in the Buttman schtick, if you're looking, world weary and ready to be heartbroken. Only later, after other people pointed it out, did I discover how being doleful was the Stagliano way, no matter how great or badly things are going. How this routine with fans writing in, telling him his life was heaven and him seriously doubting that fact, was par for the course. "Yeah sure, John's really got it bad," jokes Brandy A, "We'd all love to have some of John's problems, the ten day trips to Cannes, the stopping off in Paris for the fun of it, the lust fest in Amsterdam, all his money, his success.... I don't wish to sound heartless, but John's always been feeling a little bit sorry for himself, it's part of his charm, it's part of the whole Buttman thing. He says this was the first time he's been around death. But he knew Savannah — the famous porno actress who committed suicide — so why didn't he feel it when she died? There have been other people too. To be honest it's all part of that charmed life he thought he could go on having for ever."

Alexandre is a little impatient of her ex-lover. Though they remain pals, they have had their run-ins. They even went to court

once. She had this dispute with Stagliano over money. When Evil Angel first got started and she was going out with Stagliano, she says she was not only acting in some of the movies, she actually worked for the company, she scripted stuff, took stills, was involved in the early promotional work.

"I did a lot of PR for E A and John's movies. I really worked it, schmoozing a lot of buyers and press people. The good-looking, hot porno chick working overtime to make them buy good 'pieces' of Buttman stock. I really pulled out the stops to get John recognised."

They agreed back then that on certain titles she'd get a small commission on all cassette sales over a certain amount. After they split up and she stopped working with him, the particular titles kept selling, but the cheques dried up. She filed a complaint in the small claims court. Which is when the hit TV show People's Court picked up on it. They got in touch with her, but she told them this was a story about pornography, and they didn't want to cover it. They said they certainly did. So, Brandy and John went on People's Court in the full glare, and she won. Stagliano took a lot of persuading to go on and she hears he was pretty pissed off about losing, but has never said anything to her. They remain always amicable. She still tells him he owes her money, and he says he doesn't. She says he doesn't understand, he says he doesn't agree. And they haven't got any further in their dispute.

Brandy was the only woman in porno to produce, write, direct and star in the same movie. She did this a few times in movies like Cop a Feel and Best Butt(e) in the West. The success of these titles, she feels, ultimately backfired on her. The patriarchal porn honchos got their egos hurt and were resentful when one of 'the female talent', whom they associated mainly with big hair and blow-jobs, made some hit movies just as raw and dirty as anything they could muster. According to Brandy, the stereotype of porno women held by the rest of society is, unfortunately, held by too many men in the industry. "Some of them, they fall for that idea that the women are stupid, dippy, too sexual, too hormonal, probably psychologically damaged — just like the feminists say about us."

She claims that a lot of porno men think it's only them that can make fuck films; that it's a guy's thing, and women aren't really ballsy enough to make it hot on screen. "But I did exactly that. I showed them. And they didn't like that." She's convinced she was blackballed and is now out of the industry and has been for a few years. Funnily enough, being underrated, she says, is one of the things about porno she really misses. That and the sex, of course, and getting to really let rip every so often. In porno she'd get a lot of plaudits for not being dumb. When they saw her blonde hair, her body, people assumed she'd be stupid, when they found out she was bright and articulate and could organise and opinionate, she'd pick up a lot of praise and approval.

"In the real world, it's not such a big deal. If you do the kind of work that require brains, then nobody praises you for being intelligent — it's expected."

Alexandre worked off-screen on some of Stagliano's early movies. Her contribution to *De Blond*, which she wrote, and co-directed, gained her a lot of praise from women, she says, who liked the movie for its plausibility. But women also loved the rough house sexplay featured in the movie. They thought it was hot. I wondered out loud about how many porno watchers were female. The oft-quoted figure is about a third of rentals in America are either by women or couples, but like all statistics it's hard to prove. Certainly you do see women in video stores in America, by themselves, in groups, or with partners. If it's no big deal, it means it's hardly a rare sighting. Brandy said she didn't know for sure how many women rented, but she had certainly met a fair few. Other actresses in the industry told me how they used to watch porno with boyfriends before they got into the industry. Stagliano says Krysti Lynn used to watch his stuff a lot, by herself, when he wasn't around, and would complain that of-

ten the work wasn't strong enough. In *Talk Dirty to Me*, her personal account of being a happy porno lover, Sallie Tisdale mentions watching a Stagliano movie called *Wild Goose Chase* and being aroused as well as being moved by the scene where Joe Silvera's character responds to a woman's rejection by claiming there's tons of other girls in his life, then returns home to pull out a drawer full of pictures of women cut out from magazines.

Stagliano himself is clear about the fact that the bulk of his market are men, but reckons that there are also some women viewers out there. "Some women watch porn by themselves. I would say a small percentage of my market, about ten per cent are women-only viewers." Having said all this, Stag still questions how many women really like porn, suggesting how it's not really in their nature. This immediately got me wondering. Has porn helped him understand women any better?

"Yes," he says emphatically, before a long pause, "And yet in other ways, no." He still doesn't have a clue, he confesses, why women do what they do. He thinks they have a whole different perspective. "I can't say I really understand women. They're wired differently."

Stag finds his views on women and gender relations confirmed and underscored by Camille Paglia. He's a very big fan. Paglia's sexual worldview sees men and women as separate and pretty much at odds, positing a great big gender gap which finds the modern urban male and female being driven to act by unseen forces beyond their control. If it's not the deep space of the neo-Freudian psyche doing it, then quite likely it's the shape of our genitals, driving and determining our actions.

Altogether anti-environmentalist, in Paglia-land we act not through choice, but through destiny, and culture is all that keeps us from succumbing to the deluge of nature. Men and women have different genitals; they urinate differently. Pissing, for men, is "a kind of accomplishment, an arc of transcendence. A woman merely waters the ground she stands on." (*Sexual Personae*) From this starting point we become binary opposites. Forget conditions and learned behaviour, women are earthen and fecund, whilst men are bold powerhouses getting things done. Men and women are never in accord, always in disharmony, and yet required to mate. Thus wars are made.

It is via Paglia that Stag has concluded that if Krysti Lynn revelled in the attention her beauty and her lustiness attracted, she was responding to her primeval need to attract the male of the species. That whenever she saw Stag look at another woman and went ballistic with jealous rage, it was because that woman was her procreative rival. Hormonally yours. I wanted to suggest to Stag that maybe this had less to do with his ex being totally in accord with her hormones and nature, and more to do with the fact that porno's an industry that puts a high premium on looks and desirability, maybe not as inflexible or as punishing as Hollywood and the fashion industry, but tough all the same, and so whenever his eyes wandered her assets might have felt questioned.

Stag wonders if it might have helped him and maybe helped Lynn herself, if they'd known more of what Camille knows. He keeps meaning to write Paglia a fan letter. I tell him he really ought to, that maybe they could script a movie together. When you think about it, the marriage of Paglia and porn is made in heaven. Whenever she raps on about beauty as power, porners are bound to sit up and listen. But it's not just what she says, it's the way she says it — the critic James Wolcott once compared Paglia's construction of a chapter as a relentless build-up towards orgasm.

Until he read Paglia and got wise, Stag used to judge women by his own standards, by male standards. He wanted to be active, successful, to make money and do all those things, and if he met a women who wasn't driven like him, then he wasn't interested. Now, he realises that women aren't like that, they have different priorities. "As Camille says, a woman can just be, she doesn't have to prove herself. And this is biological fact. I think the fact my dick gets hard when I see a butt is totally related to biology, it is a sign that she's fit and healthy and will reproduce well". Furthermore, "What stops a lot of women getting into porn is the repression of their natural exhibitionism that women as the female of the species naturally require to attract a mate.

"One of the things I like about the porno business is that the women are so interesting, much more interesting than the average women on the street. The reason I say this is that because of the stigma thing. Stigma is so great a thing for the women. And for a woman to stand up and say 'I know all this, I know this is going to piss a lot of people off, and cause me a lot of problems'. And they still do it, basically saying, 'I don't care what other people think, I don't care what the consequences are, I think this is something I want to do right now and I'm going to do it'. I respect the hell out of that…"

What does he think about the claim that women in porno are psychologically damaged, are maybe trying to sort out, or runaway from something in their background, their childhood. He doesn't think this is necessarily the case. But then he doesn't rule it out either.

"A lot of performers get into porn for the wrong reasons, but then again this happens all over the place in life. People do many things for the wrong reasons, get into a quick marriage because of a bad homelife, for example, and no one's going to blame marriage for this, but porno will be criticised even when it is the exact same motivation…"

Like several porno producers spoke with about this, Stagliano demonstrated a genuine concern for newcomers to the industry and issues of social stigma. "For a lot of people it's not good to be in porno… if a girl is not approaching the issue that if she's getting into porno she'll suffer stigma and lose friends, then she shouldn't be getting into it. I have often queried girls at casting calls if they seem to have doubts or are avoiding some of the issues. When they say they don't think they'll tell their fathers. I say that's not good, you should think of doing one or two things, either telling him (because he'll find out one way or another) or don't do porno. Having said that, if I see a pretty girl I really want her in my movie, I don't work too hard to put her off."

Until Wendy McElroy came along researching her book *XXX* — which features an amusing dinner party scene involving Stagliano, McElroy and John Leslie — Stagliano didn't much recognise a feminist threat to his livelihood. Though he knew that there were women who didn't like his line of business, Stagliano was not aware that there were feminists who wanted him put in jail, saying that the movies he made were a crime against women. "Early on in my career, I used to try and write women characters for my scripts who were really independent. I thought that that was what feminism was all about. It's what it was all about in the early seventies. But people like Andrea Dworkin took feminism in another direction, to having all males as being oppressive of women. I don't understand this."

Otherwise, Stag has little to offer on the matter, other than to mention the fact that porners cannot depict rape scenes now because of the pressure from certain feminists. This would get them into trouble. "Rape is a big sexual fantasy, especially for women. I would say that if I did a rape scene, and I did it right, it would appeal more to women than to men. A lot of women want to dream about being taken, about being overwhelmed, and if you can relate that in drama, I think it is a good thing to let a woman live such a thing out in fantasy."

What about talk of violence and coercion in the making of porn? How much of this goes on in the industry?

"Generally speaking, in strict definition of coercion, there hasn't ever been any to my knowledge — in the sense that someone was physically forced to do a porno movie. That being said, there are other ways to convince a weak-willed person to do something they didn't really want to do, and that happens, on occasion. It's not something I want to be involved in, and I believe that is a very, very small percentage.

"People get into this industry with their eyes wide open, no one signs a model release

and then later says 'oh I didn't know that meant you could show my picture all over the place'. That just doesn't happen. I've never heard of it in all the time I've worked in porno. People know that if they have their picture taken, it's going to be shown all over the place. A girl is not forced to do anal, oral. There has never been any physical force used in this business that I know of."

I move on to ask about the religious, moral objections. When faced with the criticisms of the religious right, Stagliano proves more circumspect. "My biggest disagreement I'd have with the religious right would come down to whether I think I have the right to tell other people what to do with their own lives, when they're not hurting anyone else.

"That apart, I understand their problem with porno. I understand better than they'd expect a pornographer to. For the religious right their big thing is family values. This is biological. Promiscuous sex is not good for the family. It's true. It's no good for my genes. So, their values are the natural values, and porners like me are anti-nature, likewise feminist values that would have women being something other than breeders. So they're partly right, because porn is bad for humankind."

It's the Paglia-worshipping part of Stag coming to the fore again.

"I believe that there is a conflict there, and I understand their objections. And yet I think you must acknowledge that women are flirtatious and like to show off. Whilst men, young men, like to screw around a lot, they will screw anything that moves. And this is a natural part of life, a biologically driven part, that should not be repressed. Porn is a good way of helping people out with these needs in fantasy rather than in real life with all of its complications.

"The fact is, on the whole, I don't behave in real life like I do in my movies, because it complicates my life too much. I like to keep mostly monogamous relationships, although this is not always possible, and then in my fantasies, when I want to jerk off, promiscuity is very erotic for me, it's a real turn on.

"Having said this, I am sensitive to the

fact that what I do offends some people. Parents with small children want to protect their kids from sexual images. I think that is wrong, personally, but I can understand their point of view. It makes them feel uncomfortable. It makes me uncomfortable when I see it in front of a child. Worst part of that is that the adult is uncomfortable, far more than the child is ever going to be."

I asked Stagliano about talk of filmed killings and so-called 'snuff' videos. It seemed like as good a time as any to pop the question. When you ask people about snuff you feel a fool, you know how pretty much everybody else knows by now how the stories of snuff is just stories — and if they don't know, then they really ought to. Knowing full well how the factual origins of the myth are well documented and have been thoroughly gone into, you know that asking about snuff makes you sound either like some sleazy journo, or some kind of innocent dope. But the thing is snuff and porno are two words that have an unfortunate habit of going together in a lot of people's minds. When I told a friend I was going to do some research into porno and that I was going to meet some porno makers, he asked me what I was going to actually do, and before I could answer said they'd probably kidnap me and take me out into the desert and use me to make a snuff video. The association is stuck there. You can understand how sick and tired of it some people in porno are. When I asked one porn executive about snuff, what harm it might have had on the industry, a person who'd, until that point, been so voluble and ready to discuss anything, really frosted over with me for a few moments and effectively declined to comment. Even an answer that would expose the myth for what it was, would also sustain the link, keeping the word association in tact.

Having said all this, I still asked. You have to really, for the sake of completion if nothing else. So, snuff, what about it, what do you reckon? — "There has never ever been such a thing as snuff videos, anywhere, to my knowledge, when there was a porn film where someone was killed and it was sold to someone else. I have never heard about it, I've never seen it.

"The actual movie, called *Snuff*, that caused the stir and birthed the myth, I've talked to one of its producers, he told me how they mixed onto a plain ordinary porno movie a dramatisation of someone being killed, being killed like in any other horror movie, and they played on the fact that to some it looked like for real, that some thought it was for real. They played on that to make money, pure and simple. They didn't immediately come out and say no, no this is just fiction, because they had moviegoers queuing round the block in NY wanting to see *Snuff*. Other than that, I know nothing."

Does he wish these people hadn't ever made the movie, and whipped up all this fuss. "Who cares that they made this movie. Maybe it was a bad thing. They let people think it was real, but otherwise people make money off of violence all the time."

Don't you think it has somewhat blighted the industry?

"A little, but the thing is with snuff, it can be settled with a few pertinent facts. Child porn is much more of an issue. When politicians are talking about repressing pornography, they put 'child' in there straightaway to gain support and leverage, it has emotive force and enables them to justify efforts to censure the activities of adults. They throw it in, and ninety-eight per cent of the time there's none of it involved."

Most porners feel they're a lot better off with a Democrat in the White House. No matter that Clinton's passed laws against the internet, and fired his surgeon general for coming out as pro-masturbation, porno people are sticking with Bill. They've got good reason for feeling this way: historically Republicans and porners do not get along. During Reagan and Bush top people in the industry went to jail. Under Clinton, the industry has expanded. Paul Thomas, the former porno actor turned director told me four more years of Clinton would do just fine. "Another term, and afterwards they can elect whoever they like, because I'll be out of the industry by then".

Stag takes the longer view. "With Clinton, there seems to have been less pressure, it's true. But whoever's elected, they will do what people in America want. And what the people in America want is to be free, and they don't want laws against pornography in general. And if a presidential candidate wants to ride on that, ride on some Christian thing, he'll find that he'll drop in the polls because that's the way it is in America."

Stag's sure of this. "Those who see the Christian right and say it's going to get worse, lack perspective. In the fifties porn was repressed, in the sixties it got a little better; the seventies, a little better; eighties, overall, a little better still, so too with the nineties. They may pass a law tomorrow that puts us all out of business, but in two-three years we'll be back." He thinks about this for a second. "I just hope that if they do pass a law, they don't send me to prison for too long.

"Whatever happens, however, the general trend's heading a certain direction. We're going towards freedom. Freedom leads to benevolence, porn creates benevolence, creates a loving atmosphere. Censorship, restriction, creates bad will in all kinds of ways, creates aggression in all kinds of ways."

Bearing in mind how I'd already asked Stag if he thought porno was good for him, I asked if porno had changed him at all.

"In what way?"

Has it made sex seem more important to you in the general scheme of things than it might have otherwise?

"Yes, I think about it a lot. It's such a big part of my life. You know, there was a time when in '85, '86, I thought I don't really want this to be such a big part of my life, and thought about getting out of it. But then I knew myself, and knew I'd get horny and aroused and dream about making porno movies again. I've always had this conflict."

Is porn addictive?

"I'm totally addicted to porn, for sure. I probably use it as an escape. Great thing about porn, is that once you've used it, you want to get away from it. 'Oh God let me get on with some work now'."

This benign form of addiction, his conflictual relationship with porno too, these are the things that make Stag the kind of porner he is, giving him the edge he needs to get the good porno shots that bring the punters in. They may also however, be the reasons for his inertia, his sluggishness with getting started on his long planned and long-stalled regular movie. For, in the end, if he were making a regular movie, he wouldn't be making porno.

Back in 1992, according to the big plan, *Face Dance* was to be Stag's launch pad. Not simply there to be amazing in its own right, he made it to prove to himself how he could still do a high end kind of movie in porno, the only way he knew of checking if he was ready to go and make a non-porno feature. Instead what happened was he kept on making Buttmans. *Face Dance* was the dry run for a movie that's still to be made. During '93 and '94 Stag regularly took time out from the 'grind' of doing Buttman to write a script. It'll be a film about stripping, male and female strippers and the world of erotic dancing. But, unlike *Showgirls* or *Striptease*, "my movie will get to the truth about the world of stripping and won't feed on preconceptions, on sleazy, moralistic clichés, in order to make some money."

He is as sure about this, as he is sure that he'll in two, three years time he will still be dilly-dallying and shilly-shallying around with his project and not really getting anywhere. The problem is, he's not as driven as he used to be. Having always thought his ambition was to save money to make a regular low budget movie, now that he has the money, the time, the opportunity, he finds he's partly lost the desire to do it; not sure anymore what it is he wants to be, does he want to be an artist, a business man, a Buttman, or just a bit of a lazy git.

With Buttman the eternally, fretfully concupiscent young male — his greedy eyes pressed close up against the shop window, ogling all the forbidden goodies within and wishing they were his, you also have Stagliano. This was his fantasy, the fantasy he turned into porno movies, which sort of turned his fantasy into a reality for him, and into a consumer package, which he then sold on and made a fortune from. Nice work if you can get it, where everything could not have been better. But what about now. You hesitate about coming over all philosophical at this stage, but what happens once you've done all that, had everything you wanted, what do you do next?

There was a time when Stagliano was the Young Turk in porno, an eager beaver with new ideas, but he can't really call himself that anymore. Now, he's top of the heap and there are probably people just starting out who dream of emulating him, guys with new ideas. He admits, for example, he hasn't got into computers in a big way. He's doing a CD-rom, but you can tell his heart isn't really in it. Evil Angel have been very slow to get onto the world wide web beyond advertising its product. Stag finds the net to be gimmicky, "a very poor delivery system for pornography", and feels that nobody's used the new tech in an interesting fashion just yet.

Stagliano admits how the next big new thing in porno probably won't be coming from him. How could Buttman stay cutting edge, when he spends half his life being CEO at Evil Angel. Brandy A thinks Buttman is in decline: "He's become a caricature of a caricature, like Buttman doing Buttman. It used to be he was a shy guy who had to work for his conquests, now he's a caricatured shy guy who barely has to wait before the goodies start putting out for him." Certainly with a movie like *Buttman's Wet*

Dream, one gets a creeping sense of self satisfaction, of Buttman being too pleased with what he's got, a kind of complacency that doesn't fit with the earlier neediness and hang dog world weariness. Stagliano himself concedes that maybe at a certain point he stopped pushing himself creatively, thinking he was

John Stagliano — lost inside the B-hole

going to be needing his ideas for other projects, that it's possible that Butt's stuck in a rut.

And then you see a movie like *European Vacation III*, Buttman and Rocco Siffredi reunited and on the prowl in Prague and Barcelona, and you remember how witty they can be sometimes, how well they play off each other, and you realise that maybe Buttman's got some life left in him still.

In the summer of '96, during the election season, Republican presidential candidate Bob Dole stated that cigarettes were no more damaging or addictive than milk. This ludicrous claim made Dole the subject of some intense agitation from the anti-smoking lobby. This included having a man dressed as a cigarette and called 'Buttman' following the lugubrious candidate from town to town around the election trail.

Meanwhile the Video Software Dealer's Association held its annual awards ceremony in Los Angeles. This rare occasion for straight and porno industries to share a platform, found Buttman's *European Vacation III* being voted the best video in the adult category. Stagliano dedicated his award to Krysti Lynn. Whilst the rest of the prize winners including actor Robin Williams made sure to get a crack in about wanting to be Buttman. Shortly afterwards Stag was off to Europe again to film *Vacation IV*, whilst his latest release was hitting the stores. The new release was called *Buttman in the Crack*.

It was Amber Hollimbaugh who once so poignantly wrote about how she regretted waiting for so long into her adult life and adult sexuality before coming to the conclusion that her fantasy life was something she shouldn't be ashamed of, or something she should seek to police, rather it was something she should find fun, comfort and pleasure in. John Stagliano seemingly has never had this problem of ruinous self censorship where fantasy and creativity are concerned. With *Buttman in the Crack* he took his lifelong fascination with posteriors to the next stage, to another place altogether, where he won't be needing his passport. Talking about things like where next for Buttman, and getting stuck in a rut, *Buttman in the Crack,* literally finds him in the crack, up there, and stuck there.

"This is not really your average Buttman movie, it's different."

That's putting it mildly. "Basically, what happens is I get myself stuck in the crack. I meet a girl on the street, and I get so into her butt, that I actually put my camera down and get up really close, and all of a sudden my head just pops into a her butt-hole, and I'm kind of like just stuck there. Actually I'm on the set then, with red parachutes draped all over and red flashing lights, it's very kind of surreal. Some girls walk over and step over my face, and then a little later there are butts all over the place, and they sit on my face. Basically I have someone film me with my head popping up inside the crack and then a couple of other guys pass by, they're already in the crack, they ask me if I really want to come in, because the crack's really addictive, get it."

At which point according to the demonic logic of this storyline coined by the former Catholic altar boy, the intrepid Buttman is pulled inside, camera in tow, and ready to film a series of set-up scenes, like the one involving the dominatrices walking leashed guys on all fours all around the place. "There's another scene with a couple of girls taking a leak and there are three toilets, and inside each toilet is a guy's face sticking up, and they play a kind of musical chairs, only thing is the loser each time is the seat that doesn't get sat on. There are also some transvestites, nuns, some male self flagellants, and a Buttman altar dedicated to the worship of butts, and a lot of other stuff, basically Buttman in the Crack!"

So where does it all end, does Buttman return, or does he stay forever stuck within the crack? The fact that other Buttman movies have subsequently been made and released is a bit of a give-away. You do wonder whether this isn't rather a shame, that maybe he should have bowed out this way. It's the best possible end-place for him: John Buttman Stagliano, stuck in the butt-crack, gleefully lost inside the B-hole.

Laurence O'Toole is the author of **Pornocopia** (Serpent's Tail, 1998). The above article was initially undertaken for inclusion in that book, but ultimately space wasn't permitting. **Headpress** wishes to thank Laurence O'Toole for allowing its publication here, and also John Stagliano, H E Sawyer, Jeff Marton at E A Productions, and Rebecca Gray at **AVN** for their help & courtesy in bringing it to print.

In Body Worlds

Adrian Horrocks

While royalists and tourists wait in four-hour long queues just to get a glimpse of a coffin (the Queen Mother's), in the Atlantis gallery in Brick Lane, visitors have the opportunity to peer within the casket...

A display of real, dead human bodies, preserved using plastination, "an impregnation technique where tissues are completely saturated with special plastics in a vacuum", Prof Gunther von Hagens' anatomical display Body Worlds has toured to acclaim in Europe and Japan, but his decision to bring it to London inevitably sparked an unnecessary controversy over whether it should be granted a licence to be seen. In the end, the flayed corpses have been given permission to enter our capital, but perhaps only because they were to be confined to the East End.

The Atlantis gallery is a dark, glass-and-cement modernist block. A giant poster of a skinned man is displayed outside, a come-on that evokes the carny and freak show more than art or science.

Inside, the exhibition starts small-scale, a few skinned feet and tiny bones displayed in glass cases. People cluster round, but it's hard to give them more than cursory glance —

where's something more dramatic, shocking? There is a full skeleton to one side, one eye still in its socket, the other empty, tendons sticking out. This is more like it, but still merely preamble.

A flight of dark stairs leads to a large, airy, space, where a selection of full bodies are posed around the room, surrounded by large, green plants. The living wander silently amongst the dead. The corpses are not in cases, and although a 'do not touch' message is etched into the base of each exhibit, you can get as close as you want. And most people do.

The first full body sets the tone for what follows. He's been flayed, his muscles dry, deep red, and flaky. In places, the muscle has been cut away, revealing the white bone beneath. The muscles look highly developed, no out-of-shape flab, probably because the fat has been removed, revealing the structure beneath. No need to be a body builder, just have the ultimate liposuction. The dead man's balls hang droopily on long tendons, his small dick hangs sadly between legs that have been stripped down to muscled wires. He's short, as they all seem to be, but maybe everyone is after this treatment. His face has been skinned too, and the eyes that look vacantly out are probably glass. His mouth is pursed, like a cross between Ian Brown and a PG Tips chimp.

Like seeing hardcore porn for the first time as a kid, your mind won't take it. It isn't real, it's some sort of fake. But why would anyone bother making such an elaborate fake, when it's so much easier to do it for real? If Prof Von Hagens reveals in a few years time that they were all plastic dummies, it wouldn't be

with skin. But if they're all characterless, the exceptions are the skeletons, who either grin maliciously or, (in the case of one whose bones are sliced vertically by several long thin pieces of plastic), seem to scream in hellish agony.

Some corpses are arranged in contrived poses. One plays chess, his veiny brain exposed, his face less ape-like, almost thoughtful. A caption invites us to follow the chess player's sciatic nerve, which looks like a bike chain that's come off. The so-called 'muscle man' is a skeleton with evil eyes, his arm on the shoulder of his musculature, which stands in front of him, pig-meat red, with a mask-like, Leatherface-style face, empty holes

- -

- -

surprising. There's no gore, no bile. Nothing glistens, and it's all very dry and clean and acceptable. The only smell is a faint indistinct odour similar to the inside of a fridge, and that's probably the air conditioner.

But if it at first looks fake, small details convince: dirty fingernails, fillings in higgledy teeth. Who are these people? Where did they come from? What were their lives like? What brought them to this point, where they're so exposed and vulnerable before us? They're almost all male: all standing there with the same dangly dicks, some a bit thicker looking, but all recalling Sylvia Plath's line about turkey necks. Their balls look like white plastic Kinder eggs. One has had a testicle cut in half, a cruel touch, and not surprisingly perhaps, he's making the most extreme Ian Brown face of all. No more monkey business now. Either to protect the anonymity of the donors, or to render the bodies generic, all faces have been removed. It's distancing, and I realize I want to know what they looked like

where the eyes once were. The duo stand sideways, but the ideal view is facing them head-on, from where the skeleton seems to point a nasty accusation.

Clumps of white grease are stuck on the skeleton's skull, provoking unbidden thoughts of chicken fat, and it's suddenly obvious that we're not much different from the beef in the butcher's window. Anyone who has cut up a chicken will find much that looks familiar here. The red, dried-looking muscle that the corpses all have reminds me of a salted Danish salami I was once quite partial to. Cannibalism now begins to make sense, after all, just look at all that meat! The exception is the brain, a dark forbidding clump covered in blue veins similar to those in the wrist, it practically screams poison.

Renaissance drawings of skeletons and skinned men are displayed around the walls. The pictures are exactly right, the corpses are their doubles. But the pictures have equal power with the exhibits, and make them seem almost unnecessary. Different bodies are sliced to expose the various internal organs, especially interesting is a guy with the various bits all mixed up. It didn't affect him apparently, but here is, headless, his weird guts on display.

Around the central area of full bodies, there are dismembered bits and bobs in glass cases. These are more interesting than the foot, as they are mainly concerned with various illnesses, although they have a moralistic edge. A healthy, white pair of lungs looks like it's been carved out of polystyrene. The blackened one next to it comes from a smoker. A little lesson for us all, but it'd be interesting to see the lung of a non-smoking Londoner, and compare it with that of a country dweller. The liver doesn't look any different from the pig liver I was forced to eat as a kid, and the healthy specimen is followed by one suffering from sclerosis, a result of 'intemperate'

drinking we're told. A caption advises us to note how the side of a heart that has suffered an attack has actually ripped apart. But if all this makes you want to give up booze and cigs, the various tumours and strokes and ulcers are there to tell you there's no real escape.

Finally, a female corpse appears, the Swimmer. Cut in half down the middle, her two halves are pointed in opposite directions, limbs outstretched in a swimming pose. She seems to be wearing a dodgy Elton wig, a last nod to female vanity, or possibly the remains of her own real hair. She looks pretty, much better than the men, although this is probably because the fad for ultra-skinny models makes a skinned female look strangely idealised. Her body looks young, her breasts small, all hint of age stripped away with her skin.

One corpse has had swathes of skin left on his bare muscle, like a M C Escher picture. Looking closer, the cross section shows skin, red muscle, and then down to bone. It's fascinating, and I stare at it, my brain trying hard to process the information, to accept and apply it to my own body. Everyone spends a long time silently staring at the exhibits, and many get very close-up, as if by looking they hope to get power over the bodies, and maybe over their own. As Camille Paglia says, "to see is to know, to know is to control". But it's an illusion, one underlined by those diseased body parts. We have very little control over our own bodies. Nevertheless, watching the contrast of living faces almost but not quite touching the exposed dead muscle is itself interesting.

One man gets obsessively close to the corpses, even getting on the floor for a good look at the underneath of a seated body. At one point he gets so close to a standing corpse that seems about to kiss its face. A sudden urge to push him from behind comes over me, and I imagine him crashing headlong into the body, embracing it as they tumble to the ground. I begin to doubt the wisdom of the exhibition's emphasis on children coming along, as I'm suddenly sure that my child-self wouldn't have resisted the urge. A young couple stand looking at a display of the diges-

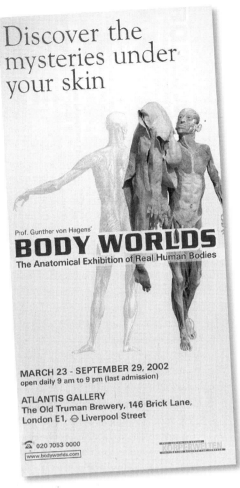

Discover the
mysteries under
your skin

Prof. Gunther von Hagens'

BODY WORLDS
The Anatomical Exhibition of Real Human Bodies

MARCH 23 - SEPTEMBER 29, 2002
open daily 9 am to 9 pm (last admission)

ATLANTIS GALLERY
The Old Truman Brewery, 146 Brick Lane,
London E1. ⊖ Liverpool Street

☎ 020 7053 0000
www.bodyworlds.com

human body to challenge and shock putting them far ahead in this particular game.

The captions accompanying the exhibits are all fussily medical in tone, and they go a long way towards making the exhibition seem to be all above-board, non-exploitative, and academic. Had the captions been more imaginative, perhaps simply titles like 'Snapshot of Hell', the exhibition would have had much more power, but would have forfeited any claims to legitimacy and educational value. The contrived poses of the bodies are obviously an attempt to harness the exhibitive power of displaying them in a gallery, while the captions stop that same power making the displays irreverent. It's a clever trick to pull, and it just about gets away with it. Even I find myself picking up a few stray medical facts almost by mistake.

The final piece upstairs is the horse and rider. A skinless horse rears up, its dick jutting out like a missile. The human rider holds his brain out, some sort of comment on the mental superiority of mankind. Or something. Skinning the horse must have been a big task. Imagine the Prof, wading through gore, a crazed look in his eye as he methodically and precisely plastinated this giant lump of a thing. The effect should be impressive, but somehow it's got less impact than the men. Perhaps because we've seen stuffed horses in museums before. Perhaps because animal lives have always been cheap.

Downstairs again, and a 'expanded' man, his body parts suspended from metal wires recalls the climax of Hellraiser. There is also a sliced-off face, finally, revolving slowly in a glass cube, reminiscent of Eyes Without a Face. It's very creepy, the missing element of humanity denied the other bodies, its eyelashes and lips eerily real, its sex unguessable. But it's been painted gold, in a final attempt to disguise and distance it, making it look like some sort of demented Easter egg from hell, one that would definitely not make a welcome kiddie's treat.

Then comes the male reproductive organs, in a glass case. Sigh, not again, yes, there are those same sad bits, laid out on their own

tive system. They start kissing, seemingly inspired by the sight of the dismembered guts before them.

Another corpse has been sliced into vertical pieces. He's got large tattoos on his arms, and it looks like he was a punk, as there's a screaming mohican skull on one shoulder. The tattoos give him some personality, as does the skin that can be seen on his back and chest. His dick still has public hair, and looks relatively normal, upsetting one woman: "how disgusting!" His face is still missing, though. He easily outdoes Damien Hirst, whose supposedly shocking sliced shark instantly looks both tame and childish. But if Brit-art looks parochial after "Body Worlds", it gives a new respect for genre cinema, as effects that previously looked unconvincing are now revealed as pretty much right. It's hard to avoid thinking of David Cronenberg and Clive Barker especially, their use of the

this time. But next to them, finally, the female reproductive organs. And a womb with a tiny foetus hidden within. Following this Prof Von Hagens' has saved the most exciting, and most frightening section for last: mutant babies. The babies are whole, all have faces, and some of them bear expressions of pain and fear, making them both endlessly tragic, but compulsively fascinating. There's a pair of Siamese twins, joined at the chest, one of the faces contorted with pain. A baby born without a brain looks like a bizarre human-rottweiler crossbreed. On the other side of the room, the development of a healthy baby, week by week, is represented by something the size of a dot at one week, moving up to an inch long miniature baby by week eight, and then to bigger babies, the larger of whom have elongated heads, presumably caused by shoddily wielded medical implements. All girls, the expressions of disappointment on the faces of these 'untimely ripp'd' infants is poignant indeed.

At the end of this small room, a heavily pregnant woman, arranged in a reclining 'Venus' pose. Her skin removed, her stomach cut open to expose the eight month old foetus curled inside her. The foetus is perhaps most haunting of all, its eyes tight shut, snuggled in its mother's belly, still eagerly dreaming of a life that will never come. The free brochure assures us that the bodies on display were donated freely by the subjects. But what about this woman? Did she know she was dying while pregnant? Did she decide to offer her body, and then fate played an ironic trick? Does the act of offering to donate trigger a quick demise?

After the peaceful, dead expression of the baby, there's nothing left but the gift shop, and an example of plastination, illustrated graphically by a brain bubbling in a vat of liquid. After all that's gone before, I half-expected the brain to start addressing us directly, from its tank, revealing itself as the real Prof Von Hagens.

Von Hagens' technique of removing his exhibits' faces means that while crowds of people see the exhibits so intimately, none of

the bodies get any real after-life celebrity, nor do they get to overshadow Von Hagens' own contrived Joseph Beuys image. Would they be disappointed to know they're missing out? But if ordinary people don't become celebrities by allowing their corpses to be put on display, would celebrities become ordinary if their dead bodies were revealed to us? The chance to see a selection of dead film stars, pop idols and soap actors, up close, naked, stripped, and exposed inside and out to our curious gaze would be utterly irresistible. How wonderful if dying celebrities would consent to plastination, rather than being buried, frozen or blasted into outer space. Prof von Hagens' would then have an attraction that would far eclipse Madame Tussaud's. Michael Jackson, so keen to buy the bones of the elephant man, would surely agree, although he looks like he's already had it done. Margaret Thatcher could return as a real mummy. A plastinated Queen Mother, posed ironically with a boned fish perhaps, would surely secure the future of the monarchy indefinitely, and draw even more tourists than at her funeral, while truly giving the people what they came for.

In Body Worlds

Will Youds

It's April 20, my partner Rick's' birthday and for a treat I take him and his twelve-year-old daughter Jazz to see Prof Hagens' Body Worlds exhibition in London.

We make our way with anticipation of the spectacle we're about to encounter. I become suddenly aware that these back streets of Whitechapel — in which we are lost looking for the old brewery where the exhibits are currently on show — are oddly enough the same streets that Jack stalked with his bag of trusty surgical instruments. I swallow and cast it to the back of my mind.

We arrive and join the silent, yet long queue, the same look on all faces: nervous, unaware and unsure. We pass the box office and carry on our tour.

In all honesty it's hard to explain what you're greeted with. Full-scale human bodies, opened, exhibited, displayed in vitriolic splendour. You gaze upon eyes without eyelids. Instinctively you cannot accept at first what you're viewing. It's familiar, but distant. It's hard to accept that what stands in front of you are human. Carved, sliced and diced.

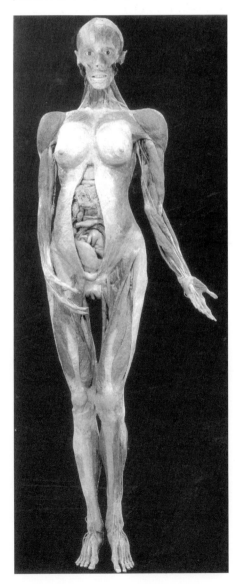

Equally hard to come to terms with is that each piece has a 'job'. The swordsman with his missing skin, elongated muscles and defensive stance. Nothing between you and the man. No glass coverings or velvet rope to distance you. The swimmer, split in two, that you can walk straight through, taking in the sights of the heart, kidneys, lungs and blood vessels. The chess player who sits behind his board surveying his finished game — you may notice the player is in checkmate; the cap of his head lifted off to reveal his brains.

The apocalyptic horseman who sits astride his stallion that has been painstakingly sliced in half. Larger than life, this vision is mythical yet real. He holds aloft the brain of the horse.

The carcasses become horrifically real, sometimes you are reminded of actual life and this shocks you — a tattoo of a lover's name, the dirt under the nails or the smell of the hair.

Jazz becomes disturbed and chooses to stay with the man holding up his skin as we venture into the 'cycle of life' room. A corridor that displays the beginnings of life. We are taken from fertilisation through to birth via the extreme view of looking through the opened stomach of a pregnant woman with eight-month-old foetus inside her womb.

Around me everyone is silent. Contorted faces try to reason the spectacle we all desperately try to take in.

We shuffle round more. We come to a stand where a pleasant lady asks us if we want to hold cancerous lungs and alcoholic livers. An invitation all three of us agree to take.

It's an emotional awakening for myself. The fragility of life, the spiritual questioning. The sombre mood of the living contrasted with the animation of the dead. It's on one hand a freak show, on the other artistic genius.

This exhibition is more than a glimpse into the world of the atomically body. It blends both science and art beautifully. It allows us, the viewer to see this great taboo that is essentially ourselves.

Its very existence signals a progress in society. A step forward to explore an avenue of death never experienced in life.

Prof. Gunther von Hagens

in conversation with Jörg Buttgereit

translated by Roland Davies

You've dedicated your life to the conservation of human bodies. What fascinates you about this?

That's certainly to do with the fact that plastination is my spiritual child. With my discovery I can illustrate things that had never previously been capable of being made visible in this wealth of detail. It is for me very satisfying and motivating to make available new ways to view the internal organs of corpses without feeling disgust.

Plastination is a chance discovery that I have made and whose worth I immediately saw during kidney research work. For twenty years I was frustrated by the barbaric preservation methods used on human corpses. In practice we weren't further ahead than the Pharaohs. Formalin makes the human corpse gruesome. As a student of medicine I was really shocked by anatomy. Portrayed in smell and appearance was an anonymous corpse, and a horror of one's own body resulted. One associates the body with horror films, decay and negative emotions.

The whole-body plastinations are frozen in spectacular poses. Where does the inspiration come from?

I always try to approach plastination conceptually. What do I want to show? For me the form underlies the views of aesthetic instruction. It should be prepared in an aesthetic, dynamic memorable way. I don't want any school anatomy, rather a display of the living; true to life; life like. Emotional anatomy. An illustration of emotion is often most impressive. It takes away the fear of death, which I don't need. For instance — HORSE AND RIDER. As the rider blends with the horse, a close bodily relationship ensues and I can compare the muscle masses.

I want to compare the organs and therefore open up man and horse. With the man who holds up his skin in his arms, I want to show that the skin is man's largest organ and how vulnerable he looks without it.

I didn't want the skin to be stretched out like the hide of a wild pig.

With the pregnant ones I wanted the eye to be drawn to the fruits of the body. I had to drape the woman so that one did not have the feeling one was looking into a cooking pot. Also she must not appear like a pin-up girl.

The expansion of bodies and the opening up of bodily cavities has been made possible through plastination.

This procedure tightens up any soft parts of the bodies. I arrange showrooms of the internal organs of the bodies without taking anything away, thereby presenting body plastination in its entirety. The body is not chopped-up or dehumanized.

Do you see yourself primarily as an artist or as a medical practitioner?

I see myself as a discoverer. I need the creativity of an artist and the sharp, logical, discursive thinking of the scientist. Therefore I am between the realms of science and culture. For myself — understanding. I can't relate to art as I haven't learnt it. I was deeply shocked when I found that people accused me of wanting to be portrayed as an artist.

More than 3,000 people have so far donated their bodies to the institute of plastination. Why do people donate their bodies?

Many donors have told me that after visiting the exhibition they have lost their fear of death. They see an alternative to the cemetery. One knows that the body is dead, but one exists beyond this... For the first time it is possible to keep the body and show it to future generations without any religious connotations.

Do you intend to have yourself plastinated?

Of course; preferably in slices. In this way I could, if only passively, teach at a number of places.

A number of displays / exhibits have something of the cartoon about them. Can one approach death with humour?

You've understood me well here. I'd also like to take death not so seriously; to make it more reconciliatory and emotional. Mortality can also be accepted with a smiling eye.

I had the opportunity in 1998 to visit both the first Body Worlds exhibition in Mannheim and the last in Oberhausen. The Mannheim visitors were shocked and unsettled, and held their distance from the exhibit. In Oberhausen they were less awkward and more relaxed. What had changed in people in those three years?

Those prepared to hold shock and disgust at bay in favour of their own curiosity, who want to know what actually holds them together — they will be amazed and experience a kind of aesthetic shock. Awareness sets in; I like to describe it as a new definition of bodily self. Contemplation of plastination gets under one's own skin. The actual success of Body Worlds is not that so many visitors come, but that so many now discuss what the layperson is allowed to see. There is a popularisation and democratisation of anatomy.

How long does it take to construct a full body plastination?

About 1,500 hours of work. To date the most lavish plastination is the HORSE AND RIDER, which has taken 5,000 hours. The plastination is naturally more than a one-man show. The plastination institute has about 300 full time employees, amongst them twenty-nine preservers. I draw up the shape of the plastination and then at the end supervise. I'm again present for the definitive final positioning.

How far has your work affected your relationship to your own death?

For me death has become so natural that I no longer need to fear it. The longer one thinks about unpleasantness the less threatening it becomes. That helps calm me and makes me more aware of life.

Because you know that, yourself, you will survive?

Yes. We fear bodily death. We practice spiritual death each night as we fall asleep.

PAN books **M108**

SOMETHING MORE LIKE GODS
THE OUTSIDER FICTION OF

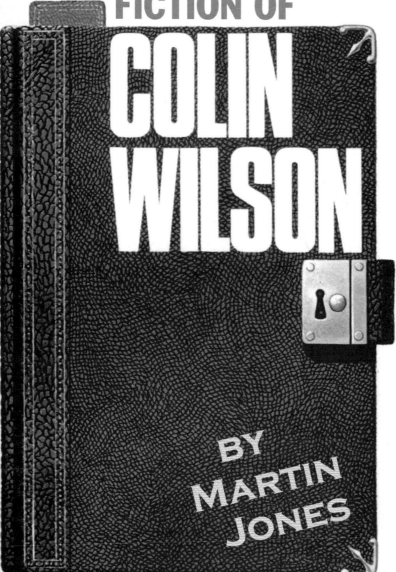

COLIN WILSON

BY MARTIN JONES

5/-

And then it came to me with great clarity: my business and the business of all writers: to refuse to be a part of everyday life, to stand aside, even if this demands a pose of brutality or nihilism. We must not be absorbed. [1]

A t first sight, the Outsider is a social problem. He is the hole-in-corner man.' So begins *The Outsider*, Colin Wilson's 1956 debut, a non-fiction 'inquiry into the sickness of mankind in the mid-twentieth century'. In the grey atmosphere of post-WWII England, those opening sentences began a short-lived literary phenomenon. Aided by a wreaking crew of alienated artists — Hermann Hesse, T E Lawrence, Fiodor Dostoevsky, William Blake *et al* — Wilson's book emerged at a time when the young shoulders of Britain were squirming under the firm fingers of the responsible uncles who had guided them through the war. Although mistakenly drafted into the emerging Angry Young Men group of writers, Wilson's work was in fact the culmination of years of 'otherness', fuelled by every spare moment spent reading, a life lived on the poor-employment breadline (famously, *The Outsider* was written in the British Museum, and every night Wilson would sleep on Hampstead Heath to save money [2]), and a sense of purpose installed by hearing Bernard Shaw's play 'Man and Superman' on the wireless at the age of fourteen. If the job of good writing is to lead the reader further afield, to areas beyond their current perspective, then *The Outsider* achieved — and still does achieve, in many ways — that goal. It is an existential primer, a page-marker's dream, a leaping board to a vast further reading section, peopled by a virtual Who's-Who of those 'not at home in the world'. Despite — or perhaps because of — the rapid advance of the twentieth century around him, Wilson's concerns were internal, searching for desires that had no physical shape:

Most men have nothing in their heads except their immediate physical needs; put them on a desert island with nothing to occupy their minds and they would go insane. They lack real motive. The curse of our civilization is boredom. [3]

In that last sentence, Colin Wilson set up what was to become his life's work. For over forty-five years, through over one hundred books, Wilson has tried to grasp something that is not within physical reach, something that has — like the elder gods of H P Lovecraft's horror stories — been buried by the immediate needs of mankind, the 'getting and spending' material trivialities that take up so much of our time. Every time man makes new discoveries, he has to put the waste soil somewhere: Wilson searches for what is under that soil. He has given this ethereal quest various names ('Faculty X' being the most famous), but they all return to one thing: Wilson is a cerebral ghost-hunter, searching for fragments of proof to show to people. Like the skins of exotic, rare beasts, these fragments are hung, stretched and displayed in his books for all to see.

The fame accompanying the publication of *The Outsider* soon turned sour when critics realized that Leicester-born twenty-four-year-old Wilson was not going to get down

lishing world, Wilson carried on writing. And writing. Encouraged by the good press he received in Europe (where interviewers actually wanted to hear the *ideas* of his books explained), Wilson set about expanding the themes he had set up in *The Outsider*, pulling out its tendons and stretching them across his subsequent work. Most writers are one-trick ponies, but some learn to become master of that trick: Wilson was one such writer, skilfully attacking his subject from every direction, bouncing ideas off the walls made by a triangle of his three literary deities: Friedrich Nietzsche, H G Wells and

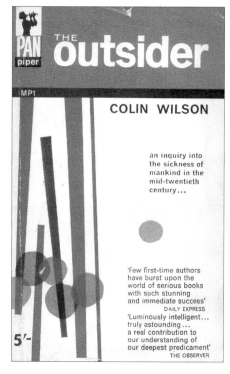

off the intellectual high-horse he had ridden in on: lurid newspaper headlines, boozy parties and sweeping statements of "genius" scattered across interviews — most famously to the broadcaster Dan Farson[4] — did not endear him to the critical classes, and, by the time his second non-fiction book, *Religion and the Rebel* (1957) was published, the British press had adopted their rigid 'build-them-up-knock-them-down' stance. But, unlike the six-figure-advance casualties of today's pub-

Shaw. It is perhaps in some of the novels that followed his initial exposure that the message is displayed clearer and more exciting than it ever was in *The Outsider*, or any of its non-fiction successors.

If we were honest, we'd acknowledge that life is a series of moments tied together by our need to keep alive, to defeat boredom. Our experience is all in bits. But the Surbiton businessman sticks it together by believing that the purpose of life is to get him a bigger

just for the murders; Gerard Sorme is the first of many authorial voices, although the only one to live on in a further two novels. These men (always men) spend their lives doing nothing much, and so are prime candidates for Wilson's 'otherness', his cerebral search parties. They find their anchor to sanity not in society and its invisible, petty codes, but in music, art and literature. They test the waters of what is labelled 'madness' by associating with those who are mad, holding up models of behaviour like a hand of cards, to remind them that they are on the right track. Upon meeting the rich homosexual Austin Nunne, Sorme tells him

car. The politician sticks it together by identifying his purpose with that of his party. The religious man sticks it together by accepting the guidance of his church or his Bible. They're all different kinds of glue, but they all have the same purpose... to impose a pattern, a meaning. [5]

Ritual In The Dark (1960) reads like such a close fictional cousin of *The Outsider* that it comes as no surprise to find that Wilson began to write it before his debut. The alienated concerns of Gerard Sorme ('Suddenly, he realised what it was that disgusted him; it was the idea of his own non-existence' [6]), the novel's protagonist, must have at some point prompted Wilson to leave the book unfinished and begin something else, something more detailed, something able to quote authors at length, rather than hide text in character dialogue and introspection. Because of this crossover, *Ritual In The Dark* is a valuable Outsider primer, and totally gripping. Although marketed as a contemporary update of the Jack the Ripper murders [7], the story barely touches on that subject, using it only as a spur for the characters thoughts and desires: "whodunit?" holds no interest to Wilson. "Why?" is the question here, and not

I am convinced that life can be lived at twenty times its present intensity...I spend all my life looking for the way to it. I envy madmen. But somehow I never get closer to it myself. But I cling to symbols. Nijinsky is one of my symbols. [8]

The ballet dancer Vaslav Nijinsky was also one of Wilson's symbols: displayed in *The Outsider*, made flesh in *Ritual in the Dark* by the Nijinsky-faced Austin Nunne. In this room-and-board London, these are men talented but unable to fix their minds on the One True Thing. But at least some of them have the opportunity: the writer Sorme has brilliant ideas for books but lacks the discipline to actually begin writing them; he finds it easier to talk away his thoughts to sympathetic ears rather than set them down on paper. The solitary painter Oliver Glasp (perhaps modelled on the artist Walter Sickert (1860–1942), often held up as a Ripper suspect) is prolific and original, but lacks the social skills and moral restraint to sell his work and himself. The romantic Austin Nunne, however, is neither writer nor painter. As a priest acquainted with all three men tells Sorme: 'Romanticism is a dubious refuge, but it is not a dangerous one. And no one remains in it for a long time.' [9] Nunne is a ro-

A shattering horror-novel in the great H. P. Lovecraft tradition

COLIN WILSON

The Mind Parasites

Panther

mantic surrounded by the novels of Villiers de l'Isle-Adam and J-K Huysmans. Like Des Esseintes in Huysmans' *Against Nature*, Nunne has his own refuge from the world — an aesthetically ordered flat — as Sorme discovers (even down to a liqueur-tasting session that mirrors the 'mouth organ' in Huysmans' novel [10]), but, like another favoured writer, the Marquis de Sade, Nunne is also a sadist, and *Ritual in the Dark*'s

modern-day Ripper. Unable to conquer a creative art, he has turned to murder, the last, most extreme refuge of the Outsider. Sorme explains:

I think being alive exhausts him. He can't accept reality... The reality of the world batters him. It bullies him. So he wants to see it from some beautifully detached standpoint. That's why he's so theatrical. Instead of real slums, he wants a stage set that looks like slums. Instead of real despair and defeat, he wants tragic actors raving about it. He has to simplify everything... If he committed a murder, he wouldn't be a real murderer. He'd be a tragic actor playing Macbeth... Murder's the ultimate taboo. In a certain mood, it could be a kind of suicide. I think that's how Austin feels. Unless he can dramatise it, the world seems unbearably alien. He wants to do something positive to justify his existence. [11]

Positivity to Nunne means nothing more than making your mark, scraping your initials into the rock of the earth so that humanity will not forget you; he can't write or paint like Sorme or Glasp, outlets that will lead to recognition in some form or another, so murder becomes escape from the outgoing persona he has built, a move on to something bigger. Nunne has remained trapped in Romanticism's dubious refuge, a place still present from previous centuries; to Sorme (and so Wilson), '...the twentieth century's suffering from a romantic hangover' [12], and people like Nunne are waking up to find they are living within a world that cannot survive in modern society. Violence is the only way to fight out. 'It's a kind of irrational resentment, I suppose,' Nunne tells Sorme. 'Not about people, or even society, but just about...the world.' [13] For all his ideals, Nunne is a true materialist who would not be out of place in the twenty-first-century: everything is at his fingertips, and yet he is trapped, stamping his feet in a petulant fit at a life made blunt at the edges by easy access to every excess. The fatted Romantic's boredom began in an era pinpointed by Wilson in other works (and blatantly attacked in his later *The Mind Parasites*); in *Vathek* — the most celebrated novel of William Beckford, perhaps a prototype for Nunne, with his high aesthetic standards, homosexual tastes, and feeling of alienation — the immense tower that the Eastern Caliph has constructed for his own pleasure is just the beginning:

> He consoled himself, however... with the thought of being great in the eyes of others; and flattered himself that the light of his mind would extend beyond the reach of his sight, and extort from the stars the decrees of his destiny. [14]

THE WORLD OF VIOLENCE

a novel

by

COLIN WILSON

His desire for riches beyond all those he has is eventually his downfall: the physical acts of Vathek and Nunne, be they black magic or murder, are attempts at expansion away from the comforts they already have. These are dangerous practises, and so it is unsurprising that they are bound for destruction. Gerard Sorme holds none of Nunne's wobbly Romanticism; he knows that this battle against boredom is not as simply defined as Nunne would like to make it. For Sorme, the hunt begins inside; again, like Lovecraft's Gods, he knows that something unfathom-

able lurks within mankind, something we have — consciously or unconsciously — neglected:

> The sleep was clear, without images. Then he began to see it: in the half darkness, in a warehouse, an animal like a crab; something flat with prehensile claws. He was aware of nothing else; only the crablike creature, moving silently into the half light; moving strangely, obliquely, but with intention, entirely itself, possessed by an urge that was its identity, entire unification of its being in one desire, one lust, a certainty. It was not man; it was what was inside a man as he waited. [15]

What lies inside man cannot remain dormant for long; its very nature requires it to burst out, to express itself. Is the 'crablike creature' violence? It's a (some might say class-based) concept attractive to writers — and now common in literature — begun by the rebellious narrators of late nineteenth-century novels, and continued up to the end of the twentieth-century. Its thread runs through the work of J G Ballard, to culminate in the business executive gangs of *Super-Cannes*; creative violence is the cathartic, fatherless punch of Chuck Palahniuk's *Fight Club*; even the is-it-real-or-is-it-imaginary narrative of Bret Easton Ellis' *American Psycho* could be nothing more than a method of relaxation for the yuppie narrator, an escape route from Patrick Bateman's labelled and ordered (and ultimately inescapable) world.

A little before the above mentioned, and a lot closer to the crushing mundanity of home, there was Wilson's *The World of Violence* (1963). The narrator here begins with a familiar outline:

> I must mention now a circumstance that perhaps sounds absurd — or almost meaningless — but which has been of central importance to me since I was very small. It is this: I have never liked human beings. I do not mean that I feel a Swiftian hatred for them. This was something different; an obscure discomfort if mixing with people was like sitting in a dentist's chair having one's teeth drilled... I have never been able to watch two people talking about the weather without a deep feeling of wonderment; I

watch them closely, expecting to see their faces crumble suddenly into horrible grief.[16]

Hugh Greene is the focus of *The World of Violence*, a mathematics prodigy whose life is related in a singular voice (from infancy to adulthood, and we can presume that he was born the same year as Wilson), and so appears old before his time. Despite his talents, Greene is searching for something more, and for a while just drifts, unable to hook onto anything of significance. Again pulling a referential tendon from *The Outsider*, Wilson makes the novel his own version of Albert Camus' *L'Etranger* : violence as another doorway to jump through, although Greene eventually lacks the nihilistic boredom of Meursault that turns that novel around halfway through. Also, unlike Meursault's solitary, fatal decision, there is always a more enigmatic character to step in the way of Wilson's narrators, to lead them down paths less trodden. Greene comes into contact with several. The conservatism of family life is tempered by contact with maverick relatives, such as Uncle Nick, a character of Charles Fort-like conviction, who tells Greene that the sun is a mere ten miles away from the earth, and giant holes in the northern hemisphere conceal entrances to worlds within worlds. Nick eventually topples into insanity, attacked by a society not yet ready for his ideas. Greene's Uncle Sam does not even attempt to fight an unsympathetic world, he simply turns his back on it, locking himself in a windowless room in his house, never to venture out again. This is not a symbolic gesture on Sam's part, a Des Esseintes-like romantic shudder directed at the philistines — this is an attack on the death of feeling. 'Have you ever tried to light a bonfire made of wet rubbish?' Sam asks Greene. 'Well, that's what God's trying to do with human beings. We're all wet rubbish, and a tiny little spark trying to set it ablaze. We never stand a chance.'[17] Sam has seen the docile human, and knows what will wake him:

The tragic thing about human beings is that they need pain and hardship. Otherwise they'd die of

boredom...That's because man's half dead...Make life unpleasant for him and he'll appreciate it when you stop — for ten minutes. Threaten him with death, and he'll be grateful for life — for ten minutes. But give him pleasure, and he's bored with it in ten minutes. This is the strangest thing about human nature — our capacity for pain is infinitely bigger than our capacity for pleasure. Where pleasure's concerned, we're all like rich men who overeat — a little of it gives us indigestion. No man is a judge of what's good, but every man knows what's bad. Never believe a man who tells you he knows what he wants out of life. The only thing we know is want we don't want. The only time a man knows what he wants is when he's suffering. Then he knows he wants it to stop. Apart from that, we're all blind and deaf.[18]

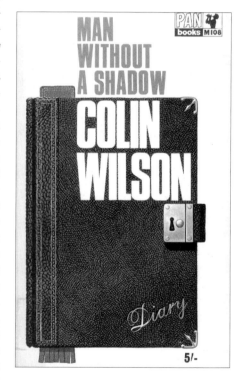

MAN WITHOUT A SHADOW
COLIN WILSON
Diary
5/-

This becomes Hugh Greene's quest, to bring order to his mind through the act of violence, to bring back feeling: exhilaration, fear, apprehension; to avoid the banality of 'horrible grief' that he knows lurks in every man. For all the apparent superiority that seeps through Greene's character (there is an irony in his later justice-quest against a local burglar and pervert, whom he calls "a dangerous man", not realising that he himself is considering murdering a local delinquent: 'I wanted to believe that I was not at the mercy of stupidity, Like Archimedes. How was this possible when one blow from a crowd of mindless thugs could extinguish my 'spirit'?' [19]) he is looking for acceptance of his emotions: acceptance that they are uncontrollable. After his wayward relatives, Greene meets two men who show him different goals in life, each with their own rewards and traps. The solitary, self-published author Jeremy opens his mind to books and music, but it is the philanderer Monty who — with his physical temptations of female flesh — leads Hugh astray in a world he was previously blind to, a place that draws him away from the logic of mathematics:

Suddenly it came to me that sex is a kind of insanity. It was too late to escape; it had caught me; but at least I could observe what was happening. What I now observed was a revelation. This world of sex had nothing — absolutely nothing — in common with the world of mathematics... Everyone was caught in this current.' [20]

Greene the Outsider is allowed access into the real world through the allure of a woman's curves; he is sent spinning in the same whirlpool that holds every other young man with lust on his mind. He is in the same space as the delinquent who he wishes to shoot because he almost assaulted his sister; but it frustrates him that sex cannot lead to progress like mathematics, and, true to the nature of Wilson's voices, he is ultimately dissatisfied with his physical lot: '...it struck me that human life is all freedom, far too much freedom. And we destroy ourselves with freedom.' [21] Ultimately, Hugh is fighting the same desires that struck Austin Nunne, that drove the Caliph Vathek, desires that bend the edges of the mind, that make our wills malleable.

If I had to define the belief that drives me to torment myself, to bully my body, to drive myself instead of drifting and 'taking life as it comes', I would express it in this way: at any moment, it is possible that we shall make the 'break-through' in consciousness, that consciousness will suddenly leap to a higher level and turn us into something more like gods. [22]

It is up to a more experienced character to expand on these sexual forces, to bring them into line with Wilson's ongoing process. In *Man Without a Shadow* (1963), Gerard Sorme returns with his 'sex diaries', an account of his encounters with the Crowley-like Caradoc Cunningham. A new ego is needed to tempt Sorme, a new attraction in which Wilson can overhaul his theories again. After all, as he himself writes in the novel's introduction: 'For me, there is one simple objection to novels: they get nowhere.' [23] (Introductions by Wilson 'explaining' his own novels would become commonplace). They each act as frames to build on: Gerard Sorme has the cold thought of a scientist ('There I go. That is also my problem; I'm too much an intellectual to stick to the 'basic facts', like sex...' [24]) that is uninviting towards great flights of imagination, but, as displayed later, imagination to Wilson is a dangerous thing: his characters are baffled by unfamiliar emotions, states of mind they cannot pin down, cannot find reference to in works of literature. At the beginning of *Man Without a Shadow*, Sorme holds familiar values, he is obsessed with 'iceberg' theories: why can't the brain be used to its full potential? Why are we not more like gods? Why can't Sorme possess every woman he meets (another tendon from an *Outsider* source: Henri Barbusse's *L'Enfer*). Sorme has become Wilson's own Angry Young Man, except that his rebellion has to be more than physical escape, as all Sorme seems to do is stay in his lodging room and have sex. Sorme admits that he is caught in 'the sexual illusion', hoping to find in it access to some greater knowledge, and knowing that pursuit is far more gratifying than the act itself. This is where Wilson begins to have fun, drags his ideas from the cold-floored kitchen of post-war Britain and adds a touch of exotic, over-the-top, and egotistical colour. Without the dark guides of the novels, main characters such as Sorme would remain in their rooms, brooding over their wasted intelligence. Oliver Glasp introduces Sorme to Caradoc Cunningham, who exposes his own theories at will:

> He said (and the image astounded me) that most men live as if they are the audience in the theatre when they don't realize that they're actually on the stage, and the gods will throw things if they don't start acting. [25]

Cunningham presents himself as a friend of Aleister Crowley, although as the novel progresses, it is obvious that Wilson has based his character solely on The Great Beast himself, with all the charisma, self-knowledge and grand gesture present: 'I believe there is some strange destiny that brings together men who will have a great effect upon the age,' Cunningham tells Sorme:

> 'Think of Nietzsche and Wagner, Schumann and Brahms, Goethe and Schiller...The great men gravitate together.' I was so flattered by this remark that I didn't point out that most great men meet when they've become sufficiently famous to be able to seek one another out. [26]

And, although blessed with a sense of humour,[27] Sorme is soon caught up — like some unfortunate acolytes of Crowley — in Cunningham's plans to intensify the sexual act, intensify consciousness, to discard 'taking for granted', and always retain the pure thrill of the 'first time': to prolong the male orgasm until the user is drawn out through the other side. Cunningham's dubious history reads like a check list of Crowley's more infamous deeds, sometimes even directly quoting the man himself:

> 'Yes, I have often thought it strange that Warwickshire should have produced England's two greatest poets — for we must not forget Shakespeare.' [28]

Elsewhere, Sorme witnesses Cunningham's trick of walking perfectly in step with a stranger so that the victim eventually does

his willing, there is talk of a farmhouse on a small island off Sardinia (i.e. Theleme), a direct steal from Crowley's fatal mountaineering exploits, and a house in Scotland (i.e. Boleskin) [29]. But all this is rather obscured by another Crowley trait, Cunningham's unfortunate vain shortcomings. As Sorme points out towards the end of *Man Without a Shadow*: '...this brings me to another point about Cunningham: his constant need to thumb his nose at society. He is *too* aware of society.' [30]. Cunningham is his own PR man, willing to stage a Black Magic ritual and then sell autographed postcards to the participants. He realises his place as the splinter under the finger of society, which creates an instant desire to rebel, and thus a constant

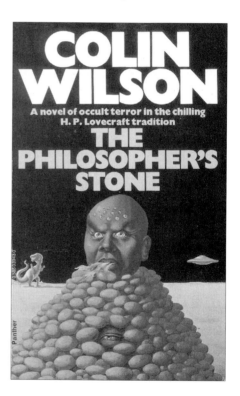

problem in maintaining a suitable image. If Cunningham had shrugged off the wants of an outside world — like John Dee and Gilles de Rais — he may well have got one step closer to a satisfactory god-like state; but is there room for gods to walk amongst gods on this earth? If we all possessed such supernatural abilities surely life would be just as 'dull'? Realising this, Sorme eventually rejects the magic that Cunningham offers, pointing out perceptively that: 'If gold could be manufactured easily, it would be as worthless as iron.'[31]

Wilson's willingness to use the novel form as the launch pad for his ideas must also be taken in tandem with his paradoxical dismissal of it as a satisfactory creative medium. A tendency to explain away his dissatisfaction with the form (as seen above in the introduction to *Man Without a Shadow*) almost acts as a spoiler; in some ways Wilson is the lone individual storming the magician's stage to tear away the velvet curtain: as he wishes to find that *something* beyond everyday life, so he wants to dismiss the 'tricks' of novelists, deflate some of *their* magic.

The Mind Parasites (1967) is as good an example as any of Wilson's saboteur tactics. He is adept at attacking a genre, as long as it is flexible to his own needs. *The Mind Parasites*, it transpires, came about through a challenge, as Wilson explains in an introduction to a later novel, *The Philosopher's Stone* (1969). His non-fiction *The Strength to Dream* (1962) included a section on H P Lovecraft, who Wilson described as '...basically an atrocious writer — most of his work was written for *Weird Tales*, a pulp magazine — and his work is finally interesting as case history rather than as literature.

> ...a copy of my book fell into the hands of Lovecraft's old friend — and publisher — August Derleth. And Derleth wrote to me, protesting that my judgement on Lovecraft was too harsh, and asking me why, if I was all that good, I didn't try writing a 'Lovecraft' novel myself. And the answer to this question is that I never write purely for the fun of it. I write as a mathematician uses a sheet of paper for doing calculations: because I think better that way... But a couple of years later, an analogy thrown out in my *Introduction to the New Existentialism* became the seed of a science fiction parable about 'original sin' — man's strange inability to get the best out of his consciousness. I cast it in the Lovecraft tradition, and it became *The Mind Parasites*, which was published in due course by August Derleth.[32]

The Mind Parasites is perhaps Wilson's ultimate metaphorical retelling of the Outsider condition, although here the characters are used to pull a previously hidden tendon from his original manifesto. In a futuristic world of the early twenty-first-century, professor Gilbert Austin has the same itch to scratch as Gerard Sorme and Hugh Greene, but now — like all good science fiction — the consequences of this insight has implications for all mankind:

> The idea that came to me was terrible. It was that the suicide rate was increasing because thousands of human beings were 'awakening', like me, to the absurdity of human life, and simply refused to go on. The dream of history was coming to an end. Mankind was already starting to wake up; one day it would wake up properly, and there would be mass suicide.[33]

The mind parasites themselves are alien invaders, just like in the works of John Wyndham, Nigel Kneale and Jack Finney; but unlike the physical threats created by those writers, Wilson's danger is a cerebral one, posed by 'vampire bats of the soul', and expounded by Austin's colleague Karel Weissman in his *Historical Reflections*:

> What it amounts to is this. For more than two centuries now, the human mind has been constantly a prey to these energy vampires. In a few cases, the vampires have been able completely to take over a human mind and use it for their own purposes. For example, I am almost certain that de Sade was one of these 'zombis' whose brain was entirely in control of the vampires. The blasphemy and stupidity of his work are not, as in many cases, evidence of demonic vitality, and the proof of it is that De Sade never matured in any way, although he lived to be 74. The sole purpose of his life work is to add to the mental confusion of the human race, deliberately to distort and pervert the truth about sex.[34]

After the initial invasion of the parasites in 1780, the 'sunny optimism' that had infused the work of Joseph Haydn and Wolfgang Mozart soon gave way to great waves of pessimism: the parasites choose men of great intelligence, and very few survive; the champions of positivism are destroyed in some way or other, and the misanthropic are rewarded with long lives. Wilson revises history to his own ends, using the parasites to point out who is with and who is against him. This is *The Outsider* as a Saturday morning cartoon, getting the message across as directly as possible. Wilson makes concessions to Lovecraft in his story, but *The Mind Parasites* is, in its metaphorical way, very simple: aliens feed on the minds of optimistic greatness, and those minds have to be extremely strong, otherwise they will die, or turn to negativity. 'The parasites probably looked with horror upon giants like Beethoven, Goethe, Shelly,' notes Austin

realizing that a few dozen of these would set man firmly on the next stage of his evolution. So Schumann and Holderlin were driven mad; Hoffmann was driven to drink, Coleridge and De Quincey to drugs. Men of genius were ruthlessly destroyed like flies. No wonder the great artists of the nineteenth century felt that the world was against them. No wonder Nietzsche's brave effort to sound a trumpet call of optimism was dealt with so swiftly — by a lightning-stroke of madness. [35]

Great men like Austin fight the parasites, perhaps unaware that in their superior defence of mankind they are still prone to the effects of the aliens: 'But it is the other men, the 'shadows', who are subject to mind-cancer. For them, human society is the reality. They are entirely concerned with its personal

THE KILLER
Colin Wilson

£20 318pp / ISBN 0 86130 110-2 / Savoy 2002
446 Wilmslow Road, Withington, Manchester, M20 3BW / www.savoy.abel.co.uk

If ever it were possible for a book to release scents when opened, then *The Killer* would be first in line. This sensation is installed early on when Dr Samuel Kahn visits the aunty of his patient, Arthur Lingard:

The dirty oilcloth that covered the table was almost colourless, and was full of cuts where she had sliced onions or potatoes without bothering with a plate. The smell of grease hung over everything.

She took down a frying pan in which grease and fragments of bacon had been allowed to harden, and set it on the gas; the kitchen filled with a slightly rancid smell. (p.49)

Lingard has drifted through life with these smells that signify the basics of his existence: hardened fat, the odour of used underwear, the scent of sexual organs beneath cold sheets. This is a 'self-enclosed environment', a trap his relations are ignorant of having fallen into, but one which Lingard escapes from through pulp fiction and, later, sex. Unwittingly, Colin Wilson's 1970 novel maps out a future of true crime reportage; its past is already within the pages: Lingard — who, Wilson writes in his introduction, is made up from various mass murderer traits — shares an upbringing grim enough to compare with Ian Brady and Myra Hindley (both mentioned); but the relationship between Kahn and Lingard calls to mind Brian Masters' interviews with Dennis Nilson, recorded in *Killing For Company*: the cultured man looks at the other and sees himself reflected, but without the education, the opportunities or the social openings. Opportunity has rejected Lingard's imagination: he is a would-be aesthete in an arena of lewdness (sexual activity between his cousins is taken as the norm), a world of uncaring randomness (one of his sister's boyfriends is killed by a falling object); and early on, the fact that Arthur loses his sister Pauline — his mother substitute — to the Enemy (his cousins, his uncle) acts like a door being slammed shut. From then on, imagination, his only creative outlet, is also pushed away by his own physical desires, and his dreams of Moriarty-like greatness. Murder is but a few more steps down the weed-choked canal path.

little values, with its pettiness and malice and self-seeking.' [36] (does this sneering at the 'shadows' around them count as a triumph for the enemy?) There is a contemporary threat, also, in the shape of Felix Hazard, whose books mark him out to the cerebral fighters as another one of the 'zombis'. Hazard, most definitely modelled on William Burroughs (a literary peer of Wilson), has no redeeming qualities in the eyes of Austin and company: he is a completely black spot on the earth. Wilson was familiar with the Beat writers, witnessing their rise from the sidelines: in *Ritual in the Dark*, Gerard Sorme meets 'Cal Teschmeyer' and 'Rudi James' — possible substitutes for Jack Kerouac and Allen Ginsberg—all Levi's, leather and unrestrained mannerisms. Sorme tells Austin Nunne:

Savoy's reissue of *The Killer* is, put simply, a thing of beauty. They have interweaved their own influences into the work of their author: so John Coulthart's visceral jacket design incorporates details from Francis Bacon paintings and book covers from David Britton's personal collection. It's more like a "thank you" than a simple reissue. Also, although any version of *The Killer* is essential reading, this edition boasts a few differences from previous releases (such as my 1970 NEL copy), which are:

■ Chapter one makes reference to the Vaseline a prison guard has used in his sodomy of Lingard. (p.24)
■ Chapter eight includes a sodomy scene during Lingard's 'seduction' of Eileen Grose, the gym master's wife. (p.203)
■ Chapter eight also includes a more explicit (oral and anal sex) account of Lingard's encounter with Simon Banks, the rich homosexual who becomes his first murder victim. Interestingly, this section has a few lines left intact in my NEL edition (pp.172–3) but missing in the Savoy edition (pp.216–18)
■ Chapter nine has a longer, slightly different account of Lingard's first 'proper' rape (pp.234-40), which again does without some text from the NEL edition.
■ Chapter ten (p.269) misses out a section on the murder of Sarah Lewis that is in the NEL edition (pp.267–8)

In an era when British crime writing appears to have been infested with airport paperbacks at one level and image-conscious 'streetwise' titles that walk in the shadow of James Ellroy at another, the republication of *The Killer* is a refreshing step above — very much alone with Derek Raymond's *I Was Dora Suarez*, as the publishers have stated themselves. Hopefully, *The Killer* will extricate Colin Wilson from the remainder bookshops and TV documentaries that he has unfortunately been placed in recently. Perhaps the collected 'Gerard Sorme' trilogy next, please Savoy? MARTIN JONES

I like them. But they don't know how to make conversation. There's no attempt to get in tune. They just fire questions and comments at you like a machine-gun. And they seem to imagine that it's all getting them somewhere interesting. I couldn't resist talking about dispossession. They're about the worst examples I've ever seen. [37]

Burroughs' considerably less-flattering incarnation in *The Mind Parasites* is blatantly transparent:

It was also during the course of that afternoon that we first heard the name of Felix Hazard. Reich and I knew little about modern literature, but Hazard's sexual preoccupations had naturally interested Fleishman. We learned that Hazard had a high reputation among the *avant garde* for his curious

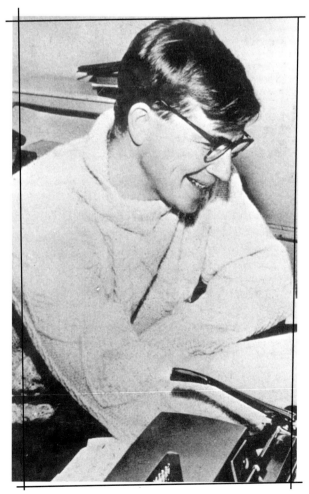

blend of sadism, science fiction and world-weary pessimism . . . Fleishman described some of Hazard's work to us, and added the interesting information that he had begun life as a drug addict, but now claimed to have cured himself. Everything he told us about Hazard seemed to indicate that this man was another 'zombi' of the mind parasites. Fleishman had met him only once, and had found it an unpleasant experience. He said that he had written in his diary: 'Hazard's mind is like a newly opened grave', and that he had been strangely depressed for days after meeting him. [38]

In Hazard/Burroughs, there is no life-affirmation for the Outsider. Wilson later wrote that 'Kerouac, [Gregory] Corso and Ginsberg were happy hipsters, drunk on the sheer size and variety of America. Burroughs had nothing in common with them, being guilt-ridden by his lifetime of failed personal relationships, and ashamed of his homosexuality, sadism and heroin addiction' [39]. Ironically, Burroughs — with his other addiction to pulp sci-fi concepts — gave high praise to *The Mind Parasites* in a 1969 *Mayfair* essay [40].

Gilbert Austin may well be one of Wilson's candidates for the Outsider, but he is still in control of his faculties, still on the intellectual cusp, like Sorme and Greene; what happens when Wilson's protagonist is faced with someone who has passed through to the other side, become an approximation of his manifesto? *The Killer* (1970) is what happens.

All human minds walk a tightrope between optimism and despair, trust and mistrust. A healthy mind, trapped in disagreeable circumstances, deliberately seeks out counterweights to its revulsion and rejection. [41]

The Killer is, as Wilson states in his introduction, an attempt to write a non-fiction novel, taking a number of murderers as its frame, Peter Kurten (the 'Dusseldorf Sadist') and Hans van Zon [42] amongst them. The composite created is Arthur Lingard: sexual misfit, murderer of one and, as prison psychiatrist Samuel Kahn gradually discovers, probably more. Lingard is no drooling, subintelligent psychopath, but a highly intelligent man whose sexually active, working class upbringing has forced him to retreat to other places in the mind. Lingard was born in London when the storm clouds of WWII were gathering; he loses both parents at an early age, and emerges into post-war Britain as a petty criminal. It has taken a particular, enclosed kind of nurturing to make Arthur Lingard what he is. The sonic waves of WWII drifted across the country until well into the 1960s. Kahn meets Lingard in 1967, but he is a man out of time, a product of the 1940s and 50s. The late critic Elizabeth Young decried the 1950s as '…a decade so awful that the very thought of it makes me tear wallpaper off with my teeth.' [43] She pinpointed an era that could have been any in the fifteen-twenty years following 1945:

At the time the very air seemed loaded with a cloying mixture of female servility and the sharp, no nonsense barking of men's voices, lapsing now and then, particularly on radio, into a contemptuous, jolly approximation of familiarity, patently fraudulent. This is certain — that the rudeness and hostility of professional men towards women and children darkened every encounter: the casual sadism of doctors, the stiff-upper-lip mockery of dentists operating without anaesthetics, everyone smug and secure in the belief that children had no emotional life. [44]

The Killer is a life fed through a miniscule terraced house, four-to-a-bed, the proximity dangerous for those stepping into puberty. Lingard and his elder sister Pauline are carted off to live with an uncle and cousins in Warrington, and the house becomes an enclosed space of 'doctors and nurses', masturbation in the dark, and, for Pauline, a relationship with the uncle. The young Lingard reacts with disgust when his sister 'goes over to the other side', to their cousins, the strangers, and he retreats further into the pulp fiction worlds so mocked by Wilson's other protagonists; but here, these imaginative pages launch Lingard into darker territory than the other Outsider candidates could ever hope to encounter: *Weird Tales* and Edgar Rice Burroughs novels, with their lurid, forbidden covers, become his escape hatch. 'He was a child whose 'emotion factory' often overproduced.' Kahn observes

If, like the young Mendelssohn, he had been a part of a warm, close family life, and had been sympathetically schooled and trained from an early period, these free-floating emotions would have found various objects, and become easy to handle. [45]

But Lingard's childhood surroundings were just the opposite:

This new, strange environment certainly provided an object for his fears… I mean the emotion — which is common to many sensitive children — of morbid excitement. It is an emotion that has something in common with poetry, for it tends to ignore the actual world, which is too commonplace and real to provide objects for it. Poe came to associate it with the death of beautiful women: Le Fanu with ghosts and vampires; Baudelaire with sin. Arthur Lingard was still young enough to feel that this family he had been forced into was inhuman and dangerous. [46]

Lingard's morbid excitement eventually

takes over, bringing him face-to-face with sex; his voyeuristic tendencies topple into physical contact (with his cousins and sister), fetishism, burglary, hypnotism, awkward affairs, rape, and eventually, murder: his science fiction daydreams of escape from a hopelessly bleak, uncaring land filled with repulsive criminals and insensitive citizens are inevitably blown away. A job as a television repair man allows Lingard a peek at a different world, a different life, with alien attitudes towards employment, possessions, and sexuality. Working in the penthouse apartment of a rich, middle-aged man, Lingard is seduced by food and drink into sleeping with him. After the sex act, Lingard becomes disgusted with the man's nerve at having him, the *master* criminal; filled with contempt for this easy access to everything, Lingard kills the man with a hammer [47]. Like Camus' Meursault (but unlike the faltering Hugh Green), he makes the crossover Wilson has guided his other narrators to, only to stop them from leaping:

What really frightened him, and caused a sense of constriction of the stomach, was the sense of putting out to open sea, of ceasing to be a child who could always retreat into a cocoon of imagination. [48]

The Killer is a novel that has been put out to sea. Unburdened of the manifesto that has snaked through his other fiction, Wilson can tell a story free from extensive literary knowledge. Arthur Lingard is a man who has followed *The Outsider* to its every word; he is every other protagonist reversed: the man not at one with the world *is* a social problem. Going against the grain of society puts him behind bars.

Lingard may have crossed the threshold, but some of Wilson's characters are still searching for the mother-lode: his alter-ego Gerard Sorme, in particular. *The God of the Labyrinth* (1970) is the final part of the Sorme trilogy, and by far the most entertaining, blending as it does Wilson's cerebral concerns with thinly-disguised personal digs at the publishing world, tongue-in-cheek self-depreciation, and a fair amount of dry humour.

By now, Sorme has become the distinguished author he so wanted to be in *Ritual in the Dark* (at a lecture he is introduced as: "...the noted novelist and philosopher, Gerard Sorme, who has been described as the most interesting British writer since Aldous Huxley and D H Lawrence." [49]), and is tempted by an American publisher to write a book on the life of a notorious eighteenth-century rake, Esmond Donelly. A fictional contemporary of Sir Francis Dashwood (leader of The Hellfire Club), Donelly, Sorme discovers, was also involved in a nefarious organisation, the Sect of the Phoenix, a Masonic-style order that counted the Marquis de Sade and Gilles de Rais amongst its members. Not that this interests Sorme to begin with; although the shadow of sex follows him faithfully, Sorme is still mainly concerned with the quest for the 'superman', the solution to the eradication of boredom, and is puzzled by the fact that most people seem to wait around until something happens to them, not seek it out:

You teach yourself to photograph 'facts' *without their meaning*...This easily becomes a habit: grasping things without their meaning. It becomes difficult to re-connect your upper levels with your instincts and feelings...You go around merely "seeing" things without their meanings. And you say: "The world is meaningless." [50]

What he is looking for, Sorme thinks is nowhere near a subject like Donelly, who he clearly places on the same level as 'Walter', the inexhaustible Victorian narrator of *My Secret Life*. But things soon change when the deeper recesses of the rake's mind begin to surface, and Sorme has on his hands perhaps the original literary Outsider, as Donelly's journal shows:

I am often the most wretched and self-derogatory creature under the sun, and my dissatisfaction often reaches a pitch where it would be a temptation to blow out my brains...Women do often complain that men lack constancy; but why should we have constancy in love when we have none in any other form of thought, feeling or desire?...this morning I read the fables of Gellert in the German for an hour before my

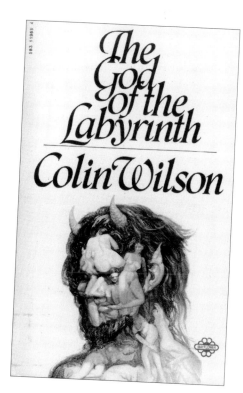

The God of the Labyrinth

Colin Wilson

usual distemper overcame me, and I became sunk in a monstrous lassitude. Since then, I can see no way in which my conscience or sense of virtue can operate upon this life consuming weariness. My conscience may tell me how to avoid doing wrong, but it cannot tell me how to escape tedium. And is there anything deadlier for a creature made in God's likeness than this same tedium? For God is God because he can create; so a man crushed by tedium is most un Godlike. [51]

From century to century, the curse of civilisation — of mankind aware of himself — is boredom ('"Boredom is to be free, but to experience no particular impulse to make use of the freedom."' Donelly writes [52]); Sorme knows that the key to man's freedom from this is through sex, as it '…gives us a glimpse of a concentration of the mind that would make us god-like if we could command it in other spheres' [53] and so he assaults the twin towers of Donelly's philosophy and his own sexual encounters (and non-encounters) that climaxes with an — what Wilson himself has described as 'absurd' — orgy in an English country mansion: 'Other figures were entangled in absurd configurations that looked as if they had been dreamed up by a pornogra-

pher with a sense of the grotesque.' [54]

The God of the Labyrinth ends with the possession of Sorme by his subject: the Outsider has come full circle, to resemble an endless loop of misfits circling a planet of 'ordinary' people, with lone stars like Arthur Lingard disappearing down black holes. And, above them all is Colin Wilson, offering his theories to as many as possible, wanting to interrupt our reality, to wake what lies inside. But we cannot all be gods — who would want to be? Reality is a dancer in a peepshow, watched from different angles by different people: each member of the audience is alone with their own personal thoughts. One might want to take the dancer out to dinner, another might want to rape her. In *The God of the Labyrinth*, Sorme realises that life for many does not stray far from their own unimaginative, petty concerns:

A girl at a party once said to me frankly: "Why don't we share a bed afterwards? It's better than masturbating in separate beds." But in the morning, I realised that it wasn't entirely true that there were no strings. Two bodies had interpenetrated; so had two worlds. I didn't particularly like her world: it was too vague and futile. Like planets that have approached too close, we had caused seismic disturbances in one another. I can no longer remember what she was like in bed; but I can clearly remember certain anecdotes she told me about the failure of her marriage, that still disturb me. I would have done better to leave her spinning in her own orbit.' [55]

Spinning in a self-created orbit, Colin Wilson is a visitor to a vague and futile world, who cannot comprehend the lives its inhabitants have made for themselves. It is a place wrapped up in a billion individual desires, with enough psychological baggage to fill meteor craters: and Wilson is still the Outsider looking in. He has removed his attention from the peepshow and seen the bigger picture: the desires of the rest of the audience. Cleverly disguised, his novels are the guidebooks from one world to another, from the reader's to the writer's. We can use them, if we should choose to do so.

ACKNOWLEDGEMENT

Thanks to David Kerekes for suggesting this article (and for supplying most of the books).

OTHER NOVELS

Necessary Doubt (1964)
The Glass Cage (1966)
The Black Room (1971)
The Return of the Lloigor (1974)
The Schoolgirl Murder Case (1974)
The Space Vampires (1976)
The Janus Murder Case (1984)
The Personality Surgeon (1986)
Spider World: The Tower (1987)
Spider World: The Delta (1987)
The Magician From Siberia (1988)
Spider World: The Magician (1992)

NOTES

1 *The God of the Labyrinth*, Mayflower, 1971, p.8
2 These pre-fame days were fictionalised in *Adrift in Soho* (1961), a hugely enjoyable provincial-boy-goes-to-London tale of a world a measure away from Francis Bacon's Coach & Horses gang. The Soho here is peopled with party girls, gutter philosophers and brutish painters — all penniless.
3 *The Outsider*, Pan, 19?? (first few pages missing in my copy), p.269
4 See pp.198–207 of Farson's autobiography, *Never a Normal Man* (HarperCollins, 1997), for a further account of this subject.
5 *Ritual in the Dark*, Pan, 1962, p.92
6 p.42
7 Like many others, Wilson would become fascinated by the Ripper killings later in his writing career; but, for *Ritual in the Dark*, his concessions to the original murders include a solution that arrives via Russia, [see pp. 296–8], and naming one of the modern victims Catherine Eddowes, thus giving her a shared surname with the Ripper's fourth victim.
8 *Ritual in the Dark*, p.17
9 p.112
10 p.107; *Against Nature*, J-K Huysmans, Penguin, 1959, chapter IV
11 *Ritual in the Dark*, pp.308-9
12 p.358
13 p.374
14 *Vathek*, William Beckford, Four Square, 1966, p.11
15 *Ritual in the Dark*, p.200
16 *The World of Violence*, Victor Gollancz, 1963, p.35
17 p.119
18 pp.119–120
19 p.168
20 p.145
21 p.214
22 *Man Without a Shadow*, Pan, 1966, p.67
23 p.5
24 p.21
25 pp.131-2
26 p.156
27 As with all serious pursuits, absurdity is but a cynical comment away; faced with a Crowley-like teacher, one character in Robert Irwin's excellent psychedelic-occult novel *Satan Wants Me* notes: 'If Satanism really works, why is Dr Felton old, fat and living in Swiss Cottage?'(Bloomsbury, 2000, p.27)
28 *Man Without a Shadow*, p.129
29 See pages 121–2, 157, 173, 174
30 p.215
31 p.163
32 *The Philosophers Stone*, Panther, 1978, p.6
33 *The Mind Parasites*, Panther, 1973, p.21
34 p.57
35 p.74
36 p.162
37 *Ritual in the Dark*, p.252 of Rit
38 *The Mind Parasites*, p.87
39 He continues: 'My distaste was not based simply on the sadism, but a dislike if his pessimistic anti-authoritarianism. This is an attitude he shares with many criminals with whom I have corresponded over the years, several of them serial killers. Society is rotten, its leaders all corrupt, and crime is a gesture of defiance at its bankruptcy. Like Burroughs, they seem incapable of grasping that, even if society is as corrupt as they think, two blacks still don't make a white... Burroughs survived as an icon largely because his contemporaries failed to see through the logical absurdity of his belief that every obscene word and gesture is an act of revolt against a bankrupt society. I suspect that, when the literary accounts of the twentieth-century are added up, we shall find that Burroughs' reputation has simply negated itself and disappeared.' —'The Nightmare Is Over', *The Daily Telegraph*, August 16, 1997
40 'The Voracious Aliens', *Mayfair*, Vol 4, No 8
41 *The Killer*, New English Library, 1970, p.98
42 Zon acts as the basic frame for Arthur Lingard. He committed seemingly random murders around Amsterdam in the mid-1960s, was bisexual, and was blackmailed by a fellow criminal into committing more crimes, which culminated in the murder of a farmer. Wilson uses all these in *The Killer*; further information: *Encyclopaedia of Modern Murder*, Colin Wilson & Donald Seaman, Pan, 1989, pp.363–4
43 *Pandora's Handbag: adventures in the book world*, Elizabeth Young, Serpent's Tail, 2001, p.263
44 ibid
45 *The Killer*, p.84
46 ibid
47 Not only do real life mass murderers stain the pages of *The Killer*: Lingard's hammer attack duplicates the playwright Joe Orton's murder by his lover Kenneth Halliwell in August 1967, almost two years before Wilson wrote his novel.
48 *The Killer*, p.175
49 *The God of the Labyrinth*, pp.228–9
50 p.25
51 pp.111–12
52 p.49
53 p.229
54 p.236
55 p.61

FURTHER INFORMATION & INTERNET RESOURCES

Dossor, Howard F., *Colin Wilson: The Man & His Mind*, Element Books, 1990 *a detailed (354 pages) investigation of the man's work and life.*
Trowell, Michael, 'Colin Wilson', *Book & Magazine Collector* #58, Jan. 1989 *good overview of the non-fiction and fiction.*
The Colin Wilson Page http://www-personal.umich.edu/ ~ jbmorgan/ cwilson.html *unofficial, but approved, site — surprisingly the only one found at the time of writing, unless you count a site for a 'Colin Wilson' who works in an office...*

by Phil Tonge

IN THE COURT OF KING KENDO

The strange and tacky golden age of British television wrestling

A seventies Saturday afternoon in the UK. A live broadcast on the ITV network shines through the economic and social gloom. In the *World of Sport* presentation studio, surrounded by bored typists and PA's in blue and yellow tank-tops, sits the raffish figure of DICKIE DAVIES (did he ever finish painting that ceiling?). Our host, smiling the type of media grin that fails to mask utter contempt, reads out a link to the next item. We cut to a live feed from a large social club somewhere in the north of England. An avuncular commentator hails us in voice-over. *"Greetings grapple fans."* It is Kent Walton, voice of British wrestling and co-producer of dreadful cinema sex comedies.[1]

As he introduces us to the bout that's already in progress, we become aware of the seedy surroundings of the venue, the Satanic half-light that only illuminates the front few rows of the audience, distorted through a grey-blue fog of Embassy Number Six and reflected in the spilled brown ale on the lino. The audience contains more than its fair share of pension age women in polyester sun frocks, sipping milk stout and chain smoking Senior Service. These are the massed ranks of the Mackeson Mafia, the Bingo Granny Battalion. Screaming for blood and waving their handbags in a mumsy threat display, they resemble none other than Mary Whitehouse[2] participating in a primal scream therapy workshop. Their gazes are centred on a starkly lit canvas-covered podium the size of the posh kid at school's bedroom. It's square and it's got corners called "corners" but everyone calls it "the ring". Three sturdy ropes connected to the vaguely padded corner posts[3] give the impression of a low-quality sheep paddock. In the paddock stands a thick set man wearing dress suit trousers, a white shirt and a black dicky-bow tie that just has to be of the type that comes fully formed on a piece of elastic. He has assumed a position, semi-crouching with hands on knees that mirrors the appearance of a hotel barman checking the fridge for mixers. However, he is not looking for Britvic 55. He is the referee and he's staring at the activities of an odder couple than Lemmon and Mattau. Thrashing around on the floor, embracing and hugging like young lovers are two binmen having a fight. One is a stocky chap with a lazy eye, regimental tattoos, a pair of hand-me-down swimming trunks (one size too small) and a neat range of pantomime put downs, the other is a brick shithouse in an Edwardian leotard, his features covered by a customised balaclava. As the pair wrestle in a delightful fantasy of amateur dramatics, farmyard choreography and shoulder popping brutalities (that would kill a rugby forward), the masked man, making a big play to the crowd that he thinks the ref can't see him, pretends to punch wall-eye in

the face. The ref stops the bout, the crowd of blue-rinsed gorehounds go mental and the public address system feedbacks into life. In a voice that only occurs when the English working class tries to "talk proper" comes the announcement...

> **LADIES AND GENTLEMEN, KENDO NAGASAKI HAS RECEIVED HIS FIRST PUBLIC WARNING!**

That was wrestling on the telly in the seventies. I *adore* wrestling — always have, always will. From as far back as I can remember it's always been there for me. Sure, I'll watch World Wrestling Federation stuff, even though it's the McDonald's / Starbucks / Man United corporate capitalist face of grappling. Even now it has it's moments, although WWF hasn't recovered from the retirement of Mick Foley.[4]

Of course there's more to US wrestling than the WWF, even if the WWF would like to make it seem that way, what with the buying up of struggling rivals World Champion Wrestling (WCW) and Extreme Championship Wrestling (ECW).

While WCW seemed to be a retirement home for aging WWF wrestlers (step forward Hulk Hogan and Bret "The Hitman" Hart) it did bring us the likes of Rey Misterio Junior and other luchadores. ECW gave the Dudley Boyz their big break and that definitely improved the state of US wrestling. The grass roots scene remains very healthy with odd little mom-and-pop operations with names like the "North Sputnumberg County Wrestling Federation". Still, never mind the yanks, wrestling is a truly internationalist pastime. I've enjoyed the painfully violent antics of Japanese women wrestlers and the acrobatic pomp of the Mexican masked superwrestlers. Ah, the wondrous antics of El Santo and his great rival Blue Demon, it's a shame that the UK is starved of the carnival that is Mexican wrestling. Except for camp documentary featurettes, usually fronted by Jonathan Ross (who, to give him credit, is a genuine enthusiast), going out at some ungodly hour on Channel 4, you won't be seeing video releases of "Mil Mascaras Versus Clodagh Rogers".

Above all it just has to be the glorious fannying about that was British wrestling. For most children in Britain, that meant watching it on television on a Saturday afternoon instead of going outside and playing. Whenever wrestling fans talk openly of their love of the game, usually in the pub, how come some utter arse butts in with what they think is an incisive and never-before-heard critique of the sport, i.e. *"Oh that shit, don't you know it's all faked, don't you know it's not a real sport, don't you know it isn't real?"* Then they sit there with a stupid smug grin all over their stupid smug faces. What stupid fucking things to say. We're aware of the "fakery" of results, but the physical effort to take part in a match would cripple yer average civilian. Wrestlers have been crippled in the ring, some have been killed there. Graeco-Roman wrestling is an olympic sport and boring as Hell to watch — that's the appeal of the professional all-in style.

It's a branch of show business, it's theatre, at worst it can be pantomime, at best it's an art form, although I sometimes wished that certain wrestlers would stay in character a bit longer. I remember my bitter disappointment after watching an exhibition match at Pontins, Weston-Super-Mare in June 1978 to see two wrestlers (you know who you are) who, twenty minutes after pretending to despise each other in the ring, were propping up the bar, chatting away like old friends.

All those wrestlers and promoters who defended the sport by denying choreographed fights, bless 'em, were missing the point. The fans don't give a shit, as long as they get their money's worth. The WWF nowadays play up this factor, concentrating on the soap opera element for the television audience, actually employing TV soap writers to provide storylines. I'm much happier with this sort of "fake"

— no-one bets on the outcome of a wrestling match as opposed to all the money blown by ordinary punters on bent boxing matches, doped horse races and thrown footy games.

Finally, what's this hang up about "real"? Real how? Landing face first on the floor of the ring after jumping off the top rope seems awfully "real" to me and just how "real" was Alan Shearer's reaction every time he got into the penalty box? No bugger's near him than BANG! He's down like there's a sniper in the stands. If you're a wrestling fan and someone says "real?" to you, pour their half of mild over their head and hit them. Hard. In the face.

Televised wrestling began in the UK on Wednesday, November 9, 1955 courtesy of ITV company Associated Reddifusion.

Kick-off was 9pm and was brought to the viewer from the luxury venue that was West Ham Baths. The first wrestlers to be featured were Cliff Beaumont and the self-proclaimed Jackie "Mr TV" Palo. Viewing figures were surprisingly large, considering the relatively small ratio of TV sets per head of population at the time and a legend was born.

Mind you the ITV watch dog at the time, the Independent Broadcasting Authority (IBA), weren't too impressed. They introduced certain guidelines for the television version, no biting, no gouging, no kneeing of the bollocks or crotch grabs and absolutely no blood. Certain holds were outlawed from the screen completely and above all, the ref had to be "seen to be in charge at all times". Well, it didn't really matter, if you wanted the no-holds-barred stuff you could always nip out to the Victoria Hall in Hanley, or the Drill Hall, Halifax, and see it there.

By its seventies Saturday heyday huge millions of devoted viewers could name all the Heels[5] and Blue-eyes[6] by heart, then follow that with a dissection of favourite moves from the Boston Crab to the simple Forearm Smash.[7]

The actual fighting was more on the technical leg-hold side and most of the wrestlers were of the "chip-shop" body shape than the oiled muscle men of today. That just added to the whole appeal. My favourite were the tag team matches.

Tag matches were fan-fucking-tastic, like mini Jacobean revenge tragedies mixed with Wagnerian opera sung by fat bastards. The set-up was always the same. Two Heels; one small and evil e.g. Rollerball Rocco and one huge and evil, usually Giant Haystacks. Opposing them, a team of one tiny athletic Blue-eye, say Steve Grey and one morally ambiguous but frighteningly hard wrestler, perhaps Kendo Nagasaki. The plot would follow the usual route, after an indifferent first round, Grey would end up in the ring having his guts stomped out by Rocco, endless cheating would ensue as Haystacks would join in the kicking without being tagged. The ref would be too busy telling Kendo to stop leaning into the notice Grey being stomped on repeatedly in the background. The battered blue eye would then make a herculean effort to reach his partner's out-stretched hand (as Kendo is too honourable to step into the ring to make the tag).

He would make increasingly desperate "if... I... can... just... reach" movements before the bulk of Haystacks dragged him off by the leg to bounce him off the floor again. This process would be repeated anything up to four times, until finally Kendo makes the tag and proceeds to beat the shit out of the bad lads. This would be doubly entertaining if one of the heels made a great play of shitting himself and making a run for the dressing room. Then it all went pear-shaped. The problem with British wrestling was that it was always in the hands of a few promoters, who (with a couple of exceptions) were only really interested in lining their own pockets. Top name wrestlers could fill the Albert Hall (yes, that one) for three nights running and make thousands for the hall and the promoter, yet even a legend like Mick McManus would come away with just under a hundred quid.

Television was even worse for its closed shop racket carried out by the Crabtree family. It was criminal how the brothers had carved up TV wrestling for themselves, Max was the promoter — you had to sign for his agency or you didn't get on the box, brother Brian got the MC job and then came the other brother... Shirley. Shirley Crabtree, better known to the world as Big Daddy.

Big Daddy. How those words burn in my guts. If you could point to the one reason that wrestling in Britain went down the shitter, there it is.. A horrible, obese, middle aged man in a badly fitting leotard, a glittery top hat and bleached hair marching into the ring carrying a small boy while chanting "Easy, easy". The horror... the horror.

He wasn't a wrestler, he was a shit gimmick. It became a cottage industry, comic strips, annuals, t-shirts, they were even going to give him his own Saturday morning kids show (replacing *TISWAS*) but luckily someone thought better of it.

He never did any work in the ring, he'd leave that up to his tag partners, he just turned up at the end of the match and went "easy, easy". Wrestling was turning into an episode of *Crackerjack*.[8]

Then he started killing people.

He had one move, the belly splash. Twenty-four stones of lard slamming on top of another fat bloke with a dodgy ticker, Mal "King Kong" Kirk (RIP). Soon TV wrestling became festooned with Daddy-clones. The old fans stopped watching and the influx of new fans trickled away to nothing. Eventually, in 1988 the plug was pulled. Wrestling in Britain still exists, albeit in a very low-key back room of the social club sort of existence. There's regular competition bouts in Leicester for instance, but the golden days of TV heaven are long dead. Probably by two falls and a submission.

The Cak-Watch! British Wrestling Hall of Fame

MICK M'MANUS

The elder statesman of Brit-wrestling. One of few men alive to look like he's wearing a stocking over his head (see also the 1973–74 Chelsea squad). Has had same jet-black dyed haircut for forty years. Sells insurance.

PAT ROACH

Hairy bloke turned actor. Appeared in *Auf Weidersein, Pet*. Still acts and occasionally wrestles on the continent and in the States.

ADRIAN STREET

Wrestled as one of those bizarre "Evil Poof" characters. Dressed like a member of glam rockers The Sweet. Master showman. Now runs own wrestling school in the US.

JOHNNY KWANGO

Inventor of the flying headbutt. Dead.

GIANT HAYSTACKS

Horrible looking beardy bloke the size of a bus. Came on to The Mighty Quinn by Manfred Mann for some reason. Became debt collector. Dead.

CATWEAZLE

Comedy relief wrestler. Dressed as then-popular TV character (created by Richard Carpenter and played by Geoffrey Bayldon). Incredibly scrawny bloke who would be paired against Haystacks. The ensuing melee would just have Catweazle being chased round and round the ring for ten minutes (a gag later ripped off in *Monty Python's Life of Brian*). Dead.

KUNG FU

A badly handled attempt to cash in on the early seventies martial arts craze. Bloke in colourful mask who goes "Hi-Yaa!" Occasionally.

LES KELLETT

Really scary. Part-time pig farmer.

KENDO NAGASAKI

My Hero. The king of masked wrestlers. You can keep Dr Death or Count Bartelli, this bloke was the master. He never spoke, he never turned up without his mask on, he never hung around the bar with other wrestlers. He meant it. Apparently Kendo would drive around for miles after a match with his mask on and only when he was certain he hadn't been followed, he'd pull over and take the mask off. Two masks, a black one for the build up to the fight and a red one to say "I am Kendo, hear me roar". I still remember the bout where he lost and had to burn his mask... heartbreaking. Then he did something a bit silly and went back to wearing the mask. A plumber from Wolverhampton tried to expose who Kendo was once... but I don't care if his name is Peter Thornley, if he lost his little finger making horse-boxes at Jennings of Crewe or if he was a junior judo champion for Britain, I'm not interested. He's wrestling's answer to Keyser Soze, "and like that... he's gone". Mind you, I'd like to see some of his rejected monikers, Karate Hiroshima anyone?

NOTES

1 Mr Walton co-owned the production firm Pyramid Film Company with Hazel Adair (the co-creator of soap-opera atrocity *Crossroads*. The television equivalent of pubic lice. No, for the millionth time, I am not related to the bloke who played Sandy Richardson. Although my mum did see the camp actor who played Adam Chance fill up his roller at a petrol station just outside Gloucester. Their films include *Clinic Xclusive* (1971), *Can you keep it up for a week?* (1974) and the legendary *Keep It Up Downstairs* (1976). Hey, we've all got to eat. **2** Hooray! Ding-Dong, the wicked witch is dead. **3** The yanks call them Turnbuckles and pad them like they expect a train to collide with them. **4** Probably the greatest wrestler the US has produced. Wrestled under the names Cactus Jack, Dude Love and Mankind. A wrestling original with a shaky grip on sanity and absolutely no concept of self-preservation whatsoever. Bucked the WWF trend for steroid style bodybuilder physiques by looking like a bloke who delivers skips. **5** Villain / Bad-Guy. **6** Good Guy. The Americans call them babyfaces or Faces. **7** I'd just like to apologise to my mate Craig Hurst whose nose I broke while demonstrating this very move in a nightclub. Sorry. **8** Corny BBC TV children's variety show, 1955 to well past its sell-by date.

ONE OF MY FAVOURITE CLASSROOM memories of life as a Catholic school boy is being shuffled, unannounced and herd like, into the science / biology lab of the Christian Brothers College in St Kilda (Melbourne, Australia), having the lights unceremoniously dimmed as we took our seats at the long, sulphur stained benches cluttered with Bunsen burners and test tubes, and treated to some antiquated but highly entertaining (to me at least — many of my classmates disagreed) short film about road safety, the perils of alcohol and / or drug abuse, how to avoid spinal injuries, or any one of a multitude of other subjects.

On rare occasions, we would even get to witness the horrible consequences that would no doubt result from any form of sexual promiscuity before marriage. This was during the late 1970s/early eighties, just prior to the widespread introduction of video into the Australian school system, when these films were still screened on 8- and 16mm film, the way they should be, with scratches, washed out colours, jumping frames, tinny sound coming out of a small box speaker, and that creepy, omnipresent creak of the sprockets as they fed themselves through the metal teeth of the projector.

By the early 1980s, classroom *films* had all but been forgotten, replaced by cheapjack video productions which — for the most part — completely lacked the charm (and impact) of their celluloid predecessors. Considered outmoded and outdated, many were simply relegated to the scrap heap, although a brief chapter in RE/Search's *Incredibly Strange Films* book (1986) kept their memory alive somewhat, as did compilation films like *The Atomic Cafe* (1982) and *Rhino's Guide to Safe Sex* (1987), which edited together some of the more memorable moments from the vintage atomic scare and sex education genres respectively. Interest in classroom films rose steadily throughout the 1990s, with several amusing episodes of *The Simpsons* paying tribute to them, and has finally reached fruition with the publication of Ken Smith's *Mental Hygiene* (1999 Blast Books/$24.95 US), the first exhaustive study of this unique genre.

THE GOLDEN AGE OF CLASSROOM SCARE FILMS

by

John Harrison

Devoted strictly to the 'glory years' between 1945–1970, *Mental Hygiene* makes for both an exhaustive, in-depth study of its subject, as well an entertaining light read for those who are not overly familiar with educational cinema. Considering many of these films have been lost for decades — and many which have survived often contain only the most basic of credits (if any at all) — Smith's degree of research is impressive (much of his data came from the archives of Rick Prelinger, a social historian who has amassed over the years a vast collection of industrial and educational films). The book's structure is very user-friendly: after giving us a brief but solid grounding on where educational films came from (conceived for the most part as shots of preventative medicine, quelling any activity or form of expression which failed to conform to the staid ideals of parents, teachers, religious groups and other authoritarian figures), Smith presents us with a useful historical timeline (placing the development of classroom films alongside important medial, scientific, social and cultural breakthroughs), followed by a primer of FAQs: *What makes a mental hygiene film?, How much money did actors earn by appearing in these films?* (usually $25 a day), *How did producers choose topics for films?*, and so on.

Smith then gets into the meat of the book, with chapters devoted to the most famous (and best loved) genres of classroom films. Further chapters examine some of the prolific producers of classroom films, such as the Coronet Studios (founded by the charismatic, Hefner-like David Smart, an eccentric playboy and hypochondriac who died prematurely whilst undergoing a risky colon examination against his doctor's advice), Encyclopaedia Britannica Films, and Los Angeles based Sid Davis, whose work is becoming increasingly more appreciated (and sought after) by collectors of vintage classroom films (David began his career as a stand in for John Wayne, and in fact it was the Duke who loaned Davis the money to make his first classroom film, 1950's *The Dangerous Stranger*, about child molesters).

The second half of *Mental Hygiene*'s 240 pages are taken up by a massive A–Z filmography, which although entertaining and informative, could have benefited from the inclusion of a little more information. For example, no mention is made of whether each film was produced in colour or black & white (although the majority of pre 1960 titles were no doubt lensed in b&w, colour photography did make a big difference in the impact which these films had on their target audiences, particularly those in the drug, sex and driver education genres). Smith devotes a substantial amount of coverage to the 1949 classic

Dating: Do's and Don'ts, yet fails to mention that the legendary Edward D. Wood, Jr is believed to have directed the film. And the running times listed for some films are incorrect (*Highways of Agony* is listed at eleven minutes, yet the print which I have runs a full twenty-six minutes). Of course, given the overwhelming number of classroom films produced between 1945 and 1970, the film understandably only manages to scratch the surface, even with Smith limiting his coverage (mostly) to American productions.

Another slight quibble is when Smith answers the question of *Where can I see these films?* with a curt *"You can't. The few copies that remain are either scattered among university and museum archives or in the hands of private collectors of stock footage libraries. At the moment, neither the public archives nor the private footage libraries seem inclined to release these films for viewing, but perhaps this will change."* At no point in the book is mention made of the volumes of vintage classroom scare films available from important companies such as *Something Weird Video* (see reviews which follow). It's hard to believe that Smith would be unaware of their existence, given the obvious amount of time and research he has put into the project. However, the fact that Blast Books — *Mental Hygiene*'s publisher — is offering their own two hour compilation tape of classroom films (advertised on the inside back cover of the book), may provide a hint as to why the aforementioned company failed to gain any sort of look-in.

These minor gripes aside, *Mental Hygiene* is simply a 'must have' for anyone who harbours a fascination for educational cinema. Even those with just a passing interest in the genre will find the book an engrossing read. It is also superbly packaged, with a clean, appropriately 1950s look to it, and is illustrated with many classic screen grabs, as well as a number of rare behind the scenes production stills, and excerpts from promotional pamphlets and trade publications such as *Educational Screen* and *Coronews* (the official guide to Coronet's educational productions).

THE FILMS

CLASSROOM SCARE FILMS Vol 1 & 3
DRUG HORRORS
Something Weird Video, US $15.00 each

These two great party tapes each compile six of the best anti-drug shorts from the late sixties/early seventies, designed to sway American high school kids away from the evil temptation of narcotics, but often having the precisely opposite effect.

Weed (1971), directed by Brian Kellman for Concept Films, kicks off Volume One. After a trippy opening credit sequence, with sitar music playing over time lapse photography of a rather pathetic looking bud growing out of the dirt, we are introduced to Charles, a seventeen-year-old high school senior who's had his stoned ass thrown into the slammer for possessing one measly joint. After this promising opening, the film bogs itself down with too much 'talking heads' footage of so-called experts espousing their views on why any form of drug use is bound to lead to our inevitable downfall. Filmed partly on the streets of Philadelphia, *Weed* also treats us to a brief history of hemp, some crude animation, and even footage of a rabbit being shot up with THC in order to observe its deadly effects.

Up Pills/Down Pills attempts to give us all the negative poop on barbiturates and amphetamines. *"I thought it was 1943, and they were taking me to the ovens"*, claims the voiceover of one demented speed freak, who according to narrator Herb Graham, supposedly went on to shoot two people dead in a drug induced rampage. A spider is shown wildly spinning its web after receiving a jolt of speed (insect and animal life were the frequent unwilling stars of many classroom films), and portraits of such famous pill poppers as Judy Garland, Jimi Hendrix and Marilyn Monroe are included to point out the fact that no one is safe from the deadly charms of mother's little helper.

The most interesting thing about *Boozers and Users* — a universal condemnation of alcohol, marijuana and tobacco — is that it is hosted and narrated by minor film/TV star James Franciscus, a fiendish chain smoker who would eventually die of chronic emphysema. *Keep off the Grass* (1970) is a vintage Sid Davis production, in which an understanding father catches Tom, his geeky high school student son, with a joint, then urges him to study dope users more carefully. Easily persuaded (thanks in no small part to a special issue of *Life* devoted to youth and drugs), he pops in on a boring stoner party, has young users begging him for small change outside the local head shop, and visits the studio of a once promising artist whose potential has been destroyed by chronic marijuana abuse. When Tom witnesses his dealer friend Mac selling a number to a small boy (*"If he's old enough to have a buck, he's old enough to blow pot. Easy money, man"*), he finally realises how evil the wacky weed really is.

"The daily drink may not be the best thing in the world, but a man who takes a drink after his day is done has worked! He has achieved! Not so the teenaged user. He desperately seeks to cop out. He uses his grass as a mental crutch because he fears to stand on his own."

Bargain basement animation is used to demonstrate the harmful effects of aspirin (and sniffing model aeroplane cement) on young people in *Drugs and the Nervous System*, before the tape rounds off with *Scag* (1970), a rather brutal and uncompromising look at heroin addiction (*"For years, confined to the ghettos and blacks, or musicians, or both"*. In other words, *we didn't really worry about it too much until it started to effect white middle class America*). Grimy pho-

tography is used to capture dead junkies lying in the gutters of New York slums, as we follow the lives of Toni, a young black girl trying to get herself off H, and Robby, a suburban white kid (who sits in his cramped, filthy bedroom listening to the Beatles' *Happiness is a Warm Gun*) in the full throes of addiction. Unlike the other films on this tape, *Scag* has not developed a 'camp' edge to it over the ensuing years, and still makes for pretty disturbing and depressing viewing.

Volume Three of Something Weird's *Classroom Scare Films* is on the whole a somewhat less enjoyable collection than the first instalment, yet is still worth seeking out for its selective highlights, chief amongst which is *The People Vs. Pot*, a b&w screamer which starts off with a memorable, poppy theme song playing under the opening montage of hippies:

Pot! Pot! Gimme some pot! Forget what you are, you can be what you're not! Hip! Hip! You wanna be hip! You're nowhere at all if you don't have a trip!

Written and produced by Sid Abel for the Armed Forces Department of Defence, *The People Vs. Pot* tells the tale of Eddy (who bears an uncanny resemblance to a young Dennis Hopper!), a turned-on soldier who is thrown into a bare room and forced to listen to the horror story of former military users. A stoned black soldier shoots three of his own GI buddies in the Nam, a spaced out airman on leave sits in his hotel room endlessly studying a length of spaghetti, and genuine war footage is accompanied by voice-overs of a high as a kite Eddy proclaiming: *"I'm floating over the whole damn universe"*. A very strange and surreal little number.

The Road Back features Florie Fisher, a middle-aged Jewish princess with a thirty year dope habit behind her, delivering a fire and brimstone lecture to a class of (mostly bored looking) New York teens. With a nasally voice that's even more grating than Fran Drescher's, Fisher is so righteous, and downright aggravating, you wish one of the students would leap up onto the stage and start pummelling her. Incredibly condescending to her audience — and constantly praising a half-way house which she's obviously been paid to represent — Fisher (who chain smokes throughout the lecture) is completely uneducated on the subject of drug use and addiction, and jumps down the throat of one poor girl who dares to challenge her view that even one puff of grass is destined to start you on a lifelong spiral of heroin addiction, prostitution and crime (according to Fischer, only six people she knew never graduated from marijuana to hard drugs — the reason being that they'd all been given the chair after committing murders while stoned on weed!). Fisher, who refers to her mostly clean-cut audience as hippies, also rolls out the old chestnut about the young LSD user who jumps out of the sixth story window, thinking she could fly (Fisher takes the anecdote one step further by claiming she actually knew the mythical person this happened to).

Smokey Joe's High Ride is a bit of an anomaly for this collection, as it seems to originate from the early-1980s, and uses the emerging video game craze as its tool of instruction. Four kids pass time in a video arcade, debating whether or not they should get blasted before heading off to the big party, when a new game suddenly materialises before their eyes. The big shot (and driver) amongst the group decides he must try the game, 'Smokey Joe's High ride', which features — surprise, surprise — four kids in a car, on their way to a party. With each successive level, the driver gets progressively more stoned, making it harder to dodge the pedestrians, trains and oncoming vehicles. Thanks to the harsh lessons dished out by this crappy game, the gang decides they better not indulge in anything until they arrive safely at their destination.

Rounding out this volume are *The Losers*, a gritty, b&w look at drugged out teeners in New York, who start out sniffing glue and smoking pot before moving onto smack and the eventual steel bar (or padded) cell, *No Smoking*, a real bottom of the barrel Sid Davis production, and *Marijuana: The Hidden Danger*, which comes across as little more

than an extended TV news segment (and, though made in the late-1970s, contains the same rhetoric which these films were spouting a decade earlier).

CLASSROOM SCARE FILMS Vol 2
HEALTH HORRORS

Something Weird Video, US $15.00

With this volume, Something Weird dig deep into the dusty old vaults to treat us to a selection of vintage health scare shorts, highlighted by the following titles:

VD: Truth or Consequences (1976, revised and updated to include genital herpes). Narrated and hosted by one Paul Goodrich (a pretty goofy looking dude in a silk shirt and sporting a magnificent early-seventies hairdo), this takes the basic 'talking heads' approach, wherein various medical and social experts expound their views on sexually transmitted diseases. The best moments of this film are the comments given by teenagers, such as the effeminate boy on the sidewalk who claims *"You can only get syph from a prostitute"*, and the shy, scared kid who approaches his horrified father on the couch and announces: *"Dad, I've got this strange discharge coming from my penis. Do you think it could be VD?"*.

With its dramatic music really piling on

the scare factor, *Smoking: It's Your Choice* could still be used as an effective tool against tobacco abuse. Particularly disturbing is the creepy mannequin which is rigged to suck down a cigarette as the putrid black tar accumulates in its 'lungs' (two glass jars with sponges inside them). A man with emphysema so bad he can't even blow out a match at point blank range is also rolled out to employ some scare tactics (he is shown watching on in wishful admiration as a healthy young boy bounces up a flight of stairs — something the man can only ever dream of doing).

Apart from a grungy short on the spinal disease scoliosis, as well as yet another warning on the evils of booze (*"one of those non-fuel extras which people take"*), this tape also features two great colour shorts on oral hygiene: *The Prevention and Control of Dental Disease* (1970) and *Your Mouth*. The former features some disgusting close-ups of mouths pulled open to reveal blackened, decaying teeth, while *Your Mouth* has some amazing x-ray footage of food being masticated and swallowed.

CLASSROOM SCARE FILMS Vol 6
KIDS IN TROUBLE

Something Weird Video, US $15.00
A double dose of classics from Sid Davis (surely the Ed Wood of the classroom scare genre) is what makes this volume essential viewing. *The Strange Ones* is Davis' colour rehash of his own paedophile classic *The*

Dangerous Stranger. 'The strange ones look just like everyone else', Mrs. Perkins, a police worker, warns Karen, a young blonde girl who has just been rescued from the clutches of a child molester (seen offering the regulatory bag of lollies in a park). As Karen sits in a chair waiting for her mom to come and collect her, Mrs. Perkins takes the opportunity to lecture the poor girl on the dangers and potential consequences of getting too close to a 'strange one'. This is followed up by an earlier Davis classic, *The Drop Out* (1962), in which a surly high school flunky (who bears a remarkable resemblance to Tony Dow from *Leave it to Beaver*) plods around his small home town in a constant state of boredom, whist the moralising narrator points out how bleak the kid's future is because he decided to drop out of high school. Like all Davis productions, these two films seem to openly flout the traditional rules of cohesive filmmaking, which — much like 60s sexploitation pioneer Doris Wishman and the aforementioned Ed Wood — give his work a signature that is unique even amongst the diverse and often delirious world of classroom scare cinema.

Other shorts featured on this volume include *Acting with Maturity*, a plea for young hotheads to keep their cool in tense situations (we see a kid smiling politely at an annoying little show off while mentally imagining that he's beating the crap out of him!), *Read the Label-And Live!* (in which we view the gruesome — albeit faked — aftermaths of a man igniting in flames after lighting a smoke while painting, and a woman whose face has been turned into pizza through the unsafe use of highly flammable hairspray), and *Headed for Trouble*, a b&w melodrama set amongst the seedy world of juvenile delinquents (the highlight of which is the performance of future *Exorcist* star Jason Miller as one of the JDs).

DRIVERS' ED SCARE FILMS Vol 1–7

Something Weird Video, US $15.00 each
It has become a sad yet concrete fact that road fatalities have solidly entrenched them-

selves as one of the major causes of death in the twentieth-century. The need for education and deterrents remains as strong as ever. In Australia, the controversial TAC (Traffic Authority Commission) advertising campaigns provide one example of the use of gritty realism in trying to teach (mostly young) people of the hazards and potential consequences of unsafe driving habits.

It hasn't always been that way, however. There was a time when automobile accidents were regarded as little more than sources of curiosity and even amusement. During the late 1930s, carnivals travelling across the American Midwest would often have special booths set up, the walls of which were lined with photographs of car wrecks and their unfortunate victims. But as automobiles developed into more sophisticated (and faster) machines, the number of road fatalities, particularly amongst younger, hot headed drivers, began to rise at an alarming pace. Car accidents were suddenly becoming a signifi-

cant cause of death, and a new genre of classroom film began to emerge to try and combat the mounting toll: the drivers' education film.

One of the earliest known drivers' ed films was a 1950 effort called *The Last Date*. A fifteen-minute fictional piece, it related the story of a pretty, law-abiding high school student, who against her better judgement accepts the offer of a ride from Nick, the local speed demon. Driving well over the speed limit, Nick (played by a young Dick York, future star of *Bewitched* and something of a regular in early classroom films) collides head on with another vehicle and is killed. The girl survives, but her face is so disfigured she smashes the mirror in her bedroom to avoid looking at her reflection.

The hokiness of *The Last Date* and several other films of a similar nature had little impact on an audience that was humoured at best by the cheesy acting and corny, forced dialogue. Meanwhile, back in the real world, the escalating road toll showed no signs of abating. A decision was made that the best way to teach highway safety rules was to simply show what happened to people who failed to follow them. Thus, the notorious era of the reality-based drivers' education film was ushered in.

Although many of these films were produced in various states across America, the most graphic and disturbing drivers' ed films came out of the Ohio city of Mansfield. Produced by Earl J Deems for his Highway Safety Films, Inc., the Ohio films are the ones most vividly remembered by horrified young teens sitting on metal chairs in freezing school auditoriums. Many of Deems' most memorable films — including *Signal 30, Mechanized Death, Wheels of Tragedy, The Third Killer* and *Highways of Agony* — are available from Something Weird video, as part of their enormous *Drivers' Ed Scare Films* series. With their monotone narration, murky photography, often piercing music scores, and unflinching, matter-of-fact depiction of the human body in various states of dismemberment and devastation, it's not difficult to understand why these films left such an indelible impression on the psyche of a generation of Americans, many of whom would be confronted by similar horrors as part of their daily routine, as the ensuing years would see them shipped off to Vietnam in increasing numbers.

(For a more thorough history of the drivers' education film, along with detailed filmography, a look at Highway Safety Films' alleged involvement in porno films, money laundering and even murder, along with an interview with Bret Wood — director of the 2001 documentary *Hell's Highway* — refer to my chapter on the subject in *Suture 2*, published by Amok).

SEX HYGIENE SCARE FILMS Vol 2

Something Weird Video, US $15.00

Next to the highway safety films, sex hygiene is perhaps the best loved and most fondly remembered genre of classroom scare films, eliciting equal doses of giggles and gasps from an audience struggling hard enough as it is to cope with developing puberty, without having to be subjected to the grotty sights on display in this tape.

VD: Name Your Contacts (1968) lays on the guilt trip hard and fast, urging people who have been infected with a dose to give up the names of all their sexual partners to their health professional, to stop the disease setting off a potential chain reaction. Lots of lingering close-ups on pained, embarrassed faces in this one, particularly on the groovy young gay guy who tries unsuccessfully to convince his doctor that he picked up his VD from a girl.

Filled with boring, predictable talk from clergymen, psychologists and parent groups about the decaying state of morals amongst our reckless, directionless youth, the undoubted highlight of *Sex in Today's World* (1966) is an early on-stage appearance by Frank Zappa and the Mothers of Invention, who are seen at several intervals playing to a small group of wildly frugging teenagers!

Pick-Up (1944) is a WWII US Army 'Training Film' which centres on Corporal John Green, a jolly rogue who rescues a damsel in distress at a bus terminal and treats her to a night on the town. Unfortunately for him, the girl was not exactly as '*clean as a whistle*' (as he boasts to his army buddies), and soon enough he's laid up in the medic ward sweating on whether his gonorrhoea is likely to develop into syphilis. The Corporal is spared that ghastly fate, but due to his convalescence has his long awaited leave cancelled, and has to face being shipped off to the Pacific without the chance to say goodbye to his loved ones back home. Despite its dose of dated cheese, *Pick-Up* still manages to pack a punch with the inclusion of close-up photographs of a penis sporting a gaping sore, a man's torso littered with syphilis infected spots, and a deformed baby borne from a mother whom had been infected with VD.

Volume Two of *Sex Hygiene Scare Films* rounds off with the double combo of *Boy to Man* and *Girl to Woman*, two shorts produced by Churchill Films which use an identical structure to demonstrate and explain the changes in the developing teenager's body. Particularly entertaining is hearing the narrator in *Boy to Man* refer to a wet dream as a '*nocturnal emission*' (although refreshingly, the film does go on to point out that masturbation is a perfectly harmless and natural activity for boys to indulge in — one can imagine this sequence being hastily edited out with a pair of clippers whenever the film was booked to screen at Catholic schools).

NOTES

Many more volumes of vintage classroom scare films are available from Something Weird Video, including *Campy Classroom Classics, Health and Safety, Mindbenders* (sixties drug education shorts), *Christian Scare Films* and others. Visit them online at *www.somethingweird.com*, or send US $5.00 for their catalogue to PO Box 33664, Seattle, WA 98133 USA / Fax: (206) 364-7526. You should also try to get hold of their *Catalogue Supplement #11* (Summer/Fall 2000), which contains a detailed listing of all their scare film compilations (a limited number of copies are available from my mail-order company, The Graveyard Tramp / email: graveyardtramp@optusnet.com.au).

Hundreds of educational shorts from Rick Prelinger's collection can be downloaded free of charge at the Internet Moving Images Archive (image quality equivalent to VHS). For information, go to *www.prelinger.com*

"THERE ARE PICTURES IN YOUR PAINTINGS!"
An interview with David X Young

by John Szpunar &
Melanie Danté

New York City. Forty blocks downtown from the hub where the music and art business sector stands, sits a building in the dynamic area where Soho, Little Italy and Chinatown meet. It was there, where for the last thirty-five years of his life, that David X Young defied the "who's who" of Pop and fine art and became a legend in his own right.

Born in 1930, Young came of age with the abstract expressionists and allowed his own work to revel in the joy of their spontaneity. But Young's was always a tethered spontaneity. Pollock heaved his brushes at the canvas to "free paint". David X Young always

kept one eye fixed on reality. Critic Juan Osaka McFelsnir noted of Young's work: "To refuse paint's picture-making aspect would be to kill a major part of the possibilities. And a major part of the fun."

The impact that the underground jazz scene of the 1950s had on Young's work cannot be ignored. The proprietor of the legendary Jazz Loft in Manhattan's flower district, he opened his doors to countless musicians and documented them in hundreds of paintings and photographs. Young wanted his brushes to go where the improvisation of jazz had gone. Night after night, he took them there.

A multi-faceted renaissance man, Young threw fashion out the window with his short film *Klaximo* (1963), a film so far ahead of its time that it is just now gaining recognition. "I knew it would be shocking, but I didn't think it would be the film that shocked the avant garde!"

Undaunted by the direction that the art world had taken in the sixties and by egotistical jabs from the New York film underground, Young kept working, producing a myriad of photographs and paintings embracing life and love in Haiti. Toward the end of his life, he completed work on his children's story *Cissimon*, illustrated with beautiful watercolour plates — magic doorways that opened wide to the joy and mystery of childhood.

Outspoken until the end, David X Young passed away on May 22, 2001. Those lucky enough to have known him will never forget his generosity, kindness, and passion. Those who didn't have something to treasure as well. Pause for just a moment and *look* at his work. The life is there, bursting forth from countless canvases, photographs, and prints. David X Young was once criticized for having "pictures" in his paintings. They're there all right, for the entire world to see. And with them is something to treasure forever.

David X Young. Self-portrait, 1958

You were born in New England in the thirties. Conservative times for an artist in the making...

DAVID X YOUNG Well, yeah. I was born in 1930 and Roosevelt was elected in 1932. My grandfather lost his fortune in the crash under Hoover. But he hated Roosevelt. So every night, members of the family would gather around the fireplace. I was a little squirt. They *hated* Roosevelt. All I can remember is the harshness. It was *very* conservative.

I imagine that there wasn't much talk of Picasso around the fireplace... No, there wasn't!

So what was your first introduction to painting? About the first thing I fell in love with was *Snow White and the Seven Dwarfs*. It was strictly Disney. But I'll tell you exactly what I felt. I knew it was drawings. I knew it was all a painting. But it was real. You believed in the personalities of the dwarfs, you kind of accepted it — it was real, but not real. It always fascinated me. Of course, we weren't exposed much to art. There was no culture — it was *Time* magazine covers and Norman Rockwell illustrations.

I know you started to draw at an early age. I used to do drawings of Mickey Mouse, because I wanted to get a job as an animator for Disney. I soon got sick of drawing a mouse with circles, so I started using squares and rectangles. My teacher said, "That looks like Cubism." So I took out a book and read about Picasso and thought, "She's right!" And then I read that Picasso had sold *The Girl Before the Mirror* to the museum of modern art for $125,000. Well, so long Mickey Mouse!

You stuck out on your own... There wasn't really much going on. I remember back in 1948, everybody wanted to be the nice Norman Rockwell. I was already fed up with him by the time I went to art school. I had teachers who thought I needed glasses. But [laughs]... I was a very hip young guy! Everyone in my family said, "You don't know how to draw."

How long was it before you were taken seriously? Well, I guess my talent was recognized quickly enough. I put on a lot of school plays and things. It was a great way of getting out of classes. One year, a guy came — this was 1947 or 48 — he was a guy whose job was to help place students in jobs. He saw

**336 Canal St.
Young's home in his later years.**

what I did, and he said, "There's this new thing starting in New York called television. I can probably get you a $75 a week job." My mother wouldn't let me go. "I'd lose a son!" Those are the breaks.

Your mother was a writer... She wrote love stories. Very pulp, very sappy. She just wrote raw emotion, she never bothered to figure out plots. Very perfumed. When I was twelve, I used to make up plots for her. I didn't know about sex or anything. A pair of identical twins falls in love with another pair of identical twins. One goes to the war and gets killed. Stupid, silly plot ideas, but she wrote them up. She smoked furiously and drank a lot of wine to get that emotion. It sort of turned me off of being a writer.

You attended the Massachusetts School of Art? My mother had this idea of keeping up with the Joneses. I went there, put on a play, and they tried to throw me out of school. That was halfway through my freshman year. Then they decided to give me a mature job at the school supply store to teach me to be responsible. So I took that job, and they were paying me seventy bucks a week. So I stuck around and stole all the art material.

What was the response to your work in school? I had one teacher who was very hip, Larry Kupferman. He took my work to a gallery in New York. He sent me a telegram saying, "Congratulations. You're going to New York." I was blown away. I'd never been to New York in my life. I didn't know about art deals or percentages. Of course my mother said, "Paint sailboats. People will buy that." But I did sell some paintings — in 1950 it was good money. Finally, I couldn't stand Boston anymore, so I moved to New York.

Did you finish art school? Yeah. I was making money. I stayed for about half a year in Boston to find out what I was going to do. I realized that I had to get out. I met a couple of people who showed me how to get along; how to get an illegal loft; how to bribe the building inspectors. How to live like an outlaw.

You first hung around the jazz crowd while you were in Boston, though... I used to hang around the jazz joints. My school wasn't that far away. The places where Bird played, rhythm and blues bands... Woody Hermann. I was soaking up a lot of jazz.

Your father was a jazz musician. Right. I was born with it. So, I got to know a lot of those guys.

Can you compare the art scene in Boston to the scene in New York? Brown was the colour of Boston. A lot of brown suits, all the buildings were very dirty. The painting was very drab. All of the art school paintings in Boston were very religious. A lot of crucifixions, painted over with yellow varnish. Not one pretty girl!

What was your first impression of the New York scene when you got there? Well... I arrived with only a few hundred dollars. And I think the first four or five days I gave away $100 to drunks and junkies. I was very innocent. But Charlie Parker used to wait for his connection on the corner of West Third and Sixth Ave. I used to see Bird every morning... It was great. All the people I admired were there. I'd go across Washington Square and see Kline and his gang. I thought that was the way things would be forever.

You did some cover art for Prestige Records. They were a cheap company and they were recording a lot of jazz musicians that nobody else would hire. They put out ten-inch records with no covers, just type — *Miles Davis Plays*. So, Jimmy Raney and Stan Getz were going to record for them. I wrote them a letter hoping to push the virtues of graphic design and offered to do the first cover for nothing. The second one was The Modern Jazz Quartet. I did that for a while.

The Cedar Bar was a popular place for New York artists at the time. Well, the Cedar Bar was three times the size of this loft. It was down on University Place and Eighth. Most of the painters, the abstract expressionists, were guys who had government support until the end of the war. And they were a pretty serious gang. They used to hang out after work at The Waldorf on Eighth Street — get together, drink a cup of coffee, talk about each other's art. Well, they tore that down. So, the nearest place to go and hang out was the Cedar Bar — it was a half a block away. The glass of beer was the same price as a cup of coffee. So they all started drinking. They all became a bunch a drunks! Today they say, "To be an abstract expressionist you have to be an alcoholic." It just sort of happened. It was a great place. I got to know Kline very well. I'd met Pollock before and he was very gentle and sweet. But at the Cedar, he was... he got very violent. He'd walk in the door and the place would be absolute chaos.

You were showing with legends DeKooning, Pollock and the sort when you and your work became considered controversial... The shit hit the fan about my work after some success in Chicago — selling to Hugh Hefner in the company of Pollock, Kline and DeKooning. All good friends. The only *controversy* was that I was intruding on the *turf* of the Poppers. They moved into the money of the art market with their trash neo-dadaism called Pop. I was about the age of most of those Poppers and thought the whole thing was just silly and stupid. When the tide turned against real painting, Jackson, Bill, and Franz had big enough names to survive on their own, but me, the beginner did not. I stuck to my guns henceforth... I *think* that made Geldzahler and company regard me as some kind of a threat. That was the only controversy involved. Of course, the kind of painting I did was generally known as controversial at the time. But that wasn't just me. Some advice: Go to law school or turn to crime! By all means stay out of the gossip of the art world. It will only contaminate the brain. Cultivate that little world of pure pleasure that making art gives you, and forget about being important. If you actually *are* important, in time people will find you out.

In 1954, you got your loft in the Flower District. Well, I couldn't find a decent place. Every place in the Village was so dark. It just so happened that there were three empty floors on Sixth Ave. They were $120 bucks. So I rented them, rented out two of the rooms. My grandfather was a plumber, so he helped me out. I got some non-union guys to help with electricity. I even had a chimney sweep work on one of the chimneys, so I had a fireplace. I heated the studio with a kerosene space heater and the back with a gas heater. I broke up orange crates and junk from the streets to heat the place. I came all the way from Cape

Dick Carey's rehearsal band. Photo: David X Young

Cod to learn how to live like a bum.

You eventually brought in a piano. Yeah. I was dead broke. I couldn't afford to go anyplace to see jazz. But I had this loft and I had all these friends who were musicians. And they couldn't afford the studios to jam. So, I opened up my doors and got all the jazz for free. I got that piano — a very good used upright — and brought it up by block and tackle! After that, I kept an open door. Anyone who wanted to play could come on up. Thelonious Monk would rehearse with Hall Overton right below my bed. I'd go to sleep at night being serenaded by those guys.

The door was open for musicians... what

about people who just wanted to hear the music? Well, there weren't that many people who were interested. Eventually, people came to realize that it was a scene. They didn't know *why* it was a scene, but they knew there was action there. I mean, we all smoked pot. There were only a couple of cases of heroin. So a lot of these squares would come in with a cheap attitude — just to get high. But we had jam sessions — Zoot Sims was playing upstairs, Monk was playing downstairs. *That* was the real shit.

How was your artwork progressing at this time? I had a few shows. I was developing. I wasn't trying to take over the world yet.

You made a few trips to Haiti during that time. Well, Charlie Parker was around. I knew him quite well. Mingus was coming to my place a lot. Mingus and Bird were very close. We were all hoping that he'd show up one day. He died on March 12, 1955, and Mingus got very upset. I can't explain it, but I felt that I had to try to get to the heart of black culture. To do that, you would normally go to Africa. But Haiti was just down the street. It was French as well, and if you wanted to do anything with art, you'd go to France. That's originally why I went.

With paints and a camera. I've always been interested in images on a flat plane within the confines of a rectangle. Never the third dimension. Sculpture always bored me. Sculpture is phallic, it sticks out at you. Painting is vaginal, it sucks you in. So photography fit that interest quite easily. After I got to know Gene Smith's level of print quality, I could see how you could do really fine work as a photographer. But for me it was always an adjunct, like spare visual parts. Movies were another dimension to photography, and I liked the storytelling climaxes and rhythms. Like music.

A lot of what you shot in Haiti has a documentary feel. I was never interested in reportage. I just kept a camera with me and when I saw something to shoot, I shot it. When I was in Haiti, I acquired a Bolex movie camera and 600-feet of colour film. It turned up in a film I did on Haiti called *Seven Haitian Moods*. Now I look back at the photos I took in Haiti and realize there is an instinctive documentary there. Of a certain hunk of lost Haitian history. But I was there before it left and recorded some of those things.

In the mean time, the loft scene was

dying. Well, let's say this: in 1963 or 1964, Pop-Art started to come in. That killed abstract expressionism where I was coming from. Then the Beatles came over here and there was no room for jazz. There was no work for musicians. The spirit was gone. They were raising the rent. It was time to do something different. I went back to the cape and made *Klaximo*.

Let's hear a little about that film. I did that film in 1963. It was way ahead of its time; I still can't get it shown.

Do you see Klaximo as industrial eroticism? For one thing, I hate the term industrial eroticism. It's an oxymoron. I made *Klaximo* as protest against that very notion. The idea that machines or computers could better the idiosyncrasies of the human psyche. The big problem was to convey the illusion convincingly, which of course meant *erotically*. And it was largely a mise en scène editing and rhythm problem. It was a challenge just like painting a leafy tree in certain lights is a challenge. No other difference. I don't see anything avant garde about it. I think it is too clear for that category.

What were you getting at? I thought I'd do something different. I didn't want to do anything unless I could carry it all the way through. Those were the days when the computer was beginning to be talked about; if you kept a computer writing long enough, it would write all of *Hamlet*. You could play chess with a computer. There was a guy I met who was around twenty-eight-years-old. He was legally blind — he had these big thick glasses and was bald. He was devising a computer that could make the trumpet sound of A flat the way Dizzy Gillespie could do it and then the sound of A flat the way Louis Armstrong could do it. This was really very different. He was going to invent a computer that could play jazz in any style, and therefore eliminate the need for jazz musicians all together. That's what mediocrity's always trying to do, to get rid of the artist by some mechanical means. I was completely horrified by the whole thing. And I started to think, "How the fuck can I express this horrible idea?" It just so happens that I was living with a beautiful blonde girl at the time. I got this idea that the most horrible thing a human could do with a machine would be to fuck it. So, I decided to make a film about a girl fucking a robot. All of my friends said, "You can't do that! How the Hell can you do

that?" It was a challenge, so I worked on it and worked on it. The movie was very convincing; the women loved it.

Why did you decide to make a film in the first place? Film was my first love. Somehow down the line, I got 4,000-feet of black-and-white Tri-Ex reversal film. I had just gone thing through the whole scene with the art world and I realized that I didn't want anything to do with the art world until Pop-Art blew over. Little did I know it would last so long. I just decided to shoot movies instead. I figured with 4,000-feet of film I could really do something.

A lot of painters have turned to film at some point. Film is a different way of approaching an audience. You had the audience's complete attention for a half an hour, an hour, or what ever. You were commanding their total *thing*. A painting is something that's on the wall. You're drawn to it or not drawn to it. With film, it's a chance to be boss for a while. Welles describes it very well: "A ribbon of dream." Something that can trigger the imagination. And I always loved things that can trigger the imagination.

Where did you find your actors? They were a bunch of guys who were party buddies of mine. They were just hanging around. It was the end of the summer and we didn't have anything to do. The clubs were closed and all that. So it was a hobby or something.

Was it difficult to direct them? Visually, I got them to do exactly what I wanted. And once the camera was on, they were very serious. But they regarded it as a party. And I don't think any of them thought I was serious. Probably the most interesting one was the old guy, who literally was a dirty old man. He loved to rent his place out to young college girls in the summer. He said to me, "Imagine you asking me to play a dirty old man in a movie!" And he did it like a trooper!

Did you process the film along the way? Whenever I had the money. Literally cashed in beer bottles and waitress tips. I'd sell a drawing for $25 and I'd process more film. I had a hard time getting the nudity out of the lab. This was 1963, before X-rated films. They thought I was a college kid making a porno.

There really isn't a lot of nudity in the film. There was only 100 feet of nudity, and it was basically bare buttocks.

Let's talk about the score. The main jazz theme was done by Zoot Sims. Zoot was at my place one day and I asked him to do something. He said, "Oh, I can't do anything..." Five minutes later, he came up with that. He'd done a jazz-blues thing that we recorded at my jam sessions. He changed the emphasis on it — it's the same notes, different stress. The other music was from — I got this guy who knew about computers. I felt a synthesizer score would be appropriate. He did all the incidental music, and I thought it worked very well.

And you composed the title track? The title track, yes. I did the music and lyrics, though Carsten Bohn did the arrangement and my daughter sang it in multiple overdub. It's actually kind of a bebop riff tune. But the rain theme Dark Clouds at the end is pure Zoot Sims, bless him, and the incidental music is Bohn.

So what did the cast think of the finished film? They loved it. They loved seeing themselves. The old man, especially.

Do you consider Klaximo a feminist film? The girl gets off without a guy— I suppose you could say that now, but there wasn't any kind of feminist movement then. That came later on in the sixties. I wanted it to be erotic, but not pornographic.

The film is beautifully lit. That's one of the reasons that the Warhol crowd hated it, I think. Because it looked so professional.

What do you remember about the New York underground film movement at the time? Well, the underground film movement was very small. There was Norman McLaren, Douglas Crockwell out in upstate New York; people like Kenneth Anger. It was very small. And most of the films weren't very good. They had things like *The Geography of the Body*, and it's a camera panning around the body of a nude guy lying on a table. About as uninteresting as you can get, unless you're gay. But I knew that that was the market to show these things. I got the idea for *Klaximo* almost simultaneously with all of that. The Warhol people were following the influence of Anger and all those people. They were all set to move in on the scene. Warhol was a very clever guy. He knew that world and he knew that there was a lot of energy that wanted to get attention. So he was like a general managing the troops.

When did you first become aware of that movement? After I made *Klaximo*. I brought the film to New York and was screening it here, trying to get some attention. Shortly after that, they became 'in'; everyone wanted to make movies. We got some pretty wretched films out of that, didn't we?

You showed the film around New York when it was finished... I showed it to the Museum of Modern Art. They rejected it. I took it to Janus Films, or something like that, a company that released a lot of the early underground films. They rejected it. Nobody had done anything that outrageous at the time. It was a real first. I thought a friend of mine at the New York Theater would do something, but he wouldn't show it. Then I took it to the Cinemateque and had a disaster with [critic Jonas] Mekas. Mekas came here several times when I was working on the film. He would never write about it... I ran into Mekas twenty-five years later and he refused to shake my hand. So, obviously, the film made some kind of serious dent on him. But I really don't know why no one would do anything with it.

You once said that you came to New York to be a part of an atmosphere that was nowhere else to be found... I think all the freedom's gone now. There wouldn't be fifty thousand kids trying to be artists if there wasn't some kind of taste of money. When we started out as artists, we didn't have any taste of money at all. We did it out of love. It was the only way we could live. That's a fundamental difference. The kids today want to be loved. They don't have the pure instinct. Big egos. They graduate from art school with all kinds of degrees, and think they have all the answers. A friend of mine was at the Cape. He said, "There's an underground movement going on right now to bring the painting back." I don't know. Maybe it's just a question of time. But the freedom, the joy, and the love for creation in this city... It's not there now. And I think it will be a long time coming.

Interview conducted by John Szpunar and Melanie Dante' between October, 2000 and February, 2001.

David X Young's Jazz Loft, a two CD box set containing over two hours of previously unreleased jam sessions featuring Bob Brookmeyer, Bill Crowe, Dave McKenna, Hall Overton, and Zoot Sims, as well as a forty-four page illustrated book, is available from Jazz Magnet Records (32 Union Square East, New York, NY 10003). For more information on David X Young's paintings and prints, please contact Eliza Alys Young at *www.davidxyoung.net*

David, thanks for everything —J and M.

The British Sitcom SPIN-OFF FILM 1968-80

by Julian Upton

YOU MIGHT BE FORGIVEN for thinking that the police apprehended the person responsible for making British sitcom spin-off films at the end of the seventies and locked him up for life. And whoever he was, this *maniac*, he got what he deserved.

He'd struck time and time again, throughout the decade, sometimes three or four times a year. And each year, with the odd exception, he left a worse mess than before. By the time *George and Mildred* hit the cinema screens in 1980, he was probably the most wanted man in Britain.

Sid James and terry Scott in *Bless This House* — the movie.

But, of course, you'd be wrong. The sitcom spin-off craze, a peculiarly British trend that lasted, in its first run, from 1968 to 1980, was not the work of one offender. Everyone was on the bandwagon: TV writers from

Galton and Simpson to Vince Powell and Harry Driver; homegrown talent from Spike Milligan to Stratford Johns; production companies from Hammer Films to British Lion. Elstree Studios was saved from bankruptcy by slapdash adaptations of TV sitcoms such as *On the Buses* (1971), *Man About the House* (1974) and *Please, Sir* (1971). And it was thankful. Crippling taxation, under Harold Wilson's Labour government, had driven most of the superstar talent out of the UK by 1975. The occasional Hollywood blockbuster utilised its stages, but no-one wanted to make serious films here any more. Nobody could afford to. Fortunately, for Elstree,

culture — the half-hour sitcom — for material. But in the1970s the sitcom, inexpensive and traditionalist, was proving itself to be the consistent ratings pinnacle of light entertainment programming and, having been deterred from exploiting more dangerous material by the consistently over zealous British film censor, it was clear that your average, enterprising low budget film producer was eyeing this success with some envy. Of course, at the time, Britain's domestic film industry, more than ever, needed this huge, conservative TV audience to stay alive. It made perfect sense, financially. If twelve million people tuned in, week after week, to watch *Bless This*

Reg Varney wasn't in the Super Tax bracket. So the spin-offs kept coming off the production line, and the punters kept going to see them.

Depending on your point of view, it was either a healthy pragmatism or a monumental lack of imagination that drove British film producers, in this newly 'permissive' era, to the country's most conservative television

House on television, then you only needed a fraction of that audience to pay to see the theatrical version to have a huge moneyspinner on your hands. And, initially, it worked. Although they were critically dismissed, these films were considerable crowd pleasers — in fact, the sitcom spin-off was the only domestic cinematic trend to see the decade through.

Between 1968 and 1980, more than thirty

British films were adapted from successful television shows. Not even the *Carry On* series had matched this concentrated prolificacy. From 1972, *Carry On* films had begun to peter out, from two a year to one a year, and in 1977 the *Carry On* backer, Rank, decided to focus on distributing Xerox machines instead of films. Similarly, the defiantly unerotic and peculiarly British exploitation comedies of the time, such as the *Confessions* series, were all but finished by 1977, after a very short burst of suburban success.

It is with the later *Carry On*s, however, that the majority of the sitcom spin-offs of the seventies are most comparable. Childishly smutty, relentlessly single-minded and lavatorially crude, many of them have nonetheless been imbued with an aura of nostalgic affection that cannot be easily explained intellectually. Like endearing but mischievous children, films like *On the Buses* (1971) and *Bless This House* (1972), like their TV sources, now seem refreshingly free from worthiness, irony and political correctness, and do not attempt to work on more than one level. On the other hand, spin-offs such as *The Lovers* (1972) and *Porridge* (1979) stand up more convincingly to modern scrutiny.

TILL DEATH US DO PART

British radio and TV comedy had dabbled with the big screen before the sixties. Vehicles for radio comedians such as Arthur Askey were fashioned in the thirties and forties, and, later, some radio and television shows led to some tenuously connected features. The Goons, for example, appeared in *Down Among the Z Men* (1951) and *Penny Points to Paradise* (1952). *I Only Arsked* (1958) was a truer spin-off (in the sense of this article), in that it focused Bernard Bresslaw's character (Sgt 'Popeye') from the ITV series *The Army Game* (1957–61). But it wasn't until the late sixties that the film industry in Britain really caught the spin-off bug.

The first spin-off of this era was *Till Death Us Do Part* (1968). Focusing on the weekly rantings of Alf Garnett (Warren Mitchell), the TV series of *Till Death Us Do Part* (BBC 1965-75) was rarely out of the controversy spotlight, bearing up to frequent attacks from the 'Clean Up TV' campaign for its aggressiveness and bad language. The film version, then, distributed by British Lion, offered a broader and less censorious forum for the show's writer, Johnny Speight, to indulge Garnett's loudmouth politics and bigotry without being accountable to puritanical harridans in fluffy hats. Speight also used the film as an 'opening out' of the confined sitcom, a noble intention given the slack padding of later spin-offs, and followed Garnett's life from the thirties to the sixties, giving him ample opportunities to rant about major political events as they unfolded. However, much of the astute rawness of the series was lost in the process, and lavatorial humour, literally, crept into the proceedings: Garnett spends a fair portion of the film sitting on the bog, conversing loudly with his neighbour in the adjoining lavvy. Perhaps this was a warning of what was to come.

ON THE BUSES

Till Death was a success at the box office, but it did not set the trend. (It did, however, lead to a sequel — *The Alf Garnett Saga* — in

1972.) What kicked the genre off properly was the release of *On the Buses* (1971). If *Till Death Us Do Part* had been filmed for vaguely 'artistic' reasons, then *On the Buses* was the opposite side of the coin. The series was a tasteless and somewhat juvenile antithesis to the abrasive realism of *Till Death*, and it was equally as popular in the ratings. This fact did not go unnoticed by Hammer films, which was now under the control of Michael Carreras who was keen to turn reverse its ailing horror fortunes. A deal was made, and *On the Buses* was brought to the screen by Hammer in a film that, instead of attempting to broaden and strengthen its TV source, merely inflated and further vulgarized it.

Coarse and anachronistic, the film version of *On the Buses* sees the ageing, brylcreemed, bus driving lothario Stan and his buck-toothed runtball colleague Jack (Bob Grant) scheming to 'put a stop' to a liberal company policy that allows the employment of female bus drivers. Although pretty excruciating to sit through today, the film's cheerful zest was, at the time, quite infectious. And it grossed over £1 million in domestic rentals in its first six months of release — an outrageous sum for a low budget British production at the time. *On the Buses* soon became the most financially successful 1971 release at the British box office, outgrossing even *Diamonds Are Forever*. This may say a lot more about British society than it does about the merits of the picture, but the returns could not be argued with. By 1973, *On the Buses* had generated two theatrical sequels: *Mutiny on the*

Buses* (1972) and *Holiday on the Buses* (1973). Arguments about taste and decency were futile — the sitcom spin-off had arrived.

Over the next nine years, Hammer and other companies such as EMI, Associated London and British Lion dipped continually into the TV pot for ideas. Among their output were sequels to spin-offs (as with *On the Buses*, the film versions of *Steptoe and Son*, *Up Pompeii* and *Till Death Us Do Part* all generated further theatrical episodes) and a handful of films adapted from popular crime or drama series, such as *The Sweeney* (1976), *Callan* (1974), *Man at the Top* (1973) and *Doomwatch* (1972).

DAD'S ARMY

Initially, the films were as lively as most of the other low budget British fodder of the time. *Dad's Army* (1971) retained some of the spark of its original series (BBC 1968–77), and saw its ensemble cast on good form; *The Lovers* (1972) was as good as any contemporary sex comedy; and *Please, Sir* (1971) was one of the earliest spin-offs to focus on a comic situation (a school vacation) that was satisfyingly beyond the scope of a twenty-five minute TV episode.

But the problems of 'opening out' a videotaped, studio-based sitcom were also immediately apparent. The school trip in *Please, Sir* set a precedent for all spin-offs that followed. The premise of sending the characters on holiday, it later seemed, was enough to justify an entire film, regardless of script. Consequently, the staff of Grace Brothers (in *Are You Being Served?* [1977]) and *Steptoe and Son* went to Spain (well, at least to an overlit corner of the Pinewood backlot), and *George and Mildred* (1980) celebrated their anniversary with a romantic weekend away (in Shepperton or somewhere — very handy). Very soon, the 'trip out' was the whole *raison d'etre* of the sitcom spin-off, and it is a device that is still being trundled out for the modern small screen equivalents: Victor Meldrew in the Algarve; Delboy in Miami, etc. In fact, years later, when Hollywood produced a big screen spin-off from *The X Files*, I half-expected the action to find Mulder and Scully on a package tour to Loret de Mar.

An early success, *Dad's Army* also reflected a number of other problems that were to dog the sitcom spin-off genre. To justify the cinematic version of the show, Columbia attempted to broaden its scope, routinely utilizing outdoor locations and bringing in characters only referred to in the series. But this achieved little except to destroy the cosy surrealism of the television format. And, quite bizarrely, some supporting parts were recast — another wacky practice that permeated the spin-off genre. In the film version of *Dad's Army*, reliable Liz Frazer stood in for regular, Janet Davies; in *Bless This House*, laid-back Robin Stewart was replaced by cheeky Robin Askwith. Weirdest of all, in *The Alf Garnett Saga*, Una Stubbs' and Tony Booth's somewhat significant roles were filled by Adrienne Posta and Michael Angelis. Contractual and commercial reasons dictated these recasting decisions, but they can't have sat easily with fans of the shows.

Nevertheless, the trend continued apace. Before long, companies were funding film versions of sitcoms that one might generously describe as pedestrian (*Love Thy Neighbour* [1973]; *Father Dear Father* [1973]), as well as those that have since sank into complete obscurity (*Never Mind the Quality, Feel the Width* [1972]; *That's Your Funeral*

[1972]; *For the Love of Ada* [1973]).

By the mid seventies, spin-offs seemed to be content to coast along on sub-*Carry On* sexual innuendo, unwashed cameos by fading variety stars and perfunctory plot entanglements. *Man About the House* (1974), Hammer's final foray into the genre, sadly wasted an opportunity to flesh out the characters of a decent, fairly daring sitcom (ITV 1973–76) and the aforementioned *Are You Being Served?* was a truly desperate attempt to stretch a mildly amusing half-hour into ninety grueling minutes.

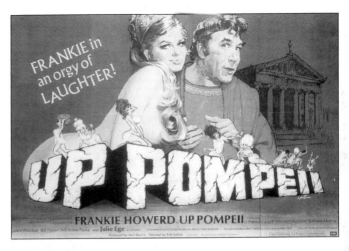

THE LIKELY LADS

Two later films did stand out from their contemporaries, though. *The Likely Lads* (1976) and *Porridge* (1979), both written by Dick Clement and Ian La Frenais, attempted to avoid the obvious pitfalls of the sitcom spin-off by actually developing and furthering the original material. Of the two, *The Likely Lads* is the more flawed film, centering as it does around a rather inane caravan episode, not unlike the lethargic escapades of a later *Carry On* or the obligatory trips of other spin-offs. But *The Likely Lads* kept the essence of the original series (BBC 1964–66 and 1973–74), which followed Bob (Rodney Bewes) and Terry (James Bolam) as they grew from adolescence to maturity, from cheerful optimism to resignation and disillusionment. Focusing on sexual escapades, boozing, factory work and the draw of marriage and class conformity, the series had been the sitcom counterpoint to the groundbreaking British movie *Saturday Night and Sunday Morning* (1960). The film, to its credit, drew on and expanded the tragicomic sense of loss and change that dominated the series' later episodes. The boy's favourite drinking haunt, The Fat Ox, is finally demolished; Terry is pushed to more desperate forms of employment in a recession-hit Britain; and Bob and Thelma's marriage sinks further into lower middle class apathy. The latter is conveyed in one of the funniest moments in any sitcom spin-off. Bob, waiting gloomily for Thelma to choose clothes in a fashionable boutique, is diverted by casually watching nubile young women undress in the changing booths. Pushed by Thelma for a reaction to her choice of dress, Bob stares wearily ahead and sighs: "I couldn't give a *shit.*"

PORRIDGE

Porridge is a better movie, perhaps because La Frenais and Clement themselves took over the producer and director roles respectively. It even gained a US release, under the title *Doing Time.* The great strength of the original series (BBC 1974–77) was the abundance of well-drawn characters, many of whom could be featured in the more leisurely pace of a feature film. This, fortunately, eliminated the need for the sudden appearance of a busybody neighbour, predatory property developer or unhinged doppelgänger to add comic conflict. In *Porridge*, the two hero convicts, Fletcher (Ronnie Barker) and Godber (Richard Beckinsale), unwittingly find themselves part of an elaborate escape plan, and have to break back into prison in order to serve the remainder of their time quietly. On film, the prison setting looks far more harsh and brutal than the cozier, studio-set TV series, but the warmth of the characterizations still comes through and the film evinces a sense of realism lacking from other sitcom spin-offs.

Despite this, the following year saw the abrupt end of sitcom spin-off. The two final

films of this era were *Rising Damp* (1980) and *George and Mildred. Rising Damp* took the safe option and simply reworked scenes that had already established the series (ITV 1974–78) as a classic, weaving them loosely into a feature narrative. Because of this, a lot of it works. But Richard Beckinsale was conspicuous by his absence from the film. He had opted out of the final series a couple of years earlier, but his death in 1979 (at age thirty-one) was a blow to British comedy and, somehow, any attempt to revive *Rising Damp* without him seemed in poor taste. Even so, the film is watchable, which cannot be said for *George and Mildred.* That anybody thought *George and Mildred* was fit for theatrical release is almost beyond reason. It is undoubtedly one of the worst films ever made in Britain. It might be the worst film ever made *anywhere.* It makes *The Ups and Downs of a Handyman* look like *Scenes from a Marriage.* The source series (ITV 1976–79) — tired marriage, lazy good-for-nothing husband, frustrated wife — was itself no milestone of TV comedy, but the film version is so strikingly bad, it seems to have been assembled with a genuine contempt for its audience. It is the archetypal example of why a sitcom should never be made into a film. Technically, it is woefully inept — it appears to have been photographed through a damp pair of Mildred's tights. To add insult to injury, *George and Mildred* was released just after the death of one of its stars, Yootha Joyce.

The double tragedy of the early deaths of Beckinsale and Joyce not only added an unintentional tone of melancholia to the films, but also seemed portentous of the fate of the genre itself. However, by this time the spin-off had played itself out and was not generating the kind of pocket-money profit the early seventies had seen. By 1980, Hammer and British Lion were all but defunct as filmmaking operations; EMI was limping along with some ill-advised US co-productions. Even Lord Grade's ITC, which was responsible for *Porridge, Rising Damp* and *George and Mildred,* was about to go down with the catastrophic *Raise the Titanic* (1981).

Further, the home video boom was closing cinemas up and down the country. 1981 saw UK feature film production at an all-time low of twenty-four films, compared to ninety-six in 1971. Similarly, admissions had dropped by roughly half in the same period.

So the critics took a relaxing breath. The future — with Channel 4 on the horizon — looked to be sparse but worthy, intense and artistic. There wasn't much danger of Channel 4 funding a big screen version of *That's My Boy* alongside Peter Greenaway's *The Draughtsman's Contract*. So the puerile sitcom spin-off, for years the scourge of sensible, middlebrow opinion, was dead. But few critics cared or even noticed that the spin-off's demise also signalled the final nail in the coffin of British popular cinema — lowbrow, cheerful and broad in appeal.

All was not lost, of course. The sitcom spin-offs of the seventies went on to prove that they had an enduring appeal almost as strong as the *Carry On*s. How many months go by without the film versions of *Up Pompeii* or *Bless This House* or *Rising Damp* being

aired? Not many. Sure, they are relegated to day time or post-midnight viewing more often than not, but then again so is a lot of stuff that is half decent. That the spin-off has reigned on television for so long is proof positive that its demise left a gaping hole in the lowbrow entertainment market. It took almost twenty years before the British film industry had the guts to greenlight shameless crap like *Guest House Paradiso* and *Kevin and Perry Go Large*. Whether this will signal a true spin-off revival is open to question, although it's unlikely. *Bean* made about thirty billion dollars worldwide, but that was six years ago and subsequent British TV comedy spin-offs can still be counted on one hand. They weren't the same, anyway.

Never mind — we can at least be confident, that, come Christmas, we can put our feet up after the pub and catch the umpteenth broadcast of *Steptoe and Son Ride Again* on BBC1. The days of traipsing to the local Odeon to catch oversized, overstretched travesties of our favourite sitcoms may be long gone, but, back on TV, where they really belong, they will probably live forever.

ANDREW SAVULICH DAILY NEWS

Show's over for last smut shop on 42nd

By MAKI BECKER
DAILY NEWS STAFF WRITER

The door has shut on the smut.

Peep-o-rama, the last sex shop on 42nd St., is closing today — putting an unceremonious end to the era of Triple X entertainment on the famed strip.

The 24-hour store that for years entertained the lonely and lascivious with its $1 video booths has been evicted — not for breaking decency laws but to make way for a soaring new office tower.

Yesterday, a steady stream of men walked to the entrance of Peep-o-rama, marked with the word VIDEO in hot pink and a sign that read "Welcome to Times Square."

Each would stop abruptly upon seeing the store's walls almost bare, then sullenly walking away.

"I just wanted to use the bathroom," insisted one man before rushing away.

While there's no more smut on the Disneyfied 42nd St., there's still porn purveyors on the edges of Times Square, most along Eighth Ave.

The Durst Organization has been buying up property along W. 42nd St. between Sixth Ave. and Broadway to construct a 1.7-million-square-foot building to be dubbed 1 Bryant Park, said the developer's lawyer, Gary Rosenberg.

"We're leaving other tenants in the site," he said.

The owners of Peep-o-rama "would have been very happy to pay us," to continue its business, Rosenberg added. "We said, 'No, thank you.'"

The owners are set to hand over the keys by 3 p.m. today.

By yesterday afternoon, Peep-o-rama employees had packed up what they estimated were about 10,000 videocassettes — many of them pornographic — into cardboard boxes.

"We all lose our job," shrugged one worker, who did not volunteer his name.

The wire shelves throughout the store were bare, save for a wall of sex toys and a display case of single-sale condoms.

"I have very good customers," said a man who said he was one of the owners of Peep-o-rama.

"Decent customers!" said the man, who wouldn't give his name. "People need sex. Everybody. Everybody! You. Me. Everybody!"

Alas, **PEEP-O-RAMA**, the last porn palace on 42nd Street, has closed its doors to make way for more office space. It is a symbolically sad day for those who remember the wild and woolly street circus freakshow days of 42nd Street and its surrounding Avenues in the seventies and beyond. I can't say for certain if I ever visited Peep-O-Rama specifically, although I'm pretty sure I must have. There was a PEEPLAND also, in the days before video took over the magazine racks and bins in the porn pits of Manhattan.

PEEP-*O*-RAMA REMEMBERED, SORT OF

by Tom Brinkmann

The sleaze carnival has left town and in its wake are a handful of adult video/ DVD stores, all with video booths in the back run by a new crop of merchants who speak with the same heavy foreign accents — commonly heard at local 7-11s — with the loud drone of some skin-vid vixen coming in the background to a porn soundtrack.

The skin-shows and adult book stores on 42nd Street and environs used to be more interactive. They used to offer a look into the semen flecked funhouse mirror of lust crazed, drunken patrons and jaded sleaze merchants with dollar signs in their eyes; married business men, sailors, perverts, creeps, drunken college kids, roaming bachelor parties, bums and tourists, swirling around in a neon disco muzak candy-coloured haze of lust and porn. Hookers squeezing your crotch out of the blue... live sex shows on a ratty stage mattress... blow job and hand job mavens working the aisles while huge genitalia go at it on screen... two-bit prostitutes spitting fresh jiz into the gutter after a quick doorway blow job... topless street walkers flagging cars on 8th and 9th Avenues... naked women in plexi-glass booths... live peep shows... drunken patrons sticking their "fuck fingers" under your nose proclaiming in a triumphant voice, *"I stuck my finger in her pussy up to here for a dollar, wanna smell?"* These are my Polaroid-like memories of the seventies on 42nd Street.

My biggest complaint is the loss of some truly strange magazine bins where all manner of pulp could be found — unimaginable stuff if not for the shops around Times Square. The walls as well were covered in multitudes of titles catering to the most diverse of sexual tastes. "Bizarre raunch" would be the operative words to describe this material to the unaccustomed. Nowadays the slick, expensive, fetish-fashion Euro-zines can be found at the corner newsstand. And the selection of magazines you find at most all of the adult video stores these days, with few exceptions, are shrink-wrapped packs containing a handful of anaemic and interchangeable back issue newsstand porn mags, that aren't worth their weight in the sperm spilled over in the booths out back.

Lap Dancing in Greece pt 2

by Jane Graham

Greece, March 1999
To recap: I've been in Greece for two nights now, and have arrived at the nightclub I've been booked to work at as striptease dancer, immediately completing my first shift. When work ends at seven in the morning, myself and another girl, Tina — who's Serbian — find ourselves sleeping in the bar manager's kitchen because there is "some problem" with the apartment provided for us...

Costas' kitchen becomes our home for the next three nights. Sharing the bed with Tina. Sitting at the tiny kitchen table eating pizza and putting on our make-up. Boiling water in a pan and drinking all the coffee in the house, waiting for the water to heat up for the shower, flicking the switch up every five minutes when it's turned itself off... There is some problem, Tina said before, and I'm thinking: too right there is, too fuckin' right...

Costas, the bar manager whose place this is, has a twenty-something son living with him who seems to spend the days smoking joints, snorting lines and watching cable TV with his friends, while we attempt to sleep after our night shift — in the kitchen, amidst apologetic tiptoes in for coffee, snacks and bottles of mineral water.

I haven't been out at all, except for work, because I have no idea where I am. The son doesn't speak to me; I don't think he can speak English. His friend Dimitri invited me yesterday into the smoky front room where I sat in front of the TV watching movies for hours, with the occasional stab at conversation, usually to ask if I was alright. Perhaps he thinks Tina and myself odd because we seem so fed up — which indeed I am; completely fed up of the situation. Yesterday he also invited me to share a joint on the balcony. I thought he was okay. Today I'm sure he's laughing at Tina and me both, eating our food and taking the piss.

Tina and I have become close in this weekend — what with sleeping together and my being reliant on her. She's quiet, trust-worthy, sensible. Works hard at her job. Drinks cans of beer, but not too much. Yiannis, our agent, was right; she has a good character.

Tina tells me she misses her dog. It is with her family in Belgrade. She misses going kayak boating in the river. She won prizes for it when she was younger.

She is looking into a small mirror, applying her make-up.

"You think I look like gypsy woman?" she asks me.

"Not really," I shrug. "Why?"

"Somebody say last night I am gypsy woman. Because my hairs is so black."

"Is it natural?" I ask her. She shakes her head.

One day I carry Tina's bag in the room from the lift because her hands are full with all her other bags. It's a leather one holding all her personal stuff, like a hand bag and I put it on the floor next to mine because there's not much room in the kitchen. Tina tells me that this is wrong. She's told me before that it's "not like woman" to put her bag on the floor. She scolds, placing it instead on the bed. I apologize, feeling somehow unfeminine for my gaff, without understanding her point. It's the first time she's really raised her voice at me.

After three nights we are finally installed in an apartment; at last I can unpack! Not that I ever really knew why we couldn't go there in the first place, except that one of the girls left and locked the room and took her key with her. I think I would still be there now, in Costas' kitchen, if we hadn't kicked up a fuss.

That night, Thanos, another of the bar staff, summons me to do a lap dance for a fat greasy man who unzips his pants and tries to push my head down with his firm fat hand towards his crotch, and all I do is smile, giving him a firm no in Greek, carrying on with the dance. I find out up in the changing room while I'm wiping myself down that he's a cop, an off duty one wanting some fun but I'm

livid — when is a cop ever really off duty? What would I have got for the suggested blow job? Why the fuck did fat Thanos tell this other girl and not me? Did he think it was funny?

Is it any wonder I'm becoming paranoid, when no-one tells me anything and nobody speaks my language and I can't go to the cops for help? When somebody finally does tell me something, it's something cryptic, like when the men say, "This is Greece, be careful, please." And I ask them to explain what they mean and all I get is, "I've said too much.

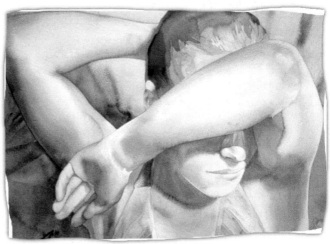

But please be careful," just repeating themselves. What the hell do they mean?

It's crazy the way the guys talk to each other, you'd think they were having blazing rows, the way they throw their arms around and shout and curse, every second word "malaka". Of course, soon they're slapping each other on the back and they're best friends again but it doesn't mean I dare throw that word into conversation, malaka, because I know it's different for a woman to say it to a man. I had a friend tell me she got chased round a car park with a knife by a man from a kiosk for calling him that. So I hold my tongue.

Whenever I say something in complaint to another girl they simply answer, "this is Greece." You had to sleep in a kitchen for three days and share a bed with another girl? This is Greece. The cops are corrupt pigs who want you to suck them off? This is Greece! I guess the girls learn to accept it because it is relaxed and the sun shines and it is such a beautiful country; because the drink is cheap and everything else is not too expensive either; because you can get cabs to the city and live like a king with your wages paid in cash every night; because the boss probably doesn't care how much coke you take, in fact he buys it for you. Am I that cynical?

I still cannot accept that this is Greece and that's it, and I'm meant to simply accept it — especially out of the mouth of a man flicking his goddamn beads or car keys around. Sometimes I have an overwhelming urge to ram their beads down their throats.

But then you have a morning like this one when I look out the club after the shift has

like what I'm used to. Somewhere to the North is Bulgaria, although all the roads stop before they reach the border. What industry there is, apparently, is in quarrying and tobacco factories. Very few tourists ever find their way here. In September, so I'm told, they hold a film festival — though how big this is or what films they show I have no idea.

I still have a Polaroid stuffed into the back of my vanity case of Katja, a friendly Russian dancer, and myself posing with two young customers. A man comes round and sells Polaroids along with armfuls of cuddly toys. He sells them to us at a discount or we get customers to buy them for us. I'm the only girl who hasn't got a room full of cuddly animals and a load of snapshots stuck to the wall by her bed.

finished while I wait for my wages and I feel a little of that Greek magic. But knowing it has that power to charm me so easily only makes me more exasperated.

"There's so many stray dogs around here," I say as we get out of the cab by the front door of the apartment building and there's a pack of skulking curs hovering around the street, not to mention the odd feral looking cat.

"There's a lot of stray dead dogs, too," retorts one of the girls, and I shudder.

I am nowhere near civilization or anything

Katja — who still smiles at me in concern and asks if I am okay — has jumped up onto one of the poles, pulling herself up higher and higher, the muscles on her slender arms straining, the leather of her boots helping to protect at least her calves. She climbs to the top, which must be at least three times her height. Her legs wrapped around the pole tightly, holding herself with only her thigh muscles, she brings her head and then her body back and downwards, her blonde hair cascading towards the ground but still high above the stage, her short dress falling from her legs and her body and slipping off over her head and slowly fluttering to the floor. Then she raises one arm, unfastens her bra and allows that also to slip from her small, bud-like breasts and follow her dress downwards. Upside down, dressed only in a g-string, Katja gradually glides down the pole, her tiny body becoming slightly larger as she nears the ground, her legs easing off the tension and opening in a wide arc above her to come together again in a backwards summersault, pulling off her panties over her knees (which are over her head) and flinging them to the side, a quick flash of pussy as she ends in the splits.

But here on the ground I've got problems of my own. The man who's just bought me a drink is sure it's nothing more than tap water in a pretty glass. I'm shocked at such an idea. I mean, *really*!

"It's not," I smile.

"What is it, then?" he asks.

"It's a special drink," I say. "I can't tell you exactly what. It's a secret. It's called a lady drink."

He tries to grab it, but I get to it a second before him.

"Why won't you let me try it, if it's not water?" he asks.

"Because," I'm thinking on the spot here, "it's only for ladies and if you tried it it wouldn't be so special. The ingredients make it look just like water and they're a very guarded secret."

He goes for it again and this time he manages to take it from me. He drinks a little, just a sip, spitting it out and shouting, "Nero! It is water!"

"No," I repeat, "It's a special drink. See, it even tastes like water. It's so clever. To make alcohol not just look like water, but taste like it too."

"I can't believe I spend too much money on water," he storms, angry now.

"Please, believe me, it's not," I say, like a wife caught red handed in an affair, discovered yet unable to stop denying it.

He dismisses it with his hand and moves his body closer to me. I guess he doesn't re-ally care if it's water. You pay for the company, not the drink.

They have this tradition here, at the weekend. First the DJ will announce: "All the girls on the stage. House party." And we all go up there, dancing around together, to Horny Horny Horny or some other stupid song. Then the DJ plays some traditional Greek music and one of the girls, usually Katja, will pull a guy up from the tables below and sit him on the round revolving circle of carpet. She'll begin to undress him, and others will join in, until he's just wearing his shoes and socks, then we all join hands and perform a traditional Greek dance around the naked male body. Like I say, it seems to be something of a custom here. But only on weekends.

I'm learning the language very, very slowly. No-one cares about English. Nobody wants to speak English. I must learn Greek, so I'm told. Sometimes I speak basic German with the men who have worked in Stuttgart or East Germany as bricklayers or in other kinds of construction work. I'm learning not only the language, but also just to smile and hold their hands and feed them peanuts when it gets silent and awkward. Learning not to think too much about them. Learning to ignore the feel of erections as I straddle their thighs, learning to hold their hands when they get a bit too boisterous, remembering to be smiling, always smiling.

Well into my last week, one of the girls is talking about work papers and I remember I never went to get my paper from the hospital. What with everything else it kind of slipped my mind. The boss has never mentioned it. I'm kind of curious about it, but more than that I'm scared. One thing's for sure; I can't manage to go there on my own. Yesterday I went to the bank and the post office and I couldn't even have managed that without the help of another girl — what chance have I in the hospital? I've only four days left of my contract, I'll just have to risk it. I discovered anyway that there's a light behind the DJ booth in the club, which flashes when the police come in as a reminder not to take your g-string off on the stage. Apparently we're not meant to be fully nude here — even though we are, four or five times a night. At least one of the girls has no papers at all so I'll do a runner with her if it comes to that.

The bank was a total farce. We went from one queue to another, and every time we reached the front they would give us a form which we would have to take to another person. The lines didn't appear to be moving; at the top sat an elderly couple who looked to be in a dispute and not going anywhere for a while. It was eight in the morning, and I'd been up all night — it was the the only time I'd catch them open. Already it had started to get hot. Behind the glass sat the bankers with their manual typewriters and great safes watched by a man with a big gun. Was this really the same Europe where everything is computerized? It seemed like nothing more than an enjoyment of bureaucracy for its own sake, as a tool to laud over people, an instrument of power in a poor country.

I'm so used to my smug British passport being able to take me anywhere in the world, allow me to work all over without problem. I'm not Russian or Polish or Romanian. No marrying nasty men for me. No hiding in cloakrooms or scurrying out of back doors into the shadowy night. I've got papers. Perhaps my smug British passport isn't enough here, for once. I must treasure my commonsense and my return plane ticket, it might be all I've got.

I've become sick, just like everyone else — the changing room's throbbing with the sounds of coughing and sniffling. It's hardly surprising, the seasons are changing and it's warm one week and the next winter has returned and it rains solidly for three days. No-one takes a day off, though — the boss won't let the Eastern girls take one, it's cheaper for him to make the rest of us have a free day, we cost him more. We have to take one a week, but nobody can afford any more. So we all suffer our way through the busy weekend, infecting half the town. Now the weather has become hot and sunny again, but it's time for me to leave.

No-one knows I'm leaving tomorrow, except for Tina and my agent, Yiannis, who played some little white lie on the boss so he'd take me for just two weeks. There was no way I'd want to spend much longer than that here. Yiannis made me promise to keep quiet, but now I'm wishing it wasn't all so deceptive — I feel like I'm running away.

It's not a night for saying goodbye; something has happened today. Something serious. The changing room is always split into two sides, the Russian side on the left and everyone else in the other corner on the right. The language on the left side is Russian and on the right side it's mainly Greek; the common language between the two sides is Greek. Tonight, everyone is talking loudly in both languages, and all I can make out is NATO, America, Clinton and Yugoslavia. It's rare that everyone should be talking about the same thing in here, so I know it must be serious.

Downstairs, by the bar, I ask Tina if everything is okay. Pretty dumb question, I guess. She answers with "No", giving me a laugh which looks like it might turn into a sob at any moment. She adds: "But there's nothing I can do about it now." Then she goes to dance. She works solid virtually all night and I don't see her again until around five.

I try all night long to say goodbye to everyone, wondering how I'm to explain my leaving so quickly, so suddenly, but it never seems like the right time. And while I'm still finding the right time it turns six o'clock. Soon we'll go home, and I'm sad because I'm leaving without telling anyone, and nobody understands why I'm acting so weird. Everybody is so preoccupied they don't seem to notice I'm clearing all my clothes and shoes out of the changing room.

The only person I manage to say goodbye to is Katja — sweet, tiny Katja who again asks if I'm okay. She says, "You know what is happened today?" I answer, "Kind of, but I don't understand!"

I'm feeling like I'm running away, and I'm due to fly over an area where a war has just broken out. In the apartment, in our room, I throw my things into my bag while Tina makes urgent calls to her family in Belgrade on the mobile a customer bought for her last week. America has bombed Belgrade, she tells me. Her family say they are fine, and she should stay in Greece and not worry, but she cannot believe that they are simply fine.

I ask her if she will stay. She doesn't know, because she thinks she will have to move to another club where there is less police presence and the authorities are not so strict. Tina has no passport. The last time they deported her they told her not to come back and took her passport away to make sure she couldn't, but she sneaked through somehow anyway. Perhaps, if she goes back to Serbia, she will not be able to return to Greece. And Greece is better. But of course she wants to be near her family…

Tina sleeps lightly, her mobile phone next to her pillow, which rings a couple of times through the morning. I can't sleep either, and sit in the kitchen, looking out of the window at the mountains in the distance. My bags are packed. I wait for the water to heat up so I can take a shower, but I end up as always showering with water which runs cold after a few minutes. For some reason I'm thinking about Tina's dog.

The sun is shining now as I leave, when just about all I've had through my stay is rain. What's more, it's a national holiday — Greek independence day, celebrating the day Greece finally freed itself of Turkish rule. I leave the apartment and call a cab from a kiosk across the road. People are out on the streets, drinking outside the cafés. No-one is hurrying anywhere. The cab arrives and we spend ten minutes traversing the short journey to the bus station, held up by a marching troupe of soldiers in full regalia. I watch a group of girls lolling by the side of the road, dressed in short navy skirts and tight blouses, their eyes thickly made-up and their hair styled up big. We crawl another hundred yards. I can see the bus station now. Boy, it's hot.

Outside the bus station, I check with an ancient looking man if this is the right stop for Thessaloniki.

He asks me if I am from Yugoslavia.

l'abécédaire chimerique
by Progeas Didier

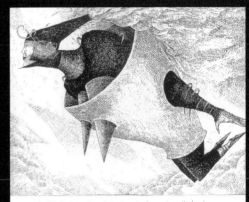

PERITOLENE : distante et introvertie, elle brule ses pensees les offronts à qui en manque

QUEZABROGLIO : adepte de l'asymetrie, on le sait casse.tête et bien souvent inabordable

RONDALAMINE : muse protectrice, elle soulage les maux climatiques et les depressions passagères

to be continued…

from Destruction to Creation

CHUCK PALAHNIUK discusses FIGHT CLUB, his latest novel CHOKE, the crumbling American Dream, and a whole bunch of other stuff.

Interview by CHRIS SWITZER

" LOOK AGAIN "

says Chuck

He's describing what he calls the "look again" game — his approach to greater detail in writing, his method for bringing more clarity to his descriptions of what we all see every day but never realize until it's pointed out to us. We are blind until Chuck shows us the light.

I'm looking at Chuck Palahniuk, the man who wrote the now legendary *Fight Club*, one of the most thought-provoking novels of the last ten years. He's been hailed as a visionary, a rebel, and the next Don DeLillo. Chuck sits across from me in a small eatery in Edinboro, PA. What I see is a gentle man, soft-spoken and exceedingly polite. He quietly orders coffee, eggs benedict, and a muffin. He offers to pay for breakfast, but I insist on paying the bill. He answers all of my questions with sincerity.

Look again.

Now, in sharp focus, I can see Tyler Durden sitting across from me, along with Tender Branson, Victor Mancini, and, yes, even Shannon McFarland. I can see the man who once got into a fistfight during a weekend camping trip and returned to work on Monday only to have his coworkers avert their eyes and conspicuously avoid asking the obvious: "What happened to you?" I can see the man who broke into the apartment of a friend dying of AIDS to remove all evidence of sexual paraphernalia, so his friend's mother wouldn't find it. I can see the man who once injected grease into a donut and watched patiently to see which one of his coworkers would take the first bite.

"That's the mantra when I'm writing. Look again. What am I not seeing? What is the telling detail about this situation that I'm not getting?" Chuck leans forward while explaining. "I was sitting on the plane playing the look again game, and when you're on a plane you're all facing the same way, so you can really study everyone's hair. The woman in front of me had really lovely blond hair. I was looking at her hair thinking, 'How would

I tongue the barrel into my cheek and say, Tyler, you're thinking of mpires.

The building we're standing on won't be here in ten minutes. You ke a 98-percent concentration of fuming nitric acid and add the acid three times that amount of sulfuric acid. Do this in an ice bath. Then d glycerin drop-by-drop with an eye dropper. You have nitroglyc- in.

I know this because Tyler knows this.

Mix the nitro with sawdust, and you have a nice plastic explosive. lot of folks mix their nitro with cotton and add Epsom salts as a lfate. This works too. Some folks, they use paraffin mixed with tro. Paraffin has never, ever worked for me.

So Tyler and I are on top of the Parker-Morris Building with the n stuck in my mouth, and we hear glass breaking. Look over the ge. It's a cloudy day, even this high up. This is the world's tallest ilding, and this high up the wind is always cold. It's so quiet this gh up, the feeling you get is that you're one of those space monkeys. ou do the little job you're trained to do.

Pull a lever.

Push a button.

You don'

The first page of Fight Club

I describe this hair? In a non-judgmental way, physically, how can I evoke the experience of this hair?' I see how every hair is a different color, and it's almost crystalline-looking, as if the hair shaft itself is a geometric shape, with angles in it, and it's refracting the light. The longer strands go one way, but the shorter strands splay across the surface of the hair, and the longer strands separate to create cleavings in the hair, and caves, and hollow dark spaces inside. I'm thinking, 'This looks just like cedar or pine when you split it.'" Chuck smiles, indicating that the punch line is looming. "I'm doing all of this, and I realize that the woman right across the aisle is her mother." He starts to laugh. "She's looking at me in a hostile way, like, 'Why are you staring at my daughter's hair so in- tensely?' The daughter has no idea, and I almost have my nose in her hair while I'm taking notes, playing this game. People are constantly catching me staring at them really hard, when in fact I'm just trying to document something about them that I want to use in a book. And then they're thinking, *Stalker!*"

It's Sunday, the day after the Chuck Palahniuk "Postcards from the Future" Conference, held at the Edinboro University in Pennsylvania. This is the first conference of his work, and Chuck is at ease, yet full of the vigor one might get from the energy of hundreds of fans. I heard about the conference several months ago, but when I saw that it was in Pennsylvania, I dismissed it as being too far from Michigan to attend. While arranging for this interview less than a week ago, Chuck asked if I was anywhere near here. Checking a map, I was surprised to discover that the drive was a mere five hours.

The next day I made the drive out to Edinboro with my girlfriend. We made good time and we checked into the lodging of choice for the conference, the Ramada Inn, Friday night. The hallways were impossibly long and bore a disturbing resemblance to the Overlook Hotel in *The Shining*. I expected Danny Torrence to come barreling toward us in his Big Wheel any minute. The room was a little on the unclean side, but tolerable. If we had known the maid would skip cleaning our room the next day we might have sought out another place to stay — if there *was* anyplace else to stay. Edinboro certainly was one small town.

The next day, the conference was in full swing, but unfortunately, by that point, it was too late to register and they weren't accepting walk-in registration. So we killed some time doing some rather mundane activities (shopping being one of them) and then cruised back into town so I could go over my interview questions. Later that evening some people from the conference trickled back into the hotel. I ran into a young college girl sitting on a couch in the hallway, reading *Invisible Monsters*. She talked about the conference and what a great guy Chuck was. She claimed that Chuck was staying in Room 100 (which

was about fifteen feet from where she was sitting). I didn't have the heart to tell her that he was actually staying in Room 272CS (the "Captain's Suite"). Later that night, when I stepped out to get more ice, the same girl was sitting in the hallway with several more Palahniuk groupies, waiting for that fateful moment when Chuck would return to his room. They were certainly going to have a long wait.

The conference schedule did indeed look like it was impressive: ten lectures on Chuck's works and their relation to society; five roundtable discussions; thirteen panel discussions; creative works, ranging from poetry to performances to art, influenced by Chuck's works; a viewing of the *Fight Club* DVD with Q&A by Chuck afterwards; a reading of *Choke* by Chuck; a keynote luncheon and after dinner party. Not something a serious Palahniuk fan would want to pass up.

The conference coincided with the release of Chuck's new book, *Choke*. Perhaps not surprisingly, it's already been optioned for a movie. It's the first novel he's launched since his fame surrounding *Fight Club*. It's about a sexaholic, Victor Mancini, who pays for his mother's hospital bills by pretending to choke in restaurants. The twist: the rescuers occasionally send Victor money, not the other way around.

Now, with Chuck sitting before me, he explains. "It's all about creating an outlandish premise, and then trying to create a false reality around it that holds it up. How about a club where people go and intentionally punch each other out? Then build a whole argument within the context that supports that." Far-fetched as it sounds, it works. Little by little, the narrator spouts his ideology to the reader throughout *Choke* so that it all makes sense. In the world according to Chuck, Victor does the rescuer a favor by giving him the chance to shine as a hero.

The act is noticeably altruistic for a Palahniuk protagonist. Indeed, *Choke* marks a distinct change in Chuck's work as being his most uplifting novel yet. When asked what caused the change in tone, Chuck talks about meeting Trent Reznor last spring.

"Nothing Records called me in Portland and said, 'Trent Reznor is coming through town and he'd really like to meet you on tour. Would you like tickets and backstage passes?' Yeah! So all of my friends went and we went backstage, and I sat through the concert. I really wanted to hear the song from *The Fragile*, his new album, 'We're in this together,' but he didn't play it. It's such a departure from all of his really dark music. It's his first baby step toward something positive, toward

you've got to pull your guts up and actually create something in the culture and stand for something. And I saw Trent doing that with that song. That's what I wanted to do with *Choke*, was risk losing all of my readers who liked the nihilist stuff, because you've got to move on at some point and actually stand for something. Even if it's putting one rock on top of another rock, it still has to end on something positive like that, something constructive, rather than continually destructive."

Chuck Palahniuk

creating something instead of tearing things down. I really missed it. When I went backstage, I said, 'Why the hell didn't you play it?' Trent said, 'Man, you know, I've worked on that song more than all of my other songs put together, and it still doesn't sound right. I'm still not comfortable with it.' I can't help but wonder if it's just the fact that it does take that leap of faith, that Kirkegaardian step away from standing for nothing, to actually standing *for* something. It's really easy, you can spend your life criticizing and tearing down the culture, but at some point,

Sounds strange, coming from the man whose characters usually end up disfigured at the end of each novel. Chuck elaborates a bit on this change in tone with Victor Mancini's mother, Ida, who during her younger days had committed herself to a life of random mischief; think of a kinder, gentler version of the Project Mayhem Space Monkeys from *Fight Club*.

"I wanted to have a Tyler Durden character that tears things down — and that's Ida Mancini — who realizes that her entire life of rebellion and anarchy has been fun, but boy, she never did take that next step of actually standing for something. So I wanted to make Victor the generation that would move beyond attacking constantly to creating something."

But does it make a difference if the thing being created has a concrete function or purpose? Not at all, says Chuck. "I really like causes that are not about doing something to fulfill a need. Nobody said if we get to the moon it's going to do anything. Getting to the moon was a romantic gesture. It was

about all the things that we discovered along the way, while trying to get to the moon, all the things we had to invent, in order to do this useless thing. It's not like we were going to bring back gold. It was not doing something in order to obtain something. It was doing something just for the doing of it, and it generated so much union, and so much

mutual cause, and so much identity, and so much pride, and so many beneficial things along the way. Now it seems like we've lost that ability to just do these seemingly pointless romantic gestures that are not about achieving something; they're about the process itself, and what the process brings us. I know people who will write a book. The book may never be published, but it's all of the joy that they've had, all of the things they've learned about themselves and the world, all of the ways they've had to be vulnerable, and meet people and know other writers; everything along the way has changed their lives. It's almost superfluous about whether or not the book gets published, it's about what this task is going to teach us. I love that part of writing. Once there's a cover on it, it's really dead for me."

It seems that the transition from destruction to creation plays a larger role in Pahlaniuk's novels than previously assumed. Perhaps that's why the most significant issue tackled in *Choke* is religion. From Tender Branson (The Book of Very Common Prayer) to Shannon McFarland ("Sorry, God"), all of Chuck's novels address religion in some fashion, but the allusions in his previous novels pale in comparison to the ones in *Choke*. Chuck talks a little bit about role of religion on the main character in *Choke*, Victor Mancini.

"Victor was just supposed to be an everyman who handled his problems in unique ways," he says. "Still, he's caught in the paradox of Christianity. It tells us we're the wonderful children of God, created in His image. But it also tells us we're tainted by original sin and must be cleansed regularly or re-born. Okay, religion people, which is it? Are we good or evil? Or maybe we should just decide for ourselves. Also, I wonder a lot about the set up at Calvary. If Paul or anyone had run forward to save Christ, maybe shoved some Roman aside and rescued Jesus, or if Paul had been killed trying, would God have been pissed? Did God set it up so no one would botch the scene? If so, God seems a little manipulative. All in all, it seems as if everyone was so passive at the Crucifixion. Getting back to Victor, in a way he's a Christ figure, but an *active* one. He seeks people out, and puts his life on the line (seemingly) to prove to them that they are brave, smart, strong, etc. Even after they find out he faked choking, that doesn't totally negate their heroism in the face of emergency."

It's obvious that religion has had a major influence on Chuck's writing. I ask him if he thinks religion is a benefit or a detriment to society.

"I think it's a benefit in that serves a real social purpose and it brings people together in spiritual inquiry," he says. "That, in and of itself, is incredible, just to bring people together in the face of mystery. It's something I really have against what was done in the Vatican II, with the Catholic Church. By taking the mystery and the pageantry out of Catholic mass, by putting it in English, by making it accessible, we create the impression that we can actually understand and comprehend God. Which is not the point — the point of faith is that it is incomprehensible, and it is an act of faith. It's not something you're supposed to be able to understand, and therefore believe in. It's something that you can never understand, and yet believe in. By making God understandable, and putting God in our terms, and making God our best friend, you no longer require faith if you know God. In that way, bringing people together in inquiry about this completely incomprehensible thing — that's the glory of religion. In a way, the conference this weekend had that same energy of bringing people together — not so much about my books, but about ideas, and about a lot of ideas presented, and having people in inquiry and discussion about the concepts of reinventing mythology and the concepts about violence, or materialism. Just having people together, talking about these ideas, excited, talking about these ideas. This is not something that happens in the world a lot. So that's what religion does best."

One thing is certain: the influence of religion on his work is distinctly Christian. I ask

Chuck how he feels about Christianity in particular, if he feels that Christianity gets an unfair top billing out of all the religions, and everything else just kind of plays second fiddle. He stops to think.

"Well, I don't know. I haven't thought about these things, so I don't want to talk about them just right off the top of my head." He drinks his coffee, ponders this question some more. "I think Christianity has some real inherent faults in some of the metaphors that it uses, and those are the things that I like to play with. If we try to identify God using metaphors from our culture, like fathers and lambs, then what happens to our connection with God? Most human beings never come across a lamb. A lamb is a totally abstract thing to me. I saw a lamb once at a petting zoo. So 'Lamb of God'... Okay, that's what a lamb looks like. In our culture where fathers are sort of absent, and where fathers are no longer a huge item of respect, or discipline, or whatever — if we've already been using that metaphor to describe God, and then the real thing in society, the father, breaks down, what happens to our idea of God? This shortcutting to comprehend God by using our world breaks down our idea of God when our world breaks down. That's what I don't like. That's what I'm always attacking in my books. In *Fight Club* I talked about that a lot."

Despite the profound subject matter, however, *Choke* is his most humorous novel yet. Perhaps that's why it works so well to get its message across. In one scene, Victor participates in a rehearsed, simulated rape that produces absolutely hilarious results.

"The day I brought that into workshop, I expected to get crucified on that. And people laughed their eyes out. People were laughing so hard, that I thought, 'Well, maybe I'm just being too sensitive about it.' Then I sent it out into the world and I thought, 'I'm still going to get crucified on this.' But no, what I was hearing back from editors and readers, men and women — *especially* women at the movie studios that I knew — said that that was the scene that they laughed at the most.

Then I thought, 'Well maybe it works, and it's not quite so threatening.' But I did fully expect to get people objecting to that."

At this point, a waiter approaches our table and asks Chuck, "May I recommend the clam chowder today, sir?"

Chuck puts his hand to his forehead and groans. "Oh no, not on a Sunday. Should I not be eating this?" The waiter laughs nervously at his joke, then leaves. Word gets around and everyone's acting out scenes from *Fight Club*.

Several minutes later, a waitress approaches and tells Chuck that Ryan (the waiter) really wanted to ask for his autograph but he was too embarrassed — so he's taking his fork instead. Chuck gasps. "My fork? For

DNA testing? Have we come to *Gattaca* already?" Chuck tells her to bring over a piece of paper and he'll autograph it. Which he does happily.

Getting back to the interview, Chuck addresses the issue of sexual addiction in *Choke*. "From what I understand about sexaholics, and the whole pathology of it, is that they use sex as an anesthetic," he says. "In the groups that I attended, it wouldn't be each person was constantly like some sort of gourmand out there trying to discover as many different sexual things as possible. Each of them seemed to have latched onto one thing. There were these guys who whacked off eighteen times a day, and there were these guys who went to lingerie modeling parlors five times a day, and guys who went to prostitutes eight times a week. And, no pun intended, they were in a rut. Cute pun though. They used it as an anesthetic. They didn't want something new and different every time. They found the thing that worked for them, so they just went and did that thing. It wasn't so much an exploration as they just wanted the same old same old. A heroin addict is very happy with heroin. He doesn't screw around once he finds heroin."

Similarly, in Colonial Dunsboro, an historic park of sorts where Victor works as an Irish indentured servant, many of his coworkers are drug addicts. Even Victor's mother, Ida, throws LSD to the animals at the zoo. The punishments for the addicts in *Choke* — whether the addiction be drugs, sex, or general mischief — seemed futile. "My family is a portrait of compulsive behavior. My brother exercises compulsively, I exercise compulsively, my mother gardens compulsively. We all are compulsive in so many ways. Even when we get

CHUCK PALAHNIUK

FIGHT CLUB

MISCHIEF. MAYHEM. SOAP.

NOW A MAJOR MOTION PICTURE

BRAD PITT EDWARD NORTON

HELENA BONHAM CARTER

'A great début, hypnotic...pitiless and told brilliantly'
BRET EASTON ELLIS

together, we all have to be doing something while we're together as a family. Shelling peas, shelling walnuts. We can't sit still. I wanted to demonstrate as many ways that people use the things that they use to keep from moving on in their lives, whether it's constantly attacking and tearing things down, like Ida, or whether it's using drugs at the same time that you dream about putting together the band that you're never going to put together. All the things that these people use because they're too afraid to create their world. It's so much easier to stay in stasis than it is to make that leap, to say, 'This is what I'm going to do with my life,' to make that choice, to make that commitment, and to eventually make that contribution to the world. It's so much easier to hide out in drugs or in anti-social teardown behavior. I wanted to find as many ways as people hide out as possible, and demonstrate those in *Choke*."

As usual with Chuck's novels, all of the issues seem to tie together to focus on one omnipresent theme: the disillusionment of the American dream. "My friends who are teachers say that their students see their parents as achieving everything that they were taught to achieve in terms of money, possessions, success, status — and their parents still aren't happy. In fact, their parents are unhappier than their own parents, who had nothing. So these kids are suddenly going, 'Oh my gosh! If we're all supposed to be chasing achievement, status, money, and we're seeing it not work for our parents, what the hell? What does success mean for us? If success isn't money, what is success now?' I see people in crisis about not wanting to chase the money thing, because it's obviously not working for so many people who have the money thing. They're not sure what to chase now. In a way, that's part of the ongoing inquiry in process. What does 'success' mean now, in the world? What will 'success' mean for the next generation? I just see the American Dream breaking down in terms of success as money and achievement. What is the next definition of success?"

In Chuck's opinion, this is the theme to-day's writer's should be tackling as well. "Despite the highest standard of living in the world, most people aren't very happy. And a large chunk of these people are about to get old and die. And the children of those people are seeing how money and power might not be the master key to success. And in that case, what is success? What will bring happiness?" A sobering thought for this generation, because there's no easy answer.

Chuck shows his light-hearted side by telling a few amusing anecdotes, including a story that David Fincher told him about how the slum-tenants were throwing bags of piss and shit on Brad Pitt during the filming of the alley chase scene in *Se7en*. (The people yelling "Shut the fuck up!" in the background? Those are for real.) Then he proceeds to tell me about the time he was sitting in a Portland restaurant with a photographer, and their waiter — not realizing "the *Fight Club* guy" was right in front of him — described how Chuck lives in a castle on a cliff above the ocean with a former Miss Oregon, how he hates people and refuses to sign books (none of which is true). That probably falls in the same category as the time a writer got the courage to ask him if he was "really Bret Easton Ellis' secret lover" (Chuck's never even met Bret).

Chuck's had what most people would consider to be an adventurous life up to this point. He's interviewed celebrities, including Juliette Lewis. He's watched cadavers being dissected. He's used steroids. He's had a conference on his works. And of course, he's had one of his books made into perhaps the most provocative film of the nineties — *Fight Club*.

But it really all started with what Chuck describes as a "shabby, thin version" of *Invisible Monsters*, which nonetheless garnered a huge amount of attention in the publishing industry. It's a freakish story about a infomercial model, Shannon McFarland, who teams up with transsexual Brandy and her lover after her own face gets blown off by a shotgun. "People really seemed fascinated by it," he says. "But ultimately all these publishing houses that were so excited, none of them would buy it, because they said it was impossible to market. They said they didn't even know what shelf it would go on in the bookstore. After all this foreplay (as my agent would say), I was ultimately just left with everyone telling me, 'Your work is too dark. It's too outrageous. It's too risky. It's too offensive.' At that point I was thinking, 'Well, should I tone it down?' And I thought, 'No, what if I make it even more offensive, and more dark, and more risky? They'll never publish it.' I had really given up hope. I was never going to get published so I might as well write what I want to write. That's when I wrote *Fight Club*. Because I never thought it would be published, but I thought, 'Well, at least it'll sort of shock these people, and entertain them maybe.' I thought for the rest of my life I was going to be writing for publishing house readers, who would ultimately reject me, but would still look forward to my manuscripts, because they would be something different."

I asked him if he feels any resentment for having difficulty getting his "dark books" published, when numerous other authors have had much darker material published. Chuck responds, "When you cite 'dark books,' they're pretty much automatically not Oprah Winfrey books. They're not those comforting best-seller books that everyone is going to rush out and buy because they touch a chord in their heart so readily. Maybe when they're saying 'too dark,' they're saying 'not commercial enough.' That's what I'm hearing. 'Dark' doesn't translate into a lot of profit."

But at some point it *did* translate into some profit, because soon after the *Fight Club* movie was released, the two novels Chuck had written previously — *Survivor* and *Invisible Monsters* — were published. Granted, although Chuck's "dark" material had finally found its way into the public eye, he still thinks there's a cutting off point. "Lois Rosenthal, the editor of *Story* magazine (which she shut down several years ago), at one point really loved to publish some of my short stories. I sent her a short story that

became parts of *Survivor* — about the man running the fake crisis hotline — which actually became chapter two of *Survivor* almost verbatim. She sent it back, saying, 'No, this is too dark.' Later I was talking to her and she said, 'I don't know what it is with people, but if one more person sends me a short story about having sex with their German Shepherd, I'm just going to go insane!'"

Chuck clarifies with an example as to what he finds gratuitous. "I was sort of appalled by the book, *The Alienist*, which was a best-selling novel about the birth of psycho-analytical detective work on homicides, around the turn of the century, New York. In it, a series of male child prostitutes are being killed by someone, and so, using fledgling Freudian ideas and psycho-analytical therapy, they identify what type of person this is doing the killings, and track them down. Most of the book is written in sort of a glib, stereotypical way, but then whenever they find a dead child, the camera zooms in and every detail is picked out, and it just seems like a travelogue used to connect these fantastically detailed scenes of children with their entrails strewn all over, and butchered in fantastically grotesque ways. As I was reading it I was thinking, 'Is this just an excuse for us to get this incredible thrill of seeing butchered children?' It just seemed like the plot was only a device for presenting these incredibly, masterfully done, hideous scenes."

When I bring up Bret Easton Ellis' *American Psycho* as a parallel example, Chuck disagrees. "*The Alienist* was a very horizontal story. We're going to catch this killer, and along the way we're going to fall in love. A to B. *American Psycho* had that metaphorical comment on society that allowed it to transcend the plot line and actually rise in meaning, so it was about accomplishing something. Even *Silence of the Lambs* was about accomplishing something and completing an aspect of the protagonist's personality. *The Alienist* was just dead child, dead child, dead child, love, dead child, dead child, romance, the end."

Getting back to his work, I mention how

Tyler Durden

his novels seem to tackle a lot of themes, and he laughs. "Everyone in Los Angeles says, 'Oh my God, we could get ten screenplays out of this novel! We don't even know where to start!' In Portland, we have these old department stores called Newbury's, like dime stores from the 1920s. The windows at Newbury's are always packed and crowded and cluttered, full of rotting manikins wearing plastic dresses. The joke in Portland is that the window dressing philosophy at Newbury's is 'If it doesn't look right, put more in.' That's the way I think about my books. If it's not working, put more in. That's why they end up getting so crowded with stuff."

When asked if this is why he considers *Invisible Monsters* to be his "weakest" novel — because it doesn't take on as many themes as his other novels — Chuck explains his original concept for the novel. "I wanted to do a linear novel, but to break it up, so that it would say to jump from chapter one to chapter seventeen, to chapter thirteen, and you would physically have to jump back and forth throughout the book. Hopscotch . It's been done before. What I really wanted to do was to write a half-dozen incredibly exciting, linguistically bizarre and beautiful chapters that the plot would never pass through. As you physically had to leap through the book to

Chuck chokes

find the plot, you would pass through scenes: Brandy on a submarine, Brandy on the Titanic, or whatever. Just some outrageous scenes that you would assume that eventually the plot would pass through, but by the time you got to the end of the book you'd realize, 'You know, I never did see that Brandy on Mars chapter. Did I miss something?' It would be like those fashion magazines — no matter how many times you read that fat magazine, every once in a while it will fall open to something that you never saw, and you'll realize that this chaotic, beautiful thing is ultimately unknowable, like a person. Every once in a while you'll see your wife across the floor at a party or at a department store, from an angle, and you won't recognize her. You'll think, 'Who is that beautiful woman?' Then you'll realize, 'Oh my God, that's my wife!' You'll realize that that person is ultimately unknowable, that you'll never completely know that person. That's what I wanted the

book to be, something that would imply the unknowability of beautiful things."

Unfortunately, that's not how it worked out. "I had a friend read it, and she said, 'Oh, I hated that jumping back and forth. It was just too confusing.' So I went and put it back together as a more linear novel. I think that's why I feel like I failed. I should have presented it the way I wanted to present it." Although it still jumps throughout the timeline in the novel, Chuck feels that it doesn't quite go over the edge. "Again, like with *Fight Club* — you can do dark, but if it's not dark enough, it doesn't work. You can do confusing. If I had boosted the confusion, and the extravagance just a little bit more, it would be a masterpiece. Right now, it's just not confusing and extravagant enough. I could have made a point with structure that would have been much more eloquent than any point made with content. I didn't do that. I pulled up short. I shouldn't have."

I assure Chuck that it's still a great novel. "You're just saying that," he laughs.

One significant thing about *Invisible Monsters* is that the main character is female. When asked what kind of problems he encountered writing in another gender, and if he thinks he was successful, Chuck says, "The main character in *Monsters* is more a person than a female. No way was I getting into a faux description of cramps or her period or anything bluntly 'female' to prove she was a woman. In that way, my character is a failure, but because this is a book about ideas, surreal ideas, is reality all that important? When my life is going fast and furious, I'm not much aware of my balls. My guess is women don't rush around, living life, always aware of their genitals either. *Invisible Monsters* was a 'reverse Cinderella story' where a character gains power by losing her looks. In the real Cinderella story, I don't remember the title character obsessing over her period." Indeed, despite the lack of stereotypical tell-tale signs of femininity, the narrative voice of Shannon McFarland is convincingly female.

On a similar note, Chuck's first novel addresses a theme that appears in all of his works: homosexuality. In *Invisible Monsters*, Shannon's parents disown her gay brother because of their own homophobia. "The gay thing in *Invisible Monsters* is a take-off on the IKEA thing in *Fight Club*. People are so desperate for a complete identity, an instant identity, they grab one off the shelf. Black. Gay. Feminist. Home-owner. All these labeled lifestyles are easy to embrace. Nice off-the-rack identities. Like IKEA furniture. But by accepting them, don't we limit our own capacity for creating a more personal, powerful identity?"

As usual, Chuck makes a compelling argument. To drive home the point even further, he brings up the theme of identity again in *Survivor*, the story of Tender Branson, the last surviving member of the Creedish Death Cult who dictates his life story into the flight recorder of a doomed 747. In the novel, Tender describes in detail how his case worker would change his identity every week, simply by picking a different diagnosis out of her DSM — Diagnostic and Statistical Manual of Mental Disorders. It's the perfect example of society searching for quick and easy answers

to problems that don't have quick and easy solutions.

In the Creedish Death Cult, the children are all referred to as Tender. "Like money," Chuck says. "The children are raised and sold as a commodity, so in a way the children are legal tender. The way that Beanie babies are now legal tender, I think." I ask Chuck how he feels about his novel sharing the same name as a certain highly rated reality TV series. Chuck groans. "That was originally called *Unnatural Disasters*. I really loved that title. God bless him, but my editor at the time, Jerry — who's now my editor again with *Choke* — really liked the title *Survivor*. He lobbied like crazy. 'Just one word. It's perfect.' If you did a search on the title *Survivor* it would already bring up sixty books. I hated the idea, but I finally knuckled under to Jerry, and let it be called *Survivor* instead of *Unnatural Disasters*."

Chuck's novel and the TV series actually have a little bit in common in the respect that they both take people who aren't really ready for fame and who are essentially manufactured into celebrities. Asked if he thinks fame has the potential for some kind of major psychological or emotional damage, Chucks says, "It seems like some people are really threatened by the idea of being recognized. They're very spooked by the idea of losing their anonymity. I talked to Juliette Lewis about that moment when you realize that you've lost your anonymity in the world, and when you walk into a place total strangers know who you are. That can be really, really frightening to people. I think that's the worst part of it — losing the ability to be just alone in public, and not being watched and being disregarded, because no one knows who you are." Chuck himself has only experienced a loss of his anonymity (other than at this conference) in Portland, because it's such a small town. "That's the nice thing about being a writer or a movie director. There's this old Fran Lebowitz line: 'Nobody knows who you are, but you still get a good table at restaurants' — or something like that."

Fame and prestige are key elements in *Survivor*. Tender Branson's employers are middle-class snobs obsessed with knowing proper etiquette for every possible occasion, which they ask Tender to find out for them. "What I understood was that there wasn't a

CHOKE

Chuck Palahniuk
ISBN 0 09 942268 9 / £6.99 239pp
Vintage 2002

EVERY ADDICTION... WAS JUST A WAY TO TREAT THIS SAME PROBLEM. DRUGS OR OVEREATING OR ALCOHOL OR SEX, IT WAS ALL JUST ANOTHER WAY TO FIND PEACE. TO ESCAPE WHAT WE KNOW. OUR EDUCATION. OUR BITE OF THE APPLE.

Like **Fight Club**, **Choke** is to some degree a book composed of set-pieces. Palahniuk doesn't go for an obvious a-b-c narrative but gives us (for the most part) self-contained incidents in different times and places. However, these are not hermetic but combine cumulatively to give us a portrait of a loveless man stranded within his own desolate sex addiction. The author does not strike a pointlessly nihilistic Gen X pose, nor does he wallow in addict-culture self-pity like the truly vile Elizabeth Wurtzel or Dave Peltzer. Instead, **Choke**'s miserabilism works in tandem with its ultra-black humour to an ultimately redemptive effect.

This is not an ostensibly cheerful book. The narrator, Vincent, describes how his lunatic mother abducted him from care to explain her garbled philosophies before being arrested once more. The only time he felt loved in childhood was when he choked in a restaurant: recovering from the Heimlich manoeuvre, he was warmed by the sight of concerned adult faces around him. Now a med school dropout, Vincent wanders from one cold sexual experience to another (usually with other members of his sex-addict recovery group), visits his now-moribund mother, hangs out with his flabby loser mate Denny, and fakes choking fits in restaurants to feel loved and to fund his life. By the end of the story his carefully constructed barriers have all come crashing down around him, but he has at least some hint of salvation; it's a well-judged ending, hopeful without being inappropriately optimistic.

This novel, like the author's previous ones, is packed with ideas, wordplay and humour (with an eye on the fundamental ludicrousness of most sexual encounters, Palahniuk renders hilarious a mocked-up rape scene) as well as a bleak cynicism; however, this pessimistic outlook on modern life is tempered by a human heart beating within the book's pages. The narrator does not want to be like this; his numbness is a self-conscious avoidance of the dangerous business of feeling for another human being. It never works, so why risk the misery? Better to stick to the familiar safety of feeling nothing, and react against anyone who might perceive one's capacity for loving and being loved.

lot of etiquette until the Golden nineties — the Industrial Revolution, after the Civil War — when suddenly, there was a new rising, an American aristocracy. They had an enormous amount of money, but it was America, and it was a democracy, and there was no innate way, inherent way to differentiate between the lower classes and the higher classes. So they started creating these codes of behavior, codes of etiquette, by which they could differentiate between low-class people and high-class people. In so many countries, there is an accent that differentiates the classes, but in America, we had nothing. So we started creating all of these really innate, ritualistic codes of behavior — all these different forks, all these different ways of conducting dinner parties, all these ways of resenting ourselves that would automatically let you know who was 'in' and who wasn't, by whether or not they knew the intricacies of this behavior." A secret handshake, so to speak. Chuck agrees. "I wonder, with all of our new instant-Internet wealth people, the high-tech money, all these people — what sort of rituals will they create, whether it's language, or whether it's rituals of behavior or appearance? What will they create that will differentiate their class from the people not in their class?

'Maybe our generation has found its Don DeLillo'
BRET EASTON ELLIS

choke

A JONATHAN CAPE ORIGINAL
by the author of
FIGHT CLUB

CHUCK PALAHNIUK

IF IT COMES DOWN TO A CHOICE OF FEELING UNLOVED AND BEING VULNERABLE AND SENSITIVE AND EMOTIONAL, THEN YOU CAN JUST KEEP YOUR LOVE.

This perennially deadly choice is the source of much narrative fiction (P T Anderson's magnificent **Magnolia** springs immediately to mind), and runs throughout this book. Faking death as a way to feel loved through making others feel heroic... picking up sex addicts as easy fucks... actors in a colonial American theme park bombed out of their heads on drugs... a man on a web cam training a monkey to stuff nuts up his ass as an act of bravery and nobility... the idea that Vincent might be the reincarnation of Christ revealed as one huge, cruel MacGuffin... these people are trapped by their own fears and failures, and would rather stick with that familiar

numbness than jump into an unknown black hole of possible feelings and emotions.

Such self-hatred works on a extra-textual level here — Palahniuk the author, speaking as Vincent the character, addresses the reader in the second person, telling them not to read the book, to stay away from the book (and therefore Vincent), that the book will do them no good. It's a literary device also favoured by Jim Goad, of whom Palahniuk is a fan; interestingly, **Choke** and **Shit Magnet** (Goad's most recent — and stunning — book) mirror each other. On page sixty of **Choke**, Vincent encourages other characters to use him as a receptacle for their own guilt and hatred, and to blame him for various historical disasters; Goad does the same in the opening chapter of **Shit Magnet**. On page 118 of **Choke**, Vincent decides that since he has so often been cast in the role of evil male aggressor

that he may as well play it with gusto; the idea is one upon which **Shit Magnet** frequently touches. At one point (p.123), Vincent even refers to Denny as a "shit magnet"! I do not suspect that there is plagiarism afoot on either writer's part; rather, their world views and writing styles are close and so a certain amount of overlap might be expected. Other ideas here are also familiar from **Fight Club** (the support groups, the consumer terrorism of Vincent's mom screwing around with supermarket goods, the two weirdoes living together and obsessing on various projects), but this book has more than enough inventive energy and raw imagination to be worth your time. Pacy, entertainingly nihilistic, unnervingly truthful and blindingly funny, the book also allows the author's humanity and all of its attendant weaknesses to show through the veneer of misery.
ANTON BLACK

In the eighties, when so many people were rising so quickly and creating so much money, in that Donald Trump-type way — suddenly we saw the resurgence of Miss Manners. That's when she really came to the forefront and people were really fascinated with manners and etiquette again, and they were obsessed with the right fork, for the first time in decades. I couldn't help but think it was just because people want to create that invisible way of identifying who's who in our culture."

Indeed, divided social classes are a key element in all of Palahniuk's novels. But it was his third written (and first published) novel, *Fight Club*, that really delved deep into the issues of a polarized society. The story of Jack, who starts a "fight club" with his newfound friend Tyler, can be interpreted in many different ways, but there are glaring social/political symbols that can't be ignored. When asked if *Fight Club* is all about the repudiation of capitalism, Chuck says, "It is in the respect that I don't like the way capitalism splinters people and puts them all against each other. By splintering society and driving us all apart and forcing us all to compete against each other, I think it alienates us, makes us unhappy. We never really achieve the great things that we could achieve. That's what I don't like about capitalism. All of my books are about bringing somebody from self-imposed pseudo-happiness of being isolated — in a way, we all want to be Howard Hughes, and live in that penthouse and never have to deal with anybody else — but in reality, that dream is like hell. That would be misery. So it's bringing people from this isolation back into community, forcing them back into community, whether it's with support groups or whether it's with them being on the lam in *Survivor*, and running the crisis hotline. In some way these people are all being dragged out of their lonely lives back into interaction with people. I think capitalism does force us into that 'us against the world' thing, by pitting us all against each other."

Yet Chuck is a relatively famous author who happens to be profiting well from capitalism. Asked how he feels about it in that respect, it's clear that Chuck is not motivated by greed. He talks about how he would like to create a foundation that will eventually fund a writer's retreat, or writer's colony, which the West Coast really doesn't have. He's not above helping out his friends occasionally either. "I don't want the success to drive me away from my friends," he says. "I want it to bring us together. I don't want it to drive us apart."

But his own altruistic ideals aren't always seen in his works. *Fight Club* has the most ominous ending of all his novels. As a result of his frustration of not getting published, Chuck displayed a level of anger in *Fight Club* that's not present in his other works. "I was never going to be published at that point. There was no hope. It was a novel written out of anger at publishing. Damn it, I was writing exactly like Stephen King and they still weren't publishing me. I had that Stephen King thing down and they still weren't publishing me."

I ask him to explain what he means by that "Stephen King thing."

"I was writing those perfect sentences, and those perfect thriller plots. I had modeled my writing after successful writing, trying to copy successful writers so well. I thought I was following a pattern of success, when in fact my work was completely unremarkable because I following the pattern so closely. Rather than writing the stories that I would tell in real life, the stories that I loved, I was writing the stories that I thought would sell — more 'marketable' stories — and they were getting shot down. *Fight Club* was written out of the frustration and anger of so much rejection. It was also written out of the freedom and resignation that I would never be published, so therefore I could write anything. If you have nothing to lose you can do anything," he says, "and that's what *Fight Club* is about. At that point I had nothing to lose."

And again, *Fight Club* deals with the issue of homosexuality. In the novel, when Jack and Tyler meet for the first time, it's on a nude beach. Was he consciously attempting to create a homosexual undercurrent throughout the book? Chuck laughs. "I wanted to play with that, so people would be squirming, thinking, 'Oh God, am I reading a queer novel? Oh God, I'm reading a queer novel! Oh God, I'm *enjoying* a queer novel!' Then they get to the end and they think, 'They're not queer, they're just insane!' There would be that huge rush of relief. I also wanted to play with the idea that we have all these buddy movies, where we're never supposed to broach the idea: 'What is it that keeps Butch Cassidy and the Sundance Kid together for so many years?' We're never supposed to broach that aspect of those relationships, what's innate in every buddy movie. Fincher just went crazy with it, ramping it up even more." But the scene on the nude beach isn't in the movie. "No," says Chuck, "but I sat there for hours while Fincher was trying to get Brad Pitt to put the gun in Edward's mouth and cock his hips in such a way, so that, from the camera's angle, it looked like nothing but…" He trails off, laughing, leaving the rest to my imagination. "Fincher was playing with that dynamic to make people squirm."

On the commentary track on the *Fight Club* DVD, Chuck mentions that he was disappointed that the recipes for napalm and bombs that he researched for so diligently were changed in the book, but for obvious reasons. In that respect, I ask him if he feels that writers should exercise some responsibility in their writing.

"Boy, I could go so many places with that," he says. "First of all, in a really literal sense, I've read so many books like *Heartburn*, where they would put recipes in the books. It seemed like there was this whole genre of novels that had recipes written in the narrative. So I thought, 'Hmm, how about a guy novel, with guy recipes in the narrative? What would be a guy recipe?' My brother was visiting from South Africa, and he's an electrical engineer. He spent seventy-two hours coming up with all these different recipes for explosives. I just put them as this sort of jokey comment on novels with food recipes. I was amazed it made it all the way to the final proofreading before W W Norton said, 'Maybe this isn't such a smart thing. Could you change one ingredient in each one to make them useless?' So I did, and it wasn't that much of a heartbreak."

There have been other instances, however, where the burden of responsibility wasn't such a clear line. "When I was talking about splicing the porno into the movies, I mentioned that to some friends, and one of my friends said, 'Please don't write about that. If you write about that then people will do it. It'll just make the world a worse place.'" He laughs. "So I went ahead and wrote about it. Since I wrote about it, David Fincher himself, when he was a high-school projectionist in Ashland, Oregon, said he used to that. There's nothing I could conceive of that a million people aren't already doing. In *Survivor*, some of my friends — the ones who told me about how crematory urns aren't examined before you board an airplane, and how that would be the most effective way to get a gun on board — said, 'Don't put that in there.' I think it's much better to be the person who points out that faulty situation in the world, than to wait until some malicious person does it. I'd rather be the person saying, 'The emperor's not wearing any clothes,' than letting somebody take advantage of the situation.

So, I think you have responsibility to bring it out there, because if you have that idea, millions of people have that idea, and it needs to be recognized in the culture and dealt with."

When asked what he thinks about the *Natural Born Killers* lawsuit (that was eventually thrown out of court), he says, "I was talking to Juliette Lewis about that, and she was saying that there's a director's cut — that I don't think I've ever seen — which is even more over the top, that really makes its message clear, and you totally get that this is a satire. It's very much like *Absolutely Fabulous*, the British comedy, where it effectively makes fun of this thing that it seemingly supports, that you never want to do it. You watch *Ab Fab*, you never want to do drugs. So I think it's a case like with *Invisible Monsters*, where if you don't take it too far, then you've failed. I think, talking to Juliette, it wasn't taken far enough. It wasn't extreme enough, and that's why it failed."

One issue that hasn't been discussed much is Jack's insomnia. In the world of *Fight Club*, Jack's inability to sleep seems to be the symptom of a much larger, deeper problem. Indeed, his attendance at various support groups only offers a temporary cure. I ask Chuck if he feels that sleep deprivation is a sign that we need to slow down.

"We really need to be aware of what we want from our lives, what we really want to be doing, so that our job is not just our job, so that it's the thing that fulfills us, it's our life," he says. "So we don't feel like we have to rush around and get that thing done and then still go off and live our life. A way of integrating what you do with who you are and with what your entire life is, so your entire life isn't your job. By compartmentalizing these things, it's like we're constantly rushing to complete one thing — we're rushing to complete our vacation, and then we're rushing to complete our work, so we can get another vacation, and rushing to complete our vacation again — and then we're dead. If there was some way to focus on what we really wanted, rather than doing all these things that we settle for, then we would need so little in our lives. Now

that I'm writing for a living, I need so little money, I need so few possessions, I need so little everything. My life is this really monk-like life, because I don't need to compensate with a lot of extra things. I'm so fulfilled and so happy with what I do for my living. That's what I wish people could get in society — to be doing what they want to do, rather than be doing what they don't want to do and trying to compensate with a whole bunch of other stuff. I have wonder if so many destructive addictions — whether they're drinking, or sex, or shoplifting — are because that person would really like to be a painter, but doesn't have the guts to be that creative painter. So they anesthetize that frustration, that sense of failure, that fear, by doing the destructive thing. It's a huge act of faith to put yourself out into the world and say, 'I'm going to create.'"

Chuck talks about when it finally clicked for him, when he realized that there was more to life than just waiting for paychecks. "When I was working full-time and writing, yeah, I could do my job. Suddenly I was happy doing my job because every day I could get a few sentences in, and my life wasn't just about filling the bank account so that at the end of the month I could pay bills, and the bank account would be empty, and then filling the bank account again. I hated that. You sit down, you write those cheques, and then you see you're right back where you started. That was just so crippling for me. At least this way I was getting a sentence a day or a word a day, and it seemed like I was building something beyond just paying the bills. My head was full of a narrative and I was actually creating something, and it was like the greatest Prozac. It really kept me from going insane in the job I hated."

It seems that the real message of *Fight Club* is encapsulated in one truly moving scene: When Jack (in the movie, Tyler) holds the gun to Raymond K Hessel's head and tells him that if he's not on his way to achieving his life's dream — becoming a veterinarian — in three months, then he will be dead.

The unexamined life is not worth living, or so they say.

Chuck laughs when I bring up the scene. He's had people approach him at book signings and tell him things like, "That was the scene that made me go back to school and get my Master's degree." This is Chuck's life dream, this is what he wants to see: for people to stop sucking up to shit-ass jobs and do what they want. And being a writer, he certainly can relate. "I've joked that there should be creative writing programs where, instead of having these nurturing workshops, they put a gun to your head and they say, 'If you don't have a novella done in six weeks, you will be dead.' The kind of energy that that would suffuse into not empowering people to living their life's dream, but *sentencing* people to living their life's dream. Because whether or not there's a gun there, there *is* a gun there. Nobody's going to live forever. That gun is there, whether it's cancer, or a gun, or whatever."

On The Writer's Cult web site (address later) is a quote where Chuck says, "I write now because I find fewer and fewer books that interest me." Asked what it is that he dislikes about today's fiction, he says, "So much of the fiction is too slow and too reflective, not enough happens plot-wise. It involves too much thinking. Brew a cup of tea, sit in the window, watch the leaves fall. Give me a break. Either that or it's too full of popular culture references. It seems to be trying too hard to be really hip and flip and cynical and glib, without ever bringing me to a deeper meaning, bringing me to heartbreak. It sort of skims along the surface without ever really breaking my heart. Those are the two things I kept on running up against."

Without question, Chuck feels that good fiction needs to have some sort of deep commentary on society. "Otherwise it's just a sketch, a movie pitch," he says. "It never moves beyond that point A to point B horizontal plot line. It never gradually rises."

I ask Chuck what he thinks are the benefits of his own writing style — basically first person, present tense — as opposed to the traditional — third person, past tense. "A couple different things," he says, rolling his eyes.

I ask him if he dislikes reading novels written in that style.

"Not if they're written by Tobias Wolff," he says. "Jeez, I would read his shopping list. Tobias Wolff's third person, omniscient viewpoint, past tense, is gorgeous. It's beautiful. But one of the tenets of minimalism — which is what I studied and which is what I write — is that someone has to be responsible for the story. This can't be God telling the story. Because we know anymore who's telling the story shapes the story as much as the events of the story. And in what context is the story being told shapes the story. And the reason

why the story is being told shapes the story. All these things shape the story as much as the events themselves. Establishing those things is sometimes the hardest part of writing one of my novels. It's really easy to come up with a chain of events, but to come up with a context and a reason and a person that is the only way in which the story can be told is most important. So that's why I like first person, because there's someone owning the story. *Choke* is really my first foray into third person, in sections. I think Socrates condemns writing because he says, 'Speech is the closest thing to thought, and therefore is the most true thing.' Writing is once removed from speech, which is even farther removed from thought, so therefore, it's even more likely to miscommunicate. So I try to make my writing as close to speech as possible, and to entertaining speech. We don't say, 'Once upon a time, a nun walked into a bar and she sat down next to a penguin.' We say, 'Okay, okay, a nun walks into a bar and she sits down next to a penguin, she says, she says, this is what she says.' We talk with so much more of an immediacy, and that's how I want the stories to occur, with that same conversational immediacy, so that they appear even closer to thought."

Charles Baxter, noted Michigan author and writing instructor at U of M said that all authors/writers steal or borrow from their idols and then break away into their own style. Does Chuck think this applies to him? If so, what authors did he borrow or steal from, and how is that incorporated into his novels?

"Chuck Baxter is a god," Chuck says, "But he's too well-known to steal from. I steal everything from Amy Hemple. Short stories are miracles; they do something in seven pages that takes most writers 300 pages. So, I steal from short story writers. Hemple. Thom Jones. Mark Richard. Bret Ellis' collection *The Informers*. Denis Johnson's *Jesus' Son*. And I steal non-fiction forms from everywhere: household hints, rules, recipes, prayers, haikus, beauty tips, fashion magazine copy, epitaphs, graffiti. I steal any convention that will help ground my ludicrous world in reality."

Chuck's most recent project is *Lullaby*, which came out September 2002. He feels it's his strongest work yet. "It's a horror novel that re-invents Wiccan culture as a means to give people the power of life and death. In a way, it's really about my struggle over whether to recommend the death sentence for the man who killed my father. In a book sense, it's about how as we get power, we want more power. And how if we have the power of life and death, we tend to use it more and more often. This is demonstrated by many cases of serial medical murder where caregivers killed out of sympathy at first, then killed increasingly out of annoyance, whim, cruelty, boredom. The research on this one's been chilling."

Wrapping things up, he says, "The greatest thing a book can do is push you to write. (I hate the word 'inspire.') My dream is, people will see the possibility for new literature, film, paintings, dance, music, everything, and I can sit back and watch a flood of work — maybe spurred by my work — but a thousand times better. I look forward to reading myself blind."

This is Chuck Palahniuk: positive, creative, sincere.

I'm disappointed that I missed a great opportunity to experience the first Chuck Palahniuk conference, but I'm glad that he's taken the time for this interview. It's helped to bring his latest work, *Choke*, into focus. No longer a spokesman for total nihilism, Chuck's made the transition into something stronger; *Choke* represents a new generation that moves beyond attacking to creating. "That's what I really see after this turn of the century, especially at this conference," he says. "I've written off young people as TV-drained with no creativity. Now I'm seeing the incredible possibility that they have so much more talent and intelligence and thought than their parents, than my generation. So it makes me very excited by the future. That's what I wanted *Choke* to be about, and that's what I'm seeing fulfilled in so much of the work I'm seeing now from people. I can't wait for the future now, instead of just dreading the future."

This article first appeared as a slightly different version in turtleneck.net, the Online Journal of Literary Culture. Visit the Writer's Cult at www.chuckpalahniuk.net

YOUNG GIRLS CAUGHT UP IN A WORLD OF

$1.50

LOVE-IN

ADULTS ONLY

HELL
OUTDOORS!

BLOOD

BIZARRE PARTY!

KICKS

A BLOOD SPATTERED STUDY IN THE MACABRE

BAD MAGS

a regular guide to
the obscure
periodicals of
yesteryear

by Tom Brinkmann

INTRODUCTION

The cover of this unusual Seven Seventy publication pro-
claims: "Young Girls Caught Up In A World of LOVE-IN."
Seven Seventy published adult magazines in the sixties, mainly
of the sensational-sexploitation shock value variety with titles
such as *Shocking World*, *Banned*, *Raunchy*, *Barred* and
Shocker. Even though the above title sounds very hippie-like,
the picture and blurbs on the cover contradict that notion.
(The publishers gleefully making known their feelings with
regard to the different youth sub-cultures of the day, perhaps?) Seven Seventy rarely included copyright dates in their
indicia, so pin-pointing the year on some of these mags is
problematic, but I'd guess in this case it's the late sixties,
around 1967–68. That said, *Love-In* would pre-date the
Manson Family's bloody antics and the tragic concert at
Altamont, making the cover blurbs particularly poignant.

THE COVER

The cover depicts a man's spread legs framing a semi-naked
woman who is lying face down in shallow water, a bloody halo

LOVE-IN

Vol 2 No 4 (contrary to the
issue number, it's unlikely any
other issues were published)
No date, circa 1967–68
Seven Seventy Publishers
**P O Box 1081 Magnolia Park
Station, Burbank, CA, U S A**
$1.50   72pp

starting to form around her head. Beneath this is the caption: "A Blood Spattered Study In The Macabre." This image belongs to a set of pictures that can be found throughout the Seven Seventy stable of publications, and are touted variously as stills from a movie called *Thrill Killers*, or *Ghastly* — "a picture that shocked the film crew!" (see *Shocker* Vol 1 No 4). The same set of photos were also used by other publishers. In *Exotic Cinema* Vol 1 No 4 (Press Arts, Inc; March 1967), for instance, they were used on the cover and in an article called 'The Devil Take Them' (where they were supposedly taken from the flick of the same name) about "How the Mod Movie Makers Create Their Gore". This is obviously going to be a strange page flipping trip.

"GHASTLY" A PICTURE THAT SHOCKED THE FILM CREW!

CONTENT

As it turns out, anyone taking cues from the cover and looking for the "blood spattered study in the macabre" will be out of luck — the whole magazine is one non-stop hodge-podge montage of hippies and bikers, i.e. the youth at the time, sitting outdoors, smoking pot, dancing, freaking out and making out.

Also included are pictures of protests, flag burning, love-ins, happenings, body painting, flute, bongo and sitar playing, meditation, camp art, swingers, gang girls, topless gyrating hippie chicks, biker mamas and so on — the stereotypical images of hippies, except these are the real thing and in some cases are situated in or around such familiar landmarks as Pandora's Box on the Sunset Strip and Ye Olde Psychedelic Shoppe. Sprinkled throughout are clip-art and cartoons of hippies and swingers.

The blurbs in the various layouts are priceless. (What can you say about such mindless drivel as: "Zipper means action stations in hippieville!" or "Today's breed gone berserk… just for kicks"?) The inside front cover is a good indicator of what to expect from the rest of the magazine. Across the top of the page are the words "Hallucination Generation" next to clip-art of an iron cross. There is a photo of a pregnant hippie girl, a "Stop The War Now!" poster and a painting of an embracing couple with text that reads:

> The daring breed of today is frantic… frantic for answers, why are some called up, others skipped over?! Some in colleges buying grades. It is worth lowering their moral standards to be with the "group" is non-conformity really classic conformity. Beards or crew cuts frantic for fast cars frantic for material things they can't afford frantic for social standing frantic for kicks motorcycles, sportscars, surf-boards and bronzed maidens!! This is The Story of a Psychedelic Circus… Beatniks… Sickniks and Their Wild Experiences!

(Grammar and punctuation are unchanged, as with all the quotes that follow.)

After three pages of photos of young people hanging out, there is a three-page article on "Haight-Ashbury". This comprises mainly of quotes from Lt Curran of Park Station SFPD in Golden Gate Park. The twenty-nine year veteran of the force says of the hippies, "The original hippies were all right — real writers and artists. Now we're attracting the LSD crowd." He also gives an interesting little anecdote about wild life in

FReAk-OuT!

SNAP THE PUBLIC'S MIND . . . HAVE A FREAK-OUT! THIS
MEANS ANYTHING THAT IS SOCIABLY NOT DONE!?

the park: "We had one incident over here the other day. Our men discovered some hippies sleeping in a foxhole they'd dug in the sand. It had a trap door with camouflage and everything." Such was life in hippie-filled Golden Gate Park.

Love-In goes into a lengthy article about "Incredible Swap Clubs" — several text pages with a few pictures of "swingers" going at it — constituting a "case histories" type of thing common in adult publications of this period. Sociology and psychology in the service of sexology. The article incorporates tales of swinging couples and how they got into the scene. From the Hollywood Hills to Malibu, the difference between the two locales is slim, according to the writer, merely different hosts and different faces. It ends with this aside:

Malibu has seen many swinging parties. The 'pornography king' of North America, recently murdered in Hollywood, made his home in Malibu, and often gave 'bare' parties for promoters and business cronies. True sharing is the Swappers credo!!

"Going To Pot" is a two-page article on — you guessed it — smoking marijuana! Images of a pair of hands rolling a joint and another of a couple on a bed are inset (bewilderingly) with smaller, high-contrast photos of Andy Warhol and Nico.

Motorcycle gangs and their "mamas" feature throughout *Love-In* — including a short list of their slang and its definitions for the novice — all seeming to belong to the same club, namely the Jokers Out Of Hell from Michigan, which the text claims have come all the way to Hollywood Blvd from their home state to check out the newest crop of biker gang movies! Indeed, one picture shows a group of bikers admiring one such movie poster. (A poster of Peter Fonda astride a chopper in the 1966 movie *Wild Angels* can be seen in the window of a headshop.)

The bikers are referred throughout as Angels and Wild Angels, which is the kind of thing that turned the Hell's Angels' name into a cover-all euphemism for outlaw biker gangs, even if they were totally unrelated clubs. One layout opens with a Nazi flag pasted above a photo of bikers — a completely separate image which, presumably, the publishers added in order to cement the two themes together in the mind of the reader.

There are many pages of photos taken at festivals or in parks with the stereotype barefooted hippie girls shaking their money-makers around. The centrespread is in color and features several various locales with the ever present hippies. One of the images is from the same "film" as the cover photo, and depicts a nude girl bound at the wrists to a horizontal bar outdoors. The caption states: "Part of a hippie rite!"

There are two pages of "Camp Art": old mannequins, reassembled with doll parts and other found junk, with paint dripped on them.

One blurb, in response to the headline "Mad", goes:

Yeah, mad with STP, the groovy new drug... it really turns the beatniks on!!? Today the kicks come in macabre ways. These two "needle high" weirdos took woodshop in school... hence knowledge of the rip saw and what it can do to a beautiful young hippie!

The image that accompanies this revelation has a car in which we see two couples inside, and a third couple on the roof, no rip saw anywhere to be seen! This blurb would be *completely* inexplicable if not for another Seven Seventy magazine (*Banned* No 8) where the exact same blurb is used for a picture of two guys forcing a tied-up, terrified hippie girl head first towards a rip saw!

The writer of the article titled "Flower Teens" talks about the problems presented by youths hanging out in store parking lots in the nearby San Fernando Valley communities of Granada Hills, Sun Valley and North Hollywood, listing the streets and

HOT PASSIONS IN A HOT SUMMER!?!

AT 3 A.M. THINGS ARE JUST STARTING TO MOVE!

SNAP THE PUBLIC'S MIND . . . HAVE A FREAK-OUT! THIS MEANS ANYTHING THAT IS SOCIABLY NOT DONE!?

neighborhoods specifically. The youths, i.e. hippies, block cars from parking and leaving, drink beer, take narcotics, harass women shoppers and so on. Those pesky hippies!

From "Freak-Out!" onwards, *Love-In* loses all sense of a layout completely and turns into a mess of blurbs, clip-art and photographs (of "Way out nuts, kooks, goons and flower people!").

The magazine ends with five pages of "Strange Gang Girls" ("Rip off that dress, baby you are about to go bedside... and not for sleep! Experienced to give. Nice girl sliding into bad ways... won't be long 'till she is 'Way Out'.") in which the text reports "Twelve Arrested After Cycle Booze Run". It reads like a newspaper item (and it probably was), detailing how a weekend "booze run" for motorcyclists at an isolated hilltop house on Sierra Highway, ended with a dozen arrests.

Deputies report that the Galloping Goose Motorcycle Club staked the "booze run" — a party consisting of drinking, barbecuing and racing — for about seventy-five members of Hell's Angels from San Bernardino, the Knight Riders of Highland Park, Satan's Slaves of San Fernando and Questionnaires of Oxnard. The arrests were made at "check points" the Deputies had set up in anticipa-

tion of the booze run, and even gives the names and addresses of those people who were arrested (for various things like alleged possession of marijuana, suspicion of motorcycle theft and impersonating a police officer)!

The layout, and magazine, concludes with more motorcycle outlaw pics and the ever present wacky blurbs:

Wild and with it! Beat generation that prefers two wheels and handlebars, spokes, grease and a wonderful "don't give a damn attitude." Roaring into trouble ride the girl outlaws! Push the knife in cry the drug high cycle kooks!

CONCLUSIONS

Of particular interest now is the fact that *Love-In* coincides with the height of hippiedom, and as a consequence is made up of all the elements of that era: the bikers, swingers and hippies that ran hog wild with the new sexual morality that was being born — or reborn, as the case may be. Also of note is that, located in Burbank, the publishers utilized local youths (as in the "Flower Teens" article). But for all of this, they seem to have had a semi-hostile, tongue-in-cheek, and at times moralizing attitude towards the youth of the day, while at the same time reveling in their milieu and accusing them of loose morals and violence. The very same publishers of course were responsible for some of the most sleazy and sordid magazines to come out of this time period!

All of Seven Seventy's publications have the same raw lack of design — photos laid on the page with text and clip-art thrown in for no purpose but to fill any blank space. The result has a random, slapped-together, frenzied feel to it. *And that's why you gotta love 'em!* The back cover photo shows two hippies blowing horns, and pronounces: "The call is out... for America's two most unusual, up to date magazines! Read Love-In Psychedelic HIPPIES." Whether this is to say there exists a magazine by the name *Psychedelic Hippies* I just don't know. If it does then I have yet to see a copy.

5 Minutes to Live video & dvd
International Art-House! Forgotten 60's Classics! Bizarre T.V.!

Find rare & unusual videos; collectible DVDs; books; magazines; vintage fil
posters and music from electronic to rare soul!

Read movie reviews plus in-depth articles and interviews with such legend
filmmakers as Timothy Carey, Russ Meyer and Alejandro Jodorowsky!

visit us online www.5minutestolive.com

vhs: Killer of Sheep; Mister Freedom; Manson Massacre; Lost Gay Tapes of John
Holmes; Skidoo; Bunny Lake is Missing; Young Playthings; Figures in a Landscape;
Emerald Cities; Murder Inc.; Dateline Diamonds; Steambath; Histoire De Melody
Nelson T.V. Special & many more titles!

dvd: Punishment Park; El Topo; Battle Royale; Last House on Dead End Street; Dark
Water; Alucarda; Blood Freak; Ichi the Killer; Viva La Muerte; Street of No Return;
The Deathmaster; Ginger; The Eye; Naked Lunch; Dead or Alive; All Ladies Do It;
The Wind Will Carry Us; Image; Satan Was a Lady & many more!

LECH KOWALSKI, BORN IN LONDON TO POLISH IMMIGRANTS AND RAISED IN AMERICA, Is best known for his 1981 film, *Dead On Arrival* (aka *D.O.A.*), which documents the Sex Pistols' chaotic tour of America.

Twenty years on and Kowalski is scheduled to show another fateful rock'n'roll story at the Raindance Film Festival. *Born To Lose: The Last Rock'n'Roll Movie* — concerning the life of Johnny Thunders — is not a new film, just a new version. But it never actually plays the cinemas, nor at Raindance, because of last minute copyright wrangles.

It is fortunate that *Born To Lose* is not Kowalski's only film at the festival. He has also completed a documentary by the name of *Boot Factory*, which stars a group of punks that Kowalski met when he was showing *D.O.A.* in Krakow. ("Imagine if the Sex Pistols had made boots instead of music," is how the director describes it.) *Boot Factory* starts off like a regular fly-on-the-wall documentary, but quickly descends into another tale about the destructive powers of heroin.

Boot Factory is the first part of a 'Polish trilogy' of films collectively titled *The Wild, Wild East*. Headpress spoke to Lech Kowalski shortly after the completion of his second instalment in the series, *Invasion on Hitler's Highway*. The final instalment will be *The Fabulous Art of Survival,* which focuses on the many prostitutes currently walking the streets of Poland.

Invasion on Hitler's Highway Photo: Lech Kowalski

B O O T FACTORY TO H I T L E R ' S HIGHWAY AN INTERVIEW W I T H LECH KOWALSKI

By Stuart Wright

What have you been filming in Poland?

KOWALSKI

The name of the film is *Hitler's Highway* and its about an important highway that the Nazis started to build before the war, for tanks to invade Eastern Europe. It's quite famous in Poland. The highway actually starts in Berlin and stretches into the Ukraine, and is now a highway for trucks, gangsters, all kinds of weird things. I spent three months on this road filming its characters and stories.

THIS PAGE AND NEXT
Images from *Hitler's Highway*

What stories evolved from it?

It's a story about Bulgarian hookers and mafia guys, Russian mafia guys and gypsies. I spent a month with gypsies. And it's a story about the new invasion of eastern Europe — the invasion is from the West and from the East. What takes place on this highway is some indication of what is happening in this Poland. Something the West has no idea about.

It's contemporary. It is a very hard movie, a transitory life on a road built by the Nazis. It's also a historical piece. For instance, on this road very close to the German border was the biggest Russian military base, where they had nuclear weapons trained at the West. It's abandoned now but is still guarded. We managed to get in there to film. There are Russians and Ukrainians living in these bunkers, hiding from the police. These are the kind of stories I was filming.

How do you approach the stories?

The crew is basically myself and a driver. We had a Suzuki jeep and I was doing the shooting, and I just go there and hang out. People see me a few times and I start speaking to them and eventually I find the characters that I feel would be good for the film. I slowly start filming with them and eventually we become — not friends, but they sort of get use to me and they let me film them. Then I start getting a story around their lives and activities. With some of the gangsters there were certain things that I couldn't shoot, but with the prostitutes they let me shoot everything. The only line I drew was I didn't show the prostitutes fucking the customers, because that is a little bit too much and I didn't want to do that. But everything else I filmed.

I spent a long time travelling with one particular Gypsy village — these are gypsies that

Photos this page and next Lech Kowalsi

lost people during WWII; they lost family and friends in gas chambers in concentration camps. I filmed those stories and what is going on with the younger people and how they live and what they are about. So, the film is a road movie that takes place across geographical terrain, but it is also a road movie about history.

Both things have a connection. For instance I found bunkers on the German border that very few people know about. They were built by the Germans and this one particular set of bunkers stretches for 40 km underground and they are in the same condition as were when they were built in 1940 by the Nazis. I spent a lot time down there and people live down there now. At one point the Russians did nuclear testing down there. They wanted to build fallout shelters for nuclear warfare and there is all this weird shit that goes on.

Were you ever scared?
You have to be careful. For instance, I was filming with prostitutes and one hid from her pimp so she could escape to Paris. They came after her with guns and it was not a safe situation to be in. These are Bulgarian pimps that talk Turkish, basically Muslim, and they come with their women to make money. So it is an economic reality for them.

Who are they making money from?
Truck drivers and policemen and people who are driving from the East to West or vice versa. There is literally fifty, sixty, seventy women working the highway there and they charge the equivalent of $10 for a session. They go into the trucks or into the bushes and have sex, and that's how they make their money. They usually have between five and fifteen customers a day. And they make much more money doing that than working in their hometown.

Did you come across the idea of Hitler's Highway after Boot Factory?
When I was doing *Boot Factory*, I went to the biggest rock'n'roll festival in Poland. There

were 250,000 people there. I went to the festival because the boot guys were selling their boots there, and it was on the way that I discovered this road and decided to make *Hitler's Highway*.

This road is divided and the mafia runs different portions of it. If you are a pimp and you have three women, you pay the mafia to have three women there working. During the day you have Bulgarian women; at night you have Russian, Ukraine and Polish women working. So you have different pimps, and the pimps have to pay the mafia for a section of road, and the women have to pay the pimps, and so on down the line, and then they pay out the cops. So it's like this whole infrastructure that is built around making money.

It's a fairly large economy. The important thing is whether they are criminals or not and I would argue that not all of them are criminals. These are essentially people who are escaping from reality and don't know what to do with their lives.

Tell me about this festival you attended

All Polish rock'n'roll bands. It was a three-day festival and they had bands from noon until 4 AM. They had a line up of about forty bands per day, everything from hardcore to eighties influenced music, pop, sixties Woodstock music. A lot of hardcore music. A lot of punk music.

THIS PAGE AND NEXT
Boot Factory

Are you a fan of punk music?

I am a fan of it to the degree that it has a vitality to it. I can't say that I listen to it all the time. There's a little bit of it played in *Boot Factory* — you can hear it in the background. Some of the better groups will mix in a little bit of reggae, a little bit of heavy metal. So it's still vital and perhaps more vital than it is in the West. In the East they are playing it because they really need to have this kind of music-activity going on in their lives, whereas in the West it's like a product.

One thing that is really interesting with this rock'n'roll are the lyrics. You know the rock is the beat, but the lyrics are… in the East there is a longer tradition of poetry, of literature and they bring some of that into their lyrics. What they are expressing is very

important because they are expressing how they are feeling. You have a lot of Western influence coming in very quickly and a lot of people are angry about it. These songs are basically influenced by punk music from the West, but they are singing about their own problems in the East.

How did the Boot Factory happen?

I went to Krakow to an underground film festival where I showed some of my films. I showed a working copy of the Johnny Thunders movie, plus I showed *D.O.A.* The guys who came to see these movies were all fans of the Sex Pistols, and as soon as I met them I realised that I should make a film about them. They told me the story about the boots. We connected because primarily I could speak Polish, but also because we were both fully into the music, into rock'n'roll and into punk. And because I was into punk and had made a film about the Sex Pistols I quickly became friends with them in a way that an outsider couldn't be friendly with them. I actually hired a couple of Polish camera people to work with me in the beginning and on the first night of shooting they actually beat the camera crew up. So I decided to film the entire film by myself with one assistant.

They beat them up?

I had hired Polish cameraman who basically kind of looked down on them. These guys are blue collar and the guys that I hired were middle to upper middle class people who went to university, So there was this clash and the boot guys immediately just jumped on them. One guy was beaten pretty badly.

The people in Boot Factory appear to be caught in a time warp with their fashion and music

Its weird. You can't call it a time warp because it's just a different type of reality. And this was interesting to me. When I first saw them I thought "Wow, where am I!" I myself thought I was in a time warp! But you get an understanding that they are just living out a certain period that they were not able to live out before. They are really into this music.

There are other types of music that are very popular in Poland — you know, the kind of music that plays on the radio in England — but these guys are still trying to push their own thing.

So, it's a resistance to Eminem, Limp Biskit and other MTV type music?
Absolutely. But you know, all over Europe there are a lot of pockets of this type of music — in France, in Spain... These guys were listening to a lot of Spanish and Italian punk music.

How long was it into the filming of Boot Factory before you realised you were making another movie about the destructive powers of heroin?
This was an unpleasant surprise for me. When I started making the movie I kind of realised that there were some problems going on, as there always seems to be with young people like that. But I didn't realise that heroin was going to play such a big part in the film. When

I look back it doesn't surprise me, because somehow rock'n'roll and the people that I am drawn to always have these kind of elements.

I get to Poland and take a cab to the boot factory and they tell me that Wojtek was strung out on heroin. So I immediately grab another cab and I found him in a hallway copping very awful Polish heroin, which is very strong. So here I am in a hallway with him shooting up, and people are looking at us, blood all over the place. At that moment it really drained me. I felt that "Here I am again". I could have been in London or New York or Paris in some other building, but it was exactly the same paradigm and it was difficult. I had to work my way out of it. But I didn't want to make the film into a heroin story — I had to make it as honest as I could, and I did.

I think that the guys in *Boot Factory* are struggling. There are social problems, economic problems and price problems, but I didn't want to show them in the film. I wanted the film to be a real microcosm of what's going on. A lot of the time, filmmakers go to

Johnny Thunders in *Born To Lose*
NEXT PAGE Posters for earlier Kowalski films

eastern Europe or some exotic culture and they make these films that show the 'greater reality', and I find that really boring because they are just lies. I just want to go as deep as I can. And the new film, *Hitler's Highway* is a much bigger picture. I show the greater culture and hopefully balance the culture.

How much do you think that banality contributes to documentary filmmaking?

I know what you are talking about. It's an interesting question. As a film progresses you have to have banal moments so that the other moments stand out. I think that this is where the art of film making comes in. You make the story of the film move forward by creating all these elements together. Banality is really important because it's a way of pacing the film. One thing I don't like is when documentaries are cerebral. I'm not talking about intellectual or intelligent but rather 'thinking in dialogue'. I like to make films where people can feel something emotionally — and you need banality to feel something because the greater part of life is banal. What I try to

do with these films is find people who are struggling with banality. I think the characters that I choose may have problems, but their biggest struggle is with banality.

How do you feel about the rise of the docu-soap culture?

What has happened is that capitalist ideas have been incorporated into our culture to the point where we no longer know what is real and what is not real. Television is basically about selling a product. Everything is a product in life right now, and reality has become a product.

All these television programs are eavesdropping, and it's forcing people to look at something that is unreal. That, I think, is ultimately very destructive. I know that all over the world for the last thirty years people have been watching TV shows, people all over the world watching people with refrigerators and big cars in all these soap operas. And all these TV shows have ruined the minds of the people in the Third World countries. You can draw a parallel between that and the new kind of reality in these TV programmes. And what

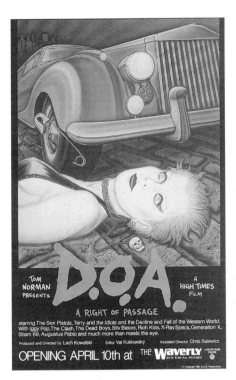

is going to happen is that these reality shows will have to get more outrageous because people are just going to get bored of them. The underpinnings of all these reality shows is sex and money. It's pathetic.

Why is heroin an integral part of rock'n'roll?

You know, that is a question that I have been thinking about for years. If you go into rock'n'roll you are going to take on all the good and bad things that rock'n'roll has to offer, and sometimes the good may actually be the bad. I will leave it at that.

Why do you consider your Johnny Thunders film to be the 'last rock'n'roll movie'?

I wanted to be provocative with it in one aspect, but in another aspect I wanted to depict how Johnny Thunders' lived, and how he fits into the history of rock'n'roll. All rock'n'roll rebellion from Johnny back to Elvis Presley has a certain naïveté to it —I'm not being derogatory; it's healthy. I think we have outgrown that kind of naïveté. We will

never be able to have that kind of rock'n'roll again. The next stage of rebellion to come will have another aspect to it, it will be naïve in another way but it will never be exactly the same as thirty or forty years ago.

A recent article in Blueprint magazine argued that there is no generation gap and this is stifling youth rebellion.

This is the new youth culture, and I think one of the big things that Johnny had to struggle with was that he had to figure a way to age gracefully. It's very hard to age gracefully. I know that because I have to age gracefully and I think about it a lot. How do you age gracefully? You can't wear the same fashions because you look like an idiot and you can't have your hair style the same way as you used to as a teenager. But how do you progress?

Invasion on Hitler's Highway — commissioned by Luciano Rigolini for La Lucarne on Arte, produced by Blanche Guichou for Agat Films — premiered at the tenth Raindance Film Festival in October 2002. Details: www.raindance.co.uk

Thanks to Dominic Thackray and Raindance for supplying all images used in this interview.

culture GUIDE

edited by Micky Murphy

Josh Simmons'
God is Happy
See page 135

BRUTARIAN 34
84pp $5 / Order from: PO Box 210,
Accokeek, MD 20607, USA

This is a well-established alternative culture mag, put out quarterly by one Dom Salemi, and offering a mixed bag of reviews, interviews, fiction and comics. Specifically, this issue contains, amongst other things, some pretty good comics (I particularly liked *Gaylord Frigg's Book Nook* by Johnny Ryan — a witty way of dealing with the zine reviews), a short story by Graham Joyce and a couple of opinion columns. There are book reviews featuring Robert Anton Wilson and Alex Toth, DVD reviews of films like *Teenage Gang Debs, Night of the Living Dead, Who Saw Her Die?* and *The Curious Dr Humpp*, and reviews of music from the likes of Lunachicks, Swell Maps and Rocket From The Crypt. There are also interviews with genre fiction author Joe Lansdale, rockabilly chanteuse Wanda Jackson and The Ubangis, trash rockers who must get sick of being compared to The Cramps, and who may be familiar to some of you as suppliers of soundtrack music for a number of Jess Franco's recent productions (*Lust For Frankenstein, Vampire Blues, Blind Target*). The highlight of this issue for me, though, is Holly Day's (yeah, right) interview with the world's oldest toddler, Iggy Pop. If there is a more entertaining human than Iggy anywhere on the face of the planet, I'm unaware of the fact, and he consistently gives good interview:

MAYBE GOD IS A GIANT ROACH IN THE SKY THAT IS ACTUALLY CONTROLLING WHAT WE THINK AND RUNS THE UNIVERSE, AND THIS ROACH HAS A PLAN FOR ME, JUST KEEPS DECIDING, 'IT'S NOT TIME TO KILL OFF IGGY POP YET.'

OK, Iggy, whatever. Or what about this gem from his tour rider:

IGGY HATES WALT DISNEY, SO HE WANTS SEVEN DWARVES DRESSED AS THE SEVEN DWARVES FROM SNOW WHITE TO BE WAITING FOR HIM SO HE CAN TERRORIZE THEM BEFORE THE SHOW.

Brutarian is a satisfying read on a number of (low) levels, and I'm eager to see another issue. Oh, and last but not least, there's a special bonus nude photo of Jennifer Tilly on page three. Schwing!
SIMON COLLINS

BRUTARIAN 35
84pp $2.95 / Order from: PO Box 210, Accokeek, MD 20607, USA

Now that the essential ingredients of 'low brow' or 'trash' culture (as it likes to refer to itself as) have been appropriated by the mainstream, what's left for those who want to feel like they're 'out on the edge'? Either you admit that there is no edge and shamelessly and happily indulge your interests or start immersing yourself further into the nether-regions of Western culture where you are inevitably left with C90's of bad noise made by ugly men in their bedrooms and zines praising Ted Bundy for being a real man.
Brutarian is one of those rare titles that remains outside the mainstream — partly down to production values — but can still provide a thrill for the curious who don't feel their nuts are being cupped by FHM skim-jobs on hot rods or Mexican wrestlers. Don Salemi has managed to keep it and his enthusiasm truckin' down the highway for thirty-five issues which is as solid testament as any to his steely-eyed resolve and unwavering commitment to things that excite and interest him.
On the surface it seems to be predictable enough — Mitch O'Connell cover and interview, Nick Zedd interview (yes, for the thousand, millionth time), obscure horror films — but what saves the title is the healthy attitude and sense of humour displayed by the contributors. The whole exercise buzzes with enthusiasm and a sense of play that make just about everything else look like a list of guests at a funeral. It starts off with an amusingly irreverent Letters Page that features mail from the likes of Mike Tyson, Ariel Sharon, The Pope and even George W himself. From then

on you've got a gist of the tone but it's not all superficial humour — the Mitch O'Connell interviewer actually gets the man to talk about his work and his techniques and doesn't just riff on about 'martini's and floozies and kitsch'. There's a totally unexpected and insightful interview with fifties Country singer Wanda Jackson and an interesting discussion of the snuff issue that comes to pretty much the same conclusions as Messrs. Kerekes & Slater did in *Killing For Culture*. Interspersed are cartoons and artwork that are *not* shit, which is an amazing feat in this day and age, and pages and pages of reviews. In amongst the inevitable coverage of no-hoper punk albums there's plenty of column inches given to smart assessments of Santana Remixes by Bill Laswell, Impulse's recent re-issue of Coltrane's last ever gig, Feral House's *Voluptuous Panic*, a Henry Darger collection, a reissue of Lautremont's *Maldoror* and even Dean R Fucking Koontz! For what is seemingly a 'trash' magazine I came away buzzing with new ideas and new things to seek out. I know the purpose of most modern magazines is partly to act as a kind of catalogue but at least Brutarian has the taste to feature things that the genuinely engaged and curious reader would want to know about. There's something for everyone here and fans of **HEADPRESS** could *not* go wrong in making the effort to get a copy. Fuck it, make it a subscription.
RIK RAWLING

FEAR AND LOATHING 53 *&* 54
32pp £1 / Order from: Andy P, PO Box 11605, London E11 1XA / andyfnl@dircon.co.uk

For many years now Andy Pearson (or "Pigswill" to give him his 'punk zine writer' name) has been putting this little mag out, and for many years now it's changed nary a jot. For your pound you will get details of where Andy's been, what friends he's met, what bands he's seen, reviews of the records he's bought... you get Andy's diary, basically. His taste has stood still too, scared to move lest any musical development of the past decade might catch his eye. The cut 'n' paste layout and dodgy printing should give it away... that's right, Andy likes Punk, and if you don't like Punk — well then mister, don't read his magazine. He spends most editorials bellyaching about the fact that

over the past twenty years punk has been watered down and co-opted by market forces and is now a style choice rather than a state of mind. Good point, Andy. He clearly sees himself as Hunter S Thompson with a Ramones collection, but unfortunately neither his prose nor his life is that interesting. Andy probably means well (though an acquaintance of his tells me he's a tight git) but his writing style dies on the page. Take his review of *Magnolia*: "The movie is pretty good. I really enjoyed it. The only problem is I didn't realise how long it was — three hours!"
Is this all he has to say about one of the most complex, emotionally wrenching American films of the past ten years? That it's too long? His music reviews are similarly lamebrained — either "it's punk and it rocks!" or, "It's lame indie shite!". He's enthusiastic to be sure and *Fear and Loathing* features the odd subject of note (The Residents, Penelope Houston, Mick Mercer), but his writing lacks any real flair or passion. He harks on about a past now long dead, oblivious to the fact that a live DJ set by the likes of Billy Nasty or Laurent Garnier — in the appropriate atmosphere and with the appropriate medication — is harder, more intense and more relevant than any of the twentieth generation punk dolts he worships. As a primer for culture beyond the mainstream this rag might lead some sixteen year old Limp Bizkit fan in a positive direction, but it serves little other purpose. ANTON BLACK

L'HORREUR EST HUMAINE 3 *& 4*
Ed. Sylvain Gérand
124pp & 60pp Eur 8 (incl p&p) / 26, rue du Tapis Vent, 79500, Melle, France

This is the kind of curious publication that can only exist on the continent — an independent zine compiling a variety of art. Not having seen issues one or two of *L'Horreur est humaine*, I can't say how they compare or whether there is a theme running throughout, but No 4 is presented as a fake medical dictionary (in that all the entries and ailments are fictitious), while No 3 is comprised almost entirely of drawings. Despite the fact that I really like the idea of a fake medical dictionary, I actually prefer the text-free latter — primarily because my French isn't good enough to sustain my interest in the wordy

PAPERBACK DUNGEON

No 4 (the text of which looks to have been printed at the wrong resolution anyway), but also because the selection of drawings in No 4 are, by comparison, much more fragmented and less satisfying. Like I said, a curious thing. DAVID KEREKES

ULTRA VIOLENT 4
Horror & Exploitation Cinema
Ed. Scott Gabbey

72pp $4.95 / UV Magaine, PO Box 110117, Palm Bay, FL, 32911-0117, USA / info@uvmagazine / www.uvmagazine.com

With a title like *Ultra Violent* you probably have a good idea that this isn't a magazine for fans of Hollywood musicals. What it does have is a bunch of interviews with the likes of filmmakers Olaf Ittenbach (*Premutos*), Roger Watkins (*Last House on Dead End Street*), Jean Rollin (*Living Dead Girl*), Fred Dekker (*Night of the Creeps*), novelist Jack Ketchum (*Off Season*), and choreographer-turned-director Busby Berkeley (*Gold Diggers of 1935*). Okay, I was kidding about the last one. DAVID KEREKES

UNRATED 1
Cinema of the eXtreme
Ed. Carl T Ford

42pp £5.95 / Unrated Press, 142 Hounslow Road, Feltham, Middlesex, TW14 0BA / carl@unrated.co.uk

This is a new publishing venture devoted to critically ignored cinema. Admirable and slick, it has one or two genuine curios up its sleeve, including an interview with Joe Christ (whose name was familiar to the pages of the long-gone *Film Threat Video Guide* and little else) and articles on the likes of Lech Kowalski's *Gringo*, Francis Von Zerneck's *God's Lonely Man* and Lodge Kerrigan's *Clean, Shaven*. DAVID KEREKES

PAPERBACK DUNGEON
Ed. Justin Bomba

24pp / Available for SAE with two first class stamps and age statement from: J Marriott, Flat 8, 21 Victoria Square, Cliffton, Bristol BS8 4ES (please do not put Paperback Dungeon on envelope)

Paperbacks weren't always an expensive commodity. Back in the seventies, publishers like NEL and Futura (but mainly NEL), were pumping out pulp novels and decidedly curious factual paperbacks for little more than the price of a school dinner. It was always a mystery how the latter ever managed to generate mass interest, dealing, as they invariably did, with end of the world scenarios, black holes, second sight, vampires and other off-kilter subjects.

The fiction titles were a different story — a good deal ended up in the schoolyard, with the authors of choice tending to be James Herbert or Guy N Smith (moving further north of England, I am reliably informed it was Sven Hassel and his WWII tales). Common to them all was the purple prose; long descriptions of steamy sex and brutal violence.

It is difficult to envisage James Herbert's *The Fog* ever making it into W H Smith nowadays. Indeed it's probably amazing that it ever made it onto the high street *back then*, given the twisted and relentless nature of its set-pieces. The book simply doesn't let up for a moment, and while the accolades bestowed on Herbert as an author have increased over the years, he has never tried to emulate the accelerated sex and violence of *The Fog*.

But the book was a bestseller, as indeed were many of the other pulp paperbacks of the day. And it is in homage to them that we come to *Paperback Dungeon*, a free — yes, free — zine from the Justin Bomba stable of publications. There are overviews of pulp authors Guy N Smith and Sven Hassel, as well as articles on popular genres such as the Frankenstein Monster revival and

the Kung Fu series of books from the seventies. Also from the same era is the inflammatory 'plantation-ploitation' novel (*Black Stud* or *Slave's Revenge* anyone?), which gets an all-too brief 'appreciation' here of under two pages. *Paperback Dungeon* is rounded out with reviews of several tawdry novels, including Pierce Nace's *Eat Them Alive*, Mark Ronson's *Ogre*, and M E Knerr's *Sasquatch*. (Pseudonyms anyone?) It's far more entertaining reading *about* this stuff now than it is reading the stuff itself. DAVID KEREKES

GOD IS HAPPY!
12pp
UGLY CUNT FUCK
24pp
ALL ABOUT FUCKIN'
44pp
Josh Simmons
www.knownothingfamily.org /
christmuffins@hotmail.com

These three independently produced dinky comic books showcase the artistic talents of one Josh Simmons. I suspect that *God is Happy* is the earliest of the comics, given the obsessive detail in the art work and the fact that the whole thing has been trimmed to size using hand scissors. It is a psychedelic manifestation of the familiar Jack T Chick school of Bible Bashing. But here the morality has been replaced with the promise that you, the reader, are happy. The penmanship is pretty amazing. Different in tone and artistic style is Simmons' *Ugly Cunt Fuck*, which features several short tales, each with a sentiment as mindless as *God Is Happy* — except that here it's taken to a different extreme. Everybody in *Ugly Cunt Fuck* hates one another (and themselves), and the stories are a relentless, vitriolic preamble with beatings, rape, torture, murder and suicide. The panels are very bold with plenty of black, and the overall look is akin to a more harder-edged Chester Brown. The final comic, *All About Fuckin'*, is different again, in that the panels comprise of staged photographs with crude pen-and-ink drawings on top. The stories are a rather extreme interpretation of — well, figure it out — with women getting it on with Lovecraftian like creatures in several of the strips, and what appears to be an act of genuine bestiality between a man and a dog in another. While *All About Fuckin'* may

be lacking the penmanship of the former two titles, I'm very much intrigued as to what Simmons could possibly do next. DAVID KEREKES

EXTREME ISLAM
Anti-American Propaganda of Muslim Fundamentalism
Ed. Adam Parfrey
ISBN 0922915784 / pb / 317pp $16 / Feral House 2001 / PO Box 13067 Los Angeles, CA 90013 / www.feral house.com

It is the age of the virtual state, where a handful of demagogues can beam their incantations around the world, a magic of speed and fire with the power to command workers to jump from the summits of their cities. The impact on WTC Towers One and Two, like tuning forks of steel and glass, will echo for ages to come.
How did this happen? What brewed in the minds of the men who inspired these acts? This book now means that no English speaker has an excuse to be ignorant. Here is a window inside the Jihad: its justifications, its reasoning, its edicts and epistles, its replies to correspondents. And words direct from the mouths of those arch-nemeses of the moment: Bin Laden, Saddam, 'the one-eyed' Mullah Omar, Colonel Quadaffi, and the forbears who inspired them with their words, the first weapons of any spiritual war.
The concise extract from *The Neglected Duty*, 'The Book that Killed Anwar Sadat and inspired Bin Laden's Holy War' makes its point. A list of restrictions imposed by the Taliban makes for grim reading. The axis is on the political tracts rather than the religious, so don't expect to be stupified by theological pin-head dancing. The meat of the book is arguments, cogently thought out and more often than not, expressed with grace. The final section dealing with Al Queda is the most intense. Bin Laden's 1998 fatwa. Transcription of an interview with Mullah Omar, pulled from the airwaves on the recommendation of the NSC, America's 'invisible' listening agency. How to make poison from Castor Beans, yum. How to survive an interrogation — what they'll do, how to use strategies such as pretending the pain is worse than it really is, no heroic posturings in this first-hand advice. And in the days leading up to the September hijackings, the actual mental disciplines the holy warrior must stay true

to in order to fulfil the words of his masters. Recovered by the FBI, these letters were left by hijackers on three of the four September flights. Even until the moment the aircraft merges with nature, each second is proscribed in word, from protection-breathing spells, recitations, and points of main actions, until the hijacker will hear every creature in the universe singing sweet songs to his deeds. This song to suggestion is the Rosetta Stone of the mentality of those who did and would again go to a joyful death in the skies, with no word or thought spared for any other soul but their own. In Death's Comely Reward we see the delights awaiting the suicide bomber — a pornucopia of girls with transparent bodies. 'The marrow of her bones is visible like the interior lines of pearls and rubies.' She looks like 'red wine in a white glass' and her shin marrow is 'visible to the eyes, and whose large breasts 'are not inclined to dangle.' She does not perform any bodily function (other than fucking, we assume). And surprise, surprise, the girl does not have to wear a veil or be covered by anything other than transparent skin, which sounds less like the ultimate vision of carnal sport than something Herschell Gordon Lewis would cook up. Maybe the translator missed a few points.
For those not blessed with the creatures of paradise, the final section is an uproarious vision of The Infidel Hell, painted with a surrealist distortion of human bodies, scales, and demonically cunning torments. The blasphemers have their tongues stretched out for up to nine miles and on every inch dances a demon. In another banquet of torments the damned are hungry, so they are given *Zaqqum*, a thorny plant which would get stuck in their throats. Now crying for water, they are given boiling water from another level of hell, thus being scaled to death, regenerated, then subjected to it all over again, ad infinitum. The boiling water is put to many good uses in other regions where an 'extreme sport' twist is added. 'In hell,' we are told, 'the part between the shoulders of an infidel would be equal to a distance of three days' journey, by a horse rider. His jawbone would be as big as the mountains of Uhud and the thickness of his skin would come to a distance which can be covered in three days.' (One demon lord's plan

to build a resort complex in this remote outpost is expected to provide a full range of facilities, including giant octopus-infested swimming pools. And yea!, it will have all the channels with full live coverage of all Hell's major events, such as TERRORISTS EXPLODE 'DIRTY BOMB' MADE OF BIBLES, and SHAITAN DECLARES ONE FEMTOSECOND RELIEF FROM TORMENT, INSTANTLY RESCINDS IDEA AS 'TOO GENEROUS.')

As well as the fascinating text, the pictures are worth mentioning. Eight pages of colour photographs showing anti-Zionist cartoons, stamps, and posters, plus Iranian and Iraqui currency, printed large… enough to permit forgery. Wait, Feral House a CIA-affiliated company? Perish the thought! The B&W pictures shows pages from a pro-Palestinian 'martyrs handbook' quality anti-superpowers cartoons, and loads of others including a raffish shot of Colonel Qaddafi and the Taliban execution of a woman. A four page final glossary contains dozens of Arabic words pertaining to sex, religion, and ritual. Every page of this book contains interest. Parfrey has done another outstanding trawl of data, presented here in its bare face and without a distorting commentary. With *Extreme Islam*, Feral House maintains its reputation as the most courageous and incendiary publisher in the US.
JEREMY GLOVER

DEEPENING WITCHCRAFT
Grey Cat
ISBN 1550224956 / pb / 359pp $19.95 / ECW Press 2002

MAGICKAL WEDDINGS
Joy Ferguson
ISBN 1550224611 / pb / 185pp $21.95 / ECW Press 2001

PHILOSOPHY OF WICCA
Amber Laine Fisher
ISBN 1550224875 / pb / 268pp $19.95 / ECW Press 2002

WITCHCRAFT AND THE WEB
M Macha Nightmare
ISBN 1550224662 / pb / 271pp $16.95 / ECW Press 2001/ www.ecwpress.com

---

I would like to be as kind as possible to ECW Press, after all we're not all cut out for descending into the underworld of the Tunnels of Set, or conjuring the malevolent automata inherent in Austin Spare's system of sentient sigils, are we? Even so, it's difficult to relate to the mind-numbing New Age quality of these books which are ostensibly about witchcraft and magick (spelled with a 'k', no less, as if in homage to the profound system devised by Aleister Crowley!) but seem so saccharine and homespun that it's mortally difficult not to discount them as twaddle, without even getting past the pastel shaded covers! That being said (though I can't understand why anyone over ten years old would want to call themselves Grey Cat), *Deepening Witchcraft* is a fairly sensible read, in the present context, offering some reasonably well argued insights into the group structuring of Wicca. Similarly, Amber Fisher's shorter *Philosophy of Wicca* is basically sound, if far from inspired. The less said about the other two volumes, the better! All in all, though there seems to be a lack of good, balanced material on the occult these days, with more and more commercialised recycled rubbish filling the shelves, I can't in all honesty recommend these books from ECW as a viable alternative.
STEPHEN SENNITT

FASTING ON SPAM
& other non-aligned diets for our electronic age
Stewart Home
ISBN 0954006313 / pb / 56pp £3.75 / Sabotage Editions 2002 / BM Senior, London WC1N 3XX

Back when I was at uni, I would find myself at those typical undergraduate parties where a wide array of humanity would gather to get completely maggotted. Without fail, there would be a type who I came to identify as the Philosophy Bore. I won't bother with a detailed physical description because that would be petty, but suffice to say the Philosophy Bore would be there, red wine in hand, spluttering about Foucault and making everyone within a six foot radius feel like vomiting on him. Stewart Home, I suspect, was also aware of the Philosophy Bore, and was taking copious notes. *Fasting on Spam*, a collection of articles, reviews and interviews, has some good moments and there is no doubt that Home has a many interesting ideas, but his prose can be completely indigestible. Yes, yes, I know that the bad style is his thing, it's part of his grand plan as agent provocateur of the arts world, but you would have to be a serious devotee to make it through these fifty-six pages. Predictably, vacuous Gen Xer that I am, I found the articles already published in the mainstream press the most interesting — read he had a word limit, a focus and an editor. I was also delighted to see him desecrating the shrine of Patti Smith, but the extended theoretical rambles left me cold. Parody is like walking a tightrope, and unfortunately Mr Home often just ends up sounding like the Philosophy Bores he seeks to subvert. NORA CHOP

INAPPROPRIATE BEHAVIOUR
Ed. Jessica Berens & Kerri Sharp
ISBN 1852426853 / pb / 271pp £10.99 $15.00 / Serpent's Tail 2002 / www.serpentstail.com

---

Who could resist a cover depicting sexy red devil girls licking ice creams in the bowels of Hell? Well, not me anyhow. After such a visual treat it's not exactly all down hill from here, but just about, as the texts comprising this anthology of mad scribblings by self-confessed Bad Grrrls do on the whole tend to be too flippant to be as irreverent as they would like to be, and too insubstantial to really grab the attention fully. However, with a list of contents as diverse as this (Satanism, matricide, guns, anti-Jennifer Anniston beauty tips, etc) there's bound to be something to appeal, and for me it's Penny Birch's Lovecraft-inspired essay, 'Squiddly Diddly' (honest) mentioning good old Cthulhu and his minions, and even the obscure booklets issued by occult group, the Esoteric Order of Dagon. Go on, give it a go! STEPHEN SENNITT

SEXUALITY, MAGIC & PERVERSION

FRANCIS KING

THE MAMMOTH BOOK OF WOMEN WHO KILL
Ed. Richard Glyn Jones
ISBN 1841193887 / pb / 558pp £7.99 / Constable Robinson 2002 / www.constablerobinson.com

Back at the dawn of recorded history, when I was at university studying literature, it became necessary for me to write a couple of dissertations. Being a **HEADPRESS** kind of guy, I decided that one of my dissertations would be about the symbolism of dismemberment in western literature, and I spent a happy few weeks reading authors like Edgar Allen Poe, Alfred Jarry, Joe Orton and of course the Marquis de Sade. I also read, for comparative purposes, a lot of true crime accounts. Some of these were classics of the genre like Brian Masters' *Killing for Company* and Flora Rheta Schreiber's *The Shoemaker*, but others were, I must confess, just what

I happened to find at charity shops and on market stalls. Thus, it came to pass that I became one of what must surely be a very select band of people to have cited *The Mammoth Book of Murder* in an academic paper. Amazingly, the university authorities let me graduate anyway. Years have passed and here I am, writing about *The Mammoth Book of Murder*'s sister volume. There are quite a number of these *Mammoth* books now, covering topics as diverse as chess, erotica, the SAS and UFOs, though disappointingly there doesn't seem to be a *Mammoth Book of Mammoths* yet.

The *Mammoth* books I've seen all follow a similar format — big doorstops of books, formed from many short chapters by many different authors, in the case of *Women Who Kill*, forty-nine chapters by thirty-four authors (including J Edgar Hoover,

who writes about Ma Barker). All your old favourites are here — Myra, Lizzie, Rosemary — though at three to fifty pages a pop, many of the chapters are too short to really give you much insight into the often complex and fascinating cases they describe. What is surprising, given the number of different authors involved, is the uniformly terrible quality of the prose — a breathless tabloid style is favoured, which is often replete with howlers and inaccuracies. Consider this representative opening from Dorothy Dunbar's chapter on Lizzie Borden:

FOR SHEER ALPINE ALTITUDE IN THE ILLUSTRATIVE PEAKS OF CRIME, THE BLOOD-STAINED PALM GOES TO MISS LIZZIE BORDEN OF FALL RIVER, MASSACHUSETTS, AND HER INSEPARABLE SYMBOL, THE HATCHET.

The author then goes on to inform us that "it was written literally in blood that Miss Emma and Miss Lizzie were inheritors of $175 000 each." Really?! Literally? Miss Borden is eventually delivered to a truly Lovecraftian fate: "Did the bloodstained images of Second Street ever gibber idiotically at her memory? Did the wet footprints of the past walk through her mind?" There's a whole lot of idiotic gibbering going on, that's for sure. You can see that your chances of gleaning much information about any particular crime are pretty slim. Despite the size of this book, it's aimed at people with short attention spans — one of the shorter chapters might just about while away a visit to the loo or a bus ride. You'd do better to invest in a book covering just one of these cases in a lot more depth.
SIMON COLLINS

THE SEXUAL CRIMINAL
A Psychoanalytical Study
J Paul De River
ISBN 0965032426 / pb / 448pp £13.99 / Bloat

A sleazy-as-hell-epic of sexual degradation courtesy of J Paul De River, the founder — in 1937 — and director of the Sex Offense Bureau of the LAPD. In a lengthy biographical introduction Brian King offers a portrait of De River, who emerges as an archetypal noir figure, a man who wanted to examine every sex-freak, sicko, pervert, and deviant arrested in order to catalogue all the moral

offences in LA, and create a kind of legitimate psychopathological *One Hundred and Twenty Days of Sodom*. Working with the LAPD, De River had exclusive access to the human cesspool he desired, and freedom to indulge in his psychological fascinations. In the end — like a character from a pulp novel — De River tried to 'fix' his 'theories' a little too much and got willingly dragged into the Black Dahlia mystery, from which he was unable to fully extricate himself. In the following scandal numerous untruths were exposed and De River's tenure at the Sex Offense Bureau was over. However, despite this, De River was able to write and publish his 'research' in *The Sexual Criminal* in 1949. De River's fascinations, as articulated in *The Sexual Criminal*, reveal two basic elements. The first is a clear realisation of Foucault's nosological gaze as articulated in *The History of Sexuality* and *Power / Knowledge*. The second element De River's work reveals is that his fascination with the sexual abnormalities of criminals, and sexual crimes in particular, was particularly voyeuristic. To these ends *The Sexual Criminal* presents the reader with crime scene photos, descriptions of victim's wounds, descriptions of the criminal physiognomy, and reprinted Q&A sessions between Paul De River and criminal. This is an incredible book, reading it you enter a world where no one comes up smelling of roses — just rotting flesh and disinfectant.
JACK SARGEANT

SEXUALITY, MAGIC & PERVERSION
Francis King
ISBN 0922915741 / pb / 208pp $16.95 £12.99 /
Feral House 2002 / www.feralhouse.com

Damn, with a title like this how can you go wrong? Those are three of my favourite things, right there. And when you open the book and find that Chapter One is called 'A Dildo for a Witch'... well, that doesn't hurt either.
In fact, I was particularly happy to get a review copy of this book — *Sexuality, Magic & Perversion* was originally published in 1971 and has been out of print for decades, with second-hand copies fetching silly money. I used to own a tatty old paperback copy, but I lent it to someone and never saw it again. Thank you, Feral

House, for making this book available again! *Sexuality, Magic & Perversion*'s cult reputation rests on its status as a fairly innovative and ground-breaking work. The late Francis King was a well-respected authority on the occult and author of other works such as *Ritual Magic in England*, *The Magical World of Aleister Crowley* and *Satan and Swastika*. In the late sixties, he shrewdly judged that the British public was ready, indeed eager, to hear about the extensive links between sex, magic and the history of witchcraft. *Sexuality, Magic & Perversion* is not a scholarly tome but a popular history, and it covers a lot of ground, from the pagan orgies of the ancient Greeks to the sacramental shagging of the Fraturnitas Saturni, a particularly dour-sounding German wing of the OTO (Ordo Templi Orientis) who swapped sexual positions according to the alignments of the zodiac. In between, we learn about such disparate topics as the supposed medieval witch-cult and the actual modern one, the Black Masses celebrated in seventeenth-century France by the Marquise de Montespan, mistress to Louis XIV, the Rosicrucians, the Knights of the Garter (was the Garter actually a sanitary towel?!), and the Knights Templar with their Baphomet worship and their *osculum infame*, eastern traditions such as the left-hand path of Tantra and Chinese sexual alchemy, Jayne Mansfield and Anton LaVey's Church of Satan, Wilhelm Reich's orgone energy and the Theosophist chicken-hawk Charles Leadbeater. And of course, there's plenty about the Old Crow himself, Aleister Crowley, who scandalised polite society during the first half of the twentieth century and got lumbered with the sobriquet 'The Wickedest Man in the World' for generally carrying on like an moderately dissolute rock star seventy years before Led Zeppelin existed. Incidentally, I was amused recently to see that Crowley appeared in a list of one hundred Great Britons voted for by BBC viewers!
A panoply of rare photos and illustrations, as well as lengthy quotations from obscure volumes you and I are unlikely ever to see, increase the worth of this book to occult researchers. Inevitably though, it shows its age a little, not only in King's rather sniggering attitude, but also in what is not mentioned. There is nothing

about Chaos Magic, TOPY or the satanic ritual abuse myth, for instance, though all of these have been important in the history of sex magic in recent years. Still, even with these limitations, *Sexuality, Magic & Perversion* is a minor classic. And it's hard to dislike an author who includes footnotes like this:

I, ALTHOUGH NOT POSSESSED BY A SPIRIT, NOT ONLY INSULT MY FRIENDS BUT SMOKE THEIR CIGARETTES, FILCH THEIR DRINK AND EVEN SELL MALICIOUS STORIES ABOUT THEM TO THE EDITOR OF PRIVATE EYE.

I feel that after whetting your appetites for this book, it's only fair to provide an extract for your edification and delight. So here you go — this is from a speech made by the god Mercury during an invocation performed by Aleister Crowley and Victor Neuberg in Paris in 1914:

EVERY DROP OF SEMEN WHICH HERMES SHEDS IS A WORLD. THE TECHNICAL TERM FOR THIS SEMEN IS KRATOS... PEOPLE UPON THE WORLDS ARE LIKE MAGGOTS UPON AN APPLE, ALL FORMS OF LIFE BRED BY THE WORLDS ARE IN THE NATURE OF PARASITES. PURE WORLDS ARE FLAMING GLOBES, EACH A CONSCIOUS BEING... MA IS THE NAME OF THE GOD WHO SEDUCED THE PHALLUS AWAY FROM THE YONI; HENCE THE PHYSICAL UNIVERSE. ALL WORLDS ARE EXCRETA, THEY REPRESENT WASTED SEMEN. THEREFORE ALL IS BLASPHEMY. THIS EXPLAINS WHY MAN MADE GOD IN HIS OWN IMAGE.

Blood sugar, baby, sex magic!
SIMON COLLINS

THE SHINING ONES
The World's Most Powerful Secret Society Revealed
Philip Gardiner
ISBN 9781904126003 / pb / 303pp £12.99 /
Radikal Phase Publishing 2002

A startlingly 'new' hypothesis on the hidden meaning behind hermetic and esoteric symbolism which serves the hypnotic purpose of an all-powerful shadowy elite etc, etc. If this sounds all too familiar, it's because it has been the subject of any number of conspiracy tomes over the years, beginning in 1801 with John Robison's

Proof of a Conspiracy, through the early part of the twentieth-century with Nesta Webster's *Secret Societies and Subversive Movements* (1924) and the pseudonymous *Inquire Within* (ex Golden Dawn cultist Christina Stoddart) with *Light Bearers of Darkness* and *The Trail of the Serpent* in the thirties. In more recent times we have seen a plethora of excellent books on the subject, for example Roberts and Gilbertson's *The Dark Gods* and Michael A Hoffman's exemplary *Secret Societies and Psychological Warfare*. Are any of these genre classics mentioned in the bibliography of Mr Gardiner's stultifyingly condescending book? Of course not! He would have us believe that the conclusions he has drawn from more exoteric works are the product of his own genius for discovering facts which we poor lost souls are unable to fathom!

A ready-made defence has been furnished via the author's assumption that any bad press he's likely to get will be the result of *The Shining*

Ones tampering with the minds of zombified reviewers; which makes Yours Truly nothing less than an unwitting pawn of the Power Elite. Yeah, it's not just because this is the worst example of conceited so-called scholarship I've read for years! Couldn't be that, eh? No, if anyone thinks Mr Gardiner's book is a poorly written load of junk, they must be a zombie! Of course there *is* a shadowy Cryptocracy at the apex of the pyramid; everybody knows that. We don't dislike this book because we disagree with it; we dislike it because, despite the author's claims, he is not telling us anything new. STEPHEN SENNITT

BOB FLANAGAN: SUPERMASOCHIST

Ed. Andrea Juno & V Vale

ISBN 0940642255 / pb / 132pp $16.99 / Juno Books 2000 / www.junobooks.com

Some of you will have seen *Sick*, Kirby Dick's astonishing 1997 film about the life and times of the late Bob Flanagan (he died in 1996). For those who haven't, Bob Flanagan was an American performance and installation artist whose work focused on a) his sexual masochism and b) the cystic fibrosis he suffered from all his life. Cystic fibrosis is a hereditary disease of the pancreas, which is incurable and inevitably terminal — when he died at forty-three, Flanagan was exceptionally old for a CF sufferer. This in itself would make his life remarkable and dramatic enough. What is really extraordinary and inspiring about Bob Flanagan, however, is his decision to, in his own words, 'fight sickness with sickness' and devote what little time he had left to him to sexual deviation of a really extreme nature. Progressing from solitary sickbed experimentation in childhood, through the Californian S&M scene to a 24/7 committed Mistress-slave relationship with his partner Sheree Rose, and ultimately to public performances and exhibitions documenting his sexual practices, Bob Flanagan disarmed moralistic objections to his work and lifestyle with a dry wit and total lack of coyness or guilt about what he was doing. The book *Bob Flanagan: Supermasochist* originally appeared in 1993 under the RE/Search imprint whilst Flanagan was still alive and can thus be seen as a major part of his project of total self-revelation. Flanagan also worked with rock groups Sonic Youth and Nine Inch Nails. He stars in the widely banned *Happiness in Slavery* video (stills from which appear in this book) and it is his screams which punctuate the track *Screaming Slave*.

In his work as a performance artist, Bob Flanagan bears obvious points of comparison with such people as Franko B, whose work also features feats of masochistic endurance and blood-letting related to a traumatic childhood full of religion and clinical interventions, and Ron Athey, who addresses themes of disease, religion and sexuality through grandiose Grand Guignol psychodramas. Both Franko B and Athey, incidentally, are homosexual, thereby providing another connection, via alternative sexualities, to Bob Flanagan. And of course, all these people owe a debt in common to the Viennese Aktionists of the late sixties and early seventies, who set the trend for sexual and visceral extremity in performance

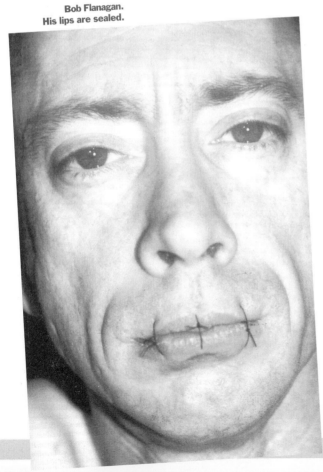

**Bob Flanagan.
His lips are sealed.**

art. Bob Flanagan's work, though, is remarkable for its lack of pretension, its frankness, and its humour. His lack of self-pity in the face of his terrible afflictions was admirable, and his acceptance of his own sexuality remains deeply inspirational for the many people crushed with guilt about their own 'abnormal' urges.

The first thing to strike the casual reader of this book is the photographs. Oh God, the photographs! Don't leave this book lying around where normal people might see it. Page after leg-crossing page shows Bob in postures of a more or less excruciating nature. He is generally naked. His penis is often erect. In the course of *Bob Flanagan: Supermasochist* we see his cock and balls shaved; tightly bound with thongs; padlocked and chained; pierced and bleeding; nailed to boards; covered in wax or clothes pegs; distended with heavy weights; sewn up with surgical sutures; and tattooed with a crown of thorns in a nicely impious gesture reflecting his Catholic upbringing. Didn't his mother ever warn him that it'd be taken off him if he couldn't play nicely?

We see Bob's emaciated and disease-ravaged form suspended in bondage harnesses, tied in a closet (was a guy ever less in the closet?!), whipped, branded, covered in food and paint, cut, hanging upside-down from the ceiling of an art gallery in Santa Monica, in rubber hoods, in hospital gowns, and, above all, in pain. And what's more, he seems to be enjoying every minute of it. As he comments on the eye-watering sensation of hanging a ten pound weight on his scrotum:

I'M IN SEVENTH HEAVEN, STROKING MY STUMP OF A PENIS AS THIS EXCRUCIATING PENDULUM SWINGS BACK AND FORTH BETWEEN MY LEGS, MY FEET PRESSED DEEPLY INTO THE CARPET, BUT I FEEL WEIGHT-LESS, HEAD IN THE CLOUDS, AS HIGH AS A KITE ON A DRUG CALLED PAIN.

Most of us will never get very near experiencing these kinds of things, nor would we all want to, but it sure makes for compelling reading! The bulk of the book consists of six long interviews with Bob and one with Sheree Rose conducted by Andrea Juno and V Vale. The interviews range freely back and forth in time to dis-

cuss his childhood, medical and sexual history, writing, music and performance, and the big-hearted character and engaging personality of the man come over very clearly. I feel the book could have used a tighter edit, though — the discursive to-ing and fro-ing makes the chronological order of events hard to sort out, and the same stories crop up in several chapters. Couldn't these interviews have been conflated into one super-long interview covering everything in order?

A much more serious fault in the book is Juno and Vale's introduction, a truly tendentious piece of PC moralising and white liberal guilt about 'Judeo-Christian brainwashing', 'genociding [sic] indigenous peoples', mad assertions that 'a third of all children have been sexually molested as children' [sic] and so on. How early nineties! A bit of this creeps into Interview Three as well, as Andrea Juno appears to encourage Bob Flanagan to join in with her critique of pioneering modern primitive Fakir Musafar — and this is from the people who published *Modern Primitives*, in which he featured prominently! Talk about biting the hand that feeds you! Apparently Fakir Musafar is guilty of collusion in:

THE INCREDIBLE EGO AND ETHNOCENTRICITY OF AMERICAN WHITE CULTURE TO ACTUALLY THINK THEY HAVE ANY DEEP UNDERSTANDING OF WHAT ANCIENT CULTURES WERE ABOUT, AND THEN TO RIP OUT OF CONTEXT 'NATURAL, PURE, PRIMITIVE' SOCIAL PRACTICES — THAT'S JUST ANOTHER FORM OF COLONIALISATION.

According to this logic, then, Bob Flanagan is more ideologically sound because he references Porky Pig cartoons in talking about his performances rather than the Lakota Sioux! Well, sorry, but I believe we live in a more complex and multilayered world than this kind of callow judgmentalism allows for. I'm also a bit disappointed that this reprint for 2000 hasn't been updated to include events since 1993, notably Flanagan's death in 1996 and the release of *Sick* the following year. It would be interesting to know what Sheree Rose is doing now, and whether Bob Flanagan's work has been exhibited anywhere since his death. (Incidentally, I read an article

by Andreas Whittam-Smith, the erstwhile head of the BBFC, recently, in which he cited *Sick* as the kind of film which demands special consideration from the censor in spite of its explicit content, because it has other socially redeeming virtues.)

These reservations aside, however, *Bob Flanagan: Supermasochist* is a great book — interesting, funny and even (dare I say it?) life-affirming. You will be amazed by what a wholesome experience reading a book crammed with explicit images of genital torture can be! The world is slightly less lively and diverse with his passing:

MINE IS THE BITTERSWEET TALE OF A SICK LITTLE BOY WHO FOUND SOLACE IN HIS PENIS AT A TIME WHEN ALL ELSE CONSPIRED TO SNUFF HIM OUT, OR, AT THE VERY LEAST, FILL HIS MISERABLY SHORT LIFE SPAN WITH MORE THAN ITS SHARE OF PAIN, DISCOMFORT AND HUMILIATION... THAT FIRST SWAT ON THE ASS FROM THE OBSTETRICIAN'S SKILLED HANDS NOT ONLY STARTED MY DISEASED LUNGS SPLUTTERING TO LIFE, BUT IT ALSO SENT A SHOCK WAVE THROUGH MY SPHINCTER, UP MY TINY RECTUM, AND STRAIGHT INTO THE SHAFT OF MY SHINY NEW PENIS, WHICH EVER SINCE THEN HAS HAD THIS CRAZY IDEA IN ITS HEAD THAT SEX AND PAIN WERE ONE AND THE SAME.

SIMON COLLINS

CONSPIRACIES AND COVER UPS
What the Government Isn't Telling You
David Alexander
ISBN 0425183831 / pb / 224pp £5.99 $6.99 / Berkley Books 2000 / www.penguinputnam.com

It's one of those books that can have two different effects on how you perceive it, of course this is depending on what kind of mood or state your head's in. If you're looking for some escapism, great! Knock yourself out as you delve into the sinister plots and twisted turns. Get to grips with Gulf War Syndrome, read the shocking truth about the Kennedy Assassination or ponder the possibilities of an extra terrestrial invasion.

On the other hand you could be thinking, 'How many fucking times do I have to have Roswell rammed down my throat?' You could groan as you're expected to believe dark plans have been drawn up and actioned by Government to control your minds for whatever purpose they see fit.

It's fairy tales for adults and quiet frankly, although sometimes fun to read you can't help but feel a sense of déjà-vu about all these stories. You've heard them before, then again, then one more time.

If you're serious about conspiracies then you need to look further for any truth as the markets are flooded with piss-poor paperbacks, published for the brain dead.

At times you even feel the author is not to sure how to approach his subject. On one hand he can appear dismissive, often poking fun at his own intrigue and then on another he appears seriously affected by his own findings. These moments of insanity are documented at the end of each chapter with his 'Impact Analysis' section, where Alexander has his Jerry Springer style 'final thought', a period for us, the readers, to reflect upon the possible outcome of these oh-so-serious cover ups!

These books are published in abundance and the only true conspiracy that I am really aware of is that these authors are shit but somehow, God knows how, they still get published. WILL YOUDS

TRICKS AND TREATS
Sex Workers Write About Their Clients
Ed. Matt Bernstein Sycamore
ISBN 1560231629 / pb / 202pp £12.99 / Harrington Park Press / 10 Alice St, Binghamton, NY 13904, USA / www.haworthpress.com

A collection of stories and recollections from people who act in porn movies, work in sex shops, hookers, outreach workers (who happen to be hookers), brothel errand boys (sadly I couldn't find the phrase "more pussy lube now" anywhere in this story, but I live in hope) and so on. These tales are interesting, and they do offer a glimpse into the sometimes unpleasant worlds occupied by some sex workers, but there's not enough meat on these bones, the stories are too piecemeal. Anybody who is interested in sex work, pornography, sleaze, depravity and verboten pleasures has already either read bios or met enough sex workers to have heard

dozens of stories. I would have been happier reading a volume about each of the occupations rather than this scattershot collection of what is essentially anecdotes. In fact, if I had to recommend anything it would be the strippers' fanzine *Danzine*, which contains better anecdotes and better advice. Plus, this book has the worst cover I have ever seen. JACK SARGEANT

UNDERWORLD OF THE EAST
James S Lee
ISBN 0953663116 / pb / 170pp £9.99 / Green Magic 2000 / www.greenmagicpublishers.com

Described as a long lost classic of drug literature, this book was first published in 1935. As far as I know this is the first 'official' reprint, though a spiral bound 'pirate' copy was doing the rounds some years ago, complete with semi-defaced library stamps, etc. I wonder whether the extremely knowledgeable Mike Jay, who writes an otherwise first class Introduction, is unaware of this fact, or not... Simply, *Underworld of the East* is a much sought-after tome, the first edition of which often exchanges hands for extortionate prices; that is when it can be found at all. It recounts the first-hand experiences of the author's travels and drug use in the "underworlds, drug haunts and jungles of India, China and the Malay Archipelago". It is clearly written, as most books tend to be from this period, exciting, gruelling and not in the least bit dated. The final revelatory discovery and experiences with mysterious substances in the jungles of Sumatra makes for breathtaking reading. STEPHEN SENNITT

GOTH CHIC
A Connoisseur's Guide to Dark Culture
Gavin Baddeley
ISBN 0859653080 / pb / 288pp £14.99 $19.95 / Plexus 2002 / plexus@plexusuk.demon.co.uk

When this tome arrived on my doorstep my first thoughts were not good. I hated the cover, some back combed, buxom young lass carrying candles and the title *Goth Chic*. I was prepared for the worse. I didn't get it. In fact it was a really entertaining read.

Gavin introduces the book with the aptly named chapter 'What is Gothic?' taking the reader on a brief history tour of all things Gothic from

the Dark Ages to Cher who is apparently flogging off 'heavy yet comfortable medievalised furniture' in her Sanctuary catalogue.

The main text of the book is concerned with Gothic media, an extensive Who's Who in the world of Goth, splitting the chapters between film / television / music and fashion.

The subjects are endless, covering the early works of Poe, de Sade and Shelley through to Clive Barker and Poppy Z Brite. *The Cabinet of Dr Caligari* to *Sleepy Hollow*. *The Munsters* to *Buffy* and Hector Berlioz to Marilyn Manson.

There are lots of great pics, I loved the one of Lon Chaney from the movie *London after Midnight* (now that would have made a great cover) and the Goth fetish wear photos from the Carnival of Souls festival.

Gavin has two other works to his name *Lucifer Rising* and *Dissecting Marilyn Manson* (reviewed in HEADPRESS20 and 21, respectively) — I may have to search them out. Release the bats and remember 'Goth's Undead'. RICK CAVENEY

AMERICAN HARDCORE: A TRIBAL HISTORY
Stephen Blush
ISBN 0922915717 / pb / 336pp £14.99 / Feral House 2001 / www.feralhouse.com

An oral history of US Hardcore punk scene by the man behind *Seconds* magazine. Using first hand interviews Blush examines the heterogeneous world of hardcore, with chapters on pretty much everybody you can imagine (including the excellent Meat Men and No Trend!), and many you can't. Midway through chapter one I was listening to Flipper and Black Flag, something I haven't done for a few years now. That such infectious enthusiasm radiates from every page of this book can only be a good thing. JACK SARGEANT

FUCKED BY ROCK
The Unspeakable Confessions of Zodiac Mindwarp
Zodiac Mindwarp (Mark Manning)
ISBN 1840680261 / pb / 208pp £11.95 / Creation Books 2001 / www.creationbooks.com

Just how is anyone supposed to review a book called *Fucked By Rock*? With a title like that, and chapter headings like 'Bucket of Piss', 'Pothead Wanker', 'Sex and Shit and Rock and

Roll' and the indisputable 'Wives on Tour. Wrong', it renders all attempts at serious critical assessment thoroughly redundant. But here goes anyway.

Released the same week as Victoria Beckham's *Learning to Fly*, this jaw-dropping confessional is the absolute galactic opposite of that hi-profile waste of trees. While Posh is all frocks and bulimic puking, our man Zod is all cocks and honking his ring up before crawling back to the bar. And coming hot on the heels of Motley Crue's *The Dirt* it's a timely reminder that when it comes to squalid indulgence and sociopathic degradation it's the British who can really show those limp-assed Yanks a thing or two about going OTT. Let's face it, we've been doing it for much longer than they have, so much so that the inclination to excess and depravity is ground into our genetic makeup like dogshit on the sole of a combat boot. Dispensing with all notions of accurate reportage and factual veracity, Zod digs deep into his foetid memory banks and retches up whatever he finds. Dates and geographical locations are ignored in favour of an excessive focus on booze, drugs and spectacularly perverted sex. Characters drift in and out of the 'narrative' as Zod regales us with amusing anecdotes, dubious philosophy and the occasional nugget of steel-hard truth, forged in the blistering fires of experience so extreme that most would scarcely dare believe it.

There's no doubt that Zod embellishes the truth somewhat — because no-one outside of the supernatural realm could have done that much fucking and boozing — but, even taking that into consideration, these stories resemble some lost chapter of the Bible. Following his previous book, the loosely-autobiographical *Crucify Me Again* this focuses solely on his life within the band — how he went from paste-up monkey at *Flexipop* magazine to bollock-throbbing Sex Fuhrer to wretch-rocker cautionary tale, in the space of ten years. Interspersed with archive photos of the band in action and gurning for press shots are some truly terrible tales: Z's first outstandingly bad trip on LSD, the band caught in a frenzied peepshow wank odyssey at the Fuckerama in Madrid, walling-up the crusty Mystery Machine tour bus in a blizzard, nearly getting bummed by their sexually insane and homicidal

Falklands veteran tour manager Gimpo, incendiary destruction of recording rooms with fireworks whilst pissed on JD and weapon-grade ganja with Lee Scratch Perry (recruited to remix Back Street Education — just imagine what that would have sounded like!), and the callously casual and systematic sexual and psychological abuse of groupies, girlfriends and grannies everywhere in the Western hemisphere. What becomes clear is that such behaviour would be expected from anyone in the same situation — trawling through the gutter of rock, forced to endlessly tour the arse-end of Europe playing every toilet venue down every shitty back street where even fat ugly Goths wouldn't go for a piss. The crushing horror of their circumstances and the accompanying boredom and frustration of being locked up in a sardine can of a tour bus eventually took its toll: booze and drugs were their iron lung, violence and wanking were an intermittent distraction from the coruscating ennui and any female lovestruck, desperate or insane enough to fall into their orbit were reduced to three holes on legs, essentially toilets for the depositing of bodily waste.

All of this is delivered in the unique Mindwarp gutterspeak that is pitched somewhere between William Burroughs, John Milton and a Leeds United boot boy pissed up and full of brag of a Saturday night. Rarely will you see the word "bugger" used so many times, along with most other expletives from the English lexicon. Buggery is clearly an obsession for the man, but unlike Burroughs, it's not ten-year-old Arab boys arses that are the focus of interest. More likely, and in the man's own words:

PERFUMED PETIT FRENCH ARSES, WINKING DOWN THE PARISIENNE BOULEVARDS. THOSE STATUESQUE DEUTSCHE JACKSIES, TIGHT BROWN SWASTIKAS BEGGING FOR A LITTLE V2 KY ACTION. DELECTABLE, WHOLESOME, SWEDISH ICEFLOWERS, CLEAN AS A WHISTLE. FUNKY, MUSKY, DARK AND DIRTY, THOSE GREASY, HAIRY SPANISH BULLRINGS.

Elsewhere, he admonishes drummer Slam Thunderhide on his towering sexual *faux pas* by shagging a woman in the conventional orifice.

"IT'S BEST NOT TO TAKE ANY CHANCES AT ALL SLAM," I CHIPPED IN, ADDING MY TWO PENNETH TO SLAM'S CRASH COURSE IN HOW TO DEAL WITH THE SYPHILITIC HEAPS THAT WERE GROUPIES. "AND DON'T USE ANY LUBRICATION EITHER, NOT EVEN SPIT, BANG THEM ULTRA FAST IN THE ARSE AND UNLOAD THE NAD JAM AS QUICKLY AS POSSIBLE. THINK OF YOURSELF AS A WWII BOMBER PILOT WHO HAS TO DUMP HIS BOMBLOAD AS SOON AS HE CAN AND THEN HEAD STRAIGHT BACK TO BLIGHTY," I CONTINUED WITH MY SAGE COUNSEL.

Does he really mean it or is it just some dark plateau of black-as-arseholes humour reached only after ten years set adrift on the storm-tossed oceans of Rock oblivion? Certainly the man is damaged by his experience but doesn't waste time pondering the significance of it all — he accepts that women and booze have ruined his chances of leading an 'ordinary' life and simply gets on with doing what he does best.

Other chapters worth a mention include the game of tour bus Cluedo triggered by the discovery of a *verboten* log floating in the chemical toilet, being holed up in Arizona and off their tits on Jack & Charlie with The Cult and The Mission and, most stomach-churningly of all, forever corrupted by a trawl through the darkest recesses of the Reeperbahn that results in the supreme horror that is 'The Choc Vid', of which I will spare you the full details lest anyone be munching on a Mars Bar as they read this. Along with such hilarious anecdotes are scintillating rants against the British establishment, the rock industry (referred to lovingly as 'The Cosmosodomistic Black Gas') and sincere responses to the eerie majesty of the Sistine Chapel and the sublime wonder of the teenage kiss. But you won't be buying the book for airy fairy nonsense like that — you want the filth, you want the sleaze, you want the stench of hogsweat and ball lightning, the feel of greasy bandaged fingers tweaking your prurient nipple — and I'm pleased to report that Zod will satisfy your darkest desires. After you've been *Fucked By Rock* you'll never be the same again. RIK RAWLING

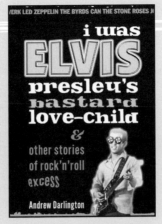

POLITICS OF THE IMAGINATION
The Life, Work and Ideas of Charles Fort
Colin Bennett (Foreword John Keel)
ISBN 1900486202 / pb / 206pp £12.99 $17.95 / Critical Vision 2002 /
www.headpress.com

This is one of the most compelling biographies you will read this year, or any year, for that matter. Despite a massive cultural and ontological presence which grows in stature at an exponential rate, Charles Fort (from whom we derive the word Fortean as a catch-all reference to all kinds of unexplained phenomena) has been the subject of only one previous full-length biographical study, Damon Knight's *Prophet of the Unexplained*, a sterling effort published in 1971, but which is now completely overshadowed by Colin Bennett's definitive and comprehensive overview.

Particularly compelling is Bennett's well-argued opinion that Fort's influence can be recognised to extend far beyond the paranormal / unexplained 'ghetto' with which he is usually exclusively associated, extending into more general culture to sit on a par with recognised cultural architects, such as Charles Darwin, James Joyce, T S Eliot, Henry Ford and Stephen Hawking. In fact, despite my life-long interest in Fort and all sorts of related weirdisms, this was the first time I had been compelled to view Fort in his true light as a really serious major shaper of popular cultural perceptions. If only for this matter, *Politics of the Imagination* is a work that demands to be read. STEPHEN SENNITT

I WAS ELVIS PRESLEY'S BASTARD LOVE-CHILD
Andy Darlington
ISBN 1900486172 / pb / 224pp £13.99 / Critical Vision 2002 /
www.headpress.com

In 1980 I was becoming increasingly fed up with the whole post-punk scene. A mate named Dale who had a dead end carpet cleaning job found an old magazine called *Planet* underneath some scruffy settee, a seemingly trivial incident which for a short time changed my life. The magazine in question comprised a special retrospective on the Fillmore scene of the late sixties, and I was galvanised by a sense of excitement I'd not felt for years! Reading about the halcyon days of rock in such uncritical,

glowing terms presented a viable alternative to that grey, cynical Joy Division scene which only days before had seemed impossible. The roster was certainly impressive by any standards: The Doors, *Anthem of the Sun*-period Grateful Dead, Iron Butterfly, Joplin, Hendrix, Quicksilver Messenger Service, Love, etc, etc.

But what grabbed my attention more than anything else was an atmospheric photo of Jefferson Airplane's Grace Slick — her crazy porcelain doll's face suggesting a strange and frightening sexuality. For the next year or so I ostentatiously rejected the contemporary music scene, in favour of collecting all the early Airplane albums, along with anything else I could lay my hands on from the pages of *Planet*. To say I lived in my own little world, scorning the current scene to the bemusement and irritation of my friends, is no understatement! But like all manufactured paradises my self-imposed exile (ha ha) came to an end with the advent of the realisation that if I kept banging on about 'ancient' groups nobody at the time was interested in, I would never get a girlfriend.

With the passing of time the follies of youth seem strange and difficult to fathom. Only a year or so later, I viewed my exclusionary pose as yet another example of a wilfully contrived and self-indulgent precocity — the unwanted ability to 'get up my own arse' that has haunted my plots and schemes ever since! What I realise now is that all this could have been avoided if there had been a book on the market like Andy Darlington's. Here we have a truly heterogonous mix of musical styles and artists reflecting the mature and considered tastes of a true enthusiast, never hidebound by obsolete questions of genre or category. Essays and interviews range between the manic oddity of Joe Meek, the cybernetic noodling of Kraftwerk and Cabaret Voltaire, the unmitigated pop of Mott The Hoople, the cool salaciousness of Robert Plant, to the manic oddity of Peter Green! Oh, and there's a nice piece on Grace Slick — twenty-two years ago the symbol of my objectless desire... Andy, where was your book when I needed it? Better late than never, I suppose. STEPHEN SENNITT

Both these books can be ordered direct from the publisher. P&P is UK £1.80 each. Or, buy both books and p&p is free. See page 160 for ordering information

COYOTE STAN AMERIKA
The Unspeakable Art & Performances of Reverend Steven Johnson Leyba

Rev Steven Johnson Lebya
ISBN 0867195053 / 178pp $24.95 / Last Gasp 2001 / PO 410067, San Francisco, CA 94141-0067 USA / www.lastgasp.com

I first read about Steven Johnson in HEADPRESS8 (1994) so it's clearly taken a while for him to get his work published, which is hardly surprising really. This is the man who's first collected book of work is entitled *My Stinking Ass* and obsesses to an almost pathological degree on all things anal — shit, rectums and the penetration thereof. Despite wholesome recommendations from the likes of H R Giger and W S Burroughs it was painfully clear he was going to have trouble getting even the most *outré* publishers to take a chance on this potentially 'controversial' work.

Seven years later and here it finally is, though Johnson has hardly been sat on his hands, dreaming about arses. Oh no, the man has been cracking on with four other handmade books in his ongoing series and this Last Gasp collection reproduces the contents of all five volumes. Johnson's technique is to use photo-montage and then overpaint and add whatever 'materials' he sees fit. It's been said that porn is 'Art's Dark Twin' and Leyba does fuse those two embryo's inside the festering womb of his imagination to produce his highly textured collage pieces that range from mesmeric and powerful to simply inane and fatuous.

In *My Stinking Ass* he was clearly making his first attempts with this method because it doesn't really work. Dark muted tones, lots of scrawls and smears and twisted torsos, it looks like some death metalhead's basement scrapbook, designed to piss off the art tutor at school with it's over-emphasis on arses, porn and decay. Maybe I'm just really jaded after a decade of 'apocalypse culture' but I don't find a single image to be in any way shocking or provocative. A double page spread of Marilyn Monroe with a tube leading from her nose to a fishnet-wrapped rectum says… absolutely fuck all. No reduction of the icon. No violation of the goddess. Just sweet FA.

The second book — *Sex & Violence* — features more vivid colours and a more adventurous and inventive use of the montage technique. The obsessions with Satanism and his Indian ancestry kicks in big style at this point so it's pentagrams, knives, feathers, nipples and lots of gaping cunts and arseholes. Not to mention all the 'distressed' depictions of the Stars & Stripes complete with swastikas, but this isn't some half-arsed appropriation like the pathetic zine imagery of the early nineties, Johnson wants to 'reclaim' the swastika and at least always ensures it's pointing east — the correct 'positive' use of the ancient symbol. Adolf and his runic bootboys had it facing West and that's where they came a cropper. Little details like that matter when you're aiming for world domination. The text pieces that accompany each image are repetitive and ultimately pointless. You can't have much faith in the clout of your image if you have to continually back it up with a running commentary of how America is shit, the Indians got fucked and corporate culture is ruining our world. If he's gone to all the trouble of slicing up his jazz mags and polaroids of his wife's arse then the least he could do is let them stand alone and leave room for some personal interpretation by the viewer. The persistent desecration of the flag gets a bit tiresome though. Whilst it makes an undeniably powerful backdrop for his works — all those primary colours blazing bright — once you've hung it upside down, wiped your arse on it, smeared it with blood and spunk then you've pretty much said all you can but the fucker is still up there flying on a hundred million flagpoles.

Book Three — *Apache Means Enemy* — is where Leyba finally gets to grips. There's a 'beautiful' use of colour and texture and a reduction in the number of splayed vaginas. 'Eagle Monster' is a striking blend of Bald Eagle head morphing into a taut scrotum and cock plunged halfway into an anus. Bits of hair and moss glued on as well. It sounds silly on paper but it really does work, giving us a wealth of symbols and interpretations to play with. Other images — cocks and corpses — come straight out of Fred West's cellar and hint at a widening of Leyba's scope.

The fourth book — *MAIM* (My American Indian Movement) — is the nastiest of the lot. Using photo's from his notorious Apache Whisky Rite (a 'performance' piece where he gets sliced, pissed on and then bloodily bummed by a dominatrix bitch wearing a JD bottle strap-on) we get an explosion of venereal yellow discharges, black stencil text, swastikas, gouged flesh, piss drinking and the Mark of the Beast. It's an angry howl from the bottom of his gut, a cut-up asylum jobbed prettied up with some poster paint like Blue Peter gone *bad*. *Coyote Amerika* — Book Five — is the most abstract of the set. The same themes are there in the detail but after the aggression of *MAIM* the tone is more subdued with more emphasis on colour and shape and symbol. He indulges the occasional knife blade or used tampon, feather or clump of hair but for the most part it's kaleidoscopic swirls of brightly coloured beads swirling through a phantasmagoric world of beast women and disembodied cocks. For the first time it seems he's trying to draw the onlooker in, not repelling them with body horror or wafting the stench of meat and grease in their faces. By banking the fires he manages to say more than he ever could by stomping his feet and pointing at his droppings.

The remainder of the book is a patchy collection of interviews and text pieces with the Reverend in various states of undress as he 'performs'. I totally understand his motives for wanting to embrace 'ritual' and tap into some spiritual aspect of his life but, stood bollock naked, covered in blood and wearing a wooden antenna on his head, the man looks like a Care in the Community case and cannot really be taken seriously — except somewhere like San Franscisco where there's a healthy appreciation of piss gargling as 'art'. His actual painted works prove he's got something to say, some message to impart. The pictures from his 'performances' suggest he's got some deep-seated mental problems that will never be addressed whilst surrounded by like-minded genitorturers and turd jugglers. As a result, the book is flawed but still worth the price of admission if bodily functions, base carnal needs and *The Lord of the Flies* are what strokes your monkey.
RIK RAWLING

GENERATION FETISH

Lee Higgs
ISBN 3980587681 / hb / 368 pp $37.95 / Goliath 2001 / www.goliathclub.com

A heavy photographic tome depicting numerous 'cute' / 'very cute' femmes tied, bound, gagged, and strapped in the usual mix of leather, rubbery and hose. Aesthetically the cunt-purples and pinks of the cross-processed photographs, the occasional use of lenses to distort perspectives, and the photographic technique is fine, but do we really need another book of goth / fetish chicks tied up? Especially because there's so little else going on in these pictures, nothing either glorifying or subverting the representation of the fetish (à la Kern or Araki — both of whom have been able to engage with and depart from the predictability of 'the scene' in order to explore their own specific interests with incredible results). For example, I would like to see the women actually looking embarrassed or ashamed or pained to have their bodies distorted by bondage and gags — if my nip-

Greg Friedler/Goliath

Four girls on Greg Friedler's *Mattress*.

ples were in a clamp it would hurt — I wouldn't be thinking about my fucking eye-liner. The quasi-moral tongue clicking of the S&M scene aside (safe words, rules for play etc) submission is about power-games, but too often now it appears as if the emphasis is on fetish fashion. The book even features an introduction by Gisele Turner that non-ironically compares the "cool, fresh" models and photos as being analogous to MTV, in my world that isn't a compliment, but it shows how mainstream this kind of scene is now. If this book is about creating / pandering to sexual fantasy then I want to see the

more contentious zones of S&M explored rather than the hipster angle. JACK SARGEANT

FUCKED UP + PHOTOCOPIED
Instant Art of the
Punk Rock Movement
*Bryan Ray Turcotte &
Christopher T Miller*
ISBN 1584230835 / hb / 240 pp £25 / Gingko Press Inc 1999 / 5768 Paradise Dr, Suite J, Corte Medera, CA 94925 / www.gingkopress.com

It cost me £25 but it was worth it because, thanks to Photoshop and the subsequent lack of excuse for anything that doesn't look at least slightly 'professional' we will never see the likes of this type of 'art' ever again. Flyers, hundreds and hundreds of them — from several personal collections — for punk gigs across the USA and Canada during the late seventies and early eighties. The imagery used perfectly complimented the music being made — hurried, botched and defiantly unprofessional — a snotty two's up to the loathed arena-filling supergroups and the airbrushed goblin-wank fantasy bollocks they wrapped their double albums with. Xerox machines allowed fast reproduction and dispersal of these images, posted to telephone poles and never intended to be regarded as cultural artefacts worth preservation. I mean, a hand-scrawled photocopy of Yoda's head for a Necro's show is so far removed from your average gallery wall smear that it may as well be in another galaxy. Which, in just about every way,

makes it more vital and relevant to the world we live in. Even that moose-faced tosspot Will Self has found that modern art shit like Damien Hirst's fishtank still can't help to sell his pointless books, whereas school jotter doodles for a Butthole Surfers show have come along, done their job and fucked off and never came loaded with all the post-modern piffling justifications of their deep and resonant artistic relevance.

Amidst the pop culture appropriations — Disney, Reagan, and B-movie scenes — there is much deformity, skateboarding skeletons and gun-toting nuns drawn by the likes of Raymond Pettibon and *Love & Rockets*' Jaime Hernandez — but the vast majority of images were drawn and designed by band members or friends of the band using anything from clippings from Tiger Beat magazine to their own bizzarro sketches and hand drawn fonts.

Of course, out of the hundreds and hundreds of images in this book there are many that are quite frankly piss poor but the compound effect of all their frenzied creativity, presented in the expected Raygun style (the seeds of which were sown in these very flyers) is totally mind blowing. Imagine sitting in a room with multiple stereos all blasting out the likes of Dead Kennedys, Black Flag, The Germs and Minor Threat and you'll come close to a similar sensory immersion. The anger and the desperation almost melts the pages. This book stands as a powerful testament to one of the last real street cultures to emerge before the mainstream blob burst and swelled out of the malls and into the gutters absorbing everything with a 'dollar potential' in its path. RIK RAWLING

MATTRESS
Greg Friedler
ISBN 3980760286 / hb / 112pp £19.99 / Goliath 2002 / www.goliathclub.com

A hard back full colour book by Friedler, the photographer behind the naked series (*Naked Los Angeles*, *Naked London* et al) depicting naked women lying on a floral mattress. According to Jordan Schaps' intro the book sees Friedler as a photographer whose work fits into wider history of the reclining nude in art, but is separate from this because it is "purer" and the photographer is more honest. The reality is that the book consists of pictures of twenty-somethings naked, often pierced, often tattooed, largely trim (of both figure and bush). This book is no more honest than any other, instead it is possibly dishonest because there's no acknowledgement that the photographer is actually foregrounding his taste (even unwillingly) — I mean, there's no fat ugly women here, no hirsute middle aged, saggy breasted grey haired types. That's not to say I want to see a book of unattractive women, but I then, I wouldn't evoke terms such as honesty and purity. That quibble aside, the general premise of the book is a good one, cute naked chicks on a dirty mattress, presenting themselves for our delectation. JACK SARGEANT

STRUGGLE:
THE ART OF SZUKALSKI
Ed. Eva Kirsch &
Donat Kirsch

ISBN 0867194790 / pb / 200pp $29.95 / Last Gasp 2000 / 777 Florida Street, San Francisco CA94110 / www.lastgasp.com

I PUT RODIN IN ONE POCKET, MICHAELANGELO IN THE OTHER, AND I WALK TOWARDS THE SUN —STANISLAW SZUKALSKI

Pretentious? Consider also the introduction to this volume by Leonardo (yes, him) and George DiCaprio where the case is made for Szukalski to be more deserving of the term 'Twentieth-century's greatest artist' in place of the man they refer to as 'Pick Asshole'. They don't have much time for that old mysoginistic paint swabber Pablo and I think they've got a point.

AS WE LURCH DAZED AND NUMB INTO THE TWENTY-FIRST CENTURY PICASSO'S WORK HAS FINALLY FOUND ITS RIGHTFUL PLACE — IN MASS-PRODUCED PRINTS ON SALE IN IKEA OR USED AS A 'SPECIAL EDITION' SELLING POINT FOR HATCHBACKS. SUCH A FATE WILL NEVER BEFALL THE WORK OF STANISLAW SZUKALSKI.

Until recently the man and his work were almost entirely forgotten by a world more inclined to accept a pile of bricks or a turd in a jar as 'art'. Which would have pissed me off had I been Szukalski because he spent much of his ninety-four years on Asylum Earth rendering some of the

most bold and potent artistic statements ever created. Ever. And he knew it! Not only that, the man managed to forge his own unique (to say the least) 'scientific discipline' called Zermatism which requires a book of its own to even begin to explain it (see *Behold! The Protong*, also by Last Gasp).

Born and raised in Poland, Szukalski bounced between his homeland and the USA, finally settling in California when the Nazis started kicking off but he never forgot his roots. Much of his work was rooted in legends and events from Polish history, giving his drawings and sculptures an added resonance beyond their own form and presence. I've never much cared for sculpture in the past, it's always appeared as a form long since adulterated by the trust fund hippies and witless piss-takers — you know what I mean, the fucking bits of cardboard and chicken wire propped in a gallery corner and called 'Untitled No.17', the lumps of slag iron welded into car crash shapes — big wastes of time for all concerned and a depressing distraction from the real possibilities of the form. Szukalski seemingly shut himself away from all that post-war avant garde bollocks and cracked on with his own ideas. He had plenty to keep him occupied after the Nazi's had trashed most of the work he produced in Poland, as he set about diligently recreating and improving some of his finer pieces that had been crushed under Das Jackboot — which is surprising as there was much in Szukalski's thrusting Teutonic lines and rampant ubermensch figurework for the likes of Albert Speer and even old Adolf himself to groove on. Szukalski's own fairly extreme and outlandish theories on art, history and culture were sometimes not so far removed from the more wigged-out sci-fi elements of *Mein Kampf* — believing as he did that Anglo-Saxon politicians, fascist Germans and communist Russians (amongst others) were direct descendents of human / ape interbreeding.

Of course, coming from a successful artist (as opposed to a failed one like Hitler) this could easily be interpreted as the more volatile part of his muse and dismissed accordingly but it was notions like this, woven into his burning commitment to Polish history and his growing fascination with the symbolic imagery of the lost

cultures of the Aegean and Meso-American empires that helped him to blossom with confidence as he charged headlong into a thunderously creative period, producing some of the best art in history.

Szukalski didn't work from life study, allowing his interpretations on the physical form to run rampant. Human figures featured prominently in his major works: writhing torsos, muscles rippling like a Terminator, sinews caught forever in rigid torment, surrounded by such potent archetypes as the soaring eagle, the sun, the eye, the dragon. Rooted in the 'Fine' arts Szukalski wasn't constrained by rigid formats or narratives, freeing him to go hog wild on mind-boggling works like the 'Rooster of Gaul' and the awesome 'Katyn'. Exquisitely detailed, every atom loaded with meaning and fashioned by an intellect that had something to say beyond "it doesn't have to mean anything — it's an installation."

Szukalski's art exposes with blinding sun-going-nova clarity the absolute paucity of imagination and talent in the likes of Emin and Hirst. Visions such as his are deeply unfashionable in these woeful times simply because they dare to stand for something but long after Emin's tent — and sweaty old Pablo's dove of peace Ikea prints — end up flapping in the breeze in some seagull shit-splattered landfill the ever-grasping claw that is Szukalski's 'Struggle' will forever be reaching out into the ether where the Mystery will always hide. RIK RAWLING

THE FANTASTIC ART
OF BEKSINSKI
Ed. James Cowan

ISBN 188339838X / hb / 72 pp£20.50 / Morpheus International 1999 / www.morpheusint.com

Another Pole, another weirdo. Behind his glasses Zdzislaw Beksinski looks like a less tormented Francis Bacon but his work is significantly different to the smears and splatters of that arch chuffter. Huge looming canvasses of alien landscapes, cathedrals of bones, withered mutants lurking through Lovecraftian wastelands of chemical epiphanies and extra-dimensional purgatory. The usual themes abound: death, God, fear of the unknown and the churning mystery at the heart of the abyss, all rendered with a painstaking attention to detail and an emphasis on the bleakest end of the palette.

Resolutely self-taught, Beksinski stumbled into painting after fumbling with other expressive mediums — sculpture, photography, writing — and he clearly found his niche with the brush and canvas. None of the works are titled, leaving the viewer even more adrift with the man's imaginative cosmology. While the bulk of the work was completed between 1970 and 1987 many of the skies and textures depicted eerily mirror those seen in the Hubble telescope shots, nebulas grinding their atoms around a surging spectrum of terrible glory. The characters that populate his works are the same feral lurkers and child snatchers of European fables but they are never caught in action, always static, brooding, shimmering with intent. Elsewhere there are canyons lined with rotting soldiers corpses, biomorphic towers looming up out of the mist and several takes on the Crucifixion including a chilling black maw, bound in webbones at the top of a telegraph pole that stands on a Golgothic plane of household detritus. A simplistic assessment would be of manic depression and religious confusion writ large as bad science fiction paperback covers but that would hardly be doing these works justice. They are, like all the best art, borne pure of the id and unhindered by crass considerations for audience and 'markets.' Any attempts to classify them as 'surreal' would be a waste of everybody's time — there's no label for this kind of art, it just *is* and 'fantastic' is about all you can say. Unsurprisingly Giger is a fan and it's got to be said that the Swiss visionary is his closest comparison. Sadly, like Giger, Beksinski has changed his style recently — to a more simplified and abstract approach — that stands as a pale shadow to his previous body of work. Worse still, he's also taken to dabbling with the 'digital arts' and the results are the usual shit we've come to expect from this fledgling medium: faces emerging out of walls, hands morphing out of heads… the same tired silly shit we've put up with from Dave McKean for the past decade. These images say absolutely fuck all and evoke nothing but a despairing wish that the man would come to his senses and stick to what he does best. Digital art, like cubism, abstract expressionism and pop art before it, will be remembered as the toilet bowl of visual creativity down which all charlatans, no-

hopers and talentless art grant monkey boys will be flushed. Or perhaps Beksinski, like Giger again, is just a spent force and is now diddling away in his retirement in much the same way as other old chaps potter around with flowers or matchstick models? Never mind, his majestic canvases will stand as testament to a great artist who did what he had to do or else go insane. Which is as it should be. RIK RAWLING

2024
Ted Rall
IBSN 1561632791 / hb / 96pp $16.95/ NBM
Publishing 2001 / www.nbmpub.com

2024, an updating of the immortal *1984*, depicts a future in which the state keeps the population numbed with TV, shopping, pornography and the like. Judging by the introduction (in which the author laments the fact that people are happy to have their freedom taken away in the nebulous

interest of national security), the book would appear to have laudable intentions. However, every page drips with just the sort of sneering cynical don't-give-a-fuck-about-anything attitude which *2024* purports to critique; hypocritically, Rall has churned out a product custom-built for the loathsome Gen Xers his book seeks to condemn. Reprehensible as this may be, the book's worst crime is that it simply isn't any good. It isn't a riff on *1984* but rather the exact same story with silly cosmetic changes. Instead of clocks striking thirteen, ironically-purchased Texas Instruments watches do so; Winston is not sent to Room 101 but made to watch Channel 101 (on which is showing a documentary

about rats); instead of loving Big Brother, he loves himself. The lack of subtlety in the writing matches the lack of originality in the concept:

THE CHAIN BAR-CAFE'S BEVERAGES WERE BITTER AND OVERPRICED, BUT EVERYONE DRANK THEM ANYWAY BECAUSE THEY WERE SO POPULAR.

The medium of the graphic novel is no excuse for this sort of lazy corner-cutting. Instead of a coherent narrative or solid characters, Rall randomly throws in supposedly 'cool' elements

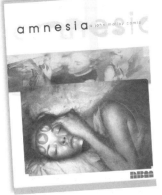

in an attempt to hold our attention. 'Anarcho-capitalism', 'Neo-postmodernism'… these neologisms mean sod-all since Rall does not see fit to explain them; that would be too much effort (as would a fluent, logical page layout). Consequently, the book is a tedious mess, lacking the thematic unity that is essentially its raison d'être. A smart arsed disclaimer ("This work contains numerous errors of omission, extraneous subplots, continuity problems, disjointed narratives…") attempts to brush this off but succeeds only in further annoying the reader. To cap it all off, the drawing style is affectedly amateurish. There is no point in reading this smarmy graphic novel whilst the immortal *1984* remains in print; that sound you can hear is Orwell spinning in his grave. ANTON BLACK

AMNESIA
John Malloy
ISBN 156163296 / pb / 64pp $9.95 / NBM
Publishing 2002 / NBM Publishing, 555 8th Ave,
Ste 1202, New York, NY 10018, USA /
info@nbmpub.com

Chloe, a young reporter from Los

Angeles, flies into Baltimore for an interview with reclusive filmmaker and novelist Ike Reuben, whose work she has long admired. Almost immediately, things go wrong. Her bag is stolen and her hire car is blown up by a mysterious terrorist organisation. When she tracks Reuben down, she finds him slipping in and out of hallucinatory narcoleptic states, and she becomes a lot more embroiled in his personal problems than is strictly wise. Meanwhile, the narrative is interrupted by Chloe's flashbacks.

This is a bare-bones summary of Baltimore-based artist John Malloy's ambitious and intriguing graphic novel. Themes of the nature of memory, flashbacks and déjà vu, the intermingling of dreams and reality and the intertwining of lives preocccupy the dense, multilayered narrative. Different graphic styles are employed to help the reader pick their way through the plotline. The stark, sinewy pen and ink work of the 'here and now' sequences gives way to modulated grey painting for Chloe's reminiscences and overpainted and manipulated photographs for Ike Reuben's viewpoint. I'd need to read this a couple more times before I could feel sure that I really understood what happens at the end — the utterances of an unearthly woman wearing an owl mask seem to be of great importance, but I couldn't really work out what she was doing there, and I found the owl mask, with its inevitable echoes of *The Story of O*, rather distracting.

I quite liked John Malloy's visual style. I was reminded of the DC Comics graphic novel *Tell Me, Dark*, written by the late Karl Wagner and illustrated by Kent Williams, and Howard Chaykin's infamous *Black Kiss* (both of which had similar noirish, *Vertigo*-esque themes of memory, desire and loss to *Amnesia*), as well as Dave McKean's influential cover work on *Sandman* and *Hellblazer* and the later work of Bill Sienkiewicz. This is surprising, given that Malloy's background is not in comics but in painting and graphic design — *Amnesia* is his first graphics novel.
SIMON COLLINS

ANIMAL MAN
Grant Morrison et al
ISBN 1840234601 / pb / 239pp £14.99 / Titan Books 2002 / titanpress @titanemail.com

A decade after its initial run, Grant

Morrison's critically rated fan favourite is back in print. The first thing one notices in the wake of *The Invisibles* and Morrison's current Vertigo series, *The Filth*, is just how dated this looks — especially in the artwork department, though of course this is hardly anyone's fault, merely the fact that comic book design has changed (for better or worse?) so radically over the last ten years. What obviously hasn't changed — only improved — in the intervening years is Grant Morrison's talent for creating dazzling and innovative stories and character situations. More than an inkling of this is apparent in *Animal Man*, though it's noticeable that in comparison to his later work this is predominantly safer stuff, and there's very little here to upset the kiddies, or, indeed, dyed in the wool traditionalists. There are, however, some of the usual clever references we've come to expect from Morrison, not least of which is the agonisingly gory reference to the Road Runner's arch nemesis, Wile Coyote. Interesting, but not an essential part of the Morrison oeuvre. STEPHEN SENNITT

BATMAN: BRUCE WAYNE — MURDERER?
Various
ISBN 1840235527 / pb / 263pp £14.99 / Titan Books 2002 / titanpress @titanemail.com

The Dark Knight. The anti-social crime stopper not adverse to bending the law in order to uphold it. Well, the concept behind this particular story is a doozey: what if the Batman — or rather his alter ego, Bruce Wayne — was the chief suspect in a murder investigation? Not unlike the O J Simpson case, on which this story appears to have some basis, it looks like the Batman — Wayne — is guilty of killing an old flame. The evidence against him is strong: he is caught on security camera buying the murder weapon and he categorically refuses to tell the police where he was on the night of the crime.

We all know that Wayne couldn't *really* have done it, and is simply covering for the fact that he was doing superhero stuff on the night in question. But as the story progresses doubt creeps in. Alas, much of *Bruce Wayne — Murderer?* is so stuck in the groove that is Wayne's resolute silence, that the reader longs for an outcome of any kind. The book is rife with big fat dry patches and fails to sustain the

intriguing dilemma of its basic premise. Highlights include Wayne kicking skinhead butt in the slammer (evidence to all that the millionaire playboy does indeed have the capacity to kill), and Damion Scott's artwork (in the Batgirl segment) which has a pleasing look to it.

The real killer? Now that *is* a surprise. DAVID KEREKES

COLLECTED PALESTINE
Joe Sacco
ISBN 156097432X / pb / 286pp $24.95 / Fantagraphics 2002 / www.fantagraphics.com

Here's the hefty re-release of the 'Landmark Work of Comics Journalism'. So now all those non-fan boy types who lament the lack of serious themes in the comic genre can hold something up as a standard. Personally, they're welcome to it; I much prefer *Biffo the Bear*, or even, at gunpoint, Garth... gulp... Ennis. STEPHEN SENNITT

FEAR OF COMICS
Gilbert Hernandez
ISBN 1560973838 / pb / 120pp £9.99 $12.95 / Fantagraphics Books 2001 / 7653 / www.fantagraphics.com

Holy shit. There is no way to deliver an adequate and coherent review of this book. It would be easier to try and fuck fog. Even Fantagraphics start their blurb on the rear cover with the warning: 'Be afraid. Be *very* afraid.' My initial impression was that this could only be the product of someone in a mental institution. It holds that potent charge of total mindfuck that you get from Daniel Johnston albums or the paintings of Henry Darger and the fact that it comes from one of 'alt.comics' more accomplished writers and artists makes it all the more surprising and intriguing. Gilbert Hernandez, together with his brother Jaime, started *Love & Rockets* back in the mid-eighties and proceeded to become the darlings of the new comics-reading intelligentsia — the types who (quite rightly) decried the likes of Marvel and DC for continuing to spew out shit and desperately wanted all comics creators to follow the examples of these new blazing talents. *Love & Rockets* was initially a breath of fresh air but readers gradually abandoned the title as the Hernandez Brothers lost their inspiration and in 1996 it unceremoniously folded.

Gilbert had always been the more unpredictable of the two. While Jaime played with his post-punk pseudo-lesbian soap opera, Gilbert immersed himself in the strange locale of Palomar (a long and complex saga that drew comparisons to Borges and the 'magical realists') and even took time out to do the *Birdland* series for Eros Comix — a totally wigged-out porno fantasy shedding new light on that which festers in the limbic core of his strange brain. But even that mad carnival of sperm and surrealism could not ever hope to compare with this collection of utterly fucking bizarre material that hurtles way beyond Dada into some nether-region of the imagination never previously charted in a comic book format. Where do I even begin? How about with the Contents Page? Here's just a few titles: 'Return of the Tzik', 'Drink, Fucker!', 'Wobbly Buttocks Frenzy', 'The Shit Eaters', 'She Sleeps With Anybody But Me'.

Already there's a big red neon flashing in your mind and once you're into the first strip 'All With A Big Hello' that neon sign explodes into a supernova of ?! spiralling out into infinity. A woman in a fifties style superhero outfit and a crescent moon on her head is on stage singing. She leaves the theatre to loud applause and gets into a car. The car takes her up into the woods above the city. Out of the woods stumbles a 'thing' best described as something out of Dr Seuss meets Charles Burns on a dark night. Next panel we see the woman half-in, half-out of her costume with the thing giving her one from behind while a crowd of other 'things' watch on from the shadows. Suddenly both characters undergo some kind of metamorphosis and in the very next panel the things are seen putting a cloak over the shoulders of a young, well-hung male human. They wave him goodbye and... well, I won't spoil the ending but it's like an episode of *The Twilight Zone*, filtered through the Phantom Tollbooth, left to fester in a Freudian swamp and then dredged up and wiped off. It's just so fucking... strange that it leaves you disturbed and exhilarated at the same time. This makes it great art but I'll be fucked if I can explain any of it.

The rest of the book is similar in tone — stark B&W artwork, a skilful use of subtly different drawing styles and a riotous assembly of freaks. It's all reminiscent in tone of some of Dan Clowes more impenetrable short strips (which Fantagraphics have noted and clearly packaged the book to look like a Clowes collection) but they all go way beyond anything even he's attempted. Childhood fetishes for gonks and masturbation fantasies over cartoon characters are allowed to blur while the 'rules' of narrative are torn up and fed to the dog. Flying women, pop-art drunks, existential jack-in-the-boxes, poisonous slugs, screaming ghosts, and, inevitably, the end of the world. The result is the best comics I've seen in years and a source of inspiration and enquiry that I'll be dipping into for years to come. Just don't expect to 'get' any of it as that's not really the point. Be more concerned if you do 'get' any of it.

It seems obvious that Hernandez was tired of the constraints of the medium and just let his imagination go wild across the page, confident its own deranged logic would see him through. This approach is in keeping with the best examples of the Underground comics of the late sixties and it would be nice to see a similar wave of experimentation triggered amongst young artists by this book. Far too many of the next generation of comics writers and artists have their eyes on the movie deal and 'franchises' which is only going to contribute to the death of the medium. We need more shameless experimentation like this to remind us of the joy of submitting to our imaginations. That's how we got to the moon in the first place so what are we doing rooting in the gutter for other people's scraps? It's time to evolve, and mutate and the less we recognise what we become, the better that is for us all.
RIK RAWLING

GILBERT HERNANDEZ
FEAR of COMICS
A LOVE AND ROCKETS COLLECTION

JIMMY CORRIGAN: THE SMARTEST KID ON EARTH
Chris Ware

ISBN 0375404538 / hb / 384pp £18 / Fantagraphics Books 2001 / www.fantagraphics.com

This collected edition of Ware's long-running series appeared on the shelves of my local comic shop during the same week as the much-heralded release of *DK2: The Dark Knight Strike Back*, a title alleged by many to be the one that will 'save comics'. Save comics from what, you may ask? Well, how about the gradual decline of the medium both in a commercial and artistic sense. Less kids buy comics these days because of the myriad other distractions — PS2, the Internet, football and lest we forget the time-
continued on p.152

DREDD!

Titan Books

Judge Death

**JUDGE DREDD
GOODNIGHT KISS**
Garth Ennis et al
ISBN 184023346X / pb / 90pp £9.99

**JUDGE DREDD
HELTER SKELTER**
Garth Ennis et al
ISBN 1840233486 / pb / 78pp £9.99 / Titan Books
(in association with 2000AD), 114 Southwark St,
London SE1 0UP / titan-press@titanemail.com

Oh no. Not one but two collections of old Judge Dredd comic strips sit before me, like miniature black holes sucking all the positive energy out of myself and the room around me. What have I done to deserve this? Haven't I already made it abundantly clear that this character is now a spent force and utterly irrelevant, except to a few dewy-eyed old school 2000AD fans who've still got a bit of growing up to do? Conceived as a pastiche of the Dirty Harry ubercop fantasy in the mid seventies by Pat Mills, the character was only effective as a straight man with Mega City One and it's bizarre denizens being the real stars. There should have been endless mileage in this approach but, some time during the early nineties, things changed… for the worse.
Goodnight Kiss is a compilation of three loosely-connected stories from those heady days. Comics had been hailed as 'the new rock'n'roll' throughout the late eighties and the medium was still enjoying a boom period which the editors at Fleetway tried to cash in on. Unfortunately they were utterly fucking clueless as to how to go about this and totally oblivious to the fact that their flagship title had actually been in decline (in terms of quality, if not in sales) for at least five years. The new obsession was with painted artwork—triggered

by the obvious natural talent of Simon Bisley whose work on *Slaine: The Horned God* had spawned a whole new generation of eager young copyists, each desperate to get some of the fame and fortune hat it seemed comics could now bring. No longer a cultural cul-de-sac inhabited by anorak-clad geeks and no-knob fat boys, now you get featured in *The Face* and, let's face it, you *can't* get any more rock n roll than that, can you? As the long-established creative teams like Wagner / Grant and Mills / O'Neill had fucked off to Yankee Land to cop for some of the action Alan Moore was getting, it was left to, shall we say, 'lesser talents' to milk the tit dry and it was these new writers and artists who were the first generation to have grown up influenced by what was now being defined as the *2000AD* 'house style'. Prior to that the writers had been in-

fluenced by a diverse range of material—from mad-ass sixties sci-fi to Hollywood's early seventies golden period—and this was reflected in the quality of the scripts. The publishers (Fleetway) were still stuck in the days of Archie the Robot and lantern-jawed Tommy's cracking the skulls of the Hun so they really had no idea what kind of new monster they had created. Once the editors and middle-management dickheads got wise on how to 'market' the 'product' it all went down the karzi and never came back. Garth Ennis was part of that new generation of writers trailing in the wake of Wagner, Grant & Mills but clearly had no idea of how to assimilate those influences into something of his own. That's clearly the case here on *Goodknight Kiss* where both stories are dull, predictable and utterly patronising to the readers. Yes 2000AD has always been full of exploding heads and men screaming "EEEAARGH!" as they die bloodily but it was the bits in-between the gore — y'know, characters, story, atmosphere, stuff like that — that kept the readers coming back. The Marshal, if you care, is a vigilante from the Cursed Earth (the radioactive wasteland that lies beyond the city limits) who is inspired by the Lone Ranger to bring his own brand of vigilante justice to what's already a totalitarian fascist society. He should blend in nicely but, as you might expect, he falls foul of Judge Dredd and, well, just have a guess how it ends.

The art job by Nick Percival is most politely described as 'workman-like'. The guy was clearly young, learning his trade and under pressure to conform to the Bisley style. Doing his best with punishing deadlines, the result is big blobs of acrylic and figurework that recalls Jack Kirby and Frank Miller at their most minimal. Meanwhile, in *Enter: Jonni Kiss* Greg Staples has totally embraced the Biz technique to such an extent that it becomes insulting. Biz, as I said, has a natural talent that throbs on the page, while his most accomplished copyists look like they're straining over each panel like constipated pensioners. The story introduces the Heavy Metal Heathcliffe alpha male that is 'Jonni Kiss' who crops up again later in 'Goodnight Kiss' where Nick Percival is back on the art chores and seemingly had more time to spend on each page as there's noticeably more detail and control on display. The villain this time around — Gideon — is a jaw-droppingly obvious rip-off of DC's Spectre, with added steroids. As for the story, well, do you care? Does anyone on this planet give a flying fuck? It's just one long procession of Arnie-film quips and threats, punch ups, gun battles and... yaaaaaaaaaawn. It's shit. It's ordure. It's excrement. It patronises and insults the reader's mental faculties and sloppily assumes that an acquiescence to the dictates of Hollywood crassness is enough to make these stories and the Dredd character resonate in the mind of the target audience. The reason why other characters like Spiderman, Daredevil and even the Silver Surfer have been so popular over the decades is because they were created and developed by writers who cared and understood what they were doing. Bearing in

mind the time they were created perhaps these strips do suffer from a certain inexperience but I'm not feeling charitable so fuck it. They're shit. Now, if *Goodnight Kiss* suffers somewhat from youthful naivety what excuse can be offered in defence of the turd that is *Helter Skelter*. It's Ennis again at the helm, only this time he's ten years older and now a celebrated author with successful series like *Preacher* and *Hellblazer* under his belt. He's got the sales to prove his talent and 2000AD is proud that this writer ("much in demand for his hard-edged, wickedly humorous style") is back to give the fans the one they've been waiting for — which is easily the most asinine and fatuous pieces of in-house nostalgia that these tired and jaded eyes have ever had to witness. 2000AD, collectively, ran out of ideas long ago and has been regurgitating past glories ever since but this is just taking the piss. 'The very structure of reality has been altered' — a plot device that creaks under the weight of its own obsolescence — allowing Dredd to face off against many of the key villains from his entire twenty-five year history. Does that sound exciting or does that sound like the biggest load of lazy-arsed bollocks you've ever heard? Yup, thought so — big, sweaty, hairy, cheese-encrusted bollocks. Every villain — from Dredd's clone-brother Rico to robot revolutionary Call-Me-Kenneth — is let loose in the streets of Mega City One on the hunt for one Darien Kenzie, the kind of BBC-approved dynamic black female protagonist that is now an essential ingredient of every shit-arsed cyberMatrixRunner sci-fi rip off bag of wank. Dyed hair, special ability, streetwise... you may have seen this before. She holds the secret to why all these entities are turning up and in an idiotically blatant reference to *The Terminator* even has Dredd save her ass and utter the line: "Take my hand if you want to live."

Am I honestly supposed to accept this without comment or complaint? I know it's 'only comics' but Come The Fuck On! This kind of stunt cannot be allowed. No amount of postmodern irony can be offered up in his defence. Ennis is utterly shameless in his plundering of the 2000AD archives and seemingly nothing is sacred — *Flesh*, *Fiends of the Eastern Front*, even *Dr & fucking Quinch* are not spared and whilst it gives the

Mack Daddy of the medium Carlos Ezquerra a chance to flex his muscles on the visuals it's all so jaw-droppingly shit that you want to burn every copy in a giant pyre that can be seen from outer space.

Comics is a stunted idiot-child medium — that's the main part of its appeal — but most of the writers now working in the medium have basically run out of ideas, run out of enthusiasm and are, for all intents and purposes, redundant.

So, fellas, there are many charitable causes out there that need your help. Go do something worthwhile instead of making bad copies of straight-to-video action bollocks. The world doesn't need your comics. The kids don't want them.

Save some trees. Save Africa. Save your souls. RIK RAWLING

JUDGE DREDD FEATURING JUDGE DEATH

John Wagner & Brian Bolland

ISBN 1840233869 / hb / 94pp £14.99 / Titan Books in association with 2000AD, 2001 / titan-press @titanemail.com

These are the more self-contained Judge Dredd strips by artist Brian Bolland, with an emphasis on the stories in which the estranged Judge Death makes an appearance. Death and his apocalyptic cohorts — Judges Mortis, Fire and Fear — believe that only the living commit crime and so have declared life itself illegal. Having wiped out the entire population of their own Deadworld, the four Judges teleport themselves to Earth on occasion where they try and further apply their fatal ideology. Judge Death is an excellent nemesis to Judge Dredd in that, like Dredd, he is a no-nonsense, two-dimensional unaffected entity.

The strips here are lifted from the pages of 2000AD, where Judge Dredd was allocated at the most eight pages an issue. Given this restriction on space, there simply isn't time to delve much below the surface of any character or situation, and in order to add some extra weight, the stories often draw on recognisable pop cultural icons or movies (for instance, the Hunchback of Notre Dame, Laurel and Hardy, Rondo Hatton, *Rollerball*, etc). Short but sweet strips, nicely packaged and with a mean villain — that's *Judge Dredd featuring Judge Death*. DAVID KEREKES

continued from p.149

less appeal of easily-plied local slags — so in a climate of diminishing returns the creative geniuses at Marvel, DC, Dark Horse etc have circled the wagons and decided to fight to the bitter end with the only weapon they've ever had that proved to be effective — superheroes.

Back in the mid eighties when Miller produced *The Dark Knight Returns*, along with Alan Moore & Dave Gibbons' *Watchmen* there was much talk of these works signifying the 'death of the superhero'.

Other creators like Pat Mills and Kev O'Neill attempted to nail the casket shut on the caped twats for good with overtly cynical creations such as *Marshal Law* where superheroes and 'gifted mutants' were hunted down, got the shit kicked out of them and were occasionally slaughtered — a gaudy display of catharsism for Mills and the thousands of readers who responded to it. At the time there was an air of expectation surrounding the medium with much bold experimentation taking place — and, yes, a lot of it was shit, but people were being drawn to the medium for its possibilities and it wasn't too ridiculous to start talking about a 'Rennaisance' for a medium that had been long ago left to stagnate in its own juices.

Unfortunately, greed and stupidity, two of the founding principles of the comics industry, triumphed in the end. The young artists ran for cover in games design or animation and it was left to a hard-core of chinless geeks in Buffy T-shirts to perpetuate the sorry mistakes of the past, in short — more superheroes.

More superpowers. More killer cyborgs. More balloon-titted ninja hacker SWAT bitches. Cheers fellas. The only viable alternative to this unmitigated tide of shit was the occasional good title published by Fantagraphics Books, comin' atcha from Seattle, USA. They themselves have published some real shit in the past, so much so that the accusations of supporting their vanity project with sales of the Eros titles started to seem plausible. I've got a lot of their books on my shelf — mostly those by Peter Bagge and Dan Clowes, as most of the other things they insist on publishing just don't appeal.

And, for many years, one of those titles that just didn't appeal was *Jimmy Corrigan: The Smartest Kid on Earth*.

I just didn't get what all the fuss was about and eventually dismissed it as the latest bandwagon for the comics snobs to pontificate about as they sneered down on the superhero fans. I even found myself coming down on the side of the geeks for a while, justifying their 'innocent' pleasures and letting them off the hook. But after week upon week of dragging my arse into Forbidden Planet to be assaulted by what was the direct result of their continual indulgence of 'innocent' pleasures (not forgetting the aforementioned greed and stupidity of publishers, distributors and the corporations that own them) I finally cracked. I gave up on comics altogether, only venturing into these spiritual hellholes if Clowes had anything new out. Fuck it, I said. The sooner they flush the toilet the better. Then someone sent me a copy of *The Imp* — an irregularly published zine, expertly written and designed

by Dan Raeburn, that focuses on particular comics creators that take his fancy. Issue three is all about Chris Ware and his comic *Jimmy Corrigan*. Dan had designed the comic along the lines of a 1920s newspaper with an almost pathological attention to detail and this feat alone impressed me to read on.

What he had to say about the *Jimmy Corrigan* saga and Chris Ware's comments on his own work inspired me to seek the title out if it ever got the collected edition it seemed to deserve. And here it is, winner of a Guardian award, all £18 of it. I don't even know where to begin to even explain

it, except to say that it's all about Jimmy Corrigan, a middle-aged man living in Chicago. There's no simple way to explain the story because it flits back and forth between past and present (and occasionally the future), sometimes within the space of a

page and relies so much on the relationship between the often sparse word balloons and panels and the specific details of each panel. In the complexity of its structure and the range of themes it explores it almost redefines the term 'post-modern' and makes literary efforts from the likes of Pynchon and DeLillo read like Shaun Hutson in comparison. No, I'm not shitting you, this book is one of *the* great artistic achievements of the twentieth-century. It will fuck with your head and make you think long and hard about yourself more than anything else you will read this year. If nothing else, it will make you realise that most of the 'art' and 'entertainment' you subject yourself to is utterly meaningless shit.

The art and design work is fucking incredible. With a highly stylised clear line style and flat shades of colour and black, each page is absolutely rock solid — nothing is extraneous, no big show-off panels, everything serving the narrative. Multiple POVs and numerous wide shots of the city reveal Ware's firm ability as a draughtsman and while his obvious love of the designs of the early part of the twentieth-century may repel those who demand everything predictably filtered via Photoshop, they help to bolster the impression that this is someone who gives a shit about what he's created. In an age of instant thrills and ideas being more important than ability, a labour of love like this might be seen as an anachronistic indulgence but it's your loss if you think that way. As far as I'm concerned this proves that the best art is produced by a singular vision, someone with something to impart that may be of value to the audience. All this from just a comic? Yes, why not? Finally, after strong hints from Dan Clowes, Alan Moore and Bill Sienkiewicz (*Stray Toasters*) the medium is being dragged kicking and screaming out of it's sperm-encrusted adolescent bed and into blazing light of a new dawn. Finally.

What has it taken so fucking long? Why are we still having to wade knee deep through mounds of shit comics to get to something good? Why is a piece of nostaligic crap like *DK2* being seen as in a positive light? The comics medium is at a crossroads now — it can take the familiar and comfortable road of the cape and the smack in the face that will ultimately lead to its doom within ten years, or it can veer off into new territory where there are no signposts, no maps and only one rule of the road: Don't Be Shit.

The choice is yours. What's it gonna be? RIK RAWLING

TRANSMETROPOLITAN
Gouge Away
Warren Ellis, Darick Robertson, et al
ISBN 184023394X / pb / 142pp £10.99 / Titan Books 2002 / titan-press@titanemail.com

Spider Jerusalem's column of investigative scandal is a bit like The Drudge Report, except with a big popular and political impact. While words are his weapon of choice, Spider also treads the poisoned path to celebrity: he is a household name beset by his own image in the form of Magical Truthsaying Bastard Spidey, a cartoon effort of counter-propaganda created to discredit him with the populous. Spider is a man of the streets (which in The City are paved with TV screens) whose column, when it comes out from under a heap of censorious orders, is flashed around the world and gets the masters of the New World Order filling their trousers.

The opening four stories ('Magical Truthsaying Bastard Spidey!', 'I Hump It Here', 'The Heroic Revenge Fantasy', and 'The Ugly Paranoid Dream') are by way of entering the unconsciousness of our hero as he flakes out on some rancid concoction. The stories are as fascinating and ugly as dreams on Strychnine-laced LSD, ameliorated with strong colours and shadows, enhanced with digital lighting effects (exactly as America's Best Comics have taken to doing in Alan Moore's *Tom Strong*). The drawing in 'The Ugly Paranoid Dream' is especially good; its clean imperfect lines are almost Durer-like. Elsewhere, the artwork takes a more Brian Bollandish approach.

'Dancing In The Here and Now' introduces his two assistant / lovers, Yelena and Channon, as they escape from Spider's apartment, get loaded and shop for guns before having a sisterly about their lives with Spider. The story is a very funny take on the always comedy premise of gals with guns, and takes pains to 3D-ise the characters. Gaiman's Death is an obvious influence on the gothicky Yelena who is a pretty much a stereotypical DC urban lass.

The next story, Gouge Away, is where the real action begins as Spider goes on the trail of a White House enmired in murder and obstruction of justice. He meets a variety of characters and uses the technology of *telefactoring*, a way of 'faxing' a person into remotely-cloned form. Before it's all over, Spider's greatest word-bomb causes the President to get the lowest ever approval rating since 'President Rodham was caught fisting kittens in the streets of Brooklyn.' It's good to see a graphic novel with a satirical edge and I look forward to future instalments. JERRY GLOVER

GUILTY PLEASURES
Ed. M Christian
ISBN 1892723026 / pb / 240pp $16 / Black Books 2002 / www.blackbooks.com

Every persuasion can find something stimulating in this collection of short stories, or as the editor would have it, a series of erotic confessions. Ultimately, however, it is each contributor's exploration of sexual secrets, weaknesses and unresolved feelings that makes the book interesting, not whether these events actually happened. M Christian is an adept editor, and each story is no more than a few pages. Perfect for when the VCR breaks down. STUART PINKERTON

LITEROTICA
The Very Best of literotica.com
Ed. Lori Selke
ISBN 1892723093 / pb / $16 239pp / Black Books 2001 / www.blackbooks.com

The Web has been a great boon to writers who otherwise would find no way to reach a wide audience, and literotica.com has been one of the more successful exponents of virtual publishing. This book collects a mixed bag of erotic writing, selected from thousands of submissions to literotica.com. Each describes a variety of sexual encounters, not all consenting or charge-free. Julie Lemolo writes strangely childlike sexual play in an attic in *Indigo*. Nicholas Travers takes a painfully honest line on sexual frustration and the humiliation felt by a married journalist visiting a dominatrix in *Vast*. Anessa Ramsey's costume-drama, *The Games We Play*, is a kind of homage to Jane Austen with shagging, and *Dirty Old Man* conjures a sexual succubus in the form of Abigail, a vivid fantasy of his ultimate lay. Three of the stories are extracts from novels.

Apart from well-described — if basic — situations, there is not much in the way of the emotional complexity that would raise the rude voltage of these stories, except in the final entry, *A Fireman's Prayer* by Dixon Carter Lee, which paints a believable and extraordinary picture of a girl with a fetish for her fireman landlord and all the scents and tastes associated with the aftermath of a blaze. Carter Lee contributes another vivid slice of life and sex in *Jazzy Girl*, but *A Fireman's Prayer* is heads above this and all the others in the collection, and has to rate on my list as one of the best short stories I have read, in and outside erotic literature. His is by far the most distinctive voice in the collection, each paragraph filled with sensitive and vivid description. Julie Lemolo also writes well, but the others I found for the most part not very exciting, too preoccupied with what-goes-where than getting to grips with the emotional nuances that make the finest erotic writing leap (or spurt) off the page. JEREMY GLOVER

BELOW THE BELT
Sarah Veitch
ISBN 0953795323 / pb / 324 pp £9.95 / Palmprint Publications 2002 / www.palmprint.fsbusiness.co.uk (the publisher's

web site offers *Below The Belt* for the discount price of £7.95 including p&p)

Listen to the sound of one hand spanking with Sarah Veitch's second novel of CP erotica (the first, *Subculture*, was reviewed by Pan Pantziarka in HEADPRESS20). The narrative follows Kerri, a spoiled yuppie bitch who invests in the wrong timeshare. Her move to Alpineglow, an idyllic-sounding (if geographically implausible) community in California, delivers her into the firm and masterful palms of Jeff Rendell, a man she has 'wronged' in the past. Jeff has evidently convinced an entire community of disciplinarian back-to-nature types to collude in his scheme to blister the bottom of everyone who has ever crossed him — if only I could do the same! Of course, many, many punishments ensue to help Kerri see the error of her ways. After her over-his-knee debut, Jeff tells Kerri, "The spanking you've just had… would score a two on my buttock correction scale," which makes him sound worryingly like one of *Viz's* Bottom Inspectors. By page twenty-seven, Kerri is being invited to, "Meet Mr Paddle, my dear. He's about to acquaint himself with your naughty bottom." And so on and so forth. If this all sounds a bit absurd, well of course it is, but what erotica isn't? For what it's worth, reading *Below the Belt* did cause my dick to get hard several times, and I ask for nothing more from dirty books. Although I can't help feeling concerned for Kerri's suede suit, which, we are informed, "the launderette washed and dried nightly". That's no way to treat suede! SIMON COLLINS

EXTRATERRESTRIAL SEX FETISH
Supervert 32C
ISBN 0970497105 / pb / 216pp $15.00 / Supervert 32C 2001 / www.supervert.com

Supervert 32C Inc is "a media company that utilises the techniques of vanguard aesthetics to research the pathology of novel perversions". Devoted to exploring the notion of exophilia — an abnormal attraction for beings from worlds beyond earth — *Extraterrestrial Sex Fetish* consists of a series of interrelated short texts (narrative fragments, philosophical speculations, diary excerpts, parodies, snippets of computer code) written in the style of a Space Age

Marquis de Sade. It's not quite as intimidating as it sounds, however, since the book's format allows you to dig in and out at will. You can follow the narrative of Mercury de Sade and his frustrated attempts to satisfy his fetish for alien sex, or you can get acquainted with philosophical speculations about otherworldly life from Descartes to Roland Barthes and back again. Personally, I found it difficult to get a foothold on the book's stylised, slightly robotic prose, though sci-fi aficionados and *Star Trek* fans may find a rare treat in the descriptions of exophiliac copulation. If it's beach reading you're after, however, I'd recommend something a little more down to earth. MIKITA BROTTMAN

SNAKE
Mary Woronov
ISBN 1852427183 / pb / 213pp £6.99 / Serpent's Tail 2000 / www.serpentstail.com

Cult film star Mary Woronov (*Eating Raoul, Rock and Roll High School*) is perhaps best known for her associations with Andy Warhol's Factory (see her interview with Jack Sargeant in HEADPRESS22), but is also a talented writer. Her debut novel, *Snake*, is the story of Cassandra, a girl whose strange affinities with nature give way to sexual and emotional abandon as she drifts aimlessly through the LA Punk scene. Trapped in an abusive marriage to a wealthy business tycoon and S&M aficionado, she dreams of freedom, finally discovering an escape route in the arms of Luke, a handsome young hitman hired to kill her husband. Hunted by both the cops and the mob, Luke takes Cassandra with him to his cabin in Idaho, where, surrounded by rednecks and survivalists, she rediscovers her connection with the natural world. But Cassandra is haunted by strange fits during which she hallucinates a series of strange scenes set in an ominous Californian clinic. Are they prophecies of the future, like those experienced by Cassandra's mythical namesake, or flashbacks caused by too much LSD? Lyrical, surreal and unsettling, *Snake* works on a number of different levels. Sometimes Cassandra's passivity can get a bit annoying — despite her many displays of prodigious inner strength, she seems drawn to hollow relationships with destructive men — but, in a way, this is all part of her mysterious complexity. Like the snake of its

title, this story twists and turns back on itself ambiguously, driven by a secret inner logic, then finally, when you're least expecting it, reveals the poisonous twist in its tail. MIKITA BROTTMAN

NIAGARA
Mary Woronov
ISBN 1852428015 / pb / 215pp £8.99 / Serpent's Tail 2002 / www.serpentstail.com

Woronov's second novel, *Niagara*, tells the sad story of Molly (Mei Li), a half-Chinese girl haunted by the sound of the Niagara Falls, which she associates with her unhappy childhood and an ancient folktale about an Indian sacrifice. When her beloved half-brother Kenny apparently plunges to his death in the Falls on the night of their high school graduation, Molly, in despair, marries his best friend Bobby and flees to arid Southern California, where, through a haze of alcohol and depression, she tries to come to terms with her destructive and confusing past. Woronov is a talented writer with the rare ability to lift this idiosyncratic tale of incest, abuse and family secrets to a resonant mythic level, where its images reverberate with secret meaning. As is also apparent in her debut novel, Woronov is best at portraying shimmering little hallucinatory vignettes. In *Niagara*, Molly's alcoholic haze evokes frightening memories of an emotionally remote family, and premonitions of a sad and lonely future. But the story ends on an uplifting note, as Molly escapes her childhood fantasies and learns how to use her strength in more healing, less destructive ways. MIKITA BROTTMAN

THE TORTURE GARDEN
Octave Mirbeau
ISBN 0965104265 / pb / 128pp $12.99 £9.99 / Juno Books 2000 / www.junobooks.com

This is a reprint of RE/Search Books' 1989 edition of Mirbeau's notorious *fin-de-siècle* novel of passion and pain in imperial China. Opening with a framing device reminiscent of Conrad's *Heart of Darkness*, the narrator recounts his flight from France in the wake of a political scandal. Voyaging to Ceylon at the head of a trumped-up scientific expedition, he meets a certain Miss Clara on the ship, a hot-blooded young Englishwoman who, we are told, 'was given to strange lapses, flights of fancy,

THE WOMAN CHASER
ISBN 1842430017 / pb / 192pp £6.99 /
No Exit 2001

MIAMI BLUES
ISBN 18422430092 / pb / 213pp £6.99 /
No Exit 2001

NEW HOPE FOR THE DEAD
ISBN 1842430106 / pb / 213pp £6.99 /
No Exit 2001

HIGH PRIEST OF CALIFORNIA
& WILD WIVES
ISBN 1842430033 / pb / 602pp £7.99 /
No Exit 2001 / www.noexit.co.uk

Willeford was one of the truly great pulp fiction writers, producing numerous noir-sleazoid classics. The best of these four volumes is *High Priest of California & Wild Wives* — two humorously grim short books in one volume, this was the book that turned me on to Willeford back in the early eighties when RE/Search issued a reprint of the 1955 edition. These two stories have a sleazy edge that positively drips from the page, especially *High Priest* — Willeford's first book — which features one of the most entertaining mean-spirited characters ever, Russell Haxby, a pussy hound and used car salesman of monstrous proportions. The original cover blurb described the book as "A Roaring Saga of the Male Animal on the Prowl", which describes not only this book but also goes someway to defining the quintessential Willeford protagonist — *The Woman Chaser* features an equally ambitious and repellent car salesman-cum-sleazebag. *Miami Blues* and *New Hope for The Dead* were written in the eighties, and are the first two of Willeford's Hoke Mosely novels, set in Miami these follow homicide detective Mosely as he stumbles through a suitably noir underworld populated by various murderers and scumbags. Stylistically Willeford sucks you into the dysfunctional vortex of his protagonists, and like Jim Thompson you don't necessarily realise how crazed characters are until the last dozen pages or so. What makes Willeford different though is his obsessions with art (according to one biographical account he studied art in France) and gleefully perverse sex — there is, for example, a hilarious scene in *New Hope For The Dead* in which a character masturbates his horny pet dog. It is good to see these republished again, but, as ever, I'd question the choice of titles. Why, for instance, republish *Miami Blues* and *New Hope*? Both have been semi-available until recently, and, ultimately, I'd rather the trashy pulp than the police procedurals. Why not new editions of the *Cockfighter*, *The Black Mass of Father Springer*, or *The Burnt Orange Heresy* — all titles that have been out-of-print and largely unavailable since the heady days of Black Lizard's reprints in the eighties? And what about the self-published *Poontang and Other Poems*? JACK SARGEANT

incomprehensible caprices and terrible desires', and who possesses 'teeth which so often have bitten into the bleeding fruits of sin'. Crikey! Does her dentist know?

Clara, is in fact a dominatrix figure, a *belle dame sans merci* cut from the same cloth as de Sade's Juliette or Sacher-Masoch's Wanda. She says things like, 'I promise you'll descend with me to the very depths of the mystery of love... and death!' It's always nice to see a French character getting instructed in the arts of love by an English one ¯ the other example that springs to mind is Sir Stephen in *The Story of O*. Hey, if you want to learn to be a pervert, ask the English! Small wonder that our hero follows her to China rather than posing as an 'embryologist' (this must have meant something very different a hundred years ago!), dredging the pelagic ooze of the oceanic gulfs of Ceylon.

Once in China, the narrator's personal heart of darkness is attained in the torture garden of the title, an exquisitely decadent anti-Xanadu, a walled compound filled with temples, gardens palaces, pavilions, and, er, torture. Lots of torture. Torture of a fiendish, oriental and minutely described variety, judicial punishment of trivial offences raised to the level of an art form. This, it transpires, is Miss Clara's favourite place in all the world, and the narrator is simultaneously disgusted and fascinated as their tainted love spirals out of control towards an apocalyptic climax (I use the term advisedly!).

The Torture Garden is very much a book of its time. Its oriental exoticism, sexual perversity and preoccupation with sin and guilt are paralleled in the works of Mirbeau's contemporaries Beardsley, Wilde, Huysmans, Swinburne and indeed the young Aleister Crowley. An unflinching willingness to question the basis of all morality aligns Mirbeau with Nietzsche, who died in 1900, just a year after the first publication of *The Torture Garden*. Mirbeau's anarchist and republican sympathies are evident right from the dedication page:

TO PRIESTS, SOLDIERS, JUDGES
— TO MEN WHO REAR, LEAD
OR GOVERN MEN I DEDICATE
THESE PAGES OF MURDER AND
BLOOD.

The opening sequence, featuring an assembly of emblematic worthies (a lawyer, a scientist, a writer, a philosopher etc) discussing the nature of murder, is highly reminiscent of de Sade's writings, in particular the *One Hundred and Twenty Days of Sodom*. A number of topical references throughout the book — to the Dreyfus affair that divided France at the time, to European colonialism — reinforce the authentically *fin-de-siècle* tone of world-weary disgust: "In China life is free, joyous, complete, unconventional, unprejudiced, lawless... at least for us... Europe and its hypocritical, barbaric civilisation is a lie."

This strand of thought connects *The Torture Garden* to the misanthropic French literary tradition of the twentieth-century, extending through Céline, Camus and Sartre to Genet. Whilst on the evidence of this book I would hesitate to place Mirbeau in the same class as these writers, this novel is still highly readable, reasonably short, and filled with enough kink and gore to titillate the jaded palates of HEADPRESS readers.

There is, though, a fundamental contradiction at the core of Mirbeau's book. On the one hand, he seems determined to produce a politically engaged indictment of social institutions, a blazing denunciation of colonial and imperial power structures, but this seemingly righteous and noble aim is fatally undermined by the slavering enthusiasm and intricately bejewelled prose with which he delineates all the torture and violence. As de Sade could have told him, condemning sin whilst simultaneously revelling in it is a very tricky balancing act to pull off, and in my view

double columns of text don't make for the easiest reading. And I must admit that the copious photographic illustrations by Bobby Neel Adams — stagy soft-focus tableaux of people in indeterminate period dress with their heads averted — didn't really add to my appreciation of the text. I would have preferred to see some appropriate Symbolist pictures by Mirbeau's contemporaries, Odilon Redon or Gustave Moreau for example.

The best reason to read *The Torture Garden* is the brilliant central conceit of the garden itself, which not only lent its name to the famous fetish club, but also stands in a noble tradition of walled gardens of more or less corrupt pleasures extending back

sian for 'hunting park'? I was also reminded of Blofeld's Japanese suicide garden in the James Bond novel *You Only Live Twice*. Even Charlie Dimmock can't make gardening this much fun!

AH, YES! THE TORTURE GARDEN! PASSIONS, APPETITES, GREED, HATRED AND LIES; LAWS, SOCIAL INSTITUTIONS, JUSTICE, LOVE, GLORY, HEROISM AND RELIGION: THESE ARE ITS MONSTROUS FLOWERS AND ITS HIDEOUS INSTRUMENTS OF ETERNAL HUMAN SUFFERING. WHAT I SAW TODAY, AND WHAT I HEARD, EXISTS AND CRIES AND HOWLS BEYOND THIS GARDEN, WHICH IS NO MORE THAN A SYMBOL TO ME OF THE ENTIRE EARTH.

SIMON COLLINS

One of the things that *Came from Bob's Basement*: The metal robot custume used in *Phantom Empire* (1935) and *Captain Video* (1951).

DVD DELIRIUM
The International Guide to Weird and Wonderful Films on DVD! Vol 1
Ed. Nathaniel Thompson
1903254043 / pb / 639 pp £14.99 $19.99 / FAB Press 2002 / www.fabpress.com

Simple ideas often translate into the most enjoyable books. Almost as often, these simple ideas generate unforeseen headaches. A book reviewing DVD films — what could be simpler? Well, if the book is comprised of over 600 pages of fine, eye-wrenching type, you could hazard a guess that it has gone through more than one author and has overshot its scheduled publication date several times over!

In the hands of any less conscientious publisher, the book would have been released on time but invariably half-baked. What we get with *DVD Delirium* is a good general guide to all manner of weird and not-so weird movies as found in the technological quagmire that is the DVD market. The reviews are informed and make for fine reading in themselves, while the DVD details are kept to a useful minimum — discussing picture and sound quality, extras, and pointing the reader in the best direction when there is more than one choice of the same movie available.

Through *DVD Delirium* I have learned that (a) the same extra footage for John Carpenter's *Dark Star* has been utilised by different DVD companies in different ways; (b) some people

Mirbeau doesn't succeed. This makes *The Torture Garden* a curio rather than a classic, though it's still worth reading.

As always with RE/Search and Juno books, this edition is well produced, although I would question the appropriateness of the oversized coffee-table book format for a novel — long

for centuries, including Coleridge's *Kubla Khan*, of course, along with the *One Thousand and One Nights*, the tales of Hassan-I-Sabbah, the Old Man of the Mountains and his *hashishin*, and Coleridge's source materials in the journals of Marco Polo. Did you know that the word 'paradise' is derived from the Per-

never learn and insist on forking out hard cash for Jess Franco product in whatever medium happens to come along, and, (c) curiously, nobody really seems to like Norman Jewison's *Rollerball* very much.

As with any expansive work there are going to be idiosyncrasies, but to me it seems odd that *Friday the 13*[th] Parts One to Seven are reviewed in *DVD Delirium*, yet none of the *Nightmare on Elm Street* films (and one solitary concert film — Talking Heads' *Stop Making Sense*). That said, there are hours of entertainment to be had trawling through this book, and I do hope more volumes are forthcoming. DAVID KEREKES

IT CAME FROM BOB'S BASEMENT
Bob Burns
with John Michilig
ISBN 0811825728 / pb / 144pp $24.95 / Chronicle Books 2000 / www.chroniclebooks.com

Bob Burns is the high grade junk collector *par excellence*! This is a massive, luxurious book full of photos of monsters from movies and T V representing a lifetime of dedicated hoarding. Burns is the actual owner of such esoteric items as Lily Munster's dress, a tunic from *The Mole People*, Glenn Strange's Frankenstein boots, the remote mind control creature from *It Conquered the World*, Paul Blaisdell's concept artwork for that awful Tobonga tree creature which featured in *From Hell it Came*, and loads of other items even more mindblowingly weird! Of special interest to me is the gorilla suit section, which finally seems to put to rest the notion that I must have dreamed about a Saturday morning show called *Ghostbusters* featuring an aged Forest Tucker, some Hispanic guy in a zoot suit and a moth-eaten 'gorilla' which nobody else ever seems to remember! Thoughroughly good fun and totally edyoocashional. STEPHEN SENNITT

THE COMPLETE FRANKIE HOWERD
Robert Ross
ISBN 1903111080 / pb / 240 pp £15.95 / Reynolds & Hearn 2001 / www.rhbooks.com

With an Introduction by stalwarts of the British film industry, Val Guest and wife, Yolande Donlan, (who say Frankie was their 'chum'), it's difficult to think who could dislike this thoroughly researched and immensely entertaining book. Though there has been a lot of material on old Lurkio over recent years, this has got to be one of the most attractive items to see light. A fantastic addition to the Reynolds & Hearn series of British film books, it should be purchased immediately... Oh, please yourself then, Missus. STEPHEN SENNITT

MOONCHILD: THE FILMS OF KENNETH ANGER
Persistence of Vision Vol 1
Ed. Jack Hunter
ISBN 1840680296 / pb / 128pp £11.95 / Creation Books 2002 / www.creationbooks.com

Kenneth Anger — underground filmmaker, author of *Hollywood Babylon*, occultist and *éminence grise* behind The Rolling Stones in their *Sympathy for the Devil* phase; associate of Bobby Beausoleil and Led Zeppelin's Jimmy Page — is finally accorded some long-overdue critical attention in this new publication from premier alternative film press Creation Books. Editor Jack Hunter's previous books include *Eros in Hell* and *Inside Teradome*, both also from Creation. Other contributors include HEADPRESS' own Mikita Brottman (who wrote the introduction), Carel Rewe and Anna Powell.

Anger's considerable reputation as a filmmaker rests on a remarkably slender body of work, the six short films of the so-called *Magick Lantern Cycle* — *Fireworks*, *Eaux d'Artifice*, *Inauguration of the Pleasure Dome*, *Scorpio Rising*, *Invocation of My Demon Brother*, and *Lucifer Rising*. The longest of these, *Inauguration of the Pleasure Dome*, is only about forty minutes, the shortest, *Invocation of My Demon Brother*, a mere eleven minutes... one hell of an eleven minutes, though — a sulphurous phantasmagoria of black magic, swastikas, Hells Angels, stock footage from the Vietnam war, soon-to-be convicted murderer Bobby Beausoleil, Anton LaVey, The Rolling Stones in Hyde Park, and a truly headfucking Moog soundtrack by Mick Jagger. This is the scariest of Anger's films by far, but they are all memorable in their own ways. Anger once said, 'Making a movie is casting a spell,' and he has evidently often approached the screenings of his films as rituals in themselves, often recutting and augmenting the

films so that no one screening is quite like any other. Free of dialogue, packed with occult symbolism, exquisite, decadent and swooningly homoerotic, Anger's films have been deeply influential in their use of colour, rhythmic cutting, montage, postmodern 'appropriation' of stock footage and clips from other films, and their pop soundtracks. This last has caused Anger to be dubbed the 'Godfather of MTV', and certainly some of his films have the vigour and impact of rock videos. *Scorpio*

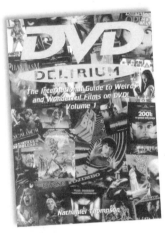

Rising (1963), the prime example of this tendency, was described by Anger as 'Thanatos in chrome and black leather and bursting jeans' and features several of the best pop singles of the early sixties — He's a Rebel, Wipeout, Blue Velvet.

The first section of *Moonchild*, 'Blue Velvet' by Carel Rewe, examines Anger's use of symbolism, both magical and otherwise, with special reference to *Lucifer Rising* and *Scorpio Rising*. The former has had a particularly vexed production history — all the original footage was stolen by Bobby Beausoleil and buried in Death Valley, according to Anger. Beausoleil says Anger destroyed it himself in a fit of pique. Remaking the film took most of the seventies, and the new version features a drugged-out Marianne Faithfull as Lilith, *Performance* co-director Donald Cammell as Osiris and a hypnotic soundtrack composed and recorded by Bobby Beausoleil in prison (this replaced an earlier soundtrack by Jimmy Page). *Scorpio Rising*, meanwhile, is arguably his most successful and complete film, though less overtly magical than some, being chiefly concerned with Anger's taste for rough trade in the form of preening teenage bikers and their gleaming choppers (actually full-dress Harleys, but let's not split hairs).

The second part, Anna Powell's 'A Torch for Lucifer', is more particularly focused on Anger's occultism, in particular on his devotion to Aleister Crowley. Every film in the *Magick Lantern Cycle* except *Eaux d'Artifice* is examined in turn. *Eaux d'Artifice*, incidentally, was filmed in the famous water gardens at Tivoli created by the Cardinal d'Estes, according to Anger, as an ode to watersports;

THE WHOLE GARDEN IS ACTUALLY A PRIVATE DIRTY JOKE — EVERYTHING IS PISSING ON EVERYTHING ELSE AND IT'S LIKE INEXHAUSTIBLE PISS. THERE ARE SPHINXES PISSING OUT OF THEIR TITS, WHICH I THINK IS WONDERFUL.

Moonchild is rounded out with a filmography, a chronology, a bibliography and an index, making it a useful reference volume rather than just a collection of essays. The wide margins created by the unusual square format of the book are also put to good use, being filled with notes, small photos and sidebar articles.

OK, enough praise, here's some moans — the Teutonic cult site used as a location in *Lucifer Rising* is called the 'Exersteine' by one author, the 'Exernsteine' by another, but no-one actually gets it right and calls it the Externsteine! Much more seriously, the otherwise detailed and exhaustive filmography by Jack Hunter unaccountably omits a plot synopsis for *Lucifer Rising* — every other film gets one, so surely some mistake? And although *Moonchild* contains a rich array of images from Anger's films, some luxuriantly spread over two full pages, I was a bit sad that the budget didn't stretch to full colour throughout, or a least a colour section. The colour of Anger's films is so opulent, and often so symbolically significant, that black and white stills don't really do them justice. It's worth pointing out, though, that both paper quality and picture resolution is far superior to those found in Creation's 'regular' film titles, which range from indifferent to appalling.

These quibbles aside, I really can't think why anyone with an interest in the enigmatic and fascinating (if undeniably rather sinister) Mr Anger

wouldn't want this book. One thing to note, though, is that *Moonchild* is not intended as a biography of Anger — for that, interested parties are referred to *Anger* by Bill Landis (HarperCollins, 1995), which as you might expect is full of scintillating information. For instance, we learn the Anger's real name isn't Anger (duh) but Kenneth Wilbur Anglemeyer — his adoption of the name Anger makes him the spiritual ancestor of Richard Hell, Johnny Rotten and Sid Vicious. He allegedly appeared as the Changeling Prince in Max Reinhardt's 1935 production of *A Midsummer Night's Dream*, though some have cast doubt on this assertion. And he had the word LUCIFER tattooed right across his chest. Rock and roll! Anger is reportedly not too happy with Landis' unauthorised book, presumably because it contains too much unhappy truth — an ironic position for the author of those masterpieces of muckraking, the *Hollywood Babylon* books, to find himself in. SIMON COLLINS

KLAUS BEYER
Hauptmann peppers einsamer herzenklub & Die Glatze
CD NO RAP 3007 & mini-CD n.UR-Kult / Prices not known / www.klaus-beyer.de / fbehnke @snafu.de / Beyer Management, c/o Behnke, Kienitzerstr. 12, 12053 Berlin, Germany

Obsessive Beatles fan Klaus Beyer is back with more crazed Fab Four renditions! Klaus records his own German vocal over the original Beatle tracks, producing pretty straight renditions in the manner that the fifty-year-old fan has been doing for a decade now (longer if you consider the home cassette recordings he was making 'before he was famous' for the amusement of family and friends). The pinnacle of Klaus' Beatle career comes with this track-by-track

'interpretation' of the *Sgt Pepper* album. It's more interesting than past Klaus-Beatle releases in that it features more of the musical cut ups — or collages — that Klaus sometimes creates in order to circumvent the original Beatle vocals. What's left doesn't always fit, but does at times touch on brilliance with its collision of repetitive guitar riffs, choppy orchestrations and clipped backing vocals. Of course, on top of it all is Klaus, who — in his own inimitable, tuneless way — resolutely refuses to let go of the melody, regardless of where the collage behind him is up to. Bonus cuts on the album include a live rendition of the *Sgt Pepper* run-out groove.

Removed from the Fab Four is Die Glatze (trans: The Bald Head), a self-penned track that features on the Klaus Beyer mini-CD, *Die Glatze*. Musically it sounds like something off a Cinecittá soundtrack, but with a maddening vocal that will haunt you to your grave. DAVID KEREKES

FLAMING FIRE
Get Old And Die With Flaming Fire
CD / contact: www.flamingfire.com

Flaming Fire are a five-piece band from Brooklyn purveying a quirky retro new wave groove. Every other review I've seen cites The Residents as their main influence — this is a fair enough comparison, but I was also reminded of Devo, Bongwater, Pere Ubu and even absurdist psychedelic mavericks like Frank Zappa, Syd Barrett and Gong. Theo Edmand's vocal on Word Up!, a delirious cover version of the eighties funk hit from Cameo, is a dead ringer for the laconic warble of Pere Ubu's David Thomas. *Get Old and Die...* gets bonus points for calling a song Pedophiliac, but then loses them all again for having a tortuously long final section featuring several minutes of silence, one of those oh-so-annoying 'secret' tracks, ten more minutes of silence and then twelve or so minutes of 'sonic exploration' i.e. a huge steaming load of irritating Nurse With Wound-like noises. God, why do bands do this shit? It's not big or clever. Your enjoyment of this album will be directly proportional to your tolerance for whimsy, zaniness and irony. I liked it at first, but I was in a funny mood, and by the time they'd finished, I'd really had more than enough. Approach with caution. SIMON COLLINS

FLAMING FIRE

CHAOS ENGINE
Escape Ferocity
CD / Wasp Factory Recordings /
www.chaosengine.com / www.wasp-factory.co.uk

Strap on your kevlar suit, cap your ears with concrete, check your anarcho-political credentials... for your speakers are about to emit Chaos Engine. Four likely lads: Lee H O'Chaos, Huw, Rawbin99, and Vere Kervorkian (do they all go to the same Sunglasses Hut?), grind, roar and twiddle their way through twenty-three tracks of 'long awaited' techno-metal. It's a lot to get through, but I drag my ears kicking and screaming all the way through this repetitive and ugly aural realm, wincing at the naff synthesiser presets, recoiling in mortal dread at the pumped-up Nordic singing, lamenting and pleading to be freed from the Bryan May-like four note guitar riffs, scattered throughout the recording like evil jingles.
Escape Ferocity is a hymn to the objective that negative talent for music and as much feel for a groove as stampeding cattle should not stand in the way of the creation of a marketable product. In this recording, the machines perform the musicians. Were they even in the studio when this offal was created in their name? The answer must be yes — no one person on their own could create such a moronic noise. Noise like this takes

a special kind of obsession, a really tin-eared love for dicking about with sequencers and overdosing on distorted feedback.

When the sequencer is tamed the results improve (well, they are faster and in sync for once), as on Jesus Christ V2.0. Let's try the lyrics... 'If Jesus Christ was just resurrected / He wouldn't have enough money to get elected... Communications systems overloaded / She [something something something] temples exploded.' Profoundities wrought in exquisite Byronic coupling, or a comical Crypto-Marxist ranting? Either way, could this be an example of the 'fiercely political' tone the press release leads us to expect? In striving to be fiercely political, Chaos Engine falls into the Catch 22 of not being so fiercely political that they don't want to insult the process they hope will make them into megastars. The politics is the by-now well-trodden package of angst against a vaguely media-engulfed capitalist nightmare. And if repeating the phrase 'This is normal' tracked alongside snippets of US news anchors constitutes a political ethos then I might pay more heed. Naphephilia is a meditation on insomnia.that turns into a nightmare. It's pretty for about fifteen seconds, then the one good idea is milked almost three minutes. The stab at guitar-trance, Don't Expect Us To Be Close After This is done no fa-

vours by an vocal impersonation of Simon Le Bon, complete with Duranic backing vocals, very heavily autotuned. Elsewhere they do the shopworn trick of the Stephen Hawking voice, and there's a *lot* of musical power-tooling about amidst glimmers of originality.

Chaos Engine aims to be a sonic smorgasbord of techno-metal, but with too many dud ideas and too much fondness for twiddling the knobs and noodling with distortion settings, something has gone badly awry. Some of these could and probably do work live but unless you're into enjoying your techno metal from a room next door to the one where it's playing, I would stay away. My advice to Chaos Engine is to catch up with the past five years of music, reboot all their equipment, and knuckle down to what we should be hearing tomorrow, not quoting what the rest of us were already atuned to back in the nineties. You've got the toys, now do something original with them. JERRY GLOVER

PAUL HARRISON
We Are All Fucking Each Other In Heaven
CD / Fiend / 2002 / £5 inc. UK p&p /
www.fiendrecordings.com

The Fiend website describes this album as containing 'intense, trance-inducing hyperbeats, circlebeats, rave surge samples and spacious caresses.' Hmm... how about revising that to 'intensely painful headache-inducing noise'? I'm not sure what a 'rave surge' is, but 'rave' sounds about right, for this is indeed music to stress out the sheep in the next field with. In between the occasional vocal sample and bleepy noise, the beat goes on. And on. And on, like the dentist's drill scene in *Marathon Man*, like Poe's tell-tale heart, like goblin blacksmiths hammering away inside your skull, on goes the bloody fucking beat, all seventy-seven miserable minutes of it. And just to add to my dislike of this album, all the tracks have Damien Hirst-style long and pretentious titles like Until You're Dead It's All Life. (I don't know what I am. What I am is unknown, but constantly revealing itself.) It's Like An Easter Thing. If someone were playing this upstairs, I'd bang on the ceiling with a broom. You'd have to be on some very bad drugs to enjoy this. SIMON COLLINS